# Deep Night

Greg F. Gifune

FIRST PAPERBACK EDITION





DELIRIUM BOOKS
P.O. Box 338
North Webster, IN 46555
srstaley@deliriumbooks.com
http://www.deliriumbooks.com

*ACKNOWLEDGEMENTS*

Thanks to L7 for fighting the power with "Bricks Are Heavy." It's even more relevant now than it was in '92. Thanks also to my wife Carol for everything, including keeping me (relatively) sane. Thanks to my sister Kim for spending numerous hours patiently discussing this novel with me from conception to completion, and for her thoughtful suggestions and loving encouragement. Thanks too to my mother Carla, and to all my friends and family for the continued support. Thank you to everyone who purchased *Deep Night*, I wouldn't be able to do this without all of you. And as always, special thanks to Shane Ryan Staley at Delirium—unquestionably the coolest cat in the business—for his friendship and tireless dedication to getting my work out there.

*For Chuckie.*
*And for Big Ern.*
*Life can never be the same without you guys.*
*See you when I get there, fellas.*

"There are more things in heaven and earth...than are dreamed of in your philosophy."

—William Shakespeare's *Hamlet*

# Chapter 1

There are many places in the everyday world reserved for the condemned, the damned, the lost and the hopeless. The holding room was but one example. Sterile, lifeless and painted a dreary off-white, it housed a long table, two plastic chairs and little else. A speaker, microphone and camera system was installed into one wall, a two-way mirror in another.

In one of the plastic chairs sat a haggard and ragged man who looked as if he'd been through a tremendous ordeal, yet possessed a strange air of composure that seemed in direct contrast to his physical appearance. His hands were shackled in front of him and rested on the table, fingers interlocked and folded together casually.

He stared straight ahead, eyes blank.

From the other side of the mirror, Detective Frank Datalia stood watching as his partner, Detective Dexter Clarke, left the man alone in the holding room and closed the door behind him. "He says he'll talk, but only to you," Clarke said with an annoyed air.

"Yeah," Datalia said, "I heard."

"It's hell to be popular, huh?"

"What's the deal with his lawyer?"

"Supposed to be a public defender on the way for him." Clarke let loose a weary sigh. "We're still recording, full audio and video. You gonna go in there and see what you can get or what?"

"Something strange about this one," Datalia said, studying the man through the glass. "Way passed composed. The flat-liner types always bother me."

"Motherfucker shows no remorse, no guilt, just sits there with that look on his face like he knows something we don't."

Datalia shrugged. "Maybe he does."

Clarke held up the file containing what little information they had to that point and looked back into the mirror. "Look at him, calm as could be. Pure psycho is what that is. Piece of shit's not even human."

"That's exactly the problem with his kind, Dex." Datalia reached for the doorknob with one hand and took the file from his partner with the other. "They're *too* goddamn human."

The man seemed to come out of his trance when the detective entered the room. He looked Datalia over, as if truly seeing him for the first time just then.

Frank Datalia had just celebrated his forty-fourth birthday, was of average height and slightly overweight, but carried it well and was dressed nicely. He wore a goatee and looked as Italian as his name sounded. His hair had begun to thin rather badly on top, and the sides were specked with gray. His eyes were perhaps his most outstanding feature, not because they were particularly beautiful or soulful, but because they were so strikingly melancholy. Though they had probably once been jovial and full of life, they had witnessed things over the years that had dulled the spirit within them, and like the battle scars they were, they showed.

"Detective Clarke said you wanted to see me?"

The man nodded. "I'd like to tell you what happened."

"You're under no obligation to speak with us until your attorney arrives."

"I agree to speak to you without a lawyer," the man said softly. "You won't believe a word of it anyway—and I won't blame you—but I'm still going to tell you because it's the truth, Detective Datalia, and nothing but the truth. So help me God."

"This session is being recorded. Anything you say can and will be used as evidence against you, do you understand that?"

"Yes, sir, I do."

"All right then." The detective took his suit jacket off, hung it over the back of the chair on the opposite side of the table then pulled the chair out and sat down. Something in this man's eyes bothered him. He couldn't quite put his finger on it, but something was askew. "What is it you'd like to tell me?"

"Everything," the man said, a faint smile creasing his lips, "and nothing at all."

# Part One: Before

"And he said unto them, I beheld Satan as lightning falls from heaven."

—Luke 10:18

# Chapter 2

He couldn't be sure why he dreamed of lightning that night, particularly during a snowstorm, but he had. At first he had no idea what it was meant to symbolize or suggest, only that the curiously violent, otherworldly storm left him feeling insignificant and strangely powerless. Later, he realized this wailing tempest of his dreams had masked other sounds, awful sounds no one should ever have to hear, like those of skin splitting, clothes tearing, and the screaming echoes of pain, horribly excruciating pain. The heavens shook, and from somewhere deep within the swathe of sleep, came the diseased murmur of ghosts, voices veiled in darkness and swallowed by the din of a blizzard wind. Just before the sky crumbled and fell, crashing down on him in pieces like a shattered windowpane, the whispers of the dead turned again to screams.

His brother was gone.

"*Raymond!*"

A violent chill shook him awake. It was cold, colder than it should have been, than it could have been had the door still been shut. Breath from his nostrils and mouth exited as mist, billowed like dragon-smoke and skipped through the darkness in search of the ceiling.

For a brief moment, Seth Roman was unsure of where he was, but as the room came into focus and he sat up, he remembered the cabin.

The moon was not particularly bright that night, but evident enough for him to make out traces of the beds next to his and the two sleeping bags on the floor between them. Louis had taken the bed closest to his own and was awake as well. He lay stretched out on his stomach, head raised slightly from the pillow, hair mussed and his face twisted into a grimace of annoyance and confusion. In one of the sleeping bags on the floor, Darian laid fast asleep, one arm protruding from the bag as he snored quietly.

Raymond had apparently slipped into the second sleeping bag at some point after they had all fallen asleep, but now it was empty, the zipper undone and the flap thrown aside as if he had exited it quickly and angrily.

The cabin door stood open. Outside, a snowstorm raged, blowing fresh flakes and occasional blasts of arctic wind through the doorway and into the cabin.

Seth stared at the door a moment, unable to initially comprehend what he was seeing. The whispers from his dreams slowly receded, left him. "What's going on?" he asked dully. Or had he only thought the words? Everything still seemed dreamlike, blurry and washed out, like sleep had not entirely freed him and was pulling him back into darkness.

While he lay there trying to make sense of things, time lost all meaning, and though his eyes remained open, memories from earlier in the day played across his mind's lens, film passing through a projector, showing him things he had already seen…

* * *

Raymond noticed her before the rest of them had, but within seconds they'd all seen her. Despite the peculiarity of the moment, as if mesmerized, no one spoke or reacted.

The woman—more a girl, really—her small frame breaking the horizon as she stumbled haphazardly over a crest of trees in the distance, appeared as if from nowhere, emerging from the thick forest at a full run. She stumbled, nearly lost her balance and fell but regained it in a forward-stagger without ever slowing her pace. She moved with the frenzied velocity of one being pursued as she travelled down the embankment toward the small clearing separating Seth and the others from the surrounding forest.

Seth looked beyond her to the forest from which she'd come, but there was nothing, no one following her. Yet she moved as if the gates of Hell had burst open behind her. The closer she got the more petite and young she appeared, her long hair scruffy and mussed, looking like it needed a good washing, as did the rest of her. Dressed in tattered jeans and an embroidered shirt reminiscent of 1970s hippie fashion, she looked like someone who had dropped out of a time warp. Despite the cold, her feet were bare and she wore no jacket, but these things didn't seem to concern her. Her eyes revealed a level of terror Seth had seldom before seen, and her movements were comparable to those of a wild animal cornered and frightened but prepared to fight for its survival if need be.

When she was within twenty feet of the cabin she

stopped abruptly with a jerking motion, planting her feet and flailing her arms like someone on the edge of a cliff trying desperately to stop and maintain their balance without falling off. Her head snapped back and forth in a rapid arc, taking in the four men she was suddenly confronted with, and she went quickly into a low stoop, hands out in front of her to ward them off as she circled back and away, keeping the men in her immediate line of sight.

"Easy now," Seth said, mind racing. "Easy."

At closer range they could see that her face was smeared with dirt, her feet had been split in places from the frozen ground and she appeared to be no more than seventeen or so. But the most troubling realization was that her shirt was not decorated with red embroidery at all.

It was spattered and soaked with blood.

Darian dropped the wood he'd been carrying. He and Louis had been gathering it from a large pile stacked next to the cabin while Seth and Raymond retrieved anything from the SUV they might need but had left there on their arrival the day before. It was probably the only time all four men had been outside at the same time since they had gotten there, but upon hearing the weather report on the radio that the severe snowstorm originally thought to hit later in the week was in fact beginning that very afternoon, they knew they'd be confined to the cabin for at least the next twelve to fifteen hours, perhaps longer.

The young woman continued her odd crouching movements, eyes wide and wild.

"What's going on?" Darian asked, breaking the eerie silence, his normally smooth voice shaky and uncertain. "It's OK, what—what's happening here?"

She said nothing, her eyes darting from one man to the next.

Louis looked to the forest behind her. "Is somebody chasing you?"

Seth moved a bit closer to her but she jumped back. He opened his hands and held them out in front of him. "It's all right. No one's going to hurt you, do you understand? It's all right, you're safe."

"She's bleeding pretty bad," Louis muttered.

"Miss," Seth said calmly, "it's OK, everything's OK, just calm down, all right?"

Louis nervously shifted his attention from her to the woods then back again. "Come on, lady, we need to know what's happening here. Is somebody after you or what? We can't help you if we don't know what's going on."

Darian glared at him. "Don't yell at her, Louis, what the hell's the matter with you? She's frightened out of her mind."

A gust of icy wind pushed through the trees and down across the clearing, cutting right through them. The gray sky threatened snow. It would begin soon.

"I'm getting my rifle." Louis headed for the cabin.

Seth motioned for them to be quiet and to stay put, but kept his hands raised and his eyes trained on the girl. Louis was right; she'd sustained a serious wound, probably in her abdomen, as the portion of her shirt covering her midsection was drenched in blood. "It's all right," he told her again. "We're not going to hurt you, miss. We want to help you, do you understand?"

When she gave no answer, Seth turned slowly and looked back at the others. Neither Louis nor Darian had moved, and Raymond, who was closest to the cabin, stood watching, some extra blankets he had taken from the SUV in his arms. There was a strange remoteness about him at that moment—even more so than usual, Seth thought—something overtly analytical in his expression. He was studying the young woman, searching her with his eyes, and within seconds something changed in his face, altered it the way a slowly dawning thought might.

The woman made a groaning sound that emanated from deep in her throat, more a growl than an attempt at cogent speech, and her posture relaxed to whatever degree it was still capable of in a slow, deflating motion.

As her shoulders slumped she looked even smaller and more fragile than she had before. She opened her mouth to speak, perhaps to scream, but this time no sound came at all. Instead, a single violent tremor shook her and her eyes rolled back to white.

Seth bolted forward in an attempt to catch her but she collapsed and hit the ground with a sickening thud before he could reach her.

"Jesus!" He slid down on his knees next to her, pushed a hand under her head and gently lifted it an inch or so from the ground. With his free hand, he quickly checked her wrist for a pulse. It was steady and surprisingly strong but she was completely unconscious. "We need to get her inside," he said, trying desperately to remember everything he'd ever known or heard about caring for someone in such a condition. "Fast, let's go."

"Moving her might not be such a good idea, man." Louis came closer. "They always say that. Never move somebody if they're hurt, right?"

"That's only if it's a neck, head or back injury, isn't it?" Darian stepped over the cords of wood he'd dropped and knelt next to Seth and the young woman.

"Well, she just whacked her head on the ground pretty goddamn hard."

Ignoring Louis's comment and still supporting her head and neck with one hand, Seth put the other on the small of her back and adjusted his position into a crouch so he could lift her. "We have to get her inside and apply pressure to the wound before she bleeds to death." As he rose slowly to his feet, the young woman lifelessly cradled in his arms, he motioned to Raymond with a tilt of his head. "Bring those blankets. We need to make her as warm as possible. Come on, hurry."

"Careful now," Louis said encouragingly. "Try to hold her neck steady."

When they reached the cabin door, Darian went ahead of them to the first bed and knocked a few spent beer cans to the floor. Louis followed, slipped inside then moved to the side of the doorway where he would be out of the way but could still watch what was happening. Seth staggered in and carefully placed her on the bed. "Christ, there's so much blood," he said breathlessly, noticing how much of it now stained his shirt as well. He crouched next to the bed and carefully peeled the woman's shirt back, away from her body. "Get some towels," he said to no one in particular.

Raymond walked through the door slowly, tentatively, the blankets still in his arms. "You better get her to a hospital."

"She'll never make it. We have to stop this bleeding or she'll be dead in minutes."

"Town's thirty minutes by car from here on a good day, and that's if the roads are clear," Louis said. "But you guys saw that place. Not but maybe fifty people in it, and there sure as hell isn't any hospital there. Shit, we'll be lucky if there's a doctor. In these parts there's no telling how far the closest actual hospital might be."

"Was she shot?" Darian asked.

"Bullet to the gut's the worst wound there is." Louis craned his neck so he could see over Seth's shoulder. "She wouldn't have been able to run the way she was if she'd been shot in the belly, trust me. No way in hell."

Seth was no longer listening to them. He was instead concentrating all of his attention on the young woman. Her shirt separated from her skin with a squishing sound, the material soaked in blood and dripping onto her stomach. He pulled it up to her breasts. She wasn't wearing a bra but the blood had not reached that high, it was centralized on her abdomen. Darian appeared at his side again, this time with a towel.

Seth carefully wiped at the pool of blood around her navel, sopping it up with the towel as he pushed it across her stomach. The woman's chest rose and fell in a steady rhythm but her body remained limp. He blinked several times in the hope of clearing his vision because what he was seeing refused to compute. "You've got to be kidding me."

"What is it?" Louis asked.

"I can't…" Seth continued cleaning the area with the now sodden towel, moving faster and with less care. "There's no—I can't find a wound."

Darian leaned in. "Where the hell is it?"

"There isn't one." Seth dropped the towel. It hit the floor with a splat. The young woman's hands and wrists were bruised, as were her ankles, and her feet had sustained several small cuts from the ground, but now that the blood had been wiped away, her abdomen was smooth and clean.

Louis backed away a bit. "Well that's *somebody's* fucking blood."

"Ray, get those blankets around her. She's still shivering and probably in shock." Seth stood up and ran a hand through his hair. Despite the cold it was damp with perspiration. "And close that door. We need to keep her warm."

"We need to get her out of here," Raymond said flatly, "and to a hospital."

Louis crossed the small main room quickly, grabbed his rifle from a closet in the corner and began checking it over. "I'm gonna keep an eye on that ridge. She was sure as hell running like somebody was chasing her."

Raymond still hadn't moved, so Darian went to him, grabbed the blankets and began covering and tucking them tightly around the young woman. "Look, we have no idea what's going on here or what may have happened. We need to call the police."

Seth started for the door. "My cell's in the SUV."

"Won't work, told you that before," Louis said. "No signal up here."

"Christ, it figures." Seth stopped in his tracks. "We better drive into town and find a policeman then, even a town that small has to have at least one."

"Problem is the snow's already falling." Louis, now positioned at the door like a sentry, the rifle held firmly in his hands, watched the forest from which the young woman had come. Though still light, the snow had begun. "According to the weather assholes it's gonna be one hell of a storm."

"According to them this wasn't even supposed to hit until later in the week," Darian said. "So listening to them might not be the best idea anyway."

"We try to make it now and odds are we won't be able to get back here until the storm passes. We'd have to wait until tomorrow once it's over. *If* it's over by then, that is."

Seth glanced at the rifle. "Will you put that thing away? You look ridiculous."

"I won't look ridiculous if I save your ass with it."

"Oh for Christ's sake, Louis, save me from *what*?"

"Well that's the whole point, isn't it?" Louis stepped out onto the front steps of the cabin, his breath trailing behind him. "We got no idea what's out there."

"Listen to me. Someone's obviously been badly hurt and—"

"Wow. See, now I never would've thought of that."

Seth was in no mood for Louis's sarcasm, but rather than engage him he paced about a bit, trying his best to harness the tension surging through him into something productive. "What do you think we should do, Mother?"

"Not sure," Darian answered. "But we need to know where that blood came from."

"Maybe she was holding someone else who was bleeding," Louis said. "Look at Seth's shirt from carrying her just a few feet."

Seth shrugged. "How she got this way is immaterial, we need to—"

"*Immaterial*?"

"You know what I mean."

"No, man, I don't. I got no idea what you mean."

"Lou, we need to get this girl to a doctor regardless. From there the authorities can handle things."

"Absolutely," Darian agreed. "This has nothing to do with us. The only thing is, if someone else nearby is badly injured we need to find them while there's still some chance we can help."

"But we got no idea where this girl came from," Louis said.

Raymond lit a cigarette, smoked it quietly.

"Could be any number of scenarios," Seth said. "A small plane crash, maybe, an animal attack or some sort of hunting accident—who knows?"

"You're not in the city now, fellas." Louis continued watching the forest, his back to them. "There's lots of small aircraft up here but if one went down we would've heard it and seen evidence of it—smoke or something—on the horizon, above the trees. If it was a hunting accident, we would've heard shots. You can hear gunfire out here for miles clear as a bell. And as for an animal attack, it's possible but unlikely." He looked back over his shoulder long enough to give the others a patronizing stare. "I know this area, OK? I know what I'm talking about."

"You borrow this place from your uncle once or twice a year," Seth reminded him. "You come up here with your kids for a weekend, cut some wood, build a campfire and walk around with that rifle and all of a sudden you're an expert?"

"More of an expert than you are, chief, bank on that."

"Fine, then how about some intelligent advice we can actually use?"

"What the hell you think I'm trying to do? This is the first time you guys have been up here. I've been coming for a few years now. That's all I'm saying, OK?" Louis resumed his guard duty at the door. "Whatever. You big woodsmen figure it out."

Raymond continued smoking his cigarette but was now looking at the floor.

"Look, people are hurt here." Darian rose to his feet. "We need to figure out what we're doing and we need to do it quickly."

"Louis, you told me once before that there were other cabins in the area," Seth said. "What's the closest one in the direction she came from, over the ridge?"

"I got no idea. I know how to get here and how to get out, that's about it. That's why I told you guys before not to go wandering off alone in the woods. It's easy to get lost out here."

"Yes but you did say there were other cabins nearby."

"There's private cabins sprinkled all over these woods, man, but it's not like there's a map or something. Only thing I've ever seen is smoke from a chimney fire a few times in the distance over the ridge, but not this trip. Not yet anyway."

"She could've come from there then."

"Could be, but unless you know exactly where you're going, you can wander around lost in these woods for the rest of your life and never find anything. That's what I'm trying to tell you. This isn't some park with a few trees like in the city. This is the deep woods, this is the wilds of Maine, man, and it's no playground out there. Shit, especially this time of year. You make a couple bad moves in these parts and you can wind up dead real easy."

"All right, then the only other alternative is to get her into the SUV and head for town. If we get stuck there due to the storm we get stuck, not much we can do about it."

Raymond finally broke his silence. "There's something you guys haven't thought of."

The others turned to him in unison.

"Couple years ago I was in this bar down in Florida," he continued. "Real dump. These two guys got into an argument over something and squared off. Everybody figures it's just two drunk dip-shits swinging on each other, right? Until this one guy pulls out a knife and stabs the other one real fast and real hard, right here." Raymond pointed to the side of his neck. "Blood sprayed out that fucker like water through a garden hose on full blast. He died before the ambulance got there. Never saw so much blood in all my life."

"What the hell's this got to do with anything?" Louis asked. "What's your point?"

"My point," Raymond said evenly, "is that when it was all said and done, the guy that did the stabbing had as much blood on him as the guy he stabbed." As a silence fell over the cabin, Raymond moved to the doorway, took a final drag from his cigarette and flicked it outside, over Louis's shoulder. "See what I mean?"

"The bottom line is we don't know *what's* happened here," Darian said. "Ray's right. She could be a victim, but she could just as easily be some disturbed person who hurt or killed someone else. We don't know either way, and as far as I'm concerned that's reason enough to get her into town. Let the police figure this all out."

The sound of coughing interrupted them.

The young woman had come awake. She was still groggy and remained wrapped in the blankets, but once the coughing stopped she tried to speak. "No police, no—no police, please." Her voice was raspy and strained, as if she hadn't used it in a long while. "*Please.*"

Louis stepped around the others. "What's going on? Is somebody after you?"

The woman considered him a moment through glassy eyes. A bit of drool slipped from the corner of her mouth. "No," she managed. "Not...not anymore."

Seth slid between them and crouched next to the bed. "No one here's going to hurt you, OK?" He gently rested a hand on hers. Her skin was cold and taut. "You came into our camp like someone was right on your heels. We brought you in here so you'd be warm. You're all right now, do you understand?"

She nodded slowly, and with great effort.

"Can you tell us what happened?" he asked, maintaining the same calm tone he'd had with her throughout. "We need to know what's going on so we can help you, OK?"

"I'm...so cold."

"The coffee's still hot," Darian said, moving toward the kitchen area. "I'll get a cup."

"I'm Seth." He checked to make sure the blankets were tucked in tightly around her then motioned to the others in turn. "That's my brother Raymond. This is Louis, and that's Darian over there."

"Christy," she said, still slurring.

"How old are you, Christy?"

"Nineteen."

Seth wasn't sure he believed her. "Are you up here alone?"

She stared at him as if she hadn't understood the question.

"Are your parents with you or—"

"No."

"Any friends then, or—"

"I haven't seen my parents in a...a long time."

Darian returned with a steaming mug of coffee and handed it to Seth. Afraid she might be too weak to hold it by herself Seth carefully brought the mug to her lips and helped her take a sip. As the warmth hit her system it seemed to instantaneously awaken her, and within a few moments she appeared far more coherent. Seth continued to assist her until she eventually took the mug in her hands and was able to hold and maneuver it on her own.

"Thank you," she said softly.

"Christy," Seth said through a staid smile, "your shirt was covered with blood."

She sipped more coffee, her eyes moving slowly from one man to the next. "He tried to kill me."

"Who did? Who tried to kill you?"

"This guy picked me up hitching not far from Portland."

"Where is he now?"

"Back at his cabin, I..." as her voice trailed off her eyes glistened with tears. "I left him back at his cabin."

"So that's his blood on your shirt then?"

"I'm from Florida originally," she said softly, "but I

left home when I was sixteen. My dad died when I was eleven, and me and my mom never got along. I had to get out of there." She held the mug closer to her face, let the warm steam wash over her. "I knew another girl from school who wanted to take off too, so we hooked up and ran away. We were together for a couple years on the road, going around from place to place, but then we got mixed up with some crazy-ass bikers in South Carolina and Jeanie—that was my friend—took off with them and left me on my own. I was like seventeen by then and I knew my way around so it was no big deal." She offered a short-lived, self-conscious smile before taking another sip of coffee.

"Yeah, fascinating," Louis said, "but we didn't ask for your life story. What were you doing running through the woods covered in blood?"

Christy's eyes narrowed, squinting groggily. "Sorry, I—"

"Never mind all that," Seth said. "Go ahead."

"I was thinking I'd go see Canada, you know? I never saw Canada before and they always say how beautiful it is. Usually in winter you got to stick to warmer places if you're on the road, but I figured I'd go north this year, maybe see Montreal, you know? I wanted to see Montreal ever since I was a little girl." She seemed to relax somewhat, and drew the blankets in closer with her free hand. "I was making my way there, hitching, and this guy picked me up a little ways after Portland. Redneck type, you know? But I've been on the road for years; I can take care of myself, OK?" Her voice cracked. She looked down into the coffee mug then handed it over to Seth as if it now disgusted her. He took it and she settled deeper into the blankets, a single tear rolling the length of her cheek.

Though she appeared impossibly young at times, clear views of her face left no doubt that her short life had been a dreadful one. A girl her age should not have had the astute, streetwise eyes and depth of sorrow she so clearly possessed, Seth thought, yet they were qualities unmistakable in her. This was no little girl playing tough, she'd lived it.

"When you're on the road sometimes you have to do things," she muttered. "You have to survive."

Louis shook his head. "We get it, you're a hooker."

"Ignore him." Seth glared at him then turned back to Christy with a far friendlier expression. "We all do."

"I'm not a hooker—not really—I mean, I've done some things I'm not proud of to survive but it's not like I'm some whore working a corner or something, I—"

"Christy," Seth said calmly, "what happened with this man who gave you the ride?"

Her face went blank, the emotion gone. "He picked me up early in the morning. Real early, like just after dawn. I don't know if I walked all night or if I stopped and slept for a while, I—I can't remember. But when he picked me up I wasn't far outside Portland. The only thing I remember about the night before was I was really tired and I had my backpack and I thought about just going off into the woods on the side of the road and going to sleep. The road was really quiet that night, hardly any cars, and it was raining. I remember…I remember the rain. It was so cool. You know that really beautiful and peaceful kind of rain? I was so tired and my legs hurt from walking—I did a lot of walking that day—and I remember how nice the rain was until…until it turned into a storm, a—a bad storm.

I was scared and I didn't really know why, I mean it's not like I was never out in a storm before. There was just something about this one that didn't seem right, I guess. Kind of trippy, you know?"

"Uh-huh." Louis sighed. "What kind of drugs were you doing?"

His voice snapped her out of the trancelike posture, and her expression again turned sad and weak. "I smoke a little weed sometimes, so what?"

"It's all right," Seth assured her. "What happened with the man?"

"I just remember him pulling over to pick me up the next morning. It was real early, like I said, and I got a weird vibe off this guy but I was so tired and there weren't any other cars around so I took the ride." Her expression grew intense as she forced herself to recall things she clearly didn't want to remember. "He said he was going all the way to Cutler, and that it was real close to the Canadian border. He told me he'd let me ride with him all the way. He didn't try anything but I knew there was something about him, something not right, you know? When you've been in as many strange cars as I have you get a sense about the people driving them. But I figured I needed the ride so I'd wait and see how it all worked out.

"After a few hours I fell asleep," she continued. "You should never do that when you're hitching but I couldn't help it I was so—so tired, you know? I just couldn't keep my eyes open. Anyways, I fell asleep. I don't know how long I was out but when I woke up we weren't on the highway anymore. That's what woke me up, the road got all bumpy and I saw we were on some dirt road going through the woods. I asked him what was happening and where we were going, and he—he never said anything. He just hit me, like all of a sudden, back-handed me right in the mouth. I couldn't believe it, and I thought: 'this guy's gonna kill me, he's gonna rape me and kill me out in these woods.' We were already out in the middle of nowhere and even if I tried to run he could've caught me easy."

Seth brushed aside a wave of anger. The idea of someone hurting her made his blood boil. "Is that how you got the bruises on your wrists and ankles?"

Christy gazed at the marks on her wrists as if she'd forgotten they were there. "He kept me tied up when he wasn't..." She bowed her head, cried quietly a moment.

"It's all right." Seth put a hand on her shoulder, rubbed it gently. "You're OK now. No one's going to hurt you anymore."

"He took me to a cabin," she eventually said, wiping the tears from her face. "Kind of like this one, only not as nice. It was older and dirty, kind of rundown. I don't know how long I was there. A few days maybe, I—I'm not sure. He kept me tied up and blindfolded most of the time. He was crazy. He kept telling me if I tried to get away or fight him he'd kill me, cut me up into little pieces and bury them out in the woods. He said nobody would ever find me because nobody would even look. He said nobody cared if some runaway whore disappears."

"We need to get this girl to a hospital," Darian said softly.

She went on, apparently having not heard him. "He had this big ax, and he got really drunk one night and said he was going to cut my heart out. I kept having these terrible nightmares, you know? Only it was like…like they weren't really nightmares because I was awake, and I thought maybe I was going crazy. I kept thinking about the rain and that storm the night before he picked me up, it—I couldn't get it out of my head. I still can't." Christy ran her hands through her hair and let out a quiet whimper. "I knew he was going to kill me that night. He took the blindfold off whenever he raped me but he usually left my hands tied. The last time, though, he didn't, he cut the ropes and left my hands free. I knew then he was going to kill me. Like a big finale, you know? He even put the ax down right near me where I could reach it. He never did that before. I think he figured I was so scared and beat up by then I wouldn't fight him anymore. But I did.

"He was really wasted, and he started undoing his pants," she continued. "It was a chance, so I took it, and…" She again began to sob.

"Jesus H.," Louis said, "she fucking killed this guy."

Her head snapped up, her eyes searching him out through the tears. "I didn't mean to, I swear to God! I just—I didn't want him near me, I—I didn't wanting him touching me again. When I grabbed the ax I just wanted him to let me leave, but he came at me and I swung it out in front of me as hard as I could. I just wanted to keep him away from me, I…" She went quiet for a time. "He ran right into it. It hit him in the stomach. He fell into me and we both fell back and he ended up right on top of me. We were lying on the floor and I couldn't get him off me. He was gagging and bleeding and I kept kicking and screaming, I—I just wanted him *off* me." She took a deep breath, slowly exhaled. "I finally got him off and then I ran out the door and into the woods. I didn't even know where I was but I just kept running as fast and as hard as I could. After a while I saw some smoke above the trees and tried running toward it. Must've been the fire from your cabin, I guess."

"When you ran, was the man still alive?" Darian asked.

Louis answered for her. "Doesn't matter, he's not alive now. Bet on it. With that kind of wound the guy probably bled out right there on the floor within a few minutes."

Christy wrapped her arms around herself and shivered.

"Lou's right," Raymond said from across the room. "He's got to be dead by now."

Seth stood up, rubbed his tired eyes. "Bastard deserved it."

"I'm not about to argue that one," Darian said. "But the fact of the matter is we have a kidnapping, sexual assaults and a probable murder on our hands. We need to get the police out here and let them handle this."

"Right," Seth agreed, "absolutely."

"Please," Christy said suddenly, "please don't call the cops."

"If it played out like you say it did you got nothing to worry about," Louis told her. "It's self-defense."

"You don't understand." She was so upset now she nearly came off the bed. "You don't understand, I can't go to the police, I can't!"

Seth returned to his crouch and held her shoulders, steadying her and gently pushing her back onto the bed. "Easy now," he said. "Easy. It's all right, it's *all right*."

Christy went limp again, laid back as more tears stained her cheeks. "I've had trouble with the cops before," she said. "I have a record; I've been arrested a couple times."

"Arrested for what?" Louis asked.

"Pot. And prostitution once."

"None of that matters," Seth told her. "This man kidnapped you and was assaulting you, threatening to kill you. You had every right to defend yourself. Your prior record has nothing to do with any of that."

"You sound like a lawyer." She eyed him with what seemed equal parts amusement and suspicion. "Or a cop."

"I'm neither," he assured her, attempting a smile. "I'm a customer service manager. I calm people down for a living."

She combed her hair from her face with her fingers. "I've dealt with cops before. They'll never believe somebody like me. Especially cops up in these parts. Everybody knows everybody else in areas like this. I've seen it before. They're all related and shit. They're not going to believe me, not over one of their own."

"Not our problem, lady." Louis strode across the room and returned his rifle to the closet. "Get a lawyer."

"Please," she said to Seth, "I've been in jail before. I'm not going back. I *can't*."

"I can sympathize with that," Raymond said.

Rather than respond to his brother's comment, Seth said, "Ray, I've got a couple old sweatshirts packed in my suitcase, grab one for her, would you? And get a pair of socks too." He motioned to Christy, indicating the far side of the cabin where the bathroom was located. "You can wash up and change out of that shirt in there. I don't have extra boots but socks are better than nothing, even if they're big."

She nodded.

"Are you hungry?"

"A little, yeah, but I'm so…I'm just so tired."

"Darian's making his world famous stew tonight. It'll be ready in a bit." Raymond appeared at his side holding an old gray sweatshirt and a pair of heavy white socks that had been rolled into a ball. Seth took them from him and held them out for Christy. "Go get changed then try to get some rest. With the storm coming in this fast nobody's going anywhere for a while anyway. We'll talk about all this later."

She took the items carefully, as if they were priceless artifacts. "Thanks."

Seth helped her from the bed, and as she stood up the blankets fell free.

The blood on her shirt had grown darker and more ominous somehow. They all did their best not to notice.

Christy walked slowly and with a degree of effort, her legs obviously not as strong or steady as they needed to be but still capable of carrying her. As if to be certain they were still there, she gave a final glance over her shoulder at the men then slipped into the bathroom, closing the door behind her.

"What the hell are you doing?" Louis asked. "She can't stay here, man."

"What are we supposed to do, put her outside?"

Darian brought them all in closer. "Keep your

voices down. This girl's already been through enough of an ordeal."

"You believe her, Mother?"

"Yes, Louis, I do." Darian shrugged. "I see no reason for her to lie."

"I believe her too," Seth said.

"But we do have to involve the police," Darian added. "We're talking about murder, even in self-defense, and I don't want any part of this. Once the storm passes we go into town and notify the police. End of discussion."

"Agreed," Seth said. "I feel terrible for the poor kid but we can't get involved in all this anymore than we already are."

"But we don't know for sure what the truth is," Louis reminded them. "Now goddamn it, this is my cabin and—"

"It's your uncle's cabin," Darian reminded him. "Calm down."

"Whatever. Point is, it's my family's property and I'm responsible for what happens here, for what goes on here while we're using it, OK?"

"Then what do we do?" Seth asked. "You're the one who said we'd never make it back once the storm kicks in full force. We're stuck here for the time being, right? I know it's a crazy situation, but what choice do we have?"

Louis folded his arms across his chest and shook his head wearily. "If this storm hits the way they say it's gonna, we could be snowed in here for a day or more. We might not be able to get to the main road until Friday. That's two days from now. What the hell we gonna do with her sleeping here and shit? What if she *is* some psycho?"

Seth thought a moment. "We'll do it subtly but we'll take turns staying awake at night, how's that? Once she goes to sleep we stay up one at a time in shifts until we know she's no threat to us."

"I don't like this, but I guess there's not much else we can do," Louis conceded.

"You've been awfully quiet through all this, Ray," Seth said. "What do you think?"

"I think I'll go have a smoke." Raymond moved toward the door, cigarettes in hand.

"Great," Louis cracked. "Thanks for your input, man."

Ray shook a cigarette free from the pack, rolled one into the corner of his mouth and lit it with a Zippo. "Storm's already here, snow's already falling, what's there to talk about? Like Seth said, nobody's going anywhere anyway." He extinguished the flame with a quick snap shut of the silver lighter then pulled open the door and stepped outside. "Least not anytime soon."

* * *

The earlier events of the day faded away, returning Seth to the cabin, to night.

He blinked away the memories and realized he was still lying there staring at the open door. "What's going on?" he asked again.

Rather than respond verbally, Louis shook his head in a slow uneven sweep, his movements rough and oddly hesitant, as if he'd yet to master maneuvering his body and was still familiarizing himself with it.

Seth swung his feet around until they touched the floor. Even in heavy wool socks he could feel the cold coming through the floorboards. He rubbed his eyes and stood up.

Louis did a half-pushup and craned his neck over his shoulder, following Seth's gaze until he could see the door. Once he realized it was open he was on his feet as well. Like Seth, he wore only long underwear, a sweatshirt and a pair of thick socks. "What the hell's the door doing open?" he asked groggily. He glanced back at the floor, to where Raymond should have been, then at Seth. "Where's Ray?"

Seth shrugged, still hazy. "I don't know, I—he must've gone outside."

"*Outside*? For what?"

"I'm not sure, I just woke up myself." The snow had formed a miniature drift in the threshold. "That door's been open a while," Seth mumbled. "I think the cold woke me."

Louis scratched his head and looked over at the fireplace. They'd made a fire in the stone hearth earlier in the evening but it had long since burned out. The cabin, though quite small, had no heat, electricity or running water, but did have an indoor bathroom equipped with a chemical toilet. "Wait," he said. "Maybe he's in the can. Might be the door wasn't latched right and blew open."

Feeling an immediate sense of relief at the possibility, Seth moved to the rear of the room to check the bathroom. The lamp inside was not lit but the door was ajar. "Ray?"

When no answer came, Seth gave the door a slight push. It slowly swung open far enough for him to see inside. The tiny room was empty. He turned back to Louis and shook his head in the negative, his relief again becoming concern. He shuffled as close to the main door of the cabin as he could without stepping in the snow and peered out into the night.

Nothing but darkness and snowflakes.

"Raymond!" he called. "Ray?"

"Why the hell would he go outside?" Louis grabbed his jeans from the foot of his bed, stepped into them with an off-balance hopping motion that would've been comical under different circumstances then began searching for his boots.

Seth turned away from the door helplessly. "I don't—I don't know."

"There must be something wrong."

The more Seth's mind cleared and distanced itself from sleep the more he felt Louis was right, something was terribly wrong. Raymond had never been up here and was completely unfamiliar with the area. To make matters worse, none of them were experienced outdoorsman. Louis was the only one who camped on a regular basis and had any idea about the wilderness—but even his knowledge was limited. At the end of the day he was a city boy like the rest of them. Add to the mix an unexpected snowstorm of near-blizzard proportions and the odds for disaster were high.

"Wait a minute," Louis said suddenly. "Christy's gone too."

The remainder of that late afternoon and early evening had been awkward but uneventful. There had been little conversation with Christy, who spent most of the time sleeping and had only come awake once to eat some stew. Later that night they built a fire and eventually turned in. Of the three available beds, Christy occupied one and the other two they had flipped a coin for. Seth and Louis won so Darian and Raymond were relegated to sleeping bags.

But even now that all seemed foggy and indistinct to Seth, like just beyond the periphery of his memory there existed things he should have remembered, *needed* to remember, but couldn't. None of it seemed authentic anymore. Were they really memories or only dreams?

At some earlier point in the evening, Seth remembered awakening to find Raymond in a chair near the fireplace, staring at the flames. As agreed, he had taken the first shift to stay awake and keep an eye on Christy.

"Ray," he whispered, "you OK?"

He offered a slight nod.

"I'll take the next shift. You take the bed, OK? When I'm done I can use the sleeping bag, it's not a big deal."

"It's OK. Wanted to watch the fire a while anyway. Not real sleepy."

He looked over at the bed where Christy lay sound asleep. "You're sure you're OK?"

"Too much to drink, that's all." Raymond held up a bottle of Jack Daniels and gave a feeble smile. He'd been drinking a lot that evening, the bottle was nearly empty. "Go ahead and get some more sleep, I'm cool."

That too seemed so long ago now, Seth thought, so distant and blurred, as if it had taken place years before rather than only a few hours.

Darian came awake while Seth and Louis were dressing but remained in his sleeping bag, shivering. "What's the matter—what—what's happening?" He fumbled for his eyeglasses, found them and pulled them on. "It's like a walk-in freezer in here."

"Ray went outside," Louis told him. "Christy's gone too."

"What? Why?"

Rather than answer, Seth pulled on his jacket and followed Louis over to the open doorway. He kicked at the snow that had accumulated in the threshold then leaned out into the night. An endless sea of flakes swirled about and mixed with a thick darkness, making visibility less than a few yards.

"Can't see any tracks but the snow's coming down so fast it'd only take a couple minutes to cover them anyway." Louis cupped a hand on either side of his mouth and shouted into the darkness. "Ray! Hey, Ray!" His voice echoed through the nearby trees, swallowed by the soft bay of the wind.

"What would possess them to go outside?" Darian asked from behind them.

"I knew we shouldn't have trusted that bitch." Louis turned to Seth. "Get the rifle. We're not going out there in the middle of the night without it."

"Don't be ridiculous. There's a near blizzard going on."

"Just get the rifle, it's in the closet."

"That's my brother out there, Louis. We need to find him. Now. Right now!"

Louis stared at him, his face tense in the dim light. "Then get the fucking rifle."

After a moment, Seth nodded and did as Louis had asked.

Still inside his sleeping bag, Darian struggled to his feet and somehow maintained his balance as he hopped over to them. "Be careful. Don't go too far."

Louis and Seth stepped out into the night.

The snow was deeper than it initially appeared, and they found themselves sinking down into it a bit as they pushed on through the curtains of flakes. Draped in white, the silhouette of Louis's SUV came into view alongside the cabin. Seth pulled his jacket in tighter around him and squinted through the storm to the nearby forest. The dirt road that eventually led to the state highway was lost in the accumulation, and it took him a moment to gain his bearings and figure out where he was. He couldn't imagine anyone lasting long out here, and Raymond had been drinking all day and hadn't slept since the night before, which only made matters worse. Visions of his little brother—slumped against a tree somewhere beyond their scope of vision, disoriented and in shock, succumbing to frostbite and letting sleep take him—flashed across his mind's eye.

"Ray!" he called. "Raymond!"

Louis continued on a few paces in front of him, crouched forward with the rifle out in front of him like a soldier on patrol. Despite the severity of the situation Seth couldn't help but notice how absurd he looked, like some child playing war games. Louis hesitated and looked in both directions.

Seth glanced behind them, glad to see the cabin and Darian in the doorway through the haze of snow.

"You see anything?" Louis yelled.

"Nothing!"

"I'm gonna circle the cabin. You stay close behind me, OK? Right on my ass."

In single file, they clomped through the snow, along

the side of the Explorer and to the rear of the cabin. There was nothing back there but more forest and a small storage shed. They hadn't seen a single track, no sign of Raymond or Christy whatsoever. The wind picked up, howling and ripping through them, and Seth shivered uncontrollably, tucked chin against chest and forced himself forward. *Where the hell are you, Ray? What's happened to you?*

Memories of their childhood came to him then, images blinking through his mind of Raymond playing and laughing, his smiling face, young and innocent and full of joy. So long ago, he thought, so very long ago.

*If something's happened, if she's done something to him, I'll never forgive myself.*

Despite the fact that his hands were stuffed in his coat pockets, by the time he and Louis checked the shed and reached the front of the cabin again, Seth had lost most of the feeling in his fingers. His nose was running and his eyes were watering so severely they hurt. *Raymond, for God's sake, where have you gone?*

Louis squinted, looking deep into the night in an attempt to see anything beyond their small encampment, but in the darkness and snow neither he nor Seth could make anything out. "If he had one of the flashlights with him I think we might be able to see a trace of it!" he called out.

Seth couldn't be so sure. "What now?"

He gave a halfhearted shrug. "I don't know, but we better get back inside!"

"We have to find him, Louis! We have to find him!"

Darian hopped out of the way as they staggered through the doorway. Louis closed the door behind him and fell back against it, breathless. Seth began warming his hands, blowing on them and rubbing them vigorously along his thighs.

"No sign of them out there at all," Louis gasped.

Darian let the sleeping bag drop to the floor then stepped out of it. "Why would they do this? Why—why would they go out there in the first place?"

"I have no idea," Louis answered. "But it's one hell of a stupid move. There's no way they're still alive if they've been out there more than—"

"We have to go back out," Seth said. "We have to go back out and try again. We have to find them."

"Yes, of course," Darian said awkwardly. "We have to try again."

"Be my guest." Louis motioned to the door. "You can't see more than a foot or two in front of you out there, and the wind's freezing, cuts right through you. If it wasn't so bad we could go deeper into the woods and look around, but on foot we can't risk it, we can't get far without getting disoriented or lost within a matter of minutes."

"What about the SUV?"

"What are we supposed to do, drive through the fucking trees?" Louis unzipped his coat and shook the excess water and snow from it. "The forest out there's too dense, the only area we could drive on is the dirt road to the main highway, and I'm not even sure we could find either one in that mess."

"We have to try," Seth said. "We have to find them."

Darian nodded thoughtfully. "He's right."

Equal parts panic and concern crept across Louis's face. "OK." He put the rifle down, wiped his face with a towel then tossed it aside. "Let's get moving then.

Time's running out on him if he's—"

"Darian, see if you can get the fire going strong again," Seth said quickly. "Louis and I are going to take the Explorer as far as we can along the road and try to see if maybe they walked up that way. It's a long shot but it's the only other thing I can think to do. If they went up into the woods instead, then..."

Darian turned away, busying himself with the fireplace.

"Then he's dead," Louis said. "By now, they're both dead."

Seth pushed by him. "Let's go."

A sudden knock on the door startled them all to silence. They all exchanged glances but said nothing until Darian broke the spell. "Well open it, for Christ's sake."

Seth yanked the door open.

Raymond stood in the doorway in his coat, a knit hat pulled down over his ears. He was covered in snow, and even his eyebrows and face were laced with ice. His skin was pale and wet, and had he not blinked, the others might have thought him dead.

"Are you guys all right?" he asked in an oddly placid tone.

Before Louis or Seth could respond, Darian took Raymond by the elbow and gently pulled him into the cabin. Raymond stared at him with a dumbfounded expression and closed the door. "Are *we* all right?" Darian asked.

Seth moved to him quickly, took him by the shoulders and sized him up. "Jesus, Ray, what the hell were you doing? Are you OK?"

Raymond nodded less than convincingly.

"Where's Christy?" Louis asked.

When he offered no immediate reply, Seth asked again, afraid his brother had perhaps slipped into some sort of shock. "Ray, where is she? Are you all right?"

Raymond stepped away from him, closer to the fireplace. He brushed snow from his coat before removing it then did the same with his knit hat. "I'm all right," he said, tossing both items into the nearby chair. "Christy's gone."

"Gone? What do you mean, *gone*?"

"I meant to wake you, Seth, like you said, so you could take the next shift, but...I must've nodded off. When I woke up she was gone, so I went looking for her."

"Why didn't you wake us up?"

"I thought...I didn't think I'd be out there long. I figured maybe she was out on the steps or something."

"Why did you leave the door open?" Darian asked.

"Didn't know I did," he answered flatly. "Sorry."

Louis stepped closer to him. "*Sorry*? Is that what you just said?"

"Yeah." Raymond's eyes watched the slowly mounting fire. "Sorry."

"Are you out of your fucking mind? You went looking for that bitch in the middle of this storm? Where? We went out there and couldn't find any trace of you. Didn't you hear us calling you?"

"Can't hear anything out there but the wind."

"Ray," Seth said patiently, "where exactly did you go?"

Raymond faced him. He already looked a bit better than he had when he'd first appeared in the doorway, but something still wasn't right. There was something off, something slightly askew. "I told you. I went looking for her. I figured she wandered off or something."

"We're in the middle of nowhere," Louis snapped. "If you'd gone up into those woods, you—man, you think the deep woods are some kind of playground? Trust me, they're not."

Raymond's eyes shifted slowly, found Louis. "You don't know any more about the deep woods than I do, Louis."

"Yeah? Well I'll tell you what I *do* know, hotshot. In these conditions and in these temperatures it's a miracle you didn't die out there. We could've gotten hurt or died ourselves looking for your sorry ass, you ever think about that?" Louis clenched his fists but kept them at his sides. "Did you, you stupid sonofabitch? Did you ever think about that?"

Raymond glanced casually at Louis's fists. "You don't want to do that, Lou."

"Look, everyone just relax." Seth moved closer to both men. "Ray, you scared the hell out of us. We just want to make sure you're OK. You're not acting right, you're not making sense."

Louis shook his head with disgust. "You better check the idiot for frostbite."

"I'm fine," Raymond said again.

"Un-fucking-believable, this guy. You weren't even supposed to be here in the first place. I let you come along and you pull this shit. Nice. Where the hell's the girl?"

"I don't know. She took off, I guess."

Seth didn't believe him and knew no one else did either. "We were out in that storm, Raymond," he reminded him. "We stuck close to the cabin and didn't last more than ten minutes. You never would've found your way back here if you'd gone even as far as the trees."

"Well obviously, Seth, I did." His face remained expressionless, but there was something more, something similar to fear just below the surface.

"What do we do now?" Seth asked, turning his attention to Darian and Louis. "We can't just leave her out there to freeze to death. She's not in her right mind and this proves it, we have to try to find her."

"There's no telling how long she's been gone." Darian knelt by the fireplace. He had the fire going strong again. "The odds of finding her at this point can't be good."

"Try nonexistent," Louis growled.

"We need to try," Seth said. "Come on, we can't just—"

"I already risked my life once tonight for *this* douche bag." Louis stabbed a finger in the air at Raymond. "If that brainless twat wants to freeze to death out there that's her business, but don't put my life on the line by being just as stupid and following her out there."

Seth and Darian looked to Raymond, fearful of what his reaction might be.

Raymond stared at him a moment before responding, then looked into the fire and muttered, "I think Louis is right. We can't help her now, best to just wait until morning and see what happens then."

"Now I know this must be a nightmare." Louis returned to his bed and flopped down onto it. "Raymond's actually making fucking sense."

"Was there any sign of her out there at all?" Darian asked. Raymond shook his head no. "Why would she do this? Why would she just pick up in the middle of the night and leave? She had to know she'd have no chance in this storm."

"I didn't trust that little bitch from the minute she got here." Louis pulled his boots off. "Maybe she tried to go back to the other cabin or something, who knows?"

"She was probably afraid we'd involve the police," Seth said. "She was terrified; the poor girl was clearly traumatized. In that state of mind you don't always make sound decisions. But what the hell do we do now? We have to do something; she could be freezing to death out there somewhere."

"Seth," Louis said firmly, "there's nothing we can do. She's a whore-sicle by now."

"Jesus Christ, Lou, you're making jokes? That girl's probably dead."

"Hey, nobody told her to take off, did they?"

Darian waved Raymond closer to the now crackling fire. "Have a seat over here for a while. You still look frozen solid."

Raymond pushed his coat and hat onto the floor and sat in the chair. He held his hands out toward the flames and smiled blandly at Seth. It was a helpless, joyless smile.

"I tried to find her," he said. "I did my best but she was just…gone."

"Way I see it, we tried to help her." Louis crossed his legs, propped a foot against his opposite knee and began to rub his toes. "I'm sorry if she didn't make it out there but in the long run it's better for us that she left. We didn't need to get involved in all that."

"Don't you think we're already involved?" Seth asked.

"Far as I'm concerned, the best thing to do is pretend none of this shit ever happened."

Darian nodded. "Seth, I think he may have a point."

"Then explain it to me."

"If what she told us about what happened was true, we're better off not getting involved at all, assuming that's still possible."

"So we just pretend she was never here?" Seth laughed but it was more a nervous reflex than anything else. "We don't even go look for the body once the storm clears? We don't get a hold of the police and let them know what happened? We don't even notify them so they can get a search party up here for her remains? We can't do that, what the hell's wrong with you guys?"

"Who says we can't?" Louis asked. "You want to get involved with the local yahoo cops up here? You want to explain to the press and your wife and the hard-ons at work what in the fuck we were doing up here in the middle of nowhere with some young girl that's got a record for prostitution and drugs? Not to mention she might've axed one of their cousins to death not far from here. And now she's probably dead too, out there in those woods somewhere. Want to explain how that happened, how or why a young girl just got up in the middle of the night and ran off, knowing she'd freeze to death in a matter of minutes? What if the cops don't buy it?"

"But it's the truth." Though Seth's tone had been

insistent, even he had begun to question what was or wasn't true. Nothing from the moment Christy had gone into the bathroom to change seemed clear or convincing anymore. Everything else had been reduced to jumbled recollections, shadowy flashes and sleepy, disquieting sensations.

"*We* know it's the truth," Louis told him. "But you got to admit it sounds weird. I mean, you looking forward to explaining to everybody how we just came up here for some laughs and relaxation on a little vacation and got mixed up with dead hookers and murdered rednecks? Jesus Christ, it sounds like a Joe Lansdale novel."

"Look, crimes have been committed here. We need to tell the truth. We've done nothing wrong; we tried to help that girl. We all know what happened."

Louis shrugged. "What happened? Some crazy girl came running into our camp covered in blood, telling all kinds of crazy stories? Maybe she was telling the truth, maybe she wasn't. Point is we helped her and she took off in the middle of the night and we got no idea why except for maybe she didn't want the cops involved, right? I say we wait the storm out and as soon as it clears and we can make the road, we get the hell out of here. None of it ever happened. Besides, there's nothing to tie us to her, no proof she was ever here."

"I gave her one of my sweatshirts and a pair of socks," Seth reminded him.

"Clothes she could buy at any department store in the country. You got your name stenciled in them or something?"

"Don't be ridiculous, that's not the point."

"That's exactly the fucking point, dude." Louis stood up, pacing about the cabin now with long, nearly theatrical strides. "There's nothing to connect her to us, so why get involved at all?"

"What about the shirt she changed out of? The bloody shirt, where is it?"

"Right here, it…it's right here." It was the first thing Darian had said in some time. Still kneeling next to the fireplace, he pointed to the shirt, which had been tossed there and now lay in a crumpled heap next to the hearth. "She must've dropped it here after she changed. Maybe she thought we'd burn it."

"We still can," Louis said.

Seth stepped forward, into his path. "That's evidence."

"Who are you, fucking Johnnie Cochrane all of a sudden? Who gives a shit? We toss it in the fire, it burns up—poof!—it was never here. Just like her, none of it ever happened. We go home and get on with our lives and forget about all this. Sooner or later somebody will come looking for the dead redneck or somebody will stumble over Christy's remains out there and that'll be that. None of it will have anything to do with us."

"It's not right," Seth said softly. "It doesn't…It doesn't seem right."

"Seth," Louis said evenly, "I got enough fucking problems, OK? We didn't ask for any of this shit. We just came up here to drink some beers, play some cards and hang out for a few days, am I right? If we get involved in all this it's not gonna change anything. That redneck's still gonna be dead, and that girl's still gonna be dead. The only thing that'll change is our lives because we'll get dragged into the middle of it. I don't need that. Do you?"

Raymond, who was still staring into the fire, finally spoke. "You need to listen to him, Seth."

Seth held his hands out like a victim of robbery. "Mother, surely you can't agree with this."

"I think maybe..." Darian looked away, back into the fire with Raymond. "I think maybe Louis is right."

"I don't believe this. I'm the only one who thinks we need to do the right thing here?"

"The right thing," Louis said through a yawn Seth found horribly inappropriate, "is to stay the hell out of this. Burn the shirt and forget it."

"I agree," Darian said.

"Raymond?" Louis asked.

Without turning from the fire, Raymond offered a slow but deliberate nod.

Seth wanted to protest further, but he was becoming tired. In the last several minutes he had felt an intense wave of exhaustion wash over him, and it was weakening his resolve. "I don't think it's the right thing to do," he said. "This is a mistake and it's lying for no reason. All we have to do is tell the truth. We haven't done anything wrong."

"I'm not gonna stay up talking about this all night." Louis moved by him and returned to bed. "I'm sleepy. I need to get some rest."

"It has to be all of us," Darian said. "Unanimous or nothing."

"You really think this is the way to go, Mother?"

He nodded. "I do, Seth."

"All right," he sighed. "Then burn it."

Darian bent over, picked up the shirt and threw it

into the fire. They all watched it burn for a while without comment. After several minutes Darian gave Seth a quick pat on the shoulder, extinguished the Coleman lantern he'd lit earlier and headed back to his sleeping bag. "I'm so tired," he said softly. "I need to sleep."

Why was everyone going to sleep? Wasn't it strange to simply be going back to sleep after all that had happened? Seth couldn't be quite sure. His head was swimming a bit and the waves of exhaustion were growing stronger. He could barely keep his eyes open.

"Don't stay up all night, you two." Darian slipped into his sleeping bag.

Seth turned back to the fire. "Yes, Mother." He watched his brother a moment, the fire now the only source of light in the cabin, and tried to figure out where he had gone for so long. He knew Raymond could sense his concern and his physical presence behind him, but he refused to look at him again. He just gazed into the fire and remained quiet, a look of reserved fear on his face. Nothing was right, even his reaction to Louis. His brother had been in numerous scrapes and could handle himself. In a fistfight Raymond would destroy Louis, but even had it not come to that, under typical circumstances Raymond would've defended himself more vehemently, more than likely to a fault. As an adult he'd never been one to avoid a fight, physical or verbal, yet he'd done just that.

"What were you doing out there?" Seth finally asked.

Several seconds came and went before he answered. "Looking for Christy."

"But you couldn't find her? No trace of her at all?"

"No."

"How were you able to stay out there so long without freezing to death?" Seth moved closer to him. "Answer me, Raymond. Where were you?"

"I told you."

"You're lying."

The directness of Seth's comment should have shaken him, but it seemed to have no impact whatsoever. Instead, Raymond seemed preoccupied, staring into the fire as if it held some special significance. After a moment, he said, "Why would I do that?"

It was impossible for him to have survived out in the storm for thirty-some-odd minutes, which Seth calculated was the approximate amount of time he'd been gone. Raymond had always had problems, but this was not like him. "Raymond," he said softly. "I need to know you're all right."

His brother said nothing, just stared into the fire.

And then it dawned on him. The SUV. He'd obviously been in the Explorer. It was the only possible explanation. He'd left the door to the cabin open by accident and went looking for Christy. When he was unable to find her, rather than returning to the cabin for some reason he had sought refuge in the SUV. When the cold eventually woke them and he saw them come looking for him, he sat quietly watching them make damn fools of themselves. He'd decided to end the charade once they returned to the cabin, probably because he was well aware that their next move might be to either check the Explorer or even attempt to search for him in it. So he'd slipped from the SUV, stayed out in the storm a few minutes until he looked properly frozen, then crept to the cabin, waited by the door and probably listened to the tail end of their conversation.

But why had he done it? It wasn't like Raymond to pull a childish prank like that. What was the point? What was he trying to prove? None of it made any sense.

"Go to bed, Seth," Raymond said. "I'll see you in the morning."

"Why don't you take the bed and get some rest? I'll use the sleeping bag."

"You take it. I'm going to stay up for a while."

Seth gave a slow nod. "We'll talk about this in the morning." He shuffled over to the bed and settled in, pulling the covers up tight. He tried to relax but the entire evening seemed beyond surreal and continued to prey on his nerves. The whole point of this trip had been to relax and get some time away from the office, from their jobs and the stress of their everyday lives, a long weekend in northern Maine at a cabin surrounded by miles of beautiful woodlands. They had planned nothing more than some drinking, card playing and some much needed downtime away from the hustle and bustle of the city, spent instead amidst the beauty and quiet of nature. Initially, Raymond hadn't been part of the plan, but when he'd showed up unexpectedly, as Raymond normally did, Seth brought him along, excited at the prospect of some quality time with his brother.

"Hey, Seth?"

His thoughts interrupted, he sat up on his elbows so he could see Raymond. He was again facing the fire. "Yeah?"

"I'm sorry if I frightened you."

"It's all right." Seth lay back, watched the shadow flames play along the cabin walls and the low, dark ceiling. "Just don't do it again, OK?"

Giving in to the exhaustion, Seth drifted quickly off to sleep. As he slipped away, he could've sworn he heard Raymond weeping. Perhaps it was only a dream, he couldn't be sure. Either way, though he did not revisit his nightmares of strange lightning, falling skies and whispering spirits, he nonetheless slept fitfully the remainder of the night. This time, during the brief intervals when he would come awake for a moment or two, he remembered only a deep darkness, a void. Nothing.

* * *

It was just prior to sunup when Seth felt someone gently shaking his shoulder. He came awake to see Louis crouched next to the bed, fully dressed, a single finger to his lips signaling him to be quiet. Once satisfied that Seth was awake, he motioned to the slowly dying fire.

Raymond was sound asleep in the chair. On the floor nearby, Darian was out cold in his sleeping bag.

Seth rolled out of bed and quietly followed Louis across the room to the small galley kitchenette on the far side of the cabin. Once there, Louis peered back at the others to be certain they were still asleep. He looked stressed and worn out. "There's something wrong, Seth," he said in a loud whisper. "Something wrong with Ray. Last night was—"

"Relax. I figured it out. He was hiding in the

Explorer, that's all. I'm not sure why he'd do that just yet, but I'm sure that's where he was."

"Not without the keys he wasn't."

"I'm not saying he started it or went anywhere, he just sat in it."

"No Seth, he didn't." He reached into his jeans and pulled free a ring of keys. "I've had them the whole time."

"But the doors were—"

"The doors were locked. I know, because I'm the one who locked them." Louis blinked rapidly, forced a nervous tic of a smile and motioned to the remote alarm button on the key ring that once pressed locked all the doors in the vehicle and gave off a loud and annoying electronic wail.

In his mind Seth saw him and Raymond unloading the last of their things from the SUV just after they'd all had stew. He saw Louis walking away, the key ring held high and aimed back over his shoulder at the vehicle. The loud beep and the distinctive clunking sound of the locks engaging in unison echoed in his memories.

"Force of habit, I guess," Louis said. "I always lock car doors. And those doors have been locked since before Ray and Christy disappeared."

"Maybe the keys—"

"They never left my jacket pocket. I checked, thought maybe she stole our wallets."

"Well then where did he go?"

"That's just the thing, man. Where the hell *did* he go?"

"He must've been out there walking, like he said."

"Seth, listen to me. No human being could survive

that long out there."

"But he did." Seth shook his head as if to clear it of distracting thoughts. "Dumb luck, maybe? The grace of God?"

"Thought you didn't believe in God."

He looked away. "I believe in God, Louis," he said quietly. "I just don't have anything to say to Him."

"I figure he was out in that storm thirty, maybe forty minutes. Did you hear what I said before? Nothing human could survive that long out there."

"Stop being so melodramatic." Seth folded his arms across his chest and leaned back against the counter. "Obviously he managed it somehow."

"From the minute that girl came here, it—things haven't been right. There's something wrong, man, something *wrong*."

In all the years he'd known him, Seth had never seen Louis this way. "It was a strange day and a strange night, no question."

Louis looked unusually pale. "I'm not gonna die out here."

"*Die*?" Seth laughed reflexively, but it was a nervous laugh laced with fear rather than humor. "For God's sake, some strange things happened last night to be sure but you're not going to *die*, Louis. Why would you die? Why would you even say that?"

"I don't know, I—I can't explain it but there's something happening here I don't like, it—I know it sounds stupid but last night all I could do was go to sleep even though I—I know it makes no fucking sense but I didn't *want* to sleep, I was scared to sleep but I couldn't stop it. It was like I couldn't control it."

Seth knew exactly what he meant but words

escaped him. He could only nod.

"I've got a bad feeling about all this." Louis rubbed his eyes with both hands then slid them down across his face as he released a lengthy sigh. "Real bad."

"It was a stressful situation with Christy and all. Sometimes stress can do strange things to you, it can alter perceptions sometimes. Then on top of it we were all drinking last night too…weren't we?"

"Yeah, but—I don't feel the same now, I feel different."

"Different how, Lou?"

"Like myself again, I guess." He ran his hands over his face, up across his forehead and into his hair. "Only different."

"There's a reasonable explanation for what happened. There has to be. Think about it. Visibility was next to nothing out there, he could've been five feet from us and we would've never seen each other." He stepped closer, put a hand on his shoulder. "Everything's all right. OK?"

Louis nodded, but Seth could tell he didn't believe it for a minute. And he didn't blame him, because Seth didn't believe it himself. Something *was* wrong—he could feel it in his gut—something horribly wrong, and like a virus not yet detected, it was silently growing, strengthening and devouring them from the inside out. He could feel it, an odd, dark and lonely feeling; a quiet sense of dread.

He wished now they'd never come here, to these woods and this unassuming cabin, because they were all going to die.

Perhaps, in a way, they already had.

# Part Two: Sleepers

"I am terrified by this dark thing
That sleeps in me;
All day I feel its soft, feathery turnings, its malignity."

—Sylvia Plath, ELM

# Chapter 3

As dusk settled, the horizon loomed above the trees, an endless canvas painted with great brush-strokes of celestial blue and black. Amidst the slowly dying light, the moon sat high in the sky like a hastily hung ornament pasted above the darkened edges, and but for the beginnings of delicate snowfall, all was quiet.

He watched her a while, careful not to reveal himself too soon.

She lay on her side at the edge of the forest, her weight supported on one elbow, her face turned to the sky. The snow increased a bit, becoming a light flurry, but she seemed unaware of it, absently blinking away flake after flake while sorrowfully gazing straight ahead, seeing everything, and nothing at all.

"Where are they?" he asked softly, still concealed in the shadows behind her. When she didn't answer he asked again, this time more forcefully. "Christy, where are they?" Like so much else here, she was familiar and foreign to him all at once. He stepped forward, allowing the moonlight to touch him. "Where are they?"

"Where do you think they are?"

"Where's my brother, Christy? Where are the others?"

"It took them," she said, this time looking back over her shoulder at him.

Her expression was possibly the most heartbreaking he had ever seen. "The snow?"

"The night."

* * *

He looked out at the vast expanse of forest, felt a subtle popping sensation in his temples followed by a gradual warm trickle. Though he already knew what he'd find, he slowly raised a hand to his nose, touched a finger to his left nostril then held it away from his face so he could see. Blood. It ran along the space beneath his nose to his upper lip, seeping in and trickling along the line of his mouth. He tasted the bitter flavor in the back of his throat, swallowed and nearly gagged.

Like always, it was then that he knew he was having a nightmare, or something like a nightmare.

The screams from the far side of the forest brought him back to the dreamscape, but by then he was falling away from it all. He could feel himself hurtling, plunging downward, as if he'd mistakenly stepped into a deep pit, the light above him shrinking into the distance, swallowing more and more of it the deeper he descended.

His fall ended quietly, and in total darkness, as always. But then came light from above, as if he were lying at the bottom of a well, looking up at the opening. Only this was no well. He was on a slab of a table, strapped down, secured with what appeared to be thick brown leather-like harnesses of some kind, various old and rusted metal contraptions littered along the periphery of his vision. The screams returned, but this time they belonged to him. He struggled violently as whatever was down there with him held him in place, and together with the restraints, made escape impossible.

"Is this Hell?" he, or perhaps someone else whispered.

He could hear breathing, labored breathing.

Something brushed against him then slid onto his head, the pressure increasing as it pushed down around his forehead, nearly covering his eyes. Cold, hard and metallic, he realized one of the strange contraptions had been forcibly fitted to his head.

*What – what's happening? What are you doing to me?* He wanted to speak the words but could only manage to think them while screaming incoherently.

Unseen hands began tightening rusted screws that had been fed through holes in the headpiece and positioned on either side of his skull. As his screams became whimpers, he heard the squeaking, grating sound of metal on metal. The screws closed on him, the tightening sensation in his temples growing stronger and stronger until he felt the metal puncturing the skin and pressing painfully against bone.

*Why are you doing this to me?*

He heard the sound of bone cracking and imploding before the pain burst through him, stabbing from his temples down into his jaw, teeth and neck. The pressure in his forehead was so severe he felt his eyes bulge and rupture in their sockets.

At the very outskirts of consciousness, he sleepily forced what remained of his eyes upward, to the opening far above him, and what little light still resided there. Through the perspiration and blood he felt something else trickling down on him in a slow steady stream. Rain? Could rain reach him down here?

His vision blurred, cleared, blurred and cleared again. A face was peering down at him, huddled over the opening. He squinted through the pain and dizziness but the face remained the same: a series of scars and open wounds in bloody raw flesh, unfinished, mutilated and tortured yet grinning like some cretin child. The being's mouth opened and it vomited, the thick, foul fluid showering down, spattering the walls and floor around him.

And then the quiet returned, bringing with it total darkness.

Until, as always, the next phase began.

The boarding house he'd been staying at of late was a gloomy and rundown building that offered the kind of meager flophouse room he could afford while washing dishes at a nearby diner. It was a place where no one knew or cared who he was; no one asked questions, no one spoke unless they were spoken to, and the world kept on just beyond its walls, noticing nothing.

A safe place to hide, he'd thought, at least for the time being.

The detail was remarkable, the room an exact duplicate in his mind, and had he not experienced this so many times before, he'd have been fooled into believing he was actually awake. But he knew better.

Lying in bed, the springs from the worn mattress poking at him through the hopelessly thin material, he remained still but let his eyes pan slowly across the room. Near dawn, the only light was that which slipped through the sides of a pulled window shade on the far wall. But he could still see that he was not alone. A humanlike shape, perched like some giant bird of prey, sat crouched on the edge of a battered old bureau, staring down upon him with calculated silence. Nude and lacking skin, the flesh beneath gleamed red, raw and wet, networks of vein and sinewy muscle glistening as if recently glazed.

Only the lidless eyes moved, gliding slowly back and forth, all the while keeping him in their line of site. But even the eyes weren't right. Not quite human.

Without moving from the bed Raymond raised a hand to his lips, palm up, and blew, as if blowing flower petals into the air. As his breath crossed the room and reached the sentinel on the bureau, the man—*thing*—disintegrated in front of him, dissolving and floating away, ash disturbed by a sudden breeze.

He watched the pieces spiral slowly downward, and sat up so he could follow their progress to the floor. But they were gone, vaporized like raindrops against hot coals.

As he continued to stare at the spot where the ashes had vanished, something else caught his attention, something small and thin and foreign along the old wooden floorboards. Cautiously, he rolled out of bed and shuffled closer to it.

He crouched, immediately realized what it was and vaulted back in horror.

A finger. A small index finger from the looks, lying

there on the floor in the center of the room, gnarled as if from arthritis or some medical abnormality and yet, the finger was so tiny it appeared to belong to a child. Like the ghoul looking down on him in the pit, it appeared not quite finished, a work raw and in progress, not fully realized.

Heart racing, he crouched down again for a closer look, then glanced above him, inspected the ceiling a moment, hoping to find a spot from which it might have fallen. Several cracks traversed the aged plaster ceiling, but none were large enough to accommodate the finger. Still, he thought, it looked as if it had been dropped there from above, thrown aside like garbage.

Slowly, he reached for the finger.

Without warning it burst through the floorboards, splintering them with loud cracking sounds as the finger became a hand, revealing a fist and a small form attached to it. From under the floor a flood of other hands and arms vaulted up into the room, reaching, grabbing at him with their tiny fingers, ignoring his screams and dragging him under, back through the now gaping hole. Their faces and bodies concealed in the darkness beneath the floor, they growled at him, yanking him down into their lightless fissure, his body folding and breaking, bones snapping before he disappeared completely, his screams silenced as an eruption of blood and bile sprayed his throat.

* * *

This time, Raymond came awake in a bus terminal. Sitting in one of a cluster of astonishingly uncomfortable plastic chairs, his eyes focused for a moment on a little girl sitting directly across from him. He knew by the look on both her face and her mother's that he had awakened abruptly and made something of a spectacle of himself.

The little girl was pretty and innocent, so precious. The moment he looked into her eyes he knew she was no danger to him, but Raymond waited a moment nonetheless to be sure he was awake, then ran a hand through his hair and let out a slow, steady sigh. His fingers came back sticky with perspiration.

The woman across from him put an arm around her daughter reassuringly and gave him a stern look. Raymond smiled at her, and then at the little girl. When neither responded in kind, he nodded self-consciously, grabbed the duffel bag at his feet and moved away, toward the exit.

Through the glass doors at the far end of the terminal he could see rain falling. *Almost time to board,* he told himself. He slung the duffel over his shoulder and strolled closer to the exit so he could get a better view of the street beyond. Plenty of cars sat parked and just waiting to be borrowed. *Never did like buses much.*

Once he'd stepped outside, he leaned his head back and let the light rain wash over him. The rain always made him feel reborn and cleansed, and this time was no exception. But the feeling abandoned him once he opened his eyes, wiped the rainwater from them and focused again on the street and those moving along it. The lonely and the lost, the unaware and the distracted, hurrying to nowhere, isolated even in the midst of brethren, blind mice all, running through an endless maze few even realized they were trapped in. He remembered Peanuts, a gerbil he'd had as a boy, and how he'd watch the little creature burrow through the shavings in his cage, or run on his spinning wheel, curious as to whether he knew where he was in the universe. Could he tell the difference between the confines of the cage he'd been placed in and the vast outside world? Did he ever wonder what else there might be out there, even beyond those times when Raymond would take him out of the cage and hold him, pet him, and let him run around the bedroom? In the end, did he care?

Something blinked through Raymond's mind, a flash like the sharpened blade of an enormous, military-style knife, glinting, reflecting a sparkle of light.

As the vision dissipated, Raymond stepped from the curb and crossed the street purposefully, his feet splashing puddles as he went.

It had been a year since the night at the cabin. Avoidance was no longer an option.

He had to go back. He knew that now. He had no choice.

# Chapter 4

Something insignificant triggered the memories, and they returned in mosaic. The recollections became stronger, more vivid and exact, until a single memory had burrowed into the forefront of his mind and taken hold.

Snowflakes.

*Tell me what you see, Seth.*

The stillness of deep night disturbed, he came awake as if shaken. The only other people in the room were fast asleep and could not have jostled him, and yet, he was certain someone had done just that. His eyes scanned the area as best he could from a prone position: shadows, moonlight—nothing more. But just beyond the darkness there *was* something more. Something he could not quite touch, see, or even hear, but it was there. It was there.

He held his breath, went still and listened carefully. In time, sounds emerged from the silence, soft noises he hadn't before noticed, like audible whispers occasionally breaking through a low hiss of static. *Movement.*

He was sure they were sounds of movement. Subtle movement. Stealth movement.

Just outside the door? Or were the sounds closer? Were they inside?

Puzzlement graduated to crazed terror. His heart crashed his chest and his body, in seizure, snapped rigid as a board. With great effort he managed to open his mouth, but all he could summon were muffled grunts and groans.

The noises (were they footsteps?) grew louder, bolder. Closer.

He shifted his eyes, struggling to make out as much of the room as possible. He knew his brother had been sleeping only a few feet from him earlier, but now the space sat vacant. "Raymond?"

A vague form shifted nearby, catching his attention. It darted past his scope of vision, altering the pattern of shadow and moonlight on the far wall.

Consumed with horror now, he again attempted to scream, but gagged out a barely audible moan instead. Was he still asleep? Could this simply be a nightmare? In some ways it felt like a dream—physically as well as psychologically—and yet he knew; he *knew* he was awake. He slammed shut his eyes, no longer wanting to see.

After a moment he slowly opened them. Darkness swirled about like rolling fog. Raymond was still gone, but the others were there in the room with him, undisturbed and still asleep.

*Seth? Tell me what you see, please.*

Something had been there only seconds before, he was sure of it.

Something malevolent. Something inhuman.

Darkness devoured everything, but in time, his vision returned, this time focusing on a night years earlier. "I see Raymond."

*And what is Raymond doing, Seth?*

"Running. He's...running."

*Are you running too?*

"Yes."

*What else do you see?*

"Raymond's crying. He's completely terrified. He—He's so frightened he's lost control of himself."

*Are you frightened too, Seth?*

"I don't know, I...I mean, it's as if I'm not really there, but yes."

*Is it day or night?*

"Night."

*What else do you see?*

"It's snowing. A light, fluffy kind of snow, it's quite beautiful, really. I try to focus on it because it's so beautiful but...but Raymond is screaming and running and crying and he's so lost, he's...he's so terrified."

*Why is he so terrified Seth?*

"I don't know."

*How old is he in the dream, Seth? How old is Raymond?*

"Little, seven or eight. Eight. He's eight."

*And you?*

"I don't know, I can't see myself but...it feels like I'm young too."

*You're four years older than Raymond, Seth. Are you four years older than Raymond in the dream?*

"I don't know. I think so. Yes, I—I must be. I must be twelve."

*What else do you see?*

"We're running. We're running in the snow. He

woke up like this, he—he had those...problems."

*Problems?*

"I told you, he...as a child he used to have these awful night terrors. He'd wake up in the middle of the night absolutely petrified. He was just—just a little boy."

*When did this start, Seth?*

"When he was seven or eight."

*The same age he is in the dream.*

"Yes."

*When was the first time, do you remember?*

"No, I...I can't remember the first time it happened. Maybe..."

*Maybe what, Seth?*

"Maybe this is the first time."

*But you're not certain?*

"No, but...I think it might be."

*Where are your parents in the dream?*

"I don't know, I—I only know they're not there. They can't help us."

*What do you see now?*

"Snow. Raymond running and crying, screaming for help and me beside him."

*Can you see where you are?*

"No, it's...just night. He's running, staggering and struggling to maintain his balance in the snow."

*Where is he running, Seth?*

"I don't...I'm not sure."

*Is it somewhere outside the house where you and Raymond grew up?*

"Yes, it—it must be."

*Is this the first time, Seth? Is that what you're seeing, the first time this happened?*

"I don't know. It's possible but, I—I don't know."

*All right. What happens next then?*

"Nothing."

*Nothing? The dream simply goes dark?*

"Like at the end of a film, the way it..."

*Fades to black?*

"Yes."

*Does the dream end there, Seth, in the dark?*

"Yes."

*How many times did you find Raymond in your backyard when you were children? How many times did he sleepwalk or awaken from one of his nightmares and run from your bedroom screaming and terrified?*

"I can't remember. It happened so many times."

*When did it stop?*

"When we were a bit older."

*Was this before or after the death of your parents?*

"Well before. Raymond was still very young. We both were. We were adults when our parents died."

*And these episodes simply stopped, night terrors and all?*

"Yes."

*He hasn't had them since?*

"Not that I'm aware of, but I don't see Raymond as often now, he's always in trouble. We've never talked about it much as adults, but no, I don't believe so, he—he's never mentioned them or anything like them again."

*What else can you tell me about the dream?*

Seth moved his arm from across his forehead, his eyes focusing on the low ceiling overhead and a hint of her at the edge of his peripheral vision. Folding his arms across his chest like a corpse, he drew a deep breath and slid shut his eyes. Returning to the darkness was always easier somehow. "That's all."

He heard her chair shift against the plush carpet, her skirt whispering as she crossed her legs. She was looking at him now—he could feel it—green eyes staring at him over those turtle shell glasses, the same small pad she always took notes on clutched in her dainty hands. "Would you rather discuss something else?" she asked in a velvety voice he had grown to love and hate all at once. Always so accommodating, she had passive-aggressiveness down to an art form. "After all, it's not really a dream. You know that, don't you, Seth."

"Yes." He sighed. "It's a memory."

"It's not unusual to remember things," she said, offering a thoughtful pause before completing the sentence, "in the form of dreams. Sometimes it's easier."

Seth opened his eyes, shifted his focus with a turn of his head, and saw her sitting just to his right. New skirt—he hadn't seen that one before—and new pumps, too. In the two months he'd been coming here she'd yet to wear the same outfit twice. "It was a usual occurrence back then, but lately the memories have been on my mind again."

"But the episodes ended as abruptly as they began, yes?"

"Yes."

"Do you think it possible one or both of you *do* know what triggered these episodes, but simply cannot, or perhaps would rather not, remember?"

"I think that's a rather obvious possibility, yes."

"And as adults you've never discussed these episodes with your brother?"

"No, not really." He forced a swallow. His mouth was bone dry and he suddenly felt like sitting up, so he did. A slight headache tingled behind his eyes. He swung his feet around and settled into a sitting position. "Raymond had...*problems*...that's just the way it was. During that time we never knew what might happen with him at night." Seth rubbed his temples, looked at her then looked away. "I've never seen anyone so frightened."

"How did that make you feel, Seth? Witnessing this so often in your brother?"

"Helpless. Frightened. Confused. All the things you'd expect." He stared at the carpet. "My parents took him to doctors, even a psychiatrist and sleep disorder specialists, but nothing worked."

"Did they ever do any of those things for you, Seth?"

He flashed a less than agreeable look. "Raymond was the one with problems."

"Of course, but they impacted you, did they not?" She raised an eyebrow slightly. "Certainly witnessing these things in your brother and having to live this way must have had a traumatic affect on you as well, wouldn't you agree?"

Doctor Farrow looked better than ever in her little skirt and matching jacket. A sheer tan blouse beneath it showed off a lacey tan bra and the swell of ample breasts. Professional but sexy, it was a look that suited her. Seth wondered why it was apparently so important for her to include sex appeal as part of her appearance. *How does it make you feel?* He wanted to ask. His eyes slid down her crossed legs to one foot that bobbed slightly, the pump dangling from her nylon-covered foot, her toes the only thing still holding it on. Something sexy about that too, only he wasn't sure what exactly.

"Seth?" she said, breaking his concentration. "Wouldn't you agree?"

His eyes found hers. She had caught him checking her out but it didn't seem to faze her in the least. She must've been used to it, a woman so attractive. She had the look of a middle-aged trophy wife, the kind of woman at home at fancy cocktail parties in exclusive social clubs; a woman who had grown up sheltered from most of the real world and who was used to being pampered in her private life even now. Spoiled, in terms less kind. But she was no empty-headed bimbo. Doc was smart, Ivy League smart. The framed diplomas on her wall told him so. She was the type of woman who could use her face and body if she wanted to, but never because she had to. Her brain was the most lethal weapon in her arsenal, if not the most immediately detectable. And in a sense, this helped to explain her somewhat cool, detached, nearly smug air. Yet when he looked at her, *really* looked at her, Seth could see something more, something beneath the carefully assembled veneer. He saw passion, traces of a woman who spent her days helping others, those like him, lost and trying to sort things out while sitting on a couch and talking about their childhoods, but a woman who spent the rest of her time trying to hold it all together herself. He wondered, as he often did, what she and her husband talked about during those rare, quiet, private moments. He wondered what she was like in bed. He wondered what kinds of noises she made, how her eyes looked, what the pattern of her breathing sounded like. Though he didn't know exactly how long she'd been married, he could tell it had been a long time. Like him, it had been a long time.

"That time had an impact on me, yes," he finally said. "It had an impact on our entire family. How could it not?"

"Exactly." She let her response resonate a while. "Did Raymond ever tell you what *he* thought was causing his night terrors?"

"He always claimed he didn't know."

"And the doctors your parents took him to?"

"This was several years ago. I suspect the medical profession didn't know as much about the phenomenon of night terrors then as they do now. They gave a slew of reasons, but most had to do with Raymond either suffering some sort of post-traumatic disorder or mental illness. I never believed that, and neither did he."

"Can you tell me why?"

"Because it only happened at night." Seth looked over at her. "People don't go crazy at night then become completely sane and rational in the light only to go crazy again the following night."

"No?"

"You'd know better than I, you're the doctor." Seth tried to mask his rising fear with something of a contentious smile. "But I've certainly never heard of such a thing."

"Actually, there are numerous disorders associated with darkness, some which manifest strictly at night. Many people, even adults, fear the dark, Seth."

"This was more than that."

She remained quiet a while, as if weighing the

validity of his statement. "Do you think it's fair to say that perhaps these episodes from your past, along with the death of your parents, of course, are contributing factors to what you've experienced since?"

Seth fidgeted a bit. His palms had begun to sweat. "Yes."

"And now you think there may be a connection between these more recent memories and dreams to a vacation you and Raymond went on..." she hesitated long enough to consult her little pad, "...a year ago?"

"I think it's possible. I haven't seen Raymond since then. We've spoken on the phone a few times and he wrote me a letter once. I've been concerned about him since then, I—I mean, I'm always concerned about Raymond, he..."

"Has issues."

"To put it mildly."

"Would you like to tell me about the vacation?"

Seth closed his eyes in an attempt to shut out images of his brother's face that night at the cabin. "It was as if he'd lost his mind." He took a moment to let the words take hold, and also to remind himself to edit out the events concerning Christy. They had agreed never to tell anyone about her and he wanted to keep his word. "We'd only been there a day, and that night he disappeared from the cabin for a while without any real explanation, or at least one that made sense to any of us. There was a snowstorm. It wasn't supposed to hit until the day after we left, but the meteorologists misjudged it and it hit early, really pounded the whole area. Raymond wandered off in the middle of it." Silence answered him, so he continued, relaying the story of that night to her in as much detail as he could recall.

Once he finished she asked, "Do you think there could be any number of reasonable explanations for what happened that night, Seth?"

"Yes, I—I even I thought of a few myself," he admitted, "but they never felt right. Nothing about that night felt right. Not then, not now. I've never been able to shake those feelings. Over time, it's only gotten worse."

"Do you think perhaps it brought back some dark memories of your youth? Your brother going off in the night again, like he had as a child frightened by bad dreams?"

"I'm sure it did."

She gave a subtle nod. "Let's change gears for a moment. After the death of your parents, Raymond's life continued to be plagued by various problems. But you eventually flourished, yes?"

"Yes, to a degree."

"But Raymond did not."

"No."

Rather suddenly she said, "Were you raised in a particularly religious family?"

"Not really. My father was a hippie. A former hippie, I suppose. He had his own way of looking at things, including religion. Mother Earth and all that." A thoughtful moment passed before he continued. "My mother was born Catholic but became a Congregationalist when she was in her twenties. She attended church regularly, sang in the choir, that kind of thing, but I never considered her principally religious—more spiritual, really. She had a way about her, a kind of spiritual purity."

"What about you and Raymond?"

"When I was a child I felt a strong connection to God. I had tremendous faith. But as an adult I became more pragmatic. Raymond was always spiritual. Then and now."

"Talk about that a moment."

Seth smiled uncomfortably. "Our Nana, our father's mother, is the only grandparent either of us has ever known. Our mother was a change of life baby and her parents died when Ray and I were quite young, so we never knew either of them, unfortunately. Nana was the most religious person in our family, but she's from the old country—Italy—and believes in a lot of the old ways. She and Ray were always very close, much closer than I was to her. I felt more of an attachment to traditional religion in those days, and enjoyed going to church with my mother. Nana's beliefs and eccentricities were better suited to Raymond than me. She used to say he was 'special.'"

"And what do you think she meant by that?"

"That he believed her nonsense, maybe. At a minimum he listened to it. Old world magic, superstitions and the rest." Seth thought a moment, remembering. "After Raymond's night terrors stopped he became more introverted than ever—even before the death of our parents. He acted like he knew something, like he could see things no one else could. He used to say he knew things before they happened; that he sometimes got these premonitions that bothered him. I don't know if it's true, I always suspected not, of course, and he must have picked up on my skepticism because he rarely mentioned it. Nana was the only one who encouraged that kind of thing in him, and in some ways I think it made Ray worse. I don't know what was going on in his head, but there *were* things going through his mind, things he found distracting somehow."

"Good things or bad things?"

"Troubling things."

"Did Raymond have a hard time as a child?" she asked. "Apart from the night terrors, that is."

"Yes." A swell of guilt shook him. "He was a strange kid, always the outsider, never really had any friends. I mean, I was never very popular either, was never a part of the 'in' crowd, but it was a lot worse than that for Ray. It was sad, but he was *so* different from everyone else he stood out. Elementary school was bad enough, but high school was very difficult for him. They thought he had a learning disorder and attention problems, probably because he always seemed so preoccupied. It was like sometimes Raymond could be sitting right in front of you but he might as well have been a million miles away. He's still like that sometimes."

"And how did Raymond's problems in school impact you, Seth?"

Seth forced his eyes shut and concentrated until his mind cleared of memories he didn't want to confront just then. "It was tough," he said. "He was my little brother, what could I do? He always looked up to me for some reason, always looked to me to be there for him, to look out for him, to defend him if need be."

"And did you?"

Another wave of guilt swept through him, this time with such ferocity it left him nauseated. "Eventually Ray learned to fight his own battles, but he took it all too far. He started getting in fights, causing trouble, doing drugs, drinking."

"How would you say other people's perceptions of Raymond made you feel?"

"He was looked at like this weirdo, a crazy kid but…" Seth took a moment to control his emotions. "It's been difficult for me too. It was especially hard then, when we were younger. There was always this pressure to make things right, to look out for him, to explain for him. Everything was always about him."

She nodded. "Talk about that a bit."

Seth shrugged, feeling trapped. "It's always been that way. I guess when you have someone in your family with problems like that everything becomes about them, or about how everything relates to them in one way or another. I always felt this responsibility not only for my own life, but for Raymond's too. And after our parents were killed he was more lost than ever. For the first time he pulled away from me. It sounds terrible, but sometimes being apart from him is easier. It gives me a break, but only temporarily, because then I worry about him and feel guilty for not doing more."

"Is there more you could do or could have done to help him?"

"Isn't there always?"

"Is that your answer?"

"I feel a lot of guilt when it comes to Ray."

"Why guilt?"

"In some ways I resented him. It made me angry that he had to be the way he was…is. But no matter what, he always looked up to me, always acted like he knew he could count on me."

"Was he wrong?"

"In some ways."

"Did you betray him somehow?"

Seth stared at the floor but didn't answer.

"Seth?"

"I love my brother," he said finally.

She watched him a moment before continuing. "After the death of your parents, did either you or your brother seek counseling?"

"No. We just handled it as best we could."

"Did it impact either of you in a specifically spiritual sense?"

Seth nodded slowly. "It killed my faith."

"And was this death of your faith permanent?"

"Yes," he said evenly. "It was."

Quiet returned to the room for a time. "You said you didn't believe Raymond suffered from mental illness as a child, do—"

"Emotional problems, possibly, but no, I don't believe he was mentally ill as a child."

"And as an adult? Do you think Raymond suffers from mental illness *now*?"

"It's a distinct possibility." Rather than make eye contact, he scanned the framed diplomas on the wall. "I think Raymond suffers from many things."

*We all do*, he thought.

Doctor Farrow jotted something quickly on the pad then placed it on a low glass table between them. "That's all for today," she said softly. "I'm afraid we're out of time. But I want you to think about how these things we've discussed today may or may not relate, all right?"

Seth nodded.

She uncrossed her legs, moved closer to the edge of

her chair and crossed her feet. "I can't do this for you. I can help, of course." Absently, she brushed a wisp of thick blonde hair from her eyes and smiled warmly. "But only you can work through this."

"I understand."

Her smile disappeared gradually, lush lips closing over beautiful teeth. "I'll be back from vacation in two weeks. In the interim, Doctor Kowalski will be covering the office for me. I've scheduled an appointment for you once I'm back, so take this break in our sessions and try to make the most of it, all right?"

Seth nodded without bothering to mention that he too would be on vacation over the next two weeks. "Going somewhere nice?"

"The Cayman Islands, actually." She seemed hopeful he might comment on her destination, and disappointed when he didn't. "Yes, well, at any rate, if you have any basic needs, Doctor Kowalski can help you. In case of an absolute emergency, should you need me, you can call my service and they can reach me. But I think you'll be fine."

It annoyed him when she said things like that. As if life was impossible to negotiate without her constant intervention. He checked his watch. "I should get back to the office."

"I'll see you in a couple weeks," she said with a wink. "Be well."

* * *

As Seth crossed the quiet, sterile lobby and stepped out into the parking lot, he was met by a burst of cold air. His mind, still locked on the memories, conjured sudden flashes of him and Raymond running in the cold night air, memories of chasing him, trying to catch him to tell him it was all right, that everything was all right. But even now, all these years later, he couldn't be certain if everything was, in fact, all right. Some, like Doc, labeled it obsessive or compulsive thinking and stress-induced anxiety, the result of depression never cured and issues never resolved, but Seth had never been so sure.

The night their parents died everything changed. Though the night terrors Raymond had suffered as a child had already stopped, his other problems escalated, and he drifted further into trouble—*dysfunction*, as Doc would say—the happy little boy he'd once been spiraling into the past, debris helplessly carried away on an unforgiving wind. And as things crumbled around him, Seth began to drown in guilt and helplessness. Angry at himself, at God, at the world, he shut down internally and did his best to move forward. Like a disoriented and exhausted swimmer giving in to the tide and wherever it might lead him, he submitted and let life take him in whatever direction it needed to. He was certain it was the only way to assure his survival, such as it was.

A curious phenomenon, survival.

Death had left the remnants of their lives shattered, raining down in shards and leaving behind rubble and mayhem where something sound and beautiful had once been, and that night at the cabin had only made things worse, more senseless and mysterious than ever.

In the last year the dark thoughts and formless, piecemeal memories of that night had grown increasingly powerful. Slowly at first, but gaining momentum over time, they had left Seth wondering if it all really *could* be chalked up to mental illness. And if so, was he destined to fall into the same bottomless pit that had claimed his brother?

Some days he believed he already had.

When Seth reached his car he stopped and looked to the sky.

There was a storm coming.

# Chapter 5

Rain sluiced along the tall windows on the back wall, blurring the parking lot and street beyond. It ran the length of glass silently, the world outside noiseless within the sealed and soundproofed corporate crypt. Instead of natural sound, nearly inaudible Muzak that could only be described as mind-numbing filtered through the area, piped in through speakers recessed and hidden in the ceiling. Like a mall in Hell, employees often joked, though few realized or appreciated the ironic redundancy of such a statement.

Seth repressed a smile at the thought then pulled off his headset, shut down his computer and took a few minutes to straighten his desk and tidy up his cubicle. He had worked in the customer service department for the Severance Stereo Corporation, an exclusive and high-end home electronics manufacturer, for the past ten years. For the past four, he'd been assistant department manager, and the powers that be still hadn't deemed him significant enough to warrant an actual office. His cubicle was a bit roomier than most, though, since he was in management after all, and class distinctions—however facile—had to be evident, lest all employees actually feel relevant and good about themselves.

"Shutting down early?"

A head peered at him over the top of his cubicle wall. Ruth Chandler, a young woman who had come to work in their department only a few months before, offered her usual cynical grin. At first, Ruth, who referred to herself as *Ruthie*, had struck him as an annoying early twenty-something with an attitude that tried a bit too hard to be cool and rebellious, but over time he had come to like her a great deal. There was something pure about her in the strangest sense. As sardonic as she could often be, she was young enough to still maintain a basic belief in the concept of hope, particularly in global, universal terms, and Seth respected that. While she reported to work each day in the requisite slacks and blouse or skirt and heels, and always appeared professional, if one looked closely the traces of the person she became on weekends and after hours was clear. The tiny hole in her nose, nearly impossible to spot under a swathe of faint makeup, sported a diamond stud on off-time, and her four tattoos (which she had described to him but he'd never actually seen), remained covered under a business attire facade. Her eyes were always adorned in black eyeliner, though not too heavy, and her lipstick looked retro, a bit too red and somewhat shocking against hair dyed jet-black and worn in a bob with bangs. Seth imagined she probably streaked it with pink and green when she was at home. More cute than pretty, she had an allure about her and a depth in her eyes that hinted she was far more introspective than she initially appeared, and a body she purposely underplayed but that still turned most heads in the office. A strict vegetarian, she volunteered much of her free time to various political and social organizations she supported, and felt the need to share most of these experiences with Seth, with whom she had formed an almost immediate bond. An odd couple to be sure, he often wondered why she liked him and seemed to view his as a sympathetic ear—even though he was management—but she did. At first he'd suspected it was proximity, as her cubicle was right next to his own, but he soon realized that despite their age difference she felt a kinship with him, a trust, like he understood not only her, but the world they were both forced to endure for at least forty hours each week.

"Yes," Seth answered quietly. "Vacation, remember?"

"Cool." She glanced around suspiciously. "Rally on Saturday, want to come?"

"Thanks, but I—"

"You'll have a blast, come on. It'll be good for your soul, dude. We're marching for peace and then protesting out in front of some media outlets—you know, TV stations, newspapers and whatnot—it'll be awesome, you should come. There's gonna be signs and chants and everything," she said with nearly lethal sarcasm. "Now how cool is that?"

Seth nodded helplessly. "Pretty cool, I guess."

"Do you good to get out there and fight the power. Lose that suit and get involved, you know?" She winked and cocked her head like a punk rock version of June Allyson.

"I'd like to, Ruthie, but I—"

"Apathy, dude, apathy—it's exterminating the human race."

"I don't mean to be apathetic, it's just—"

"What about Sunday?" She adjusted her position, kneeling on her chair as she often did so she could get high enough to rest her forearms on top of the cubicle wall. "I've got some people coming over to my apartment—all very cool. We need to get organized if we're going to stop this fascist machine running our government right now. I mean, it's worse than people think. Even the press is in on it, Seth. A free press is vital in a society like ours. Without a free press to do the job we can't do as citizens, who else is there to protect us from totalitarianism? But it's all becoming a joke. The press is corporate-owned now, and beholden to other interests, you see what I mean? That's why they don't actually act like journalists anymore. Shills, that's what they are. Fake news, reporting what the man tells them they can, never questioning anything anymore, just going along, getting ratings and not making waves, see, because waves are bad for business. It's grim, Seth, big-time grim. Things are happening and none of them are good, OK?"

He nodded dutifully. "OK."

"So you wanna come?" She grinned again. "On Sunday, I mean."

"I would, Ruthie, but I'm sort of busy this weekend." He returned her smile with the best one he could muster. "Thanks, though, I appreciate you thinking of me."

She sighed. "One of these days you'll say yes. I know there's still hope for you."

"That's good to hear."

"No, for real, I can feel it. I have really good instincts. The first time I met you I knew you weren't like all these other fucking androids wandering around here. Deep down, you're just like me."

"Yeah, we're virtually identical," he chuckled.

"In our hearts and minds," Ruth said, grin faded. "You know what I mean."

"Maybe you're right."

"You hate the way things are just as much as I do. You even hate this corporate prison the same as I do."

He looked away, tried to busy himself tidying up again. "Yes, well…"

"I know, I know, you're management, you have to support the company line. Whatever, dude, it's cool. It's just us talking, right? We can still talk, can't we?"

"Of course, I didn't mean—"

"It's just that this place doesn't help, that's all I'm saying. The concept that corporate repression crushes the individual is sort of beyond debate, wouldn't you agree?"

"You'll never last here with that philosophy," Seth said with a wink of his own.

"Who'd want to?"

"You may have a point there."

"The way I see it, it's kinda like the Piggyback Fish."

Seth stared at her dumbly.

"Piggyback Fish," she said again, this time rolling her eyes. "There's actually this long scientific name for it, some Latin name or something, but they call it the Piggyback Fish because of how it piggybacks on other fish. I saw a show on it on the Discovery Channel the other night, very cool. See, it's this rare fish that lives in the Amazon, right? It's small, about the size of my pinky finger, and what it does is, it attaches itself to other fish, bigger ones, with these little tentacles or freakin' throwback feeding things or whatever the hell they are. This scary-ass shit growing out of their undersides, OK? I forget what they call them but anyway, it attaches itself and feeds off them kind of like a parasite. Only regular parasites make the host sick but always keep it alive because if the host dies they die too, right? But not the Piggyback Fish. Nope, he feeds off the host fish until it dies, but he kills it slowly, gradually over time, and absorbs as much from it as he can before he kills it. See, the Piggyback Fish isn't really a parasite, it's a predator *disguised* as a parasite, get it? It can survive without the host, so it kills off one and just moves to another, spending its life attaching itself to other fish and slowly sucking the life out of them. Way fucking heinous, no?"

Seth suddenly felt uncomfortable. "Yeah that's uh...fascinating."

"It just reminded me of life. It's kind of like we're the poor fish swimming along trying to do our best, right, and the company, the government, whatever—fill in the blank—is the Piggyback Fish, attaching itself to us and slowly taking everything from us until eventually, we die."

"Jesus, do you think that's pessimistic enough, Ruthie?"

"It's a bleak world out there, dude."

"Well, I'll be sure to stay out of the Amazon."

"I know things bother you," she said, lowering her voice to a mere whisper and assuming a more serious tone. "I watch you sometimes and I see you thinking, I can see it in your face. This troubled look you have, I can relate, you know? You're not like most people. You're a thinker, like me."

"OK, well right now I'm thinking about getting out of here." Seth stood up and grabbed his briefcase. "I'll see you in a couple weeks."

"Bet you miss me already," she said with a resigned air. "Have a good vacation."

"I'll do my best. Be good."

Ruthie gave a wicked smile and sank back behind the cubicle wall. "But it's so much more fun being bad."

Stifling a laugh, Seth left his cubicle and checked in with Bill Jacobs, the head of the department. After a brief but uneventful meeting, he headed for the break room.

As he moved past the water cooler and a sea of cubicles, he loosened his tie and breathed a sigh of relief. Two weeks away from this place would do him a world of good.

But for Louis Dodge and Darian Stone, the break room was empty. They had agreed to meet there earlier, but since they all worked in different departments—Darian in accounting and Louis in shipping—Seth was surprised to find them waiting, as they were rarely able to coordinate their break times to coincide.

"Hey guys," he said meekly.

Louis waved him over to the table where he and Darian were sitting. "I'm going for appetizers and a few drinks over at O'Leary's after work, you in?"

"Thanks, but I can't." Seth set his briefcase down and rubbed his tired eyes.

"Why, you got something going?"

"Nope, I'm exhausted, haven't been sleeping well lately. I was planning a quiet evening alone."

"Scintillating." Louis jerked a thumb in Darian's direction. "You're getting as bad as this one, can't get him out of the house either."

Darian took a sip of coffee from a small Styrofoam cup. "Sorry if I can't match your enthusiasm for the artery-clogging delicacies at O'Leary's."

"I can only hope they kill me quickly." Louis ran a hand through his thick blond hair. Though conservatively-styled, it was one of his more striking features.

At thirty-three, Louis was the youngest of the three men. Short and a bit stocky, he had always appeared healthy and strong, but in the last few months he had slowed a bit, as if the singles lifestyle he so passionately claimed to embrace since his divorce three years earlier had begun to catch up to him. In addition, he'd gained at least thirty excess pounds, which even in his work attire—a suit and tie—left him looking frumpy and disheveled. "Fine, you old farts do what you want," he said. "I'm going for drinks and having myself some fun. You guys remember fun, right?"

"Sure, it's right between *fumigate* and *function*, in the dictionary," Darian said. "Think about it."

Louis and Darian were doing their best to keep things light, but Seth could tell they were trying a bit too hard. Neither had been quite right since that night a year before. None of them had. Louis in particular seemed shaky of late.

"You hear the latest with Becky?" Louis asked abruptly. "Got a call from her last night. You ready for this? She and her new boyfriend are moving to

Montana next month, and she wants to take the kids with them. You believe that shit?"

"Jesus, Louis, can she do that?"

He shrugged. "I can fight it in court but these judges are pricks. They almost never take kids from their mothers, and besides, even if I tried to get custody they'd never give it to me. Not after that other thing."

A few months before, Louis had been arrested for punching his ex-wife's new boyfriend over a dispute involving his children. Though the charges were eventually dropped, the incident had resulted in Louis only being allowed supervised visits with his children. In all the time Seth had known him it was the only occurrence of violence he could ever remember Louis perpetrating. He'd always been more tough talk than action, but now even that had changed. "So what's in Montana?"

"Cows?" Louis gave a humorless laugh. "Her boyfriend's old man owns a big car dealership out there and he wants to retire and turn everything over to his son. Sounds like the kids won't want for anything, but shit, I'll never see them."

His daughter Danielle was only five, his son Louis, Jr., just seven. It seemed a particularly difficult time to uproot children and make them start all over again elsewhere, Seth thought, especially so far from their father. Though the pain in his friend's eyes was intense, Seth made it a point not to stare. He knew Louis was far from a saint. He drank too much, ate too much and by his own admission had been a less than stellar husband. But one thing no one could deny was the love he had for his kids. For all of Louis's calculated bravado and tough guy swagger, Seth couldn't imagine him surviving long without his children in his life.

"What do you plan to do?"

"Not much I *can* do," he said in an uncharacteristically soft tone. "Deal with it, I guess. Tell my kids I'll see them every chance I get and hope to Christ they remember who I am."

"Maybe you should put in for some personal time," Seth suggested. "Take a break and try to sort this all out."

"I don't know." Louis shrugged. "I'm thinking about it."

"We could all do with some time off from this place." Darian stood up, walked behind the table and tossed his coffee cup into a nearby receptacle. On his way back, he reached out, gave Louis a gentle pat of reassurance on the shoulder then turned to Seth. "Be sure to take advantage of your vacation and get some rest." Of average height, with hair trimmed so close to his scalp at first glance it appeared shaved, Darian was the opposite of Louis in almost every way. Subtly handsome, he possessed a bright smile and an average but thin build, wore eyeglasses and a short goatee, and had a voice and manner that was generally so relaxed it bordered on serene. "We'll hold things together here, don't worry."

"*Me* worry?" Seth smiled, grabbed his briefcase and headed for the door.

Louis crossed his eyes comically. "Thank God for Mother."

Because he was the eldest of their group, and due to his often doting and controlled manner, Darian had been given the moniker *Mother* by his small circle of friends, and though he often cringed whenever they used it, they knew that deep down he was secretly fond of it. Darian was a quiet, confident sort, the kind of man that carried himself like he knew who he was, where he was headed, and precisely how he planned to get there. He was a company man, took his career seriously and performed his job with a nearly obsessive intensity. He could be cynical but was rarely malicious, less of a wiseass than Louis, and inherently brighter. At thirty-eight, he'd been married to his wife Cynthia for several years, and together they'd had a child, a daughter named Debra who had recently turned nine. For Darian, there was the company, his family, a few close friends, and little else, and while Seth sometimes found him almost too deliberate in his routines, he respected him enormously.

"Absolutely." Seth gave a casual wave goodbye. "I'll see you guys later."

When he headed back into the hallway, Darian followed. "Hey," he said quietly, "hold up a minute."

"What's up?"

"You're looking a little stressed."

"Don't I always look like that?"

This time Darian didn't smile. "Seriously, is everything all right?"

They'd all been dancing with each other like this for months. Approach and avoid, testing each other, reaching, trying to feel each other out. "I'm just tired," Seth said. "Like I said, haven't been sleeping well lately."

Darian looked like he wanted to say something but hesitated, seemed to think about it a moment then said, "Worried about you, that's all."

"What about you?"

"Me? I'm—I'm fine."

"And Louis; is he fine too? He doesn't look fine, Mother. He's not acting fine."

Darian nodded knowingly, and neither man said a word for several seconds. "Have you spoken to Peggy lately?"

Seth shrugged. "It's complicated."

"Yeah, I imagine it would be."

"I've got some issues I have to work through." Again, Seth waited, hoping Darian would bite. But he didn't. "I think we all do."

Darian looked around to make certain they were still alone in the hallway. "How's it going with that doctor? Does it...Do you find it helps you?"

"It's still a little early to tell, but I think so."

"Good, that's—that's good."

"Why, are you thinking about trying it?"

"I was just curious how it was going, that's all." Darian moved closer, his expression somber. "Listen, don't—I mean, you haven't told the doctor about that night, have you?"

"Some of it, yes."

"But not about..."

"Not about Christy, no. I gave my word, didn't I?"

Darian nodded vigorously. "Of course, yes. I wasn't implying you—I just—I didn't mean to pry, I just wanted to make sure you're OK."

Seth kept his expression still. "Thanks."

"Well listen, if you need to talk, I'm around."

"Same here."

Darian nodded awkwardly.

"Keep a close eye on Louis." Seth turned and

headed toward the elevator. "I'm worried about him."

"I'm worried about all of us."

Seth hesitated a moment. Though it was the most honest and unguarded thing he'd heard Darian say in nearly a year, he couldn't bring himself to respond. The fear had risen in him again, the inexplicable panic and terror. He gave a quick nod, and without looking back, made his way down the hallway to the elevator.

Why couldn't they discuss things like they once had? It was as if they spoke to each other in code now, like guilty children too nervous to look each other in the eye. As the elevator doors closed, he focused on being away from this place and all its Kafkaesque morbidity for two weeks. Normally he would've been thrilled with the break, the change of scenery, but this time he could not be so sure of what was waiting for him out there.

Once the elevator began its descent to the parking garage beneath the building, Seth caught himself replaying the session he'd had earlier with Doc.

Visions of Raymond, the snow, the two of them running, slipped through his mind like a movie reel. And his parents, they were always there too, lingering in his head like the ghosts they'd become, brooding, distant entities peering at him from some other place, some other time.

He swallowed hard and fought off emotion. Maybe it was just guilt.

If there was one thing Seth Roman was intimately familiar with, it was guilt. There had always existed in him a curious dichotomy that coupled a love of life directly alongside relentless self-loathing, and that, compounded by all that had happened, left Seth feeling like a complete failure. He felt he had failed not only himself, but in every way possible: as a son, as a brother, as a husband, and in ultimately losing his faith, he'd even failed God.

But he believed God had failed him too. He'd turned His back on them and in the process stolen the lives of his parents, destroyed his brother and left their lives in ruins. The world had gone up in flames, and only Seth's guilt remained, more powerful and unshakable than his faith had ever been.

Although he'd left a bit early, he still found himself caught in rush hour traffic on his way out of Boston, and to complicate matters, an icy rain had kicked up. Sitting in a bumper-to-bumper creep, the squeaking cadence of the windshield wipers distracted him a moment. But like all good demons, his never stayed quiet long.

It had rained that night, too. He remembered the horrible downpour as his mind raced, trying desperately to make sense of what had happened.

By the time paramedics reached the scene their father was dead. Their mother made it to the hospital but never regained consciousness and died the next day.

The look of his mother in that hospital bed—a profane hybrid of flesh and apparatus, so many tubes coming from her it was hard to tell where she ended and the array of machines surrounding her began—was something Seth had never been able to wipe from his mind. Her head a mangle of bruises and awful contusions, mouth propped open, a breathing tube protruding from it like a plastic bone burst through her body, she barely looked human.

Raymond had sat next to the bed and sobbed uncontrollably, now and then looking to Seth with a pleading expression that screamed: *Do something.*

That had always been his role, after all. He was the older brother, the protector, a role he had been assigned whether he wanted it or not. *Do something.*

Seth prayed for hours, as his mother had taught him, asking God for a sign, some explanation, or even a miracle. But no answer came.

That vision was the last memory Seth had in which his brother actually gave a damn about something. When their mother slipped away, much of his desire—perhaps his ability—to care for anything or anyone seemed to go with her.

After the accident Seth left school in the hopes of looking out for his brother, but within days of the funerals Raymond had packed his meager belongings into a duffel bag and simply walked away. Though he returned periodically over the years, for the most part, Raymond stayed gone.

Seth took a retail sales job and began to drown his sorrows in alcohol. Eventually he was able to move into his own small apartment, and in a short amount of time he'd left sales and taken a position in customer service.

For the next several years Raymond bounced around the country, spending time in numerous county jails for various petty crimes and run-ins with locals or the law. Seth rarely saw or heard from him except in the form of occasional phone calls looking for bail money or brief letters penned in some cell.

Despite a slowly worsening drinking habit, Seth managed to land a job with Severance, where he had worked ever since, and for those first several years after the tragedy not much changed. It was a lonely and sullen time.

And then he met Peggy.

With the most soulful eyes he had ever seen and a bawdy, contagious laugh, she was passionate, direct, fiercely intelligent, and had a wonderful sense of humor Seth found disarming. Though she rarely wore makeup she had a natural beauty that matched her down-to-Earth sensibilities and compassionate political leanings. Peggy was a sculptor, painter and teacher, an artist who was more comfortable in jeans and a t-shirt, sandals or an old pair of sneakers than she ever could be in a dress and heels. She wore kerchiefs and rope bracelets, funky rings on her fingers and toes, drank cheap wine and danced barefoot whenever afforded the chance.

To Peggy, Seth was a dark, brooding, mysterious and complex man she found fascinating, and while she was as far from the corporate-type as one could get, she believed that deep down, so was he. It was one of the things he loved about her instantly. She was capable of seeing not only the good in people, but the truth in them as well. Tortured as she knew him to be, she saw more than the pain of his past, she saw the person he wanted to be, the person he *could* be.

* * *

When they met at a fund-raiser for a local animal shelter, both were in their early twenties. Seth had only recently started working at Severance, and Peggy had graduated from Lesley University with a degree in Fine

Arts a few months before. As a volunteer at the shelter, she'd been helping out with adoptions, and since Seth had decided to get a dog, it became a perfect excuse to talk with her.

That day he took home a puppy he named Petey. The following night, he took Peggy to dinner and a movie. A few months and numerous dates later, while walking along the banks of the Charles River, Seth proposed.

They were married soon after in a quiet ceremony by a justice of the peace. Peggy's parents, professors who lived and taught in Cambridge, attended on her side, and Seth's Nana attended on his. Although Raymond had promised he'd be there for Seth, he'd been unexpectedly detained in some Pennsylvania town after getting into a bar fight that resulted in his arrest. In his absence, Darian—someone Seth had only known and worked with for a year at that point, but with whom he'd become close—stepped in as Best Man at the last moment. Raymond eventually blew into town, but by the time he got there Seth and Peggy had already returned from a weeklong honeymoon in Bermuda and moved into an apartment in the Back Bay section of Boston.

Two years into the marriage Peggy learned she was unable to have children. The question of starting a family had always been something Seth avoided, and though he knew Peggy wanted kids one day, she had never forced the issue or made him feel pressured to become a father. Although he liked children, parenthood was a terrifying prospect, so the news was something he found far easier to deal with than Peggy had. For her, it changed something in her being, something nearly tangible. It was neither a dramatic nor blatant change, but instead a subtle one that seeped from her quietly. She became a wonderfully attentive aunt to her sister's children, and loved them dearly, but Seth knew it wasn't the same for her. To him, as long as they were together that was all that mattered, and while Peggy believed the same, the idea of not even being able to consider children as a possibility, a concept in some future they might have together, the finality of it all, left her distraught.

"I never had a burning desire to be a mother," she'd told him one night while they lay in bed, cuddled together beneath blankets and a large comforter, "it was never that important to me. But when I met you, I thought about it for the first time in a serious light. It seemed a natural extension of us, to bring a child into the world. *Our* child. Together."

"I'm sorry," Seth whispered to her again and again, holding her tight. It was all he could think to say.

"It doesn't matter, as long as we have each other."

Initially, Peggy had given Seth reason to focus on something other than his lack of self-esteem. She'd been a reason to get up in the morning, to go to work, to do well. She'd given him the chance to care for someone, to feel alive again, even if imperfectly so, a reason to love and be loved. And though her inability to bear children had made things more difficult in their marriage, theirs was still a strong bond, and Seth believed they'd be together forever.

But then came the trip to Maine, the days and nights at the cabin, the snowstorm and Raymond and Christy's disappearance...

He'd pulled away, become more introverted and

silent, pushing Peggy away without even realizing it, and the chasm between them began to widen. The joy and unconditional acceptance that had bridged their differences and made their marriage rock solid in the early years continued to slowly decay until Seth finally decided it would be best if he moved out. After nine years of marriage, he left Peggy and moved to a small apartment complex in the suburbs just south of Boston.

"I don't want you to go, but if you don't want to be here I won't stop you."

Several months later, her words continued to haunt him, and though he and Peggy were still legally married, they remained separated. Despite their now individual lives, they continued to be oddly close in many ways. Some days their marriage—their happiness—seemed so distant, while others it still felt within reach, like there might still be hope. So he'd grabbed hold of that distant glimmer of hope and tried to sustain it as best he could. In the dark, or even in the light, it was all he had.

* * *

As the logjam of traffic finally broke, Seth's thoughts returned to the road and what would hopefully be a quiet evening ahead.

The rain was still falling by the time he pulled into the apartment complex. Using his briefcase as a makeshift umbrella, he moved quickly across the parking lot to the shelter of the building's small foyer then rode the elevator to the third floor.

He strolled along the quiet, carpeted hallway to his front door, unlocked it and slipped inside. As he flipped the switch just inside the entrance, welcoming light filled the short hallway that led to the living room.

He'd only taken a few steps when he sensed a presence in the apartment other than his own, and while that realization was still taking shape in his mind, a dark form slipped past his peripheral vision.

His heart sunk in a terrified rush as he brought his briefcase up like a shield, but even then he knew it was too late.

The intruder was already closing on him.

# Chapter 6

The intruder stepped forward, became Raymond. "Relax."

"God almighty," Seth said, his heart rate slowly returning to normal. "You scared the hell out of me, Ray."

Still partially masked in shadow, he lingered near the far wall but said nothing.

Seth put his briefcase down. "How did you get in here?"

"Invest in a decent deadbolt." Raymond motioned to the door. "That lock's shit."

Unsure of what to do, Seth looked behind him at the door.

"Don't worry, I didn't break it. I know what I'm doing."

"That's comforting." He noticed Raymond's hair was still wet and dangling in his eyes, and his clothes—a badly worn brown leather jacket, old jeans, scuffed boots and a sweatshirt—looked damp as well. He hadn't been in the apartment long. "You've become an accomplished thief, congratulations."

Quiet draped the room as the brothers stood looking at each other awkwardly.

Rain tapped the windows, filling the silence.

Raymond stepped closer. "It's good to see you, man."

Before he could prevent it a slight smile crossed Seth's face. "It's good to see you too, Ray." He leaned into him, and they hugged. "But you could've waited to come in until I got home."

"It's raining out."

Seth stepped back, looked him over. "Are you all right?"

He shrugged.

Seth moved to the couch and sat down, his nerves finally settling a bit. "Are you in any trouble I should be aware of?"

"Depends on what kind of trouble you're talking about."

"I'm not joking, Raymond. I'm sorry I have to ask these things but I don't want any problems."

"You mean *additional* problems."

Seth shook his head. His brother had always been one of his weaknesses. No matter what he did and no matter how Raymond aged or hardened, Seth couldn't help but see the young boy he'd once been. To him, Ray would forever be his innocent younger brother, the tiny sidekick who had once followed him around and idolized his every move, the terrified little boy running through the night as if for his life.

*I don't deserve your reverence, Ray. I never did.*

"The police—or worse—won't be knocking on my door, will they?"

"I'm not on parole or probation or anything if that's what you're asking."

A few months prior, Seth had received a letter from Raymond while he was serving time for car theft in a county jail in Indiana, but hadn't heard from him since. "Is that business in Indiana over with?"

"I got hammered one night and pinched a car—real box of crap, couldn't outrun a paperboy on a fucking Schwinn with this sled. The judge threw me in county for a couple months because of all my priors. I did my sixty days and walked."

"And decided to come see me?"

"I got a job for a while so I'd have a few bucks ahead of me, but then, yeah."

"How did you get here?"

"I rented a car." Raymond shuffled about nervously. "Well...more borrowed it really, but you know what I mean."

"Jesus Christ, Ray, you're thirty-one years old, when is this going to stop?"

"When's what going to stop?"

"This nonsense."

"This nonsense is my life."

"Only because you choose it to be."

"I don't need this shit from you right now, man, OK?"

Seth looked away as another wave of uncomfortable silence filled the room.

Raymond gathered his hair into a ponytail and secured it in place with a small rubber band he pulled from his pocket. "I told you in the last letter I sent I was coming home when I got out. Well abracadabra, motherfucker; here I am."

"I could've sent you the money for a bus or a train ticket, Ray, you didn't have to—"

"Jesus, I figured you'd be happy to see me. Should've known better."

Though his hair reached his shoulders when loose, once pulled back and away from his face Raymond's attempt at mysteriousness all but vanished. Just shy of his thirty-second birthday, upon closer inspection he could have passed for someone ten years older. Worn, tired, and battle-weary, Seth realized his little brother didn't look so little anymore. "Don't be an ass, of course I'm happy to see you."

Raymond looked edgy, like he hadn't yet again become accustomed to open spaces. "In case you're interested, on my way into town I stopped at the cemetery and saw Mom and Dad."

Raymond could revert to innocence in a flash, Seth thought, effortlessly referring to them with the wide-eyed wonderment of a little boy, as if they had died quietly in their sleep. Memories of their parents came to him then, and Seth embraced them. But they faded rapidly, banished to a netherworld of vague yesterdays that often seemed more fantasies born of wishful thinking than the literal history he believed them to be.

"I brought flowers for Mom," Raymond said.

He pictured Raymond standing in the rain at the cemetery, a bunch of wilted, dying flowers in his hand he'd probably stolen from a nearby headstone.

"I haven't been in years," Seth told him.

"Yeah, I could tell." Raymond eventually wandered back toward the couch, closer to his brother. "Don't they have any upkeep at that fucking place?"

"Ray, we need to talk."

His face revealed nothing. "You think?"

"I'm serious."

"You don't say."

"Can we have an intelligent conversation or are you going to crack jokes all night?"

"Some people whistle in the dark," he answered. "I've learned to laugh."

"Neither one are genuine."

A glint sparkled in Raymond's dark eyes. "You got me there."

Seth drew a deep breath. It suddenly felt as though the apartment had closed in around him. "Have you eaten?"

"Not since yesterday."

"Let's go get something then, you must be starving."

Raymond looked at the rain against the windows just beyond the shadows still covering the far wall, and cocked his head as if he'd heard something odd. "You still live here alone?"

A rush of fear slammed Seth's chest. "You know I do, why—"

"Can I get a glass of water? I need to take a pill."

"What kind of pill?"

Raymond sighed, reached down to his duffel bag on the floor and rummaged around in it until his hand came back holding a small prescription bottle. When Seth still looked at him questioningly, he tossed the bottle to him.

Seth read the label. "Accupril?"

"It's for high blood pressure."

"Since when do you have high blood pressure, Ray?"

"About a year now." His answer hung in the air between them. "Can I get that water? I'm supposed to take one every day."

Seth handed the bottle back, disappeared into the kitchen and returned a moment later with a bottle of water.

Raymond took his pill, polishing off most of the bottle in the process. "Thanks."

"Why do you have high blood pressure, Raymond?"

"They're not sure." His face remained neutral. "But they think it's probably stress-related."

"Horrible thing, stress."

Raymond nodded slowly. "Guess you've had plenty of your own lately. I was real sorry to hear about you and Peggy, man. How's she doing?"

"I haven't spoken to her in a while."

"That's too bad."

"Yes, it is."

"I always liked Peggy."

"Me too."

Raymond's face didn't even hint at a smile. "You still see her?"

"We talk now and then."

"Only now and then? It's gotten that bad?"

He shrugged.

"You still in love with her?"

"Love's overrated," he said flatly.

"Only when you have it."

Both men remained still and quiet for a time.

"Why did you ask if I still lived alone, Raymond?"

"I thought I heard something."

"Like what?"

"Like fear."

Seth felt a shiver cross his knees. "You don't hear fear, you feel it."

"But then we're all different, aren't we, bro."

"We need to talk, Ray. I can't—I can't keep doing this."

Raymond nodded. "Sure could use a drink first."

"I know a place."

Their eyes met as both men tried their best to quiet the echoes of screams bellowing in their minds—screams of relentless agony and terror—all the while ignoring the shadows growing along the walls and everything hidden within them.

Beyond their protective walls, the rain continued its assault, determined to wash the world clean.

# Chapter 7

Seth couldn't remember the last time he'd had so many drinks in one sitting. He and Raymond had gone to a quiet Chinese place for dinner and ended up staying for hours, talking and reminiscing about everything and anything but what was really on their minds. At one point Seth confessed to Raymond that he'd recently begun seeing a psychiatrist to help him sort through various issues. The more he drank the easier expressing himself became, and though it had been years since he'd been in the habit of having more than a glass of wine or perhaps a single mixed drink in a sitting, it felt good to cut loose a bit, to just let his mind and worries go for a while.

"Have you ever been?" Seth asked at one point.

"To a shrink? Been evaluated a few times when I was doing stretches inside, those types are always around. I haven't met one yet that knew what they were talking about, though. Bunch of witch doctors, if you ask me."

"That's Dad talking. You've never experienced it

outside of a jail or hospital setting."

"Why would I?" He grinned helplessly. "I already know I'm fucked up."

"You shouldn't joke about things like that," Seth said softly.

"I'm not." Raymond studied his brother like he had only just then noticed him sitting there. "You ever talk about me?"

"With Doc? Now and then."

"What do you say?"

"We've just started talking about the night terrors you used to have."

The restaurant was dimly lit, and when Raymond leaned back in the booth, away from the candle on their table, darkness swallowed him. "What's that got to do with you?" he asked in a way that sounded curiously like a challenge.

"Ray," Seth said hesitantly, "I need to ask you something. You don't have them anymore, do you?"

"Night terrors?" He shook his head in the negative. "Not in years."

"Do you ever wonder what they were, what caused them?"

"Emotional problems, remember?"

"I never believed that and neither did you."

Raymond leaned closer, allowing the candlelight to again reveal his face. "Maybe it was just the boogeyman." For the second time his tone made the words sound like a challenge. "Maybe it was a monster in our closet."

"Sometimes I wonder."

"If you're looking for something that'll make you feel better, I got nothing. Sorry."

"That's not what I meant, I—"

"Is that what you needed to talk to me about, nightmares when I was a kid?"

The candle flickered, and shadows licked the table between them.

"That all that's on your mind, Seth?"

"I've been having the strangest feelings." Seth looked down into his drink. "About Mom and Dad, and when we were kids. About your nightmares and all the weird things that happened when you were younger." He smiled feebly. "And that night at the cabin last year."

"Now we're talking." Raymond's face remained stoic. After a moment, he powered down most of his drink. "What do you think they mean? These *feelings*."

"I don't know what any of it means."

His expression grew darker just before he fell back, away from the table and into shadow. "Seth, listen to me. Most days I figure it's a miracle I'm not stuck in some loony bin drooling into a bucket, OK? The way I see it, every time I roll out of bed and make it through without completely losing my mind—or realizing it if I already have—it's a good day. You hear me? That's a *good* day."

Seth gripped his glass tightly. "Something happened, Ray. Something..."

"We can't change the past."

Seth sipped his drink; felt the warmth slowly spread through him. "Maybe we can. Maybe we can change the past by remembering it differently, more accurately."

"The future's the only thing you can fix, and even then—"

"Maybe the clearer certain memories become the more truth they reveal and the more truth that's revealed the more those memories can change from what we thought was the past to what was *really* the past."

"You think we're dealing with some encounter group psychobabble, is that it?"

"I don't have any fucking idea what we're dealing with, Ray."

"And you think I do?"

Seth stared at him.

Flashes of the blood blinked in strobe-like bursts through Raymond's mind. Blood on the walls, on the floor—everywhere—congealed into sticky pools mixed with sprinklings and smears finger-painted into three blurred words. Then just as quickly it was gone, replaced by Seth staring back at him from the other side of the table.

"When I was a kid," Raymond said, staring at the table, "right before all the bad stuff started, I met someone. It was this beautiful summer day, sunny and warm, but with a nice breeze. I was sitting on the ground in the field behind our house playing and Mom was in the kitchen and the screen door was open. She was singing one of those really beautiful hymns she used to, remember? Sounded just like an angel…or what I always figured an angel should sound like. I was playing and listening to her, when all of a sudden something moved in front of me and blocked the sun. I looked up and there was this…this guy. I could see him but not totally because the sun was behind him and sort of washed him out, you know? But I could see his eyes real clearly. I was afraid at first but when I saw those eyes I knew I didn't have to be. I knew he was a good man, I could tell. He wasn't there to hurt me. There was something about him that made me want to go with him, to be with him. And it was like he read my mind or something because he reached down and he touched the side of my face. Not in a bad way or anything, like a parent, you know? He smiled and told me I couldn't go with him, because if I did, he wouldn't be there…right there…right then…and neither would I."

"What does that mean?"

"I don't know."

"Who was this man?" Seth asked. "Did he hurt you, Raymond?"

"No."

"Did anyone else see him?"

"No. Mom was in the kitchen and Dad wasn't home from work yet. You must've been at a friend's or something, maybe in our room, I don't know. But this guy, he looked down at me and he told me not to be afraid. He told me he'd protect me. He told me not to come to the field at night, and I didn't know what he meant because it was before the nightmares started so why would I be in the field at night? He said one day I'd understand. He said not to go to the field at night, but that I should hide. Hide, he said. Make sure you hide." Raymond rubbed his eyes. "And then he was gone, just—just gone. Like maybe I imagined him or something."

"You never saw him again?"

"No, but I still think about him sometimes. I call him the man in the sun." A brief smile blinked across his face. "Kind of stupid, I know, but I used to wonder if maybe he was an angel, you know? Maybe he came down to be with me before all this fucked-up shit started. Or maybe I thought it all up. I don't know."

"Ray, how does any of that tie into—"

"This is through-the-looking-glass shit, man. I can't—I can't talk about this right now. I thought I could but I *can't*." Raymond signaled the waiter for their check. Despite his attempt at cool, traces of the terrified little boy he had once been—and still was in many ways—lingered in his eyes. He was on the run again; it was all he knew. "I need to get out of here, I need to—I got to get some air."

Seth grabbed him by his wrist. "Raymond, stop it. We can't keep running from this. I know what you're going through, I—"

"You don't know shit about what I'm going through," he said evenly, his expression changing, shifting from one of panic and terror to one more closely resembling menace. "But you will."

Seeing the look on his face, Seth released his brother's wrist. Over the years he had felt many things when it came to Raymond, but until that moment fear had never been one of them. "Ray," he stammered, "I—"

"I got to get some air, man, I'm suffocating in here."

"We can't keep running; we have to help each other."

"Don't you get it? There is no help."

As Raymond turned and left the restaurant, Seth yielded to the alcohol and his tired, frayed nerves. Closing his eyes, he felt the room spin and wished sleep would take him right there.

* * *

Darian stood at the window and watched the night. The street was slick from recent rains, the black asphalt glistening as if polished. He cocked his head for a better view of the far end of the street and the other townhouses that lined either side of it. The neighborhood was quiet, as it always was this time of evening. But for the rare pass of a car now and then, no traffic moved and the only noises were those common sounds of the city one grew so used to they barely registered, distant and removed but occasionally trickling in from far-off corners and alleys. Much the way someone in the suburbs learns to tune out the constant buzz of crickets, he thought.

"What are you doing?"

Cynthia's voice brought him back. Lights from the television painted the walls in alternating patterns of light and shadow. He vaguely remembered she'd been watching a program, a documentary. They had gone to bed together earlier, and he'd done his best to feign interest until she'd fallen asleep, but the compulsion to watch the street, something he'd been doing more and more frequently of late, had overwhelmed him as it did near every night these days, and he had slipped from bed to his position at the window, standing there surveying the neighborhood like some deranged sentinel awaiting attack. Later, he would make the first of perhaps half a dozen trips before sunrise down the hallway to their daughter Debra's room, where he would crack the door, and with the help of a small nightlight next to her bureau, check on his little girl to make certain she was still in her bed, still breathing, asleep, safe and unharmed.

Darian looked back over his shoulder. Cynthia lay in bed beneath flannel sheets and a comforter. Even after years of marriage, he still thought she was the most beautiful woman he had ever seen. More importantly, she was the best person he'd ever known, a woman of substance, intelligence and compassion, also blessed with statuesque beauty. She was his wife, lover, best friend, and the mother of his child, yet he'd never felt more alone in her presence than he had these last several months. It was as if whatever bonds had held them together were slowly dissolving without his consent, his world unraveling and spinning out of control despite his best efforts to stop it. "Just thinking," he said quietly. "It's all right, go back to sleep."

She rubbed her eyes and sat up a bit, bringing the covers with her, her movements delicate and graceful. She squinted at the television in the corner, recognized the tail end of the documentary she'd been watching. "Damn it, I wanted to see that."

"You nodded off about halfway through."

She stifled a yawn. "Baby, don't you feel well?"

"I'm fine."

"Are you ever planning on telling me why you do this every night now?" When he stared at her without answering she said, "Stand at that window, I mean. What are you looking for? Are you expecting someone? You've been doing it every night for a week or more."

His stomach clenched, and a slow wave of nausea drifted through him, settling at the base of his throat like a marble lodged in his windpipe. "I've got a lot on my mind, that's all. I couldn't sleep."

"Maybe you should take something. We have some Tylenol PM in the medicine—"

"I'm fine." He turned back to the window, adjusted his eyeglasses and continued to study the street. "Go back to sleep."

"I know you didn't just dismiss me like that."

He nodded without turning around. "I'm sorry."

"It's time we talked about it, Dar. It's time we talked about what's bothering you."

*Screams. Horrible sounds. A storm. Snow. Fear. Relentless fear.*

"I was thinking this weekend maybe we could all go to the movies," he said. "It's been a while since we've gone."

"Sounds like fun," she said matter-of-factly. "But I won't hold my breath."

Darian fought a sudden swell of tears. He'd become so emotional of late, able to cry at the drop of a hat, often without even knowing why. The simplest thing could set him off, a commercial on television, someone on the street—nearly anything. *Like some overly emotional basket case,* he thought. *What the hell's wrong with me?*

He focused on the street beyond the window until the tears receded.

His thoughts turned to his parents, and how deeply he loved them both.

They'd both worked at the same public high school for decades, his mother as a math teacher, his father as assistant principal. Darian had been raised in a happy, comfortable home, and had gone on to college where he majored in accounting and earned his degree, finishing near the top of his class. He was not a black kid raised in the projects of Dorchester or Roxbury, rather a middle-class kid from Hanover, a small, predominantly white and relatively affluent town on the south shore, a stretch of coastal towns between Boston and Cape Cod. Though most of the people he knew were white, including most of his friends, he'd always been aware that things were rarely as they seemed, not always quite as liberal and open-minded as many suggested they were. And he heard it from both sides: The quiet racism from some whites who smiled when he was looking but secretly despised him, bigots who considered him an uppity, self-impressed negro trying to play the big-shot, along with the slurs from some blacks who accused him of selling out or trying to be white. He'd heard it his entire life, and knew what it was to be alone, to be in a position where no matter what he did, he couldn't seem to win. That sense of isolation and the unfair disrespect leveled by some black and white people alike was a point he and Cynthia shared early in their relationship, since she was the child of a mixed marriage. But these other feelings…this darkness he'd experienced for some time now, was not something she could experience with him—and for that he was grateful. His feelings of helplessness and seclusion; his fear that at any moment his mind might tear and come apart at the seams was not something he wished on his worst enemy. Yet there were others who understood. He knew that. Seth hadn't acted right for months, and neither had Louis. They had all been affected, yet they were all so alone, it seemed.

In a tone that signaled her patience was nearing its end, Cynthia said, "Tell me what's going on, Darian."

*How do I tell you I'm losing my mind? How do I tell my*

*wife her husband is breaking into pieces? How do I tell our daughter her father is not the rock of strength and stability she thinks he is?*

"Is there someone else?"

His heart dropped and he again fought the rise of raw emotion surging through him. He moved wearily to the foot of the bed and sat down. "Of course not."

"You never lay a hand on me anymore, and—"

"There's no one else," he said. "Don't be absurd."

"You're so far away," she whispered, as if to herself.

"I love you, you know that. You and Debra are everything to me."

"What is it then? Are you in some sort of trouble?"

"I'm so tired," he heard himself say, voice trembling. "I'm just so tired."

"What's happened, Dar?"

The screams rose in his mind, ripping through his brain and bringing with them an uncontrollable terror. Flashes of snow, night, the woods, a storm—blink and they were gone, leaving in their wake a sense of dread he experienced so often these days he had nearly grown accustomed to it. Do the insane know they're insane? He wondered. Do they become used to how it feels? Perhaps. But do they feel they might contaminate others close to them with their disease, their madness? If not, then this isn't insanity I'm dealing with, Darian thought, it's something else, something pretending, masking itself as insanity but something far worse.

When he saw the look of confusion and concern on his wife's face, he drew a deep breath and pulled himself together as best he could. "Everything's going to be OK."

"I'm not the only one. Our daughter's been asking questions and she has a right to answers the same as I do. She's only nine. She's still a little girl who needs to know her father's all right. She needs to know he'll be there for her. We both do."

He rose slowly from the foot of the bed as his heart sank into his guts. "It's all right. *I'm* all right."

"No, you're not."

"Everything's going to be OK," he muttered.

Though he felt her eyes on him, felt her frustration and anguish hanging in the air between them like a gossamer curtain, neither he nor she said another word as he crossed the room and slipped into the hallway, gripped with the sudden and overwhelming need to check on their sleeping daughter.

* * *

The ride back to the apartment was filled with uneasy silence. Without discussing things again, Seth and Raymond turned in for the night, agreeing to continue their conversation in the morning.

Later, Seth lay in bed, swathed in total darkness. In those strange and soundless moments, he could not be sure if sleep had claimed him or not. All the thoughts from the day flooded to the forefront of his mind at once, slowly dissipating until only memories and flashes of childhood remained.

*Tell me what you see, Seth.* Doc's voice echoed in his head, only it wasn't Doc's voice, not really. It was a counterfeit version, a creation of his mind whispering to him from somewhere between the worlds of consciousness and sleep. *Tell me what you see.*

"There was something more," he heard himself say. "Before Raymond and I were running in the snow."

*You said you saw movement.*

"Yes."

*And you saw someone in the room.*

"I saw…something."

*Then you and Raymond were outside running in the snow.*

"Yes, but…"

*Do you remember something else, between the two instances, Seth?*

"Yes."

*What do you remember?*

Fear hit him like a sucker punch to the back of the head. The terror rose so suddenly and with such ferocity Seth was certain he could actually hear it exploding in his brain before wracking his entire body with violent tremors. The sound of fear tearing him apart—the literal shriek of personal demons—was deafening.

"Help me—Christ almighty, please—help me, there's something here, something in the room, please—"

*Who is in the room, Seth?*

"There's something in the room, it—"

*Breathe.*

"Help me, help—us—please, God—"

*You're crying, Seth.*

"I—please—please—"

*Who is this person, Seth? It's all right, you can tell me. Who is this person?*

"It's not a person."

Seth bolted upright in bed, feeling the bile rise from

the base of his throat. He choked it down and turned to the window, seeking it out through the darkness. But there was nothing, no one there, no one peering into the room. Trying to catch his breath, he rolled over and looked to the alarm clock on the nightstand. It was nearly midnight.

Had he and Peggy still been together, he knew she'd be there, snuggled against him, her body soft and warm, quiet mewling sounds escaping her now and then as she settled deeper into sleep. He lay back, pulling the blankets up tight under his chin and tried to picture her in his mind, her eyes blinking slowly, watching over him, protecting and loving him as she once had. Though his heart still pounded and the memories or nightmares continued to play in his mind, the liquor took hold, his eyes grew heavy and he eventually descended into sleep. Losing his grip on the visions of Peggy, the dark room, the world—everything—he fell away from it all slowly, weightlessly, an astronaut broken from his tether, gliding gradually into an endless sea of twilight.

# Chapter 8

The darkness offered artificial comfort, a flimsy shroud he hoped might hide him from all that existed beyond its scope. Snowflakes fell, dotted the black sky and distracted him from a subtle, moaning wind. Somewhere not so very far away he could see a form, a woman, moving awkwardly near the edges of darkness. The woman, or what looked like a woman, walked with a strange, otherworldly stride, and the closer she drew, the slower and more sluggish her stride became. When she finally came to a halt, Raymond realized the woman was standing with her back to him, huddled over a bit now and slowly rocking back and forth, as if in prayer.

The snow stopped. Only darkness remained.

Turning, the woman looked back over her shoulder, and Raymond gazed directly into her eyes. *Christy's* eyes, but eyes not entirely her own. They revealed the madness trapped within, the fear, revulsion, helplessness and all else that had infected this young woman before...before what?

"Christy?" he asked; voice slow and drowsy, incomplete. "What are you doing out here? Why did you leave the cabin?"

Draped in a dark and heavy blanket she wore like a cloak, Christy slowly extended her arms, holding them up like a great bird unfolding its wings. As she turned around, her robe fell open.

Faint cries called to Raymond from the surrounding night, cries similar to those of a baby. But they were not completely human sounds, rather squeals, like the noises of frenzied pigs.

Beneath the robe Christy was nude, her skin pale and taut in the cold night air. Along the side of her head, a large tumor protruded from her temple, moving in spasm-like twitches and stretching the skin and skull at impossible angles as if bubbling beneath it. "This is how it starts," she said gravely, her voice sounding as if she was speaking to Raymond from the far end of a tunnel. "Do you understand? *This* is how it starts."

The skin along the tumor began to split with a quiet ripping sound, releasing a gelatinous fluid that dripped across her cheek and neck onto the snow-covered ground. The pain seemed to disorient her, and she dropped her arms, the blanket again concealing her nudity. She doubled over and brought her hands to her head, one of them gripping the tumor. Her legs buckled a bit, unsteady as she grunted and groaned and stared at Raymond weakly.

As the side of her head burst, spraying blood, skull fragments and various fluids through the air, she screamed in agony, and her body vaulted suddenly backwards into the darkness, twisting and turning as if boneless. Plucked away by unseen hands, the night swallowed her whole.

* * *

Seth awakened in a haze. Had he heard Raymond scream just then?

He rolled out of bed groggily, listened. Nothing.

He found Raymond asleep on the sofa in the living room, the large comforter he'd given him the night before kicked away to the floor. Seth retrieved it and carefully covered him.

On the coffee table he noticed an empty glass and another plastic prescription bottle. Moving quietly, he grabbed the bottle and read the label. Anti-anxiety pills. He gazed down at his sleeping brother. High blood pressure, anxiety attacks, what next?

*Madness,* something whispered to him.

He returned the bottle to the table, swatting away his own demons as he slipped into the adjacent kitchen.

Seth turned the coffeemaker on, listened to it gurgle and belch, then returned to the living room and took up position in a chair across from the couch. He hadn't thought it possible for Raymond to look so peaceful, yet there he was, asleep like a child without a worry in the world. If only it were genuine rather than drug-induced, he might be able to believe it the way he had once believed in other things. But that ability had long since abandoned him.

*Poor Raymond,* he thought. *Poor lost Raymond. I'm so goddamn sorry.*

He watched Raymond sleep a while, uncertain as to why he felt compelled to do so. Perhaps it reminded him of how not so very long ago he'd watched Peggy sleep in the early morning hours, his favorite time, before the world awakened and all the chatter began, when all that mattered was the woman lying next to him, warm and trusting and still. Those moments of quiet certainty and affection had meant something once.

Maybe they still did, though like so much else now, he could no longer be sure.

His attention returned to Raymond. His expressionless face—the delicate rise and fall of his chest and the way his hair fell across his shoulder—revealed nothing. Yet even now, in the narcotic slumber Raymond had escaped to, when he saw his brother's face, Seth saw glimpses of the tears that so often streamed down his cheeks in their youth. And the terror, he still saw the terror, as if it were still close by, gone but not so very far after all.

Flashes of night surged through his mind, filled his eyes with rapid-fire glimpses—memories—of him and Raymond running through the snow. Like strobe lights, they temporarily blinded him, consumed him with a feverish cadence that revealed in frantic pieces another night, the night at the cabin a year before. But it vanished just as rapidly, a blur at the corner of his eye, gone the moment he turned his head.

Forcing himself to focus, he summoned the images back.

Beneath charcoal skies filled with snowflakes the cabin loomed at the outskirts of Seth's mind. The sound of labored breath and furious footfalls echoed faintly in his ears like distractions from a distant room, but he knew these things were all in his head, mur-

muring specters faded to nothing, come and gone as quickly as lightning rips across canopies of night.

*That night at the cabin...what the hell happened to you out there, Raymond?*

* * *

Louis couldn't remember exactly how long he'd been sitting at his kitchen table, but it had been dark when he'd taken position there the night prior, he knew that much. The sun had risen perhaps thirty minutes before, pushing bright beams of light through the small windows over the sink and bringing with it a promise of clarity he could only recall in distant memory. His mind rarely seemed lucid anymore, and when he sunk into these dark waters time held little meaning.

The apartment was small, cramped, and needed a good cleaning. The sink was overrun with dirty dishes and the floors were littered with debris—old pizza boxes, spent bottles of beer and cola, and the like. He'd never lived like royalty, but this place, particularly the small size, irritated him to no end. With each passing day, Louis resented the apartment more and more.

He knew he couldn't keep this facade up much longer. Sooner than later the house of cards his life had become would come toppling down and he would no longer be able to hide from those things that dwelled beneath it.

In some ways he felt like a drug addict. He'd once read an article about a crack addict, and remembered how the man had described his life coming apart slowly at first, and then suddenly, and how throughout his descent into addiction and darkness, things most take for granted became irrelevant and unimportant. Bathing, cleaning, paying bills—none of it mattered. Only the high mattered, only the escape. This was similar, he thought. It was devouring him steadily but slowly, an alpha male predator that had brought him down and now lay next to him, eating him alive and at a leisurely pace before others arrived and were granted permission to rip him limb from limb in frenzied hunger. There was something at once heartbreaking and humorous about that. Laugh or cry, he couldn't decide. So Louis did neither. Instead, he sat in the same chair he had been sitting in for hours and stared at a framed picture on the table before him of his family in happier times. Surrounded by empty beer bottles he'd consumed during the night, it seemed a fitting shrine to both the past and present—the once smiling faces of what had been a family—his family—amidst the garbage, clutter, loneliness and angry mess his life had become.

His eyes found the knife. Next to the framed photograph, it lay in its nylon sheath, a Marine Bowie Knife. Fifteen inches including the ribbed handle, with a ten-inch carbon steel blade, he had purchased this magnificent weapon at an online Army/Navy shop, and though he'd never actually used it for any practical purpose, he often removed it from the sheath and thought about many of the possibilities such a large and savage knife could yield. Like his rifle, Louis found something exciting about holding the weapon that bordered on the sexual. The weight of it in his palm, the way the handle felt against his skin, the way the slant of the huge blade reflected light when he held it at the appropriate angle—it all came together to make him feel alive and powerful—nearly invincible. Because brandishing a knife such as this changed everything. It transformed him from a manager in the shipping department at Severance into a fighting machine—a potential killer—a dangerous man to be feared and respected.

Louis rarely took the time to investigate why things like guns and knives made him feel inherently more masculine and tough, he only knew he embraced such feelings, particularly of late. In the past year his fascination with many things dark and deadly—particularly weapons—had increased dramatically. He could sit with the knife in hand for hours, his mind racing and calculating any number of violent and satisfying scenarios.

And then memories would come. Just flashes at first but then as the weeks became months, little by little, he remembered more. Slowly, he felt himself coming apart.

But he was not alone. He knew that now. He was being watched, influenced, controlled by...something. There were eyes on him…watching him, judging him, *changing* him.

"I remember," he mumbled, as in answer to questions only he could hear. "You hear me you motherfuckers? I know you can hear me. I'm remembering. *I remember.*"

He blinked, focused on the photograph on the table, on Becky. How he loved her even now, he couldn't help himself. The mother of his children, his former wife, how could he ever hate her?

"It's all right," he said, addressing the photograph now, his voice heavy and slurred with exhaustion. "It's

OK, Beck, you—you're doing the right thing."

*That's right,* a voice from deep within him said. *Fight it. Fight them.*

Still, even in those rare instances when the voice of reason escaped the recesses of his mind and offered moments of clarity, Louis couldn't shake the other side, the dark side that continued to haunt him, to goad him with promises of relief if only he'd give in and let it take total control. But he realized now this was a battle he'd eventually lose no matter how hard he fought, and like a boil that needed lancing, the pressure continued to grow, to strengthen to a near-breaking point.

He forced his eyes back to the photograph. Danielle and Louis, Jr.—his children. *His* children. "Only worthwhile fucking thing I ever did," he told the photo. Emotion rose, choking him to tears. Louis shook his head as if to ward them off as visions of Becky with that new boyfriend of hers came to him. Five and seven, Danielle and little Lou were still babies, he thought. And that guy, this new guy, he'll be their father. "Forget me," he said aloud. "Forget me."

Something whispered to him, something far away. He cocked his head, listened.

And then the fear returned, that same awful, relentless fear he'd been running from for a year hit him again like a whirlwind.

Screams. Snow. The dark—that awful, endless darkness…

Louis pushed his chair away from the table with such force it nearly tipped over. He staggered to his feet, gained his balance and leaned against the stove for support.

He was alone in the room…for now.

"Go," he told the photograph of his wife and children. "Take them and get the hell away from here, Beck, away from me, you got to go. Go!"

He snatched the knife from the table and clutched it to his chest like a child. Heart thudding, he drew a deep breath and did his best to control himself. But within seconds he felt the same odd popping sensation in his temples he had felt numerous times before, followed by a feeling of release, a release of pressure. Something tickled his nostril. He brought a finger to his nose, pulled it away and saw the bright crimson staining his fingertip. A bit of dizziness swept through him and was gone.

There were tissues in the bedroom but he made no move for them, not this time. He let the blood trickle from his nose, down across his upper lip and into his mouth. Becky, Danielle and Louis Jr. all watched from the kitchen table, eyes fixed and dead. Watched him bleed. Fucking fitting, he thought. Watch me bleed, kids. Watch Daddy bleed. This is who I am now. This. A fucking disease—that's what I am now. They'd stolen everything else. *They* were inside him, burrowing deeper, ripping through his head, twisting through his brain like tiny fingers clawing to get out.

The tears ran the length of his face, mixed with the blood.

"Make it stop." Louis slowly drew the knife from its sheath. "All of it."

Reason slipped away, lost in the darkness along with him.

* * *

Daylight filtering through the curtains on the far wall broke his concentration.

For now, the rain had stopped.

"What are you doing?" Raymond mumbled drowsily.

"I was just checking on you," Seth said, startled. "I thought you were asleep."

Raymond rolled out from under the comforter and planted his bare feet on the floor. But for the lack of boots and socks, he was still fully clothed. "When you've slept in some of the places I have, you learn to sleep light."

"I made coffee."

"Cool, thanks." With both hands, Raymond pulled his hair back away from his face and dropped it behind his shoulders. "Look, man, I didn't mean to freak out on you last night, it's—"

"Don't worry about it." Seth made a point of not looking at the pills on the coffee table. "These things happen."

"I get *attacks*." Raymond pawed at his eyes and yawned, glancing around the room as if subtly inspecting it for things not immediately evident. "Like last night, it's hard to explain but it's an anxiety thing. It's like standing on the tracks watching a train coming right at you, only you can't get out of the way, you know?"

"You're my brother Raymond, you don't have to apologize to me."

"They hit me out of nowhere sometimes. Panic attacks. Doctor told me stress brings them on." He motioned to the pills. "Anyway, I can't always control them, so if they get out of hand I take one of those to chill me out until they pass."

Seth rose from the chair, smiled politely and headed for the kitchen. "Let's have some coffee and—"

"You want to know about that night, the night at the cabin."

The response stopped him cold. He stood there a moment; let the chill run its course along his spine. "Last night you said you didn't want to talk about these things."

"Do you really think we have any choice?" Raymond patted himself down then rolled over so he could grab his leather jacket from the arm of the couch. He rummaged through the pockets until he located a pack of cigarettes and a lighter.

"Can you not smoke in here, please?"

"Christ, whatever." He tossed the items aside and let out a long sigh.

Seth stood in the doorway a while, unsure of what to do with himself. "No one's been the same since that night. If you know something, please tell me. What the hell is happening?"

"That's it exactly," Raymond said, eyes dull and lifeless. "*Hell* is happening."

# Chapter 9

With bits and pieces of that snowy night still spiraling through his head, Seth searched his brother's brooding face, hopeful it might anchor him to the present, where at least for the time being, he still felt relatively safe. The quiet of the kitchen embraced them, cradled them a moment while they drank their coffee.

"Whenever that shit used to happen to me it'd take me a while to realize I was even awake. I'd already be running, scared out of my mind, no clue where I was." Raymond brought his coffee to his mouth with both hands, took a sip then replaced the mug on the table. "Most of those days just blend together now. The field behind our house, I ended up there, what, dozens of times?"

The words triggered memories of those nights in Seth too. He closed his eyes defensively, but the darkness he found there was even more unsettling than the thoughts coursing through his mind, so he opened them and stared down into his coffee instead.

"We both remember these things happening when you were a child, but neither of us can remember when any of it started," he said. "Can you honestly tell me how or why it all began?"

"No."

The word ricocheted about in Seth's memory, replaying from the hospital room their mother had died in. So sterile and impersonal, mechanical, a place of machines and wooden people who moved about like zombies, emotionless and withdrawn from the things they saw day in and day out. It was no place for the living, the vibrant or the sane.

*"No,"* Raymond had said then too, repeating the word again and again as Seth put his arms around him while wrestling with the harsh reality of their situation himself.

Eventually Raymond had broken free of Seth's protective arms and draped himself across their mother's corpse, his tear-stained cheek pressed to her chest. "Goddamn it, *no.*"

Seth heard his brother's cries for years. Some nights he still did, though he could rarely recall his own. He could only remember the cold seeping through his body like a foreign substance injected into him without his knowledge, spreading through him from the inside out, tentacles of fluid filling his veins until no warmth could survive and his body had turned as cold and lifeless inside, as their mother's had outside.

Seth sipped his coffee; let it bring him back as he embraced the warmth. "Everything has a beginning, Ray, even what happened to you as a child."

"Nana used to say I was special," Raymond

mumbled. "Remember?"

"You told me once that you knew things before they happened." Seth put his mug aside and placed his hands flat on the table, steadying himself. "Was that true?"

"Yeah," he said faintly. "Still is sometimes."

Seth thought on it a moment, then let it go for the time being. "The earliest I can remember your night terrors was when you were eight and I was twelve," he told him. "My sessions with Doc have helped me remember that much."

"Twelve and eight," he said softly, looking as though he couldn't quite comprehend such a time span.

Just for a moment, Seth glimpsed their parents in his brother's face, their parents as they'd looked prior to the world coming apart, melded together into a single surviving entity sitting there at his kitchen table.

Their father had resembled Dennis Hopper in *Easy Rider*, eccentric and cool, with unruly hair, a renegade sense of fashion and a persona that was equal parts oblivious and magnificently profound. A former hippie, he worked for a defense contractor, a large manufacturing plant nestled into the woods of Adamston, the otherwise unassuming little hamlet just north of Boston where Seth and Raymond had grown up. "It's an assembly line of death, man, where mostly poor people build weapons the government can use on other poor people in other places," he'd told them. Because it was virtually the only employer in town, their father viewed his employment there as a personal mission to infiltrate the hearts and minds of everyone else on the payroll with his concepts of peace and love rather than bombs and violence. "One person at a time, man," he'd told them. "Just like a preacher, right? One soul at a time." Like many of his ideas, it was based more on unadulterated optimism (along with a bit of convenient self-deception) than reality, but this was their father.

The town itself was less than half an hour from Boston, a quiet and woodsy suburb solidly divided between the haves and the have-nots, and though many residents who worked at the plant arrived each morning wearing suits and ties, their father reported in workpants and a matching shirt with his name embroidered over the pocket. It wasn't until they became older that the boys realized their father's job as a janitor could be used as a source of ridicule. It was honest work, he told them. "Boys, I'm an honest man in a den of iniquity," he'd often laugh. "Got to be on my toes at all times, see what I mean?"

A freethinker, he was a man who left those who didn't know him (and occasionally those who did), unsure if they were in the presence of a fool or a genius. And in the end it hadn't seemed to matter either way.

During the course of his life he never made a lot of money or achieved even remote professional success, but neither fact seemed to bother him. He and their mother made enough for them to all live comfortably, and for their father, family was everything, being together, having one another—*that* was what life was about. The intensity that eventually surfaced in their family when Raymond began having his night episodes eventually changed him somewhat, and from then on he often seemed distracted or deep in thought. Yet even in his more pensive moments, he always had a story to tell—a tale to spin, some moral or ethical treatise about life or love—especially when he was around his sons. And that was how Seth liked to remember his father, as a reflective but happy eccentric who viewed the world on his terms and in his own unique way.

Their mother, a thin and rather gangly woman with mousy brown hair, dark doe-like eyes and a toothy smile a bit too large for her face, was the kind of person easily overlooked. She was not a woman who stood out in a crowd, except to those who knew her, had spoken to her, or had heard her sing. Though she was soft-spoken to the point of sometimes being mistaken for timid, her singing voice was soprano and angelic, more prepubescent boy than grown woman. She wrote most of the songs herself, and sang around the house while doing chores, or in the backyard while tending to her flower and vegetable gardens. The only time Seth heard his mother sing away from the house was in church. Not always as part of the choir, but sometimes as one of many parishioners hidden among the pews, singing pre-selected hymns, her voice a bit higher than the rest, a bit more melodic, at least to his ears. And when she sang she seemed happy, removed from the harsher aspects of life and the hours she spent toiling as a social worker.

As unconventional as their father could sometimes be, their mother was generally quiet, introspective, and reserved, like she carried with her the weight of tremendous wisdom but was only capable of sharing or revealing it in small, periodic increments. Though initially she appeared shy and somewhat submissive, in reality she was a very strong, intelligent and articulate woman that was easy to get along with but not easily manipulated or maneuvered. Despite being the main breadwinner in the family, it was never something she spoke about or seemed bothered by. She adored their father, faults and all, and had she ever been unhappy in their marriage, Seth and Raymond were wholly unaware of it.

Relegated to the world of dreams and memory for so long now, it was often difficult to remember them as living, breathing, fully realized human beings. They'd become bland faces watching from the dark corners of his mind, silent and passive.

In time, those faces faded, and it was only Raymond sitting before him, tired and wounded Raymond, a man and little boy all at once, pure and innocent and tough as nails in a single breath, a solitary look, or three simple words. "Long time ago," he said.

"We were just kids." Seth toyed nervously with a small napkin on the table. "But did those things have anything to do with what happened at the cabin? That was only a year ago."

Raymond held his mug of coffee, cupping it with both hands and holding it before him like a chalice. "It helped me and cursed me all at once."

"What did?"

"The change in me when I was a kid. They've tortured me for years, these things in my mind. But it helps me to see. Whether I want to or not, it helps me to see."

"To see *what* Raymond?" The napkin tore in Seth's hands. "Something happened at that place, and whatever it was it's still affecting all of us. Louis has been acting strangely ever since, and Darian—he's not himself either. None of us are. We're all..."

"Yeah." Raymond's expression revealed the extent to which his mind had wandered into the past. It also revealed the extent to which he feared it. "Me too."

"Tell me what happened out there, Ray. Tell me what you know."

He pushed his mug aside and brought trembling hands to his eyes, covering them as if hoping to block it all out.

Seth reached across the table and touched his brother's hand. "Whatever happened to you wasn't your fault, Ray. Something happened that night at the cabin that was beyond our control."

"Nana used to call me special," he said again, dropping his hands and no longer concerned with masking his tears. "But it took me a long time to understand what that meant. I'd hear things, see things and—I was sure I was crazy—and maybe I was. Maybe I still am."

"But the night at the cabin," Seth said, bringing him back from his childhood memories, "something happened to you, something—"

"Nothing happened to me at that cabin." He wiped the tears away but had regained the look of a caged animal recently freed and not quite certain what to make of it.

"Raymond, you disappeared in that storm for—"

"You don't understand."

"Then help me, Ray. Help me to understand. Please."

Dull morning light bled through the windows on the far wall, the wintry gray sky casting the small kitchen in a mélange of shadowy silhouettes and ashen hues. Through the unexpected silence, the soft ticking of a nearby clock became more apparent then receded the moment Raymond began to speak.

"What happened out there didn't happen to me," he said, voice splintering with emotion. "It happened to all of you."

# Chapter 10

Startled to silence, Seth watched his brother squirm about in the chair across from him like an interrogation victim in some low-budget crime drama. The posture took him back to their childhood, when Raymond often looked that way, confused and troubled, scared and uncertain. How had he dismissed so much of his brother's pain during those years? How had he simply looked away and paid little or no attention to Raymond's torment the way one considerately ignored a nervous tick or obvious physical handicap? Little Raymond, with no friends, a pariah— disregarded and labeled a "freak," he was a strange and isolated little boy haunted by nightmares and who claimed the ability to know certain things before they happened. And no one believed him, not even his trusted older brother.

Seth had challenged him once when they were boys. "If that's true then prove it," he'd demanded. "Show me."

"It's not like a magic trick," Raymond explained.

"It's feelings I get. I get them sometimes and then—then I know something's going to happen."

"Like what?"

Raymond shook his head, as if to deny the thoughts even then. "Bad things."

"You're making it up," Seth told him. "It's just the bad dreams you have."

All those years before he hadn't been so sure, but like a strange noise in the night better left uninvestigated, Seth had convinced himself that Raymond did not possess the ability to see the future—and in time began to believe it, to no longer fear or take seriously the things that so clearly upset his brother. And in his denial, he found a sense of safety. False as it may have been, like a child hiding beneath blankets during a thunderstorm and insisting he was not afraid, it got him through, and more importantly, it separated him from Raymond. *He* was not the one with problems. *He* was fine.

*My parents took him to doctors, even a psychiatrist and sleep disorder specialist, but nothing worked…*

*Did your parents ever do any of those things for you, Seth?*

Focusing again on the here and now, Seth said, "Ray, *you* were the one who went out into the storm in the middle of the night. *You* were the one who went missing."

"I think we should go see Nana," he said suddenly. "I need to talk to Nana."

"Try to focus, Ray. You said—"

"I know what the fuck I said."

"Then explain yourself."

"I need to see Nana."

"Why?" Seth asked, though he already knew the answer. Their grandmother was the only one who *had* believed. Even when Raymond was a child, she'd believed him, and now he was grasping for anything he could lay his hands on.

"She'll understand," Raymond said. "She'll know what to do."

"She's our grandmother, and I love her, but she's an eccentric old woman who believes in a bunch of antiquated mystical nonsense, Ray, nothing more."

"You used to believe in a lot of that nonsense."

"I *used* to believe in the tooth fairy and the Easter Bunny. What's your point?"

"It's been a long time since I've seen her." Raymond settled a bit, his nerves evening out. "Over a year."

"I haven't seen her in months myself," Seth said guiltily.

"Shame on us."

"Yes, shame on us."

Raymond turned away and stared at the shadows along the wall like he could see what lay behind them, like all the answers were playing out right there in front of his eyes if only he'd look hard and long enough. "Whatever it is I'm able to do, to see and sense, it helped me to see something that night at the cabin, Seth. Something I shouldn't have seen. Something I wasn't supposed to see. So I ran." The words caught in his throat and as his nerves fractured again, his eyes filled with tears. "I left you there, and I ran."

"What are you—I don't know what you're talking about." Pieces of the dream he'd had that night in the cabin—the nightmare about a storm, an otherworldly storm, at once so violent and beautiful—blinked in memory.

"I ran, don't you get it?" Raymond slammed a hand on the table so hard Seth was surprised the entire thing didn't collapse. "I *ran*."

"You left the door open and the cold air woke us, we went looking for you," Seth stammered. The sounds. Somewhere beneath the wail of the storm in his dreams there had been sounds. Horrible sounds. "You went looking for Christy, you—"

"No. I ran. Like a coward."

The memories receded and floated from his grasp, tendrils of fog slipping through his fingers. "Why were you running, Ray?"

"Because I knew what was coming," he said gravely.

"But nothing happened to us. *You* went outside, we were all asleep."

"That's when things happen." He grimaced and wrapped his arms around himself as if cold. "In the dark, in the night, that's when things happen."

Seth drew a deep breath, held it a moment, exhaled. "What things?"

"All that's out there in the night," he said. "Deep night. That's when we're most vulnerable."

"Vulnerable to what?"

"Those...*things*."

"What things? There's nothing out there," Seth said squarely.

"You trying to convince you or me?"

"There's nothing out there," he said again. "This is all in our minds."

"Yeah." Amidst the tears, a smile twitched across

Raymond's face. "But what's the difference?"

"You tell me."

"I never asked for any of this. I never wanted it, never wanted to see these things."

"Just relax and tell me what—"

"I don't know what they are."

The response threw him. "What?"

"What I saw that night, what I've seen ever since. I don't know what they are."

"Since that night..." Seth forced a swallow, realizing only then how dry his mouth had become. He tried to continue but the words lay wounded in his throat. Maybe Raymond was right. Maybe they both really were insane. "Since that night," he eventually managed, "nothing makes sense. I don't understand, Ray. I don't understand what's going on."

"Neither do I; not completely. But I *do* know this. They're a disease." Raymond's gaze met his. "And you're all infected."

The fingers of an icy chill swept across the back of Seth's shoulders like a scurrying spider, reminding him of the cold winds that night in the woods. "Infected?" He folded his hands and held them tightly together to prevent them from trembling. "Infected how?"

"Maybe I am too, I don't know. Maybe sooner or later we all are." Raymond pointed to his head. "This is where it starts. That's all I know."

Seth forced the emotion and terror down, did his best to bring forth some sense of logic and reason. "Illness, is that what you're saying? Some sort of mental illness?"

"Something terrible is going to happen," Raymond said, "Soon. Something terrible."

"You said 'they' before. What..." Overwhelmed, Seth struggled to sort his thoughts. Something had happened to Raymond as a child, something had happened that night at the cabin to him and everyone else there, and now, according to his brother—who may or may not have gone completely out of his mind—something else was going to happen soon. "Are you suggesting we've all gone collectively insane—you and me and Darian and Louis—or—"

"You're not listening. Insanity's subjective."

"But you said—"

"*This* is where it starts." Ray stabbed a finger into his temple. "Here, in our minds. That's what I said."

"If it's in our minds then it's some form of insanity, it—"

"I wish that's all it was, man. I really do."

Memories of the deafening storm in Seth's nightmare continued to muffle the hideous sounds still echoing through his mind, sounds of skin ripping and splitting, wrapped in screams, ungodly shrieks of inconceivable agony. "It's too much, it's—this is crazy—I—why can't I remember, Ray? Why can't I remember what happened that night? What could just wipe out my memories like that? What could do that?"

Raymond shook his head with a defeated air. "I don't understand it either. Not completely. Not yet. But then, I never have."

Silence returned to the apartment as both men wrestled with their thoughts, fears and suspicions. After what seemed a very long time, Seth said, "I don't know what to do."

"We go see Nana." Raymond wiped the tears from his eyes, pushed away from the table and stood up.

Despite the dark bags under his eyes, the wear and tear on his face and body, the discernibly profound expense this had taken on a thirty-one-year-old man, the expression he assumed was the closest thing to resolve Seth had seen him express in years. "She can help me clear my head, see things straight. I need to see Nana."

Seth felt himself nod. "OK, Ray," he said numbly. "OK."

# Chapter 11

After nearly an hour of driving, Seth and Raymond reached the Sagamore Bridge, one of the two enormous structures that connected Cape Cod to the mainland. Though Seth had been over the bridge countless times, he'd never cared for heights and always found himself nervously staring straight ahead, eyes fixed on the road and hands firmly gripping the steering wheel at the ten and two o'clock positions.

"The bridge still scares you, doesn't it?" It was the first time Raymond had spoken since they left Boston.

"I get a little nervous, that's all."

Seth noticed a large sign posted just before the beginning of the bridge, an advertisement for the Samaritans. It included a toll free phone number and the words: *Feeling Depressed*? A slogan for the suicidal, he thought. How many potential jumpers had walked right by that sign on their way to death? A final warning, a final chance ignored. In these recent days, Seth felt he could relate. There were warning signs everywhere and, yet, he could not change the direction of his fate. Not his, not anyone else's. Like the jumper destined to plummet to the deep waters of the canal below, destiny had already set the stage and written the script.

As the car climbed the initial slant of the bridge, Raymond made it a point to sit up and crane his neck so he could look down over the edge, through the metal bars and cables to the distant coastline, canal and tiny landscape. There had been a time years ago—before he'd needed anxiety pills and high blood pressure medicine, before he'd gotten frequent nosebleeds from the pressure in his head—when he'd enjoyed the kind of basic thrill crossing an enormous bridge like the Sagamore could provide. Like being on a roller coaster, it gave him a buzz, an adrenaline rush that was actually fun, something he rarely had the opportunity to experience anymore. He embraced the escape for a moment and imagined what it might be like to freefall from such a colossal height. "Do you ever wonder what it would be like to fly?" he asked.

A memory of Raymond as a child blossomed in Seth's mind. Little, pre-nightmare Raymond, skipping through their house with a small blanket tied around his neck to resemble a superhero's cape as he jumped along the furniture in the den, arms flapping furiously. "No," Seth said flatly, "I don't."

Once over the bridge, they were greeted by mile upon mile of identical two-lane highway carved into what remained of old forest terrain. This was ancient land, but like much of modern America, it retained little of the rustic appeal it had once possessed, as rest areas, exit signs and other manmade intrusions interrupted the otherwise natural setting with distressing frequency.

The forecast had called for more icy rain, and the further they ventured from Boston the darker the skies became. Just over the bridge, they encountered a belt of fog rolling in off the Atlantic that stretched across the road in thick, gray, slow-moving vapors.

"Haven't been out this way in a long time." Raymond slumped down in the passenger seat but continued to stare out the window. "Still get that same feeling whenever I cross the bridges."

Seth nodded but said nothing. He knew what his brother meant.

"Brings back a lot of memories, I guess," Raymond continued. "Always felt like I was crossing over into another world whenever I was on-cape. Still does."

All those years ago, after the death of their parents, it *had* felt like crossing into an entirely new world. Driving these lonely roads with the knowledge that once they reached their destination, it would be Nana waiting for them, a woman who had outlived her only child, her son, and yet, she had been expected to restart her life, or to at a bare minimum continue on with it, despite all that had happened. It was something with which Seth and Raymond could identify in their own way. Though most people lived with the realization that one day they would bury their parents, no one expected them to be taken prematurely or violently, and when these things did happen, the surviving family members instantly became something akin to small-town celebrities. They were the two sons everyone had heard about on the local news, the ones who had lost both parents in a terrible automobile accident. They were the people others looked at without actually *seeing*, regarding them instead with side-glances and nervous smiles, or pitiful eyes and hurried, uncomfortable, overindulgent friendliness.

For a time, their mere presence could alter the mood and feel of an entire room. Adults or children, it made no difference, when the Roman boys walked through the door, everyone stopped and immediately began scurrying for ways to occupy themselves, to appear to have not noticed, to seem unaffected. But Seth had always felt their discomfort, and knew Raymond had as well—even that of their own grandmother's.

Though he and Raymond had done nothing wrong, they were often initially treated like exiles. Their very existence seemed constant unpleasant reminders of how vulnerable and ultimately fragile human beings were, how close everyone could be to death at any given moment. *Those poor guys*, people would whisper, *poor, poor guys*.

But their pity held little meaning. *Please take our sympathy*, everyone seemed to say, *and go*.

"You sure this is a good idea?"

Raymond faced the window, watched the trees zoom past. "I need to see her, man."

They drove on in silence for a while, lost in their own thoughts.

"Are you afraid?" Seth asked.

The hot air from the car heater was stifling. Raymond cracked the window and dug his cigarettes from his jacket pocket. "All the time."

* * *

Darian awoke in a heavy sweat, but couldn't be sure if it was from the nightmares or because Cynthia had the heat turned up too damn high. Regardless, he rolled out of bed with an overwhelming need to bathe, went immediately to the bathroom, showered and returned to the bedroom to dress.

He could hear Cynthia moving about downstairs amidst the faint sounds of the television in the living room. He pictured Debra sitting in front of the TV like she did every morning before school, watching cartoons while devouring a bowl of cereal, and wondered if he'd still be alive to see her grow into a young woman, to one day marry and have children of her own.

Faraway screams called to him from distant corners of his mind, and blurred images of thick forest covered in abundant darkness swept past his vision like a movie projected through his eyes and onto the wall before him. Someone or something was running behind those trees...screams...tears...horrible sounds of things ripping and shredding. Someone screaming for help...*Help me, God – God help me*!

As the hallucinatory images and sounds slipped away, Darian drew a deep breath and attempted to focus on the day ahead, on the mundane tasks awaiting him at work. His job had once been one of the more important and defining elements in his life, but now served as little more than an occasional necessary distraction, a respite from the intensifying madness.

As he stood in front of the mirror above his bureau and slipped on a necktie, something in the doorway behind him caught his eye. He turned slowly and saw his daughter smiling at him. She was still in her pajamas and robe.

"Hi, Daddy."

"Hey, sweet pea." Even with all that was happening to him, he couldn't help but smile back at her. The magnificence of his little girl never ceased to amaze him. It seemed impossible to him that he could have been a part of creating anything so pure and perfect, and though it had been nine years since he and Cynthia had brought her home from the hospital, he still marveled at her existence the same as he had when she was a newborn. "You better hurry up and get dressed or you'll be late for school."

Debra scrunched her face into a puzzled expression. "It's Saturday, though."

Darian froze, staring at her with a befuddled look of his own.

"It's Saturday," she said again, as if to be certain he'd heard her. "I don't have school today."

He forced his fingers to move, to finish knotting the tie and to tighten it up under his collar. How could he have forgotten what day it was? Surely that happened now and then to everyone, but until that moment he hadn't realized the extent to which his sense of time and place had been anesthetized. He'd simply gotten up and prepared himself for work like a tortured lab rat awakening and scurrying through plastic mazes as it had been taught. There was something so lifeless about it all, something cold and detached. And he was so tired, so damn tired he could barely see straight. "Right," he said awkwardly. "Of course it's Saturday. I was just teasing."

Debra padded closer, arms folded across her chest. "Are you OK, Daddy?"

"He's fine, sweetheart." Cynthia appeared in the doorway, a spatula in one hand and a dishtowel in the other. "Daddy's being silly."

Debra smiled and gave her father a hug. As Darian wrapped his arms around her small shoulders he couldn't be certain if she had done it for her benefit or his. As he held her close, careful not to squeeze her too hard, his eyes lifted and found Cynthia frowning at him. "Well, I think since I have to work today," he told Debra, quickly taking his wife's lead, "it's only fair that you go to school."

Debra laughed, released him and shook her head. "No way!"

"Yup, already called the principal and he's going to open school just for you."

"Yeah, right!"

"Sweetheart, go downstairs and set the table, please," Cynthia said. "We'll be down in a sec and I'll make pancakes, but I need to talk with Daddy first, OK?"

Debra's laughter ceased, her smile quickly replaced by a look of concern indicative of wisdom well beyond her years. "OK," she said softly.

Rather reluctantly, Debra left the room.

Darian strode to the closet, pulled a suit jacket from a hangar and slipped it on. He returned to the mirror to inspect himself; straightening the creases on his lapels slowly, hopeful his wife wouldn't see how badly his hands were shaking.

"You're working today?" Cynthia finally asked.

"Thought I'd try to catch up on some paperwork," he lied. "Why, what's the big deal about me going into work for a few hours?"

"The *big deal,* is that you already made plans with your family. Your *family,*" she said, spitting the word at him like it caused a bitter taste in her mouth. "Remember us?"

Darian swallowed hard. Heart racing, a horrible sense of dread and fear welled within him then just as quickly receded, leaving behind an overwhelming feeling of paranoia. It suddenly felt as though they were being watched, listened to and gawked at like helpless animals in the zoo. "What plans?" he managed.

"The movies, remember?" Cynthia shot him a disgusted look and wearily shook her head. "You promised Deb we'd all go together. You *promised,* Darian."

"Oh, that. I didn't forget."

"Sure you didn't."

"It's not a problem." He turned away from the mirror, faced her. "I'll be home in time for us to catch a matinee, OK?"

"Where are you going?" she asked. "Really."

"This is ridiculous."

"Tell me the truth."

"These suspicions of yours are nonsense," he said through a quick burst of nervous laughter, "and I'm not about to give them credence by discussing them."

"You're acting as if you've lost your mind. You spend hours staring out the window at night. You check on Debra twenty times a night. You rarely sleep, and even when you're here, you're not here, not really. You're coming apart right before our eyes and you expect us to just stand by and watch? You expect us to be completely unaffected by all this? Did you see the look on our daughter's face just a moment ago?"

A clammy film of perspiration broke out across his scalp. "I have to go."

"Darian, obviously something's happened and you're having *problems.* We can get through this. We can go talk with someone, but you've got to let me in. You can't shut me out like this and expect me to understand."

She looked so beautiful standing there in her robe. God, how he loved her, how he worshipped this woman who, along with their daughter, made him whole.

*I don't want you to understand,* he thought. *Not this.*

Something moved in the corner of his eye. Something small, gone even before he'd completely realized it was there. In its wake came feelings of claustrophobia and terror, and Darian was gripped with a sudden need to run, to get as far from here as possible, and to take whatever evils were infecting his mind with him, away from this house and away from his family.

Ignoring a churning pain deep in his gut, he moved past her, through the doorway. "I'll be back later."

"You need to talk to me, Darian."

"I have to go," he said from the hallway behind her.

"You need to talk to me before I stop asking you to." Cynthia bit her tongue in an attempt to ward off the tears already filling her eyes. "Do you understand?" she asked.

But he was already gone.

* * *

There had been a violent thunderstorm the night before. Raymond remembered how it had awakened him, and how he had lain in bed with the covers pulled up tight, watching the blue flashes of lightning fill the windows then vanish while Seth lay just feet from him in a bed of his own, asleep and unaware of the storm. He'd eventually fallen asleep while praying frantically to God to make it all go away, and awoke early the following morning feeling tired but relieved. In the morning, the world was still wet, dripping with remnants of the heavy rains the night before, and Raymond, filled with a new sense of dread, had gone down to the field behind their house, a solitary and quiet place he often went to when he wanted to be alone or think, a place where he felt safe and at peace.

The shadowed forest just beyond the touch of the slowly rising sun bordered the field, and a small creek ran through a portion of sloped land between the two. Raymond sat atop a large rock there and watched the water trickle past. He could sit for hours and watch armies of ant soldier about, or sometimes he'd study the delicate flight of a butterfly as it bounced from flower to flower, blade of grass to branch, or occasionally even when they landed on his outstretched fingertips.

On this particular morning, however, rather than watching the beauty around him with his typical sense of wonder and awe, little Raymond sat on his favorite rock and wrestled instead with a sense of trepidation and sorrow. A tear fell free, trickled the length of his face, as he wondered why God made people like him. Different. Crazy.

"Isn't it beautiful out today?"

Raymond looked back over his shoulder and saw his mother approaching across the field, the grass tall this time of year, nearly to the tops of her thighs. Dressed in a white summer dress and sandals, her long hair pulled back and fastened with a matching white and silver clasp, she was the most beautiful woman he had ever seen.

"I figured I'd find you down here." She smiled that big smile of hers, but when she realized Raymond was crying it transformed quickly into a frown. "What's wrong, honey?" She slid up next to the rock and let her hand rest on his knee. "What is it? Why are you crying?"

Raymond shrugged.

"Did you have a bad dream again?"

He shook his head in the negative.

She gave his knee a slight squeeze and smiled up at him. "You sure?"

"I'm OK, Mom," he finally said, wiping the tear from his cheek.

"Want to go for a walk with me?"

"Will you sing a song?" he asked.

"Tell you what. I'll trade you a song for a smile, how's that?" She raised an eyebrow. "But you first."

Raymond smiled, slid down off the rock and into the waiting arms of his mother. She kissed his cheek and whispered, "I love you," then hand in hand they started off across the creek and up into the forest for their walk. His mother began to sing, her exquisite voice sweeping through the trees, and while Raymond found solace in her sweet voice, as he always did, the bad feelings that had filled his head since he'd awakened remained. Feelings of fire, a raging fire burning and destroying everything in its path, refused to leave him.

The following day, when a house in their neighborhood burned to the ground due to an electrical fire, and the Delmont family was left homeless, the feelings finally left him, replaced by those of helplessness and grief.

Memories of that day faded, blurred, and became landscape along the Cape Cod highway rushing past his window. Raymond took a hard puff on his cigarette. "I've always been different, Seth."

"Not always. For a long time now, but not always."

"Once the night terrors started I changed. They changed me. I could sense things I couldn't before. Sometimes I could see things."

"I know."

"No one believed me, and I couldn't talk about it because I…I felt like a freak." He shook his head sadly. "I guess I was. Am."

"Ray, don't—"

"It is what it is, man."

"Talking like that about yourself isn't going to help the situation."

"Sometimes I could see things. Things that weren't there, that weren't supposed to be there. But I could see them. And for a long time I dealt with it the best I could. It's fucked up my whole life. I never had half the shit most people do. A decent job, good place to live, somebody to share it with. My whole fucking life, I've dealt with it. I've lived with it. If you can call what I do living." He left the cigarette between his lips. "Only since that night at the cabin it's worse. It's darker, more extreme."

Seth stammered something unintelligible as he struggled to form his thoughts into a coherent response. "Nothing's right," he finally managed. "Nothing's been right since that night. I know things have been bad for you for years, but this is new to me, it's not something I understand, I—"

"You think I do?" Raymond asked.

"I think you know more than you're telling me, Ray."

"Is the same thing happening to you? Is that what you were trying to tell me when you said—"

"I don't know." Seth glanced in the rearview then slowly pulled over into the breakdown lane. Another car rushed by but otherwise the highway was strangely empty. Once stopped, Seth put the car in PARK but left his hands on the wheel, head bowed. "Things have been off for a while," he said softly. "When Peggy and I split things got worse. I know it was a stupid move but I couldn't stay with her. As much as I loved her—and still do—I couldn't stay with her. Things were different. *I* was different. I started to remember things... things I didn't want to remember. I started to hear things, and sometimes even see things. Not the way you normally see things, but from the corner of my eye, or I'd just sense it, see it in my mind, do you understand?"

Raymond drew on his cigarette. "What do *you* think?"

Seth finally looked at him, his face contorted into a muddle of emotion. "That's just it, Ray. I don't know. It's like someone or something is there but I don't know what it is. I'm having odd nightmares and the strangest sensations even while I'm awake. It's why I started seeing a doctor. I thought, here we go; I'm going crazy, just like..." he caught himself and stopped just short.

"You can say it," Raymond told him. "Just like me."

"I didn't mean that, I—it's just—insanity can be hereditary, you know."

"You think that never occurred to me? I think about that shit every day."

"I started to feel like I was losing it at times, Ray. I was having trouble functioning and I was afraid of what I might do. I didn't want to do what you did. I didn't want to just drop out of life—I still don't—but sometimes I wonder if I have any choice. And that makes me angry. Unnaturally angry, I'm not a violent person and yet lately I get these feelings of rage that scare the hell out of me."

Raymond nodded. He'd tried cleansing himself through violence—bar fights and street brawls—but nothing had ever washed it all away. The fear was a constant, something he had been forced to endure as both a ghost from the past and a continual reality in the present, and all of it with no end in sight.

"My time with Doc helps," Seth said a moment later. "She helps keep me focused and thinking clearly. But I know there's more to this than meets the eye, Ray, there always has been."

"I'd say that's a safe bet."

"I know something's happened. Something happened that night at the cabin, something I can't remember for some reason. I know all that as sure as I'm sitting here. I just don't know what the hell to do about it."

Ray nodded.

"And whatever it is, it's—I know this sounds crazy—but it's as if it's changing us, killing us off slowly, all of us, from the inside out."

"I told you before: it's like a disease, and that's what some diseases do. They rot you from the inside out…slowly…gradually."

Seth's expression remained still, neutral. "Why does *it* want us?"

Raymond smoked his cigarette for a while without responding. When it had burned to the filter he flicked it out the open window. The cool fresh air felt good, sobering. "I've spent my whole life running from this shit, telling myself none of it mattered, that it was all bullshit, but always afraid one of these days I'd wake up and it'd be true. I was a regular kid once, man, I was normal a long time ago. Wasn't I, Seth? You said it yourself. A long time ago, wasn't I a normal kid?"

"Sure, Ray, of course you were."

"Then things changed. That was hard enough to deal with, but then that night at the cabin things changed again. When I was a kid, I tried to fight it off, I tried to pretend for a while that if I ignored the things I was seeing and thinking and feeling everything would go back to normal. But it didn't work. It wouldn't let me go. It came out of nowhere, slowly, subtly at first, but it got stronger and pretty soon I couldn't even shake it when I went to sleep. Sometimes it got worse. The visions and thoughts would come to me in dreams, nightmares. No matter what I did or said or thought, it wouldn't stop. Whatever *this* is that I have—a gift, a curse, psychic ability, whatever you want to label it—when it changed me as a kid it changed me for good, Seth. Years later, somehow these abilities—or whatever the hell they are—allowed me to see what was happening in those woods a year ago in ways none of you could. It was like there was a time bomb ticking away that finally went off and we were unlucky enough to be there when it did. And now maybe we've all got the same time bomb in our heads. Maybe it never goes off, but maybe one day it does, and just like that, you're full-throttle motherfucking crazy."

Seth finally released the steering wheel and let his hands drop to his lap. He was certain he had never heard his brother speak so openly and honestly about anything in his life, and knew if he didn't push it further he might not get another chance to find some answers. "What happened at the cabin, Ray?"

"I don't know for sure."

"Would you tell me if you did?"

The look in Raymond's eyes answered for him. And it was in that moment that a memory flashed through Seth's mind, a memory of Raymond looking at Christy when she first bolted into their camp that day, a look on his face that could only be described as a look of recognition. "My God…you knew, didn't you? That's it, you knew. That's why you looked at Christy the way you did. She looked familiar to you…because you'd seen her before. You knew what was going to happen out there. That's why you showed up when you did, that's why you wanted to come along. You knew."

"Yeah," he said softly.

"You'd seen her before in—what—a vision?"

*Darkness. The forest. That night unfolding before him, the snow draping everything and coming down with unusual ferocity. Sounds of his boots crunching beneath him, and his own gasping, labored breathing. The flashlight in his hand bouncing and shaking, its beam cutting enough of a fissure in the night to reveal blurry views of Christy running several yards in front of him, maneuvering through the trees and along the uneven terrain, her nude body impossibly pale amidst the darkness. Another cabin coming into view, the door open…*

Raymond slammed shut his eyes, rubbed them until it all went away.

"Why can't I remember what happened, Ray?"

"Maybe we're not supposed to. Maybe we're not allowed to."

"But we have to find out," Seth said. "We have to know."

Raymond ran a hand through his hair, pulling it away from his face. "Then drive."

# Chapter 12

Lighthouse Shores was the kind of quaint little town people envisioned when Cape Cod came to mind. Picturesque, with long stretches of beautiful beach, sand dunes, pastoral homes sprinkled among miles of unspoiled countryside and an old lighthouse still in commission, it could have been lifted directly from a postcard. A place where time did its best to stand still, the permanent, year-round population was just shy of three thousand, and though that number increased a bit in the summer months with the influx of seasonal townsfolk, the increase was significantly smaller in Lighthouse Shores than in most Cape Cod communities, as for the most part, it was a more exclusive area and not one where tourists were especially welcomed. There were no department stores or strip malls in Lighthouse Shores, only a small general store and recently refurbished post office, both of which resembled something out of the last century, a small bed and breakfast, a diner, and a handful of quaint gift shops that catered more to the year-round residents than to the modest summer trade that occasionally passed through town.

Raymond felt a surge of discomfort as they crossed the town line and ventured along Main Street. It hadn't occurred to him until just then how similar his feelings were to when he'd gone to Gull's Peak, the small town in northern Maine where the cabin was located. The forest there—so thick and sweeping—watched him from the back of his mind, silent, black and unforgiving, and as the gentle sway of branches slowly increased, bending and bouncing, giving way for the emergence of something harsher than the subtle breeze pushing its way through them, Raymond let the memories go as one might release a tethered balloon. They drifted away, back into the darkness, and he focused again on the countryside gliding past his window.

Little had changed since he'd been here last. That's how people in Lighthouse Shores liked things—the same—always the same. Their previous visits here, particularly the ones after the tragedy involving their parents, had altered the sense of serenity he had always felt in this town, the consistency of things, as if in some ways their very presence and the pain that accompanied them brought about palpable changes not only in them, but in their grandmother and the very fabric of her sleepy little town as well. All these years later Raymond still felt uneasy here, nervous, an intruder trampling about in places he had no business disturbing. It was a dichotomy that had always baffled Raymond, the way pain and anguish could so effortlessly coexist alongside exquisite beauty and tranquility, each feeding one off the other with appalling symmetry. And the concept rarely seemed as ordinary as it did within the borders of Lighthouse Shores.

A hazy rain kicked up.

Seth switched on the wipers.

The incessant squeaking that followed broke the silence and shuffled Raymond's thoughts and memories back to where he kept them bound, the secret places where they were powerless and could do him no harm. He placed a hand against his cheek. Despite the heat in the car it was cool and clammy. He considered popping another anti-anxiety pill, but decided against it. He was only supposed to take two a day and wanted his mind clear as possible.

Seth drove on.

Though neither man spoke a word, the inertia of the moment fell away as they turned onto Duncan Road, the car slowing to a mere creep. Huge trees hundred of years old towered on either side of the street, branches stripped bare in the winter wind.

*Do you remember, Ray? Do you remember how the leaves in full bloom would create a canopy way up there, a ceiling of leaves? Do you remember walking this street with Nana and gazing up at those magnificent trees? Can you remember the beauty here?*

He felt himself nod, or perhaps only thought he had, eyes scanning the houses as the car skulked along.

*Do you see the beauty now, Ray? Can you still see the beauty of a barren winter day?*

The car stopped.

*Can you still see the horrible beauty of what festers beneath it, waiting, watching?*

Raymond sat up expectantly. Before them sat a presumptuously large Victorian-era residence set back from the road atop a small hill, the winding white gravel driveway, the perfect lawn and sculpted grounds and bushes out front, the curtains in the windows—everything looked the same as it always had, frozen there like a paused video awaiting their return. Beyond the small cluster of trees behind the house lay miles of sandy dunes, and further, the vast waves of the Atlantic Ocean.

Raymond could remember the day he and Seth had sat in front of this house trying to convince themselves to go inside and tell their grandmother what they already knew, that her son was dead—killed—mangled beyond recognition in the twisted metal remains of what had once been the family car. Their parents—her son and daughter-in-law—were dead, and life could never be the same.

That same gnawing feeling deep in his gut burrowed forth as he took in the house now. The house and all it represented, then and always.

*Do you remember realizing you could never escape the darkness, Ray? Do you remember it being here too, how it followed you and Seth even on your visits? Do you remember feeling it in those rambling, soulless old rooms?*

Raymond turned from the window. "You gonna park it or what?"

Always the tough guy, Seth thought. Ever since the change in him in high school, when he transformed himself from victim to fighter, he'd tried so hard to be the strong one, and maybe he was; maybe he always had been.

Seth slid into the driveway and parked behind the Lexus sedan already there. A decal of the American flag adorned the back window, but the distraction was short-lived as their attention was quickly drawn back to the house, and the large, partially open front door that faced the street.

In the shadow it cast along the front steps, stood Nana. Tall, sophisticated, and still looking twenty years younger than she actually was, she was dressed in one of her usual, rather formal dresses and a pair of tasteful heels. Her hair (dyed raven black as it had been for years) was, as always, flawless as her makeup and manicure. Though her style was somewhat dated, she possessed the fetching beauty and presence of a silent film star, and was an individual one noticed immediately, regardless of circumstance. Her high cheekbones, large dark eyes, full lips and olive skin—all trademarks of her Mediterranean heritage—only served to compliment a vibrancy rarely found in someone nearing eighty years of age, but which she enjoyed in abundance.

Realizing they had seen her, she raised a hand, offered a restrained wave and smiled coolly as she moved down the steps. In the misty rain there was something ghost-like about her grace and elegance, her presence partially obscured amidst the first stages of an imminent storm.

Raymond's emotions were so evident Seth could practically feel them himself. Just seeing Nana brought forth in his brother a look of relief and hope he'd only seen in him while in her presence. Yet in all the years of his life Seth still couldn't determine if that reaction was good or bad. As with so many things, the truth could probably be found at some point in between. "You ready?" Seth asked.

"Yeah," Raymond answered in a tone calmer and

more genuine than before.

"Then let's go," Seth said, and stepped from the car.

* * *

Alessandra Isabella Roma immigrated to the United States in her late teens, already married to Seth and Raymond's grandfather, Rocco, a man nearly twenty years her senior who died when his grandsons were just toddlers. As was the case with many immigrants in those days, due to a clerical error, the original name of Roma was changed to Roman, something that always bothered Nana and something she made a point of explaining every chance she got. "Roma," she would say to people who showed even vague interest, "means one from Rome, of course. So *Roman* becomes a rather ironic and fascinating error. Now, the meaning of my first name, Alessandra, is 'defender of man,' and my middle name, Isabella is the Italian form of Isabel, and means 'consecrated to God.' It's all so stoic and dutifully old-world *Catholic*! But rather delicious too, don't you think? People so rarely take the time to learn about their names. Pity, really. At any rate, in the end, the attempt to butcher our family name was not a success. The spelling changed but the meaning remained the same. Some may consider it miraculous but I contend you can never destroy who any of us truly are. No one has that power but God, and God would never be so vulgar as to use it, don't you agree?"

Since the death of their grandfather, Nana had remarried twice. Once when Seth and Raymond were in elementary school, she was briefly married to a surgeon from Chicago, a man they met only once and to whom she stayed with for less than a year. For the next few decades, Nana remained single then eventually settled down with her third husband, a German-born retired businessman ten years her junior named Rolf Kropp, whom she had met on one of her many trips to Europe. He was a man they had never known well, and to whom they seldom spoke. He was a quiet, private, introverted man who looked like a German diplomat direct from Central Casting. Though friendly and gracious, he often remained aloof and spent most of his time reading in his study or tinkering with plastic model airplanes he was fond of building.

As always, Nana remained the main attraction.

Though she retained a faint accent from her youth, her English was flawless, as were the four other languages she spoke fluently: French, German, Japanese, and, of course, Italian. She was almost completely self-educated, and while she and Rolf enjoyed a comfortable lifestyle, Nana conducted herself like some displaced countess, royalty in exile awaiting liberation that was surely destined to arrive at any moment.

Like Ms. Jean Brody, she was fond of saying: "One must never be *too* provincial."

In the light rain, she welcomed both her grandsons with a hug. The three stood silently joined for what seemed a long time, oblivious to the weather. In turn, she took their faces in her hands and kissed them. "It's so good to see you both," she whispered, as if fearful someone else might hear and intrude upon them. "I've missed you."

"Nana," Raymond began, head bowed and feet shuffling like a child, "there's—"

"Shhh," she said, placing a blood-red fingernail

against his lips. "Come inside."

She escorted them past the large foyer to the dining room. A large area with high, long windows draped in thick velvet curtains, the room was filled with dark furniture and an ostentatious crystal chandelier dangling over the sprawling table. Rolf appeared as if by magic from an adjacent hallway in a pressed white oxford and slacks, his silver hair slicked back and his manner awkward and overly formal. Coming just shy of clicking his heels together he shook Seth and Raymond's hands in turn, made minimal small-talk then with a slight bow took his cue and disappeared down the hallway from which he'd come.

Nana floated about the room as if she rarely spent time there. She hovered near a large hutch, one hand poised near the door handle, behind which stood numerous pieces of fine crystal. "Something to settle the nerves?" When they hesitated she grinned mischievously and motioned to a fully outfitted bar in the far corner of the room.

In a stern voice Seth said, "I don't drink this time of day, thank you."

Raymond shook his head in the negative and smiled weakly.

"Oh how tiresome." She rolled her eyes and strolled closer to the table, but upon closer inspection of Raymond, turned more somber and tenderly cupped the side of his face with her palm.

"I need to talk to you, Nana," Raymond said suddenly, emotion filling his voice, "I—"

"It's all right," she said calmly. "I know why you're here."

Seth's expression betrayed him before his insolent

sigh did. Here we go, he thought, more mystical nonsense that will do nothing but further cloud the entire situation and make things more difficult to decipher. Clearly something beyond their scope of understanding had happened, *was happening*, but he failed to see how their grandmother's melodrama could help the situation.

She ignored him as what little light there was in the room dimmed. She looked to the nearest window and considered the dark sky a moment. "You used to love to walk in the rain, Raymond."

Raymond nodded.

Nana turned to Seth, who had taken position in front of the table but had opted to remain standing. "You'll excuse us?"

He answered without looking at her. "Of course."

She dropped her hand from Raymond's face and held it out to him as the beginnings of a smile teased her lips. "Come for a walk in the rain with your Nana, my love."

# Chapter 13

Alone in the grand dining room, Seth felt more uncomfortable and insignificant than ever in his grandmother's rambling home. Though he'd never had large sums of money, he was certain he would never live like this even if he had. Perhaps his father's hippie, minimalist values were more deeply ingrained in him than he realized. He glanced around. The immaculate floors, glossy furniture, high ceilings and austere silence reminded him of a museum, though for Seth, there was nothing of particular appeal here, aesthetic or otherwise. He loved his grandmother, but Raymond had always been the one beguiled by Nana, not him.

He wandered to the tall windows on the far wall, his footfalls echoing along the floor, and gently pulled back a small section of velvet curtain to reveal a view of the grounds behind the home, the surrounding sand dunes and fog-covered Atlantic Ocean below. Amidst gray skies and a drizzling rain, waves roiled and crashed the shore, spraying water up in great misty bursts like a scene from some turn-of-the-century gothic novel.

A blue umbrella with white polka dots appeared along the path leading to the dunes and beach beyond. Despite her heels, Nana walked arm-in-arm with Raymond, her usual graceful stride unaffected by the uneven and sandy terrain. Her free hand held the umbrella to shelter them both.

They were an odd pair at best, his disheveled brother seemingly held together with chewing gum and duct tape, slowly ravaged from the inside out and struggling to hold himself together alongside Nana, with her long and fashionable raincoat, white silk scarf wrapped about her head and down around her neck á la Gloria Swanson, considerable black sunglasses—which she wore regardless of weather conditions—designer clothing and a style and flair just shy of Nora Desmond.

And what of him? What did they see when they looked at him? He wondered.

He watched them walk slowly along the path to the dunes. Raymond hesitated long enough to help Nana down onto the sand before they continued on along the beach, just beyond the reach of ocean spray.

*What happened to you that night at the cabin, Ray?*

Seth felt an odd tingling sensation in his temples. Flashes of the dream he'd had that night returned: the storm, the screams and…something else…something close and yet still just beyond his memory and understanding. There, in the darkness.

*What happened out there didn't happen to me.*

Seth released the curtain and turned away from the window. The light shifted and dimmed as the curtain fell closed, and the tingling in his head increased, became more a mounting pressure that spread up into his nose and behind his eyes. A slight dizziness emerged then left him just as quickly as a sudden popping in his head relieved the pressure, and he felt his nose begin to run.

*It happened to all of you.*

Seth reached up, wiped his nose with the back of his hand. Blood.

"Jesus," he muttered. He couldn't remember the last time he'd had a nosebleed. He found cocktail napkins on the bar, grabbed one, held it beneath his nostrils and pinched.

Tilting his head back, he sat in one of the dining room chairs while echoes of screams and storms still lingered in his mind. Seth closed his eyes, embraced memories of Peggy instead, though he couldn't be sure why he had thought of her just then. Perhaps because she represented a safe distraction—sanctuary—from all else haunting him, or perhaps because at that moment he feared he might never see her again.

The bitter metallic taste of blood dripped along the back of his throat as a distant voice in his head whispered to him. Three words. The screams and storm sounds were replaced with three simple words, he was sure of it, but they were spoken in a swirling, garbled voice he couldn't decipher.

Seth pulled the napkin away and looked at it. A spot of dark red blood about the size of a half-dollar stained the center of the cloth. He sniffled, swallowed and again tasted blood, but after inspecting his nose, realized the bleeding had stopped.

The three words in his head were spoken once more

then faded away.

This time they were unmistakable.

*Let Them Out.*

* * *

Louis lived in a small, three-story apartment building in Boston's North End. A predominantly Italian-American neighborhood known for amazing fresh food, cappuccino joints, topnotch restaurants, and in parts, its longtime and historical connection to organized crime, in recent years many of the narrow streets and quiet avenues had become home to a slightly more diverse body of residents.

Though Louis had lived there more than three years now, Darian knew how miserable he was in the apartment. It was clear to anyone who knew him how much he still identified with being a husband and father, and how difficult it was for him to exist without Becky and his children. And now, things were even worse. Louis had been on Darian's mind a lot lately, but the evening prior he'd been unable to shake his feelings of paranoia and dread concerning him particularly. He'd called twice that night but there'd been no answer, so Darian assumed Louis was out drinking or simply hiding out at the apartment and not answering his phone. That morning he'd decided to go and check on him. He knew the lie about going to work would get Cynthia off his back for at least a couple hours and hopefully buy him enough time to make sure Louis was all right.

Through a now drizzling rain, Darian found a vacant parking space half a block from the apartment building, pulled in and quickly dialed Louis's number on his cell phone. It rang four times before the answering machine kicked on.

He must still be asleep, Darian thought. Probably tied on a good one last night.

The greeting kicked on, and a gruff-sounding Louis muttered, "Leave a message."

A tone sounded.

"It's me. If you're there, pick up." With the phone still pressed to his ear, Darian twisted around in his seat, taking in as much of the area as he could, searching the lines of parked cars on either side of the street until he located Louis's SUV a bit farther up the block. "Lou, I know you're home, I'm looking at your car. Pick up the phone."

He was just about to flip shut his cell when the piercing sound of feedback screeched through the earpiece followed by a clunking sound as Louis answered.

"Yeah?"

"I've been trying to reach you since last night. Are you all right?"

"What do you want, man?"

"I'm outside. I need to come up. There are some things I haven't told you, I—"

"Now's not good."

"I'm coming up."

Louis sighed heavily into the phone but said nothing.

"Goddamn it, Louis, I need to come up!"

Silence filled the line for a time.

"OK, Mother." His tone softer now, defeated. "You might as well be here when it happens."

Darian felt a hollow ache in the pit of his stomach.

"When *what* happens, Lou?"
The line clicked, went dead.

* * *

In the dream Seth found himself on his knees in a clearing ringed by a thick forest of enormous trees. Snow blew about like dust, but just above the treetops, through the darkness and swirl of flakes, he could make out a section of cobalt sky. Breath surged in thick clouds from his nostrils and open mouth, his chest rising and falling rapidly, lungs sore from the cold and straining for more oxygen. He attempted to push himself back up onto his feet, but the freezing temperature had left his hands numb and useless. Tears from the cold, fear, frustration or all three filled his eyes, and he whimpered helplessly.

Screams hemorrhaged the short-lived silence. Exploding through the trees surrounding him in squealing waves of agony and terror, the shrieks circled and cornered him there in the clearing, a pack of ravenous coyotes closing on wounded quarry.

The sky trembled and cracked as an unearthly storm coursed across the heavens, stealing his eyes and sending him plummeting into horrible darkness.

Sounds of skin splitting and clothes tearing trailed the screams still echoing through his mind, screams from familiar voices.

*"Raymond!"*

The darkness, thick and endless, encircled him in a slow sweep, a series of black waves crashing over him, swallowing him and pulling him deeper into nothingness, it filled him like a cancer invading his body against his control. He breathed the darkness into his lungs, felt it bleed through the corners of his eyes, rush deep into his ears and absorb into his pores until there was no longer physical separation. He and the darkness had become one, the same.

*I'm so sorry, Raymond. Christ, I'm so sorry.*

Seth realized his attempts to struggle against the night he'd found himself lost in were futile. He felt the rigidity in his body slowly uncoil and release, submissive now, he became a lamb led to whatever slaughter the darkness had planned for him.

*This is home*, something whispered to him from not so far away.

As the darkness parted like a huge curtain, he saw his mother standing at the sink in the kitchen of their home. He sat at the table, his face smudged with dirt, blood, tears and snot, pieces of grass stuck in his mussed hair. His knuckles were bloodied and sore, and his jaw and cheeks ached where they'd punched him.

Their mother turned from the sink with a washcloth in her hand, moved quietly to the table and crouched before Seth. She gently took his hands in hers and cleaned them, wiping away the blood. She had done the same moments before with Raymond, cleaning his split lip, kissing him and sending him to his room to lie down for a while until she could sort this mess out.

"How many were there this time?" she asked softly, emotion scratching her throat.

"Four."

"Why do they feel the need to terrorize him so? Raymond doesn't bother anyone, why can't they just leave him alone? Why do children have to be so cruel?"

Seth shrugged.

She took his chin in her hand, slowly raised his head up so they could look each other in the eye. "You don't have to keep doing this, Seth. I know you mean well and you love Raymond—and you should defend him, you're his older brother—but getting into fist-fights isn't the answer."

"I'm not very good at it anyway," he told her. "But I got a couple of them good. I hit Tommy Hennessey so hard he fell down and started crying."

"You're only lowering yourself to their level when you do that, sweetie," she said. "You need to learn to just take Raymond and walk away. Don't give them the satisfaction." Seth nodded, but he could tell by the look in her eyes she was proud of him. This gentle and spiritual woman who would not hurt a fly was secretly pleased he had jumped in and taken a beating bullies had intended for his little brother. She kissed his forehead, her lips soft and cool against his flushed skin. "Raymond would be lost without you, Seth. You're all he has."

"He has you and Dad, too," he reminded her.

Something in her face changed, and she smiled, but it was a smile so subtle he nearly missed it for what it was. "Yes, and so do you. But one day, all you'll have is each other. One day when Mommy and Daddy are gone. I know it's hard for you sometimes, honey, with Raymond, I mean. But you're a good boy. You're doing the right thing in looking out for him. God sees what we do. Good and bad, Seth. And He doesn't forget either."

*Neither do we, Mom. Neither do we.*

Through slowly churning patterns of black and gray, his vision cleared and the dream faded, giving way to a blurred version of a high white ceiling.

"It's all right." Nana's voice, soft and sympathetic. "It's all right, sweetheart."

The room came into clearer focus, and Seth sat up a bit. He was stretched out on a large bed in one of the many bedrooms in the house that normally went unused. Ornate and mostly antique-style furniture littered the room, and the lone window on the far wall was covered with a white lacy curtain and a shade that blocked most of the light. There was a musty smell here, like an old closet that hadn't been opened and aired out in some time.

Seth turned, felt pain ricochet through his temple. "Nana?"

"I'm here." The mattress shifted as she sat on the edge of the bed next to him. Her face came into view, the white scarf still wrapped about her head and down around her neck. "How are you feeling, love?"

Seth realized the only light in the room was from a small lamp on a night table next to the bed. Beneath it was an old, small porcelain basin filled with water, a washcloth draped over the side. He blinked, the light leaving traces of dark patterns gliding across his scope of vision. "Bit of a headache," he mumbled. "What happened?"

"From all indications, you suffered a nosebleed and fainted." She dipped the washcloth in the basin then gently wiped his forehead with warm water. "We found you in the dining room."

"I'm sorry, I—"

"Don't be ridiculous, sorry for what?" She arched an eyebrow. "Have you eaten today? You look awfully pale."

He let his head lay back against the thick, plush pillow. It was soft and cool and felt good against the back of his neck. "No, I—Nana, where's Ray?"

"He's near." She smiled, put the washcloth on the night table. "You were dreaming."

Seth studied her face a moment. "Where's Ray, Nana?"

"Downstairs."

"Did you two have a nice talk?"

The slight edge of sarcasm in his tone did not go unnoticed. Rather than answer directly, she said, "He's quite worried about you."

"I'm worried about us both."

Her eyes settled on his, blinked slowly. "So am I."

"Well he was the one who wanted to…" His voice trailed off, leaving only the faint sounds of ocean crashing coastline.

"One must always say what one means, Seth." She removed her scarf carefully, so as not to muss her hair in the process. "Always."

"He's the one who wanted to come here, not me. But I didn't mean it like that, it's just—"

"I understand."

"Raymond needed to see you. He needed your… guidance."

"Well, Raymond is—"

"Special. Yes, I know."

She waved at the air as if to swat his comment away then crossed her arms delicately across her chest. "I love you both more than you can imagine, Seth, but Raymond has *special* issues, and knows I understand them and always have. And now he needs you to understand them as well, because as much as I'd like to, unfortunately, I won't live forever." She brightened a bit, which seemed peculiar in such a dingy and quiet room. "Immortality *is* a thoroughly tasty concept, though, don't you think?"

"Depends on whose life it is."

"In the early 70s, accompanied by a gentlemen friend of mine named Armando, a painfully handsome trumpet player of Cuban ancestry, I visited Egypt and had an opportunity to experience the country in all its magnificence. Ancient Egyptians fully embraced immortality as a reality. In fact, when I visited the Great Pyramids, I—"

"Nana, look." Seth sat up slowly. The pain in his head had subsided. "What does—"

"You never listen, Seth. It's one of your shortcomings, I'm sorry to say. You're always too busy talking to hear anyone else, or to see what's right in front of you."

"You're my grandmother, and I love you, Nana, but—"

"And I love you."

"—I find that criticism rather ironic coming from you."

"As the British author and poet Elizabeth Bibesco once said: 'Irony is the hygiene of the mind.'"

Seth sighed heavily. "I'm sorry, but your Auntie Mame routine never captivated my imagination the way it did Raymond's."

"Pity."

"Something's happening to us, Nana…something…"

"You were dreaming," she told him again. "Just now."

Seth nodded, hoping to dislodge the memories and

lose them forever.

Nana stood up and moved back a bit from the bed so Seth could swing his legs around onto the floor and sit up fully. "You called out for Raymond at one point."

"What did Raymond tell you?"

"In many ways, it's remarkable the degree to which he resembles both of your parents," she said fondly. "Though your father wasn't blessed—or cursed, depending on your personal outlook, of course—with the demands Raymond has had placed upon him. And frankly, Raymond is significantly more intelligent than your father ever was. You both are. If we're to be honest, and why shouldn't we be, my son was a fool, a jester, but a good soul. He always meant well, he truly did. And he loved you boys. My God, how he loved you boys. He also worshipped your mother, as any good husband should." Her expression turned stoic. "I respected your mother as well, for a great many reasons, not the least of which was it takes a truly special woman to tolerate someone as marvelously eccentric as your father was. We had little in common, your mother and I, but one thing we shared was how deeply and dearly we loved him. Your mother also had a spiritual aspect to her I respected enormously, and one that Raymond shares, though his is far deeper and wider reaching than her somewhat limited beliefs. But then he's not bound by the same religious boundaries your mother adhered to, of course."

Seth gave a sullen nod. "I miss him. I miss them both."

"As do I," she said tranquilly. "I not only lost a daughter-in-law, I lost my son, my only child. My *child*. There's nothing quite as perverse as outliving one's own child. Remember that, won't you?" She strolled to the window, her heels clacking against the floor with each step. "Raymond tells me you're seeing a psychiatrist. Is this helping you?"

"It was at first but now, I—I'm not so sure."

"Raymond's gone to doctors. They feed him pills."

"He needs those pills, Nana."

"That's the answer to everything today. Drug it." She turned from the window, looked back at him. "No drugs can help your brother, Seth. He's not mentally ill, he's gifted—special—and he always has been. Your parents couldn't reconcile it in their own minds and poor little Raymond still can't. Look at your brother closely and without judgment, and you'll see a devastated young man carrying the weight of the world on his shoulders. Look into his eyes and you'll see the soul of a man who has seen things no one asks to see, no one wants to see, but eyes that cannot look away because he, like the rest of us, has not been given that luxury. Do you think people with his abilities—*real* abilities—to see things others cannot, host insipid television shows or give tarot card readings in low-rent storefronts or at your local mall? How patently absurd."

Though he still felt a bit lightheaded, Seth slowly rose to his feet. "You've always believed Raymond was *psychic*—or whatever label you want to give it—but I never thought that kind of thing actually existed in any real sense."

"You've always simply pretended it wasn't there, and in doing so, in many ways pretended Raymond wasn't there either. You've looked for answers everywhere and anywhere except in the one place where we all know the answers truly lie. Are you still prepared to do that, Seth, to believe that?"

"I don't know what the hell to believe at this point."

"Believe this: The few people on this planet who have the gift your brother possesses are more often than not either tucked away in mental institutions or victims of suicide before they reach their formative years." She moved back toward the window, closer to the shadows in the corner. "Imagine knowing what he knows. Really, *truly* knowing it. Seeing it before it happens. It's destroyed his life. No meaningful relationships, no peace, no rest. Why do you think he was so frightened as a young boy? Night terrors. Indeed. Look to history, Seth. Your ancestors come from a land rich in tradition and knowledge of many things people dismiss now as nonsense due to ignorance and fear. Study the saints and the martyrs, if you're more comfortable dealing with a religious experience you can relate to. They all thought they were mad, particularly initially. Voices, visions, things no human should be capable of and something no human can endure without consequence." She hesitated a moment, bound by reflective thought. "Your mother knew. I believe she always did, and tried to pray it out of her son, tried to destroy it because she feared it, feared what it was doing to him. But you can't destroy it without also destroying him."

"And where does this *gift* come from exactly?"

"Well, that *is* the question, isn't it?"

"Why him?"

"Perhaps there's some greater purpose he needs to fulfill, I don't know. But what I *can* tell you, is that Raymond has never recovered from these things, and he's never recovered from the death of your parents."

"Neither have I," Seth reminded her.

"But it's time you knew something, Seth." She raised the window shade enough to allow a bit of outside light into the room. "Unlike Raymond, you didn't know it was coming. You didn't see the accident that would one day kill them night after night in your dreams."

# Chapter 14

Once when he was a child, Seth fell from a tree he had been climbing. Upon hitting the ground, all the air was knocked from his body and he lay there a moment squirming like a fish out of water, gasping for oxygen in a haze of furious panic. In those few seconds before his lungs again filled with air, he realized what it must be like to drown or suffocate, an awareness that never completely left him.

In the silence of the bedroom, he felt a similar sensation, like he had again hit the ground with such force he could no longer breathe. His legs felt weak, and he slowly lowered himself down onto the edge of the bed.

Nana, well aware of the impact of her words, fell silent and returned her attention to the sea beyond the window.

"How could that never occur to me?" Pain seared through his midsection then faded to a dull ache, which left him feeling like the victim of a punch full in the gut who had not first had the opportunity to tighten his stomach muscles. "In all these years," he muttered, "how could I—how could I have missed it? It's so obvious."

"Why would something you choose to disbelieve occur to you?" she asked him. "You never believed Raymond was anything other than a frightened and confused little boy. Later, he was mentally ill, emotionally disturbed, a young man with *problems*. Not a terrified and nearly destroyed soul with abilities he has no control over. After all, only Nana—silly and eccentric Nana—would believe such nonsense."

For just a second it seemed she had succumbed to time, and her always-perfect posture slumped. Seth was certain Nana had never looked like an old woman until that very moment, but it too passed as she caught herself and corrected it like an actor who had forgotten her line then suddenly remembered it. "Sadly, we are a repugnantly self-absorbed species. It is our nature in many ways, so of course those who choose to slog along rather than enlighten themselves have no idea what's taking place right beneath their noses, nor do they care. But believe me, there's a symphony being played by a full orchestra, you only have to listen for it. It's simply a part of life, of being a living thing, Seth, of being *alive*. And sometimes, those simple truths that ought to be obvious remain hidden because we simply refuse to see them. Somewhere along the line we convince ourselves it's easier that way, which of course, it is not."

"But he *knew* they were going to die?"

"That and other things," Nana said. "You must understand that there are countless situations and scenarios taking place all around us at all times: realities, possibilities, mysteries, riddles and the rest. Only human beings would be so pompous as to believe our existence is singular not only in terms of importance but in a literal sense. It might explain why we've managed to achieve the levels of destruction and agony on this planet no other species has come even remotely close to. When you're the only one at the party, do you really give a damn if someone pees in the proverbial punch?"

"My God." He brought his hands to his face and closed his eyes, as if to shut it all out just a moment longer. "But he knew?" he asked again. "He knew how and when Mom and Dad were going to die?"

Her lack of a reply answered the question for him.

"And you? Did you know?"

After a moment she offered a quick nod.

"How?"

"Because he told me. And I believed him."

"You told no one? You just took this information and did nothing with it?"

"What would you have had me do, Seth? Please, enlighten me as to what I should've done, won't you?" She kept her back to him so he would not see the pain in her eyes. "I prayed, I hoped he was wrong, I tried to speak to him of it whenever I could, to gain more information and hopefully some details. A date, a place, anything I might use to warn them. But he had nothing that specific, only visions of the mayhem to come."

In his own pain, confusion and anger, Seth had forgotten to take notice of the things Nana had carried with her for years, but once in possession of this knowledge, she seemed small and fragile to him, as if this revelation had unmasked or disrobed her somehow, shrouding her instead with great vulnerability wholly at odds with her larger-than-life persona. And yet, it made her more human to him, more accessible. For so many years he had seen her as if from a distance, as one-dimensional, a screwball grandmother who traveled the world, had countless affairs and adventures and spoke like a character from an old movie. For so long he felt they shared nothing in common and that he would never bond with her the way Raymond had, and though that was perhaps still true, this new knowledge altered his perception of his grandmother, and therefore of Raymond and even himself. Everything had changed. Everything he thought he knew, he would have to rethink and learn again from a new angle. Neither life nor the players in it were what he had previously believed them to be.

"There's certainly nothing new or unique about precognitive dreams," Nana said. "There are numerous accounts throughout history, some quite famous. The Egyptian pharaohs spoke of it. Mohammed, Saint John, and Joan of Arc all claimed to have had precognitive dreams. Even President Lincoln dreamed of his impending assassination, and Mark Twain dreamed of seeing his brother dead only hours before he was killed in an explosion on a steamship. Many people dream of disasters before they happen, it's not that unusual. But what Raymond possesses is different. His experiences are not isolated. These things always haunt him. Always Seth. Always."

Visions of his parents refused to leave him, their faces distorted and gliding through his mind like cheap effects in a carnival funhouse mirror. "Why didn't he ever tell me? Even now, why hasn't he?"

"Perhaps you should ask him that question, or perhaps yourself."

In fact, Seth knew his brother *had* tried to tell him many times over the years, particularly when they'd been younger, but he hadn't listened, hadn't heard him, not really.

"I'm sorry," he told her. "For all of this—for all of *us*—I'm sorry, Nana."

"So am I, love," she said, the words catching in her throat. "You have no idea."

Seth rose from the bed, slowly crossed the small room and joined her at the window. In time, he put his arm around her and left it there until he felt her lean against him.

"Pain, much like faith, is often a shared experience, but also a fiercely personal one," Nana said sadly. "Like anyone else, Seth, I've known pain too. I've had a wonderful life, a grand adventure in so many ways I've no right to complain about a moment of it. But believe you me I've had my periods of agony as well. I've always prided myself on having an open mind, and I've strived to learn as much as I can about everything this amazing world has to offer. Once we stop learning, we cease to live, and I, for one, do not wish to cease living. I am constantly in search of answers to the mysteries and intricacies of life, and Raymond knows this about his Nana. So he comes to me with these things because he understands I not only believe what others do not, but I've seen what many deny is even possible. Once while traveling through Tibet I had the good fortune to witness many…" her voice trailed off to silence and her expression shifted, washing her face with a look of futility. "Well, no point in going into all that, I suppose."

Seth gently tightened his grip on her shoulder and

gave it a reassuringly squeeze.

"I'm sorry," she said. "Sometimes I really *am* just a silly old woman, aren't I?"

Seth wanted to be angry but could only gather an overwhelming sense of sorrow. "Never," he whispered.

She gave him an uncharacteristically restrained smile and kissed him lightly on the cheek. "This family," she sighed. "We're either blessed or cursed, depending on where you're standing, I suppose. There's such a delicate line between evil and the divine. Both can be so frightening, so powerful. But one binds you and the other sets you free."

"Maybe they both bind," Seth offered.

"Maybe, though in different ways."

"Raymond came to you with this years ago," Seth said. "And now he's come to you again. He's come to tell you about his new nightmares, hasn't he?"

"Yes. More visions, more nightmares, more impending darkness."

Seth felt the shakes move through him again. "Did he tell you about the cabin? Did he tell you about that night last year?"

"He did."

"Did he tell you what happened that night? What happened to him—what happened to all of us? Did he tell you, Nana?"

"Yes, as best he could from what he knows at this point."

He reached across her, took both shoulders in his hands and turned her toward him until they were face to face. "Please, Nana, tell me what he said."

"No."

The sound of Raymond's voice startled them both.

Seth dropped his arms and looked back at the doorway. His brother stood watching them, still damp from the rain, a lost soul wandered in from the rising storm and only just then free of the prison his mind had constructed around him.

"She doesn't have to tell you," Raymond said. "I will."

* * *

Darian froze. The door to Louis's apartment was ajar.

Standing in the dark and narrow hallway, he watched bright tracers of light leak from the doorway. An unnatural and anticipatory silence filled the hallway and apartment beyond, as if the building itself were awaiting something of great significance.

Darian moved closer then reached out and gave the door a gentle push.

The place, unusually bright despite the overcast and rainy day, was a mess. Debris littered the floor and dishes were piled high in the kitchen sink. A dank and musty odor mixed with one of body odor and rotting food lingered in the air, and a damp and chilly breeze wafted about.

"Jesus, Louis." Darian crossed the threshold, eyes panning across the once dull white walls. "What the hell's going on?"

Three tall windows set against the back wall of the apartment overlooked the neighborhood and street below. Sheer white curtains danced gracefully in the breeze, indicating the windows had been opened wide, and as the curtains fluttered, Darian could see Louis casually sitting on the windowsill of the center window, staring back at him through the thin material like a ghost.

"Louis, come away from the window," Darian said softly. "I need to talk to you."

As the curtains swept up and out of the way a moment, Louis grinned at him. It was gone quickly, though, and he looked away, distracted by some other thought that required his immediate attention. He looked as if he'd neither slept nor bathed in days. His clothes were soiled and filthy, his hair mussed and matted, and his face unshaven and pallid. In one hand, he clutched an enormous knife. His t-shirt was short-sleeved, revealing a network of slashes and gory gashes on his flesh from wrist to bicep; many still dripping blood. As Darian moved a bit closer, he realized Louis's face and clothing were dotted with spattered blood as well, and his fingers were coated in it, looking like he'd dipped them in a bucket of bright red paint.

As he moved deeper into the apartment, careful to move slowly and not further disturb Louis, Darian did his best to ignore the things written on the walls. Scrawled in crimson, it was the same phrase written over and over again, a lunatic's demented obsessive mantra finger-painted in his own blood.

*Let Them Out.*

"Louis," he said, "I need you to come away from the window now, OK?"

"That's good right there, Mother." Louis raised the knife so Darian could have a better view of it through the curtains. The blade was stained and smeared with dried blood. "Just stay right fucking there."

Darian held his hands up and slowly nodded his

head. "OK, man, you got it. Just take it easy, all right? Take it easy and talk to me."

"You know what the worst part is?"

"Please come away from the window, Lou."

"I can't ever go home. That's the worst part. I can never go home." He sighed, slowly lowered the knife back to his lap. "No matter what, even if Becky wanted me back—which she doesn't, of course—I could never go home. I could never spread this to her and—and my babies." The last word snagged in his throat and his voice cracked. His body bucked and he began to cry silently, his face bent into a shivering frown.

"It's all right," Darian told him, struggling to hold his voice steady too. "We'll get through this, you and me, together. I promise you, Lou. I *promise* you. But you've got to let me help you. Will you do that for me? Will you let me help you?"

Louis stayed quiet a while, and Darian could not be sure he'd even heard him. After a moment, in a calmer voice, he said, "I met her in high school, you know. Becky, I mean. I met her senior year. She was still a junior. Hottest chick I ever saw. She used to wear these tops with one shoulder always showing, the way girls did then. Big rock-and-roll hair all teased up high, jeans with holes and tears in them—remember that look? Becky looked like that. Like a metal chick but...but she was innocent, too. She had this innocence, like all that stuff was just for show. There was something so pure about her back then. And she liked me. Right from the start, she liked me." He looked over at Darian, his eyes red, swollen and glassy. "And I loved her."

"I know, man."

"I still love her."

"She's the mother of your children, Louis, of course you love her." He tried a smile, but he couldn't hold it long. "You have to think about them right now. I want you to think about Lou Junior and Danielle, all right? They need you, Louis. You're their father and they need you. Don't rob them of their father, don't do that to them."

"I'm already gone, Mother." As the curtains blew out far enough to reveal his face, Louis returned Darian's smile with one of his own, one equally counterfeit and fleeting. "And so are you."

"We're all going through this," Darian said. "We're all—"

"It's that fucking freak's fault." His face darkened and his eyes grew wild. "Seth's brother. Raymond, that fucking freak, he did this to us. He made this happen."

Darian felt lightheaded but kept his focus on Louis. "Listen to me, Lou. Can you do that for a second? Can you just listen to me, please? You've cut yourself pretty badly in a couple spots, OK? I need you to come down out of that window and come with me so we can have somebody look at you. We can talk and have somebody tend to those wounds, OK?"

Louis seemed even farther off, like a deranged street person sidetracked by voices only he could hear. "That night at the cabin we..."

"Yes, something happened to us that night." Darian felt himself nod. "Something happened to—"

"There was something out there." Louis shook his head as his eyes filled with tears. "Something we weren't supposed to see. That bitch brought it to us, exposed us to it...spread it. And Raymond—that fucking freak, he—knows more than he's telling, Mother. Don't forget that, your hear me? Don't forget that."

"What did Raymond do?"

"He knew."

"Knew what, Lou? What did he know?"

"They show you things," he said, gasping. "Horrible fucking things, they—have they shown you yet, Mother? Have they? They will, they will. They know Raymond can see them. They know. They know everything, you can't hide anything from them, they—they're watching us right now."

"But we—we didn't do anything, Louis. We didn't do anything."

"We were there. That's enough. Raymond could've helped us, he—he should've fucking helped us but he didn't. He let that bitch infect us and now it's too late, we can't stop it. Game over, man, we're done. We're *done*."

"Who are they, Lou? What...what are they?"

"You'll know soon."

Darian moved a bit closer, careful not to make any sudden movements. He knew if he could get perhaps two or three steps closer, he could grab hold of Louis before he could do anything else to hurt himself. "There are some things I haven't told you," Darian admitted. "I haven't told anyone. I didn't just forget about that night and pretend none of it ever happened. I tried, I—I've tried so hard to understand, to make sense of it all."

"You will. Deep down, you already know, you just haven't freed it yet."

Hoping the conversation would keep Louis focused on him, he continued. "I subscribed to a couple newspapers," Darian told him. "Newspapers that cover Gull's Peak and the surrounding areas. I poured through them from the moment we got back and they started to arrive. Every week, I'd check them front to back, looking for anything new, any mention of Christy or the man she talked about. I wanted to tell you guys, but it's crazy. It doesn't make any sense. A few weeks after we got home I found some articles. They found that man's body at a cabin not far from where we were."

"I know."

"He didn't die the way Christy said he did, Louis."

"I *know*."

"There are things with her that don't add up, too."

Louis looked away.

"What have they done to us, Lou?"

He blinked slowly, compliantly. "They're here."

Darian had an overwhelming urge to look behind him. "I don't—"

"Look around, Mother. Read the walls."

"We have to stick together." Darian took another step. "Don't do it, Lou. Please."

"I can't fight it anymore," Louis said, voice cracking again as the tears spilled from his eyes and ran the length of his cheeks. "I just want it to stop, I—I have to make it stop."

"Come away from the window."

"It has to stop."

"Please, man, please come away from the window."

Louis dropped the knife. It hit the floor with a dull thud, and served to distract Darian just long enough to prevent him from taking a third and final step closer.

"I'm sorry, Mother."

Darian looked up in time to see Louis offer one final sad smile just before he leaned back and toppled out the open window, the curtains swirling about like arms unable to quite catch him, fluttering in the breeze as he vanished beyond the ledge.

"Louis, no!"

Darian ran for the window but Louis was already gone, already plummeting to the street below, his t-shirt rippling in the open air just seconds before he crashed against pavement, his body twisting at impossible angles and bouncing to the curb before coming to rest near a parked car.

Somewhere further down the block, a woman began to scream.

* * *

On her way out of the room, Nana stopped long enough to give Raymond a peck on the cheek. He responded with a quick one-arm hug, and Nana escaped through the doorway, leaving them alone in awkward silence. After a moment Raymond asked, "How you feeling?"

"A little lightheaded," Seth answered, "but I'm all right."

The rain outside had grown worse, its beat against the windows louder and more intrusive than before.

"Nana told me about—"

"I know." Raymond stuffed his hands in his pockets like he'd done as a child whenever he was nervous.

"I'm sorry you had to go through that alone."

"I wasn't alone. I had you."

*God sees what we do. Good and bad, Seth. And He doesn't forget either.*

With remnants of his mother's voice still dripping in his mind Seth remembered the hallway leading to the locker room in high school. Senior year. Raymond's freshman year, and once again apart from the rest, standing out even more than the rest of the frosh population and targeted for various initiation nonsense, rituals passed from generation to generation, from one mindless and sadistic bully to another.

He remembered the hallway, how dark it was even in the middle of the afternoon, and how deep in the old school building the shadows were so thick one could hide undetected in a corner or along the stairwell leading to the nearby cafeteria.

"Keep your eyes open," Seth had told his little brother prior to the start of the school year, already cognizant of what many would have in mind for someone deemed as weak and strange as Raymond. "High school's a lot different, Ray. If you let them a lot of guys will bury you, understand? Try to fit in. Just try, OK? It'll be easier for you, trust me."

Raymond had promised to try, but within the first few days he was labeled an outcast. He spent lunch at a table alone, isolated and self-conscious, and walked the halls with his head bowed, books clutched tight against his chest. In classes, word was he was quiet and rarely interacted with anyone. He wore his hair longer than most kids even in those days, and it tended to fall in his eyes a lot, covering a good deal of his face. Seth had heard the rumblings, even seen some older kids pick on Raymond, and he'd done his best to step in whenever possible. But the pressure was mounting for both of them.

That day in the hallway near the locker room, he had hesitated in the shadows, listening to three seniors huddled near the locker room door, football players who took particular glee in terrorizing freshmen. Unnoticed, Seth slipped deeper into the corner and listened. Apparently Raymond was the last person in the locker room, running late and still showering after gym class. They'd been watching him, these three, and waiting for an opportunity to get him alone.

One of the boys pulled a tube of toothpaste from his jacket pocket and held it up like a prize. The others, both equipped with cans of shaving cream, began to laugh.

Seth knew these guys, could probably talk them out of it. He was hardly a popular student himself, but still, they knew him and if he asked them to grant his little brother a break from initiation they might agree.

But he never moved from the shadows. Even when they slipped into the locker room, Seth never moved.

"I always knew that," Raymond said, bringing him back. "I always had you."

"Yeah," he managed, pushing the memories away, "well I should've—"

"I'm going to tell you some things," Raymond interrupted. "Hard to believe things, things you won't want to believe. But you need to understand that I don't always know all the answers myself, OK? I can't always explain everything completely. Sometimes, but not always."

His thoughts focused on the here and now, his guilt

subsiding as memories of that day in high school dissipated in favor of dread more recent. "What happened at the cabin, Ray? What happened to us that night? What's happening to us right now? Were we just in the wrong place at the wrong time?"

"We were born in the wrong place at the wrong time." Raymond paced a bit, one hand running feverishly through his hair again and again, pulling it away from his eyes then letting it fall. "At least I was. You were right before. I knew something was going to happen, and I went with the idea of protecting you. I figured maybe if I knew what was coming I could somehow help to stop it but I *didn't* know, not really. I kept hoping the whole time at the cabin would be just what you guys wanted it to be, some drinking and card playing. Spent my whole fucking life hoping...but then Christy showed up and I knew it was all true. I wanted to stop it but I failed, man. I failed all of you."

Seth left the window and returned to the bed, where he sat on the edge of the mattress and attempted a casual pose. "I'm trying to grasp what you're saying here, honestly I—"

"You're not supposed to be able to see them." Raymond made eye contact that lasted more than a second or two for the first time since he'd entered the room. "I shouldn't be able to see them either, but I can. And so could she."

"Who, Raymond? See *who*?"

"I'm not sure what they are. Not yet."

Seth sat quietly, determined to make sense of what his brother was so obviously struggling to explain to him. "All right," he said hesitantly. "Go on."

"There was a storm that night."

"The snowstorm, yes."

"That wasn't the only storm." He shook his head with frustration. "There was another one, a different kind you can't see but some people can feel and are affected by. I don't understand that much about it myself but it has to do with magnetic energy and solar winds. I've been reading up on it and trying to figure some things out. All I know is, these storms help make them more powerful."

Glimpses of the otherworldly storm flashed in his memories. "These…things?"

Raymond nodded.

"And they're—what—not *human*? Come on, what—"

"No, they're not."

"Raymond, I don't—"

"They exist, but not in the same way we do."

Seth stared at him dumbly.

"Between." Raymond pulled his hands from his pockets. "Imagine a wall right here in the center of the room, only you can't see it. But it's definitely there. Things exist on both sides, but not together. If you're human and you want to see or move to the other side of the wall there's only two ways that can happen. The first is if you're some goddamn accident like me or—"

"Don't say that."

He moved closer to Seth in a manner nearly threatening. "The *first* is if you're some goddamn accident like me."

"All right," Seth said softly. "And the second?"

"If you're one of them."

"But…"

"They move in the psychological world, not the

physical one. I think that's why they need us."

Seth held his hands to either side of his face. "What have they done to us, Raymond?"

"They're disguised as insanity."

"You think we're insane then?"

"Do *you* think you're insane, Seth?"

"No, I do not."

"Then you need to be prepared to believe the things I'm telling you."

"I'm doing my best, Ray. This isn't making much sense so far."

Raymond seemed to deflate a bit, as if the topic itself sapped him of energy. "I know."

"Who are *they*, Raymond?"

"I'm not sure. They don't always look the same. Sometimes they look human and sometimes they look like—like things you don't ever want to see."

Seth sighed. "What do they want?"

"In." Raymond pointed to his temple. "Here. Then they sleep until we let them out."

*Let Them Out.*

"I don't, I can't—"

"That's how they move and spread: through our minds."

Seth tried to catch his breath but the words refused to come for several seconds. "All right," he finally said, "so we're being pursued then? By what?"'

"I don't know."

"But—"

*"I don't know."*

Seth released an involuntary eruption of nervous laughter. "This is—it's like—I mean it's like something out of a horror movie, for God's sake. It's not..."

"Reality?"

"Yes, goddamn it. It's not reality."

"You're right, it's not." Raymond returned his hands to his pockets; let his shoulders slump a bit. "Not *this* reality anyway."

Seth felt his hands go cold. "This madness, this can't be happening."

"It won't stop," he said sadly. "Christ, it's only just starting."

Seth rose to his feet, legs shaking beneath him. "What do we do?" Before Raymond could answer Seth's cell phone began to ring. He glanced down at the small phone clipped to his belt then pulled it free. Darian's cell number crawled across the caller ID screen.

"Answer it," Raymond told him.

"It's Darian. I can call him later."

"Answer it."

Seth swallowed, hard. "Tell me why."

Raymond glared at him. "Because something terrible has happened."

With an air of optimistic defiance, Seth answered the phone and brought it to his ear. "Hello?" His expression changed from one of fear and frustration to one that more closely conveyed outright horror. "Jesus. Is he alive?"

"There's blood all over the walls," Raymond said, turning away from his brother's pale face. "Ask him what it says."

"Darian, is he alive?" Seth listened, nodded. "OK, I'll—where did they take him?"

"Ask him what the blood says," Raymond said again.

"All right, we'll meet you there. I'm more than an hour away but we'll be there as soon as possible." He nodded into the phone. "Yes, we—we're leaving now."

"Ask him what the fuck it says!"

Seth held the phone close to his ear, eyes fixed on his brother throughout. "Darian, was there blood on the walls?...Just tell me, was there?...What did it say?...I'll explain later." Seth reiterated their plans to meet him at the hospital. He disconnected the call but his hands were shaking too violently to clip the phone back to his belt. "Louis…he…he threw himself out a window."

Raymond nodded impassively. "Did he tell you what the blood on the walls said?"

"Yes."

Before Seth could reveal the answer, Raymond did it for him. "Let Them Out."

"Louis might die," Seth mumbled. "Will he? Will he die, Raymond?"

"I don't know."

"Tell me."

"I just did. I don't know."

"So this power of yours comes and goes, is that it? What the fuck good is it?"

Raymond approached him again, this time coming so close Seth could feel his breath on his face. "You want a sideshow mystic, find a fucking carnival."

"How do you…" emotion took hold of him and he stopped a moment. "How do you *live* like this?"

"Take a good look at me, man. What do *you* think?"

"Here's what I think, Ray." Using one hand to steady the other, Seth clipped his phone back to his belt. "I think that for my own sanity I'm going to follow some basic logic here, and basic logic dictates if you knew all these things then you must know how this all ends."

Raymond turned away and stood by the window, watching the rain as it hit, spattered and ran the length of the window, blurring the world beyond. "Maybe you're the one who knows, only you just don't realize it yet."

"Not me, *you*. You know, don't you," Seth pushed, though it wasn't a question and both knew it.

Raymond said nothing, but when he finally turned and looked back over his shoulder at his brother, eyes brimming with pain and sorrow, Seth had his answer.

# Part Three: In the Night Season

"Terrors are turned upon me: they pursue my soul as the wind: my welfare passeth away as a cloud. And now my soul is poured out upon me; the days of affliction have taken hold upon me, my bones are pierced in me in the night season: and my sinews take no rest."

—JOB 30:15-17

# Chapter 15

From his position on the bed he could see her in the small adjoining bathroom.

Sleep had not yet fully released him but the soft rays of light peeking through gaps in the window shades signaled morning had arrived.

The rain had finally stopped.

Peggy stood near the doorway, one bare foot on the closed lid of the toilet, a white half t-shirt stretched snugly across the curve of her small breasts. Unaware that Seth had awakened, she took a can of shaving gel from the medicine cabinet and squirted a generous amount into her hand. Working it to lather, she bent over and ran it across her shin, coating her leg with a thin layer of soapy foam. Carefully, she removed the plastic guard from a disposable razor and began to shave.

Seth rolled onto his side, propped himself up on an elbow and let the side of his face rest in his palm. It was little things like this, the intimate moments he missed, and the fact that she hadn't yet realized he was awake and watching her only heightened the experience. There was something uniquely exhilarating about taking in a scenario while remaining undetected, even when the scenario was, under normal circumstances, somewhat mundane. What was it about that, he wondered, that stirred his senses so?

Seeing without being seen, perhaps there was comfort there, safety—the ability to witness and live in a moment without consequence or direct involvement—like sitting in a darkened theater watching a film. There was something comfortably isolated about it, being alone without really being alone, voyeurs all, watching alternate realities captured on celluloid and playing out before them in the safety of darkness, only to lose it the moment the houselights came up and the story was over.

But what of those *being* watched? Now that he experienced a sense of this nearly constantly, it held no fascination for him whatsoever. It supplied only fear—unease—his privacy and most intimate thoughts no longer his alone, but shared, displayed whether he wanted them to be or not.

They were peering into his mind and he could do nothing to stop them.

He let the thoughts go, spiral away to nothingness.

Peggy's hair was pulled back into a ponytail and fastened with an elastic band, allowing a clear view of her face. Seth studied it for a time before dropping his eyes across her stomach, lingering on her navel before continuing to her waist and hips. A thick patch of neatly trimmed brown hair filled the gap between her legs, lips still slightly swollen from their earlier lovemaking visible beneath it. Traces of a milk-white bikini tan line, still evident from the summer prior, offered a contrast to the gold, silken skin along her thighs, calves and finally, the foot of the leg she was shaving. A modest arch, delicate toes and a small rough patch of skin around the back of her narrow heel were the sorts of details Seth noticed, and the things he often visualized when he thought of Peggy. She came to him as much of the world did, in pieces, and though over time those pieces gradually melded to reveal a bigger picture, more discernible, she—like so much of life—remained slightly obscured. As well as he knew Peggy—or thought he did—could any person ever *wholly* know another, or like an incomplete puzzle, the theme of which is ultimately realized but never quite fully understood, did there forever remain pieces missing, questions unanswered? Seth had always suspected the latter, and in the past year had come to have no doubt.

But he also believed the mysteries and secrets all human beings held did not always necessarily carry with them nefarious or even negative implications. Along with Raymond, if there was one person on Earth Seth felt he could trust, it was Peggy. In many ways, he trusted her even more.

Peggy's mysteries were whispers. Raymond's were screams.

She finished shaving both legs. A smile creased his face as she turned for a towel on the edge of the sink. Two perfectly round buttocks returned his gaze, a small red and yellow butterfly tattoo along the slight curve of her lower back. Though well into her thirties, Peggy still possessed a body most women ten years her junior would've killed for, yet her physical splendor was still organic—effortless—and she often seemed barely cognizant of it.

Seth visualized the night before, only a few short hours ago, Peggy facing him, riding him slowly, her palms pressed flat against his chest, breasts rising and falling with each breath, her body slumping forward in time and that same breath warm in his ear and along his neck as her lips brushed his, the tips of their tongues gently tangling, slipping in and out of their mouths.

Though separated for months, once intimate it felt like they'd never been apart, and now, while gently caressed by the emerging sun of a new day, he was content to watch her quietly and replay the images in his mind of the night prior, his coming here to her new place, and the subsequent lovemaking that followed.

Peggy had eventually left their apartment in the Back Bay as well, in favor of a small place in Plymouth, the historically famous town just under an hour from Boston where sites like Plymouth Rock still lured tourists each summer by the thousands.

The cottage itself was small, cramped and located at the end of a lonely dirt road that overlooked the nearby Atlantic Ocean. Countless odd works of her art—mostly sculptures and a few paintings—were scattered about in typical Peggy fashion, some completed and others still in progress. Most of her pieces had a dark and ancient look that Seth found curiously familiar and disturbing all at once. Her work had always fascinated and somewhat repelled him, and that had not changed. Beyond the pieces of work lying about, she had furnished the cottage modestly, and it bothered him that her new home had a very personal, individual feel that related solely to her. The woman who lived here might have still been legally married, but her living quarters strongly suggested she had already moved forward, had already reached that new life that no longer included him. No trace of him existed here, no artifact concerning their lives before. Peggy, much like himself, had become a loner, which perhaps explained their need to make love again so quickly. An unspoken recognition of one's own solitary existence mirrored in the lonely eyes of another was unmistakable. Besides, why else would they have risked sleeping together so soon, even before anything in terms of reconciling had been discussed, much less agreed upon?

With all that had happened, Seth knew that softening the agony, even for a short time, was worth the risk of opening himself up to more eventual pain, and could only presume she felt the same. But for now, the anguish and fear had subsided somewhat. Life reverted to the way it had been before the darkness had stolen it from him, and though he understood it was temporary, at that moment he and Peggy were just a couple again, two people in love and sharing space in the waking hours of morning, together; their bond understood and resolute.

Peggy grabbed a towel from the sink, wrapped it around herself and cinched it beneath her waist. Noticing he was awake, she smiled and softly said, "Good morning."

"Morning."

"I was trying to be quiet. Did I wake you?"

"No, it's OK."

She strode into the bedroom. "There's coffee on if

you want some."

"Thanks," he said, forcing himself into a sitting position and planting his feet on the floor. For a moment, in the silence of morning, he'd felt a part of this, a part of her, but was already regressing, again feeling like a visitor. "Been getting quite a bit of work done, I see."

Peggy glanced around the room, revealing subtle signs of self-consciousness. Discussion of her artwork often elicited in her an odd reticence Seth had never quite understood. "I've been sculpting a lot lately," she said a moment later. "I don't know, maybe I need the physical interaction, the actual feel of the piece in my hands. Painting can be a bit more removed at times. It's a different experience. Not better or worse necessarily, just different." She seemed to catch herself, as if suddenly realizing this was not new information to him. She'd explained and discussed her creative processes in detail many times over the years, but this time had done so as if they'd only just met.

Seth's head began to clear somewhat, shining light on memories of the day and night before. He tried to think of something to say that might continue the conversation in a more original and meaningful way, but failed. Old patterns were difficult to break, and maybe for now that was best, because there was comfort in them as well.

"Were you able to sleep all right?" Peggy asked, rescuing him.

"Yeah, I think so, for the most part."

"You were snoring a couple times." She smiled the way she had when they'd first met, when many things still embarrassed her.

"Sorry." He remembered drifting off to sleep with their arms around each other, and how for the first time in a very long while he hadn't been forced to rely on memories of how she felt snuggled against him in the night.

"It's OK. It didn't really bother me."

He knew that was untrue, and recalled nights when she would none-too-gently elbow him awake and growl that his snoring was keeping her up. But he appreciated her effort. "I was just so exhausted. I barely remember falling asleep, actually."

*I felt safe here*—he'd wanted to say—*rescued.*

"Did you dream?" That had always been one of her favorite questions. Peggy was a great lover of dreams, but then, she could still afford to be.

"Probably," he muttered. "But if I did I don't remember."

Peggy slowly ran her palm across her cheek, along her chin and down to her throat, finally resting it against her collarbone. "I dreamed of these strange patterns and textures…colors. But they swirled and moved like liquid."

She even dreams like an artist, he thought.

Peggy sat on the corner of the bed. Had she extended her arm completely she could've touched him with her fingertips, but from her position enough space remained between them to give the illusion of breathing room.

"Do you want to talk about it?" she asked a moment later.

He didn't, but knew he'd have to in some context.

* * *

The night before at the hospital, he had sat for hours with Raymond and Darian in the emergency room waiting area. The ride from Cape Cod to that Boston hospital had been mostly quiet but as oddly surreal as the hours leading up to it. Seth did his best to concentrate on the road and the rain while dozens of things fired through his mind at once, all of them patently absurd. He remembered a time he would've prayed for Louis, for God to protect him and to not let his injuries in the fall be life threatening. But he hadn't said a single prayer since the night his mother died. He no longer saw the point of it. Whatever happened was going to happen regardless of anything he might say or think or hope for. That's what he believed now. And that was all he believed.

*Thought you didn't believe in God,* Louis had said to him that morning at the cabin, the morning after Raymond had disappeared.

*I believe in God, Louis,* he'd said quietly. *I just don't have anything to say to Him.*

As he drove, remembering their exchange that morning in the chilly cabin, Raymond broke his concentration. "The more you push something into the shadows the darker it gets," he said. "I didn't make the rules, man. It's just the way it is."

Later, at the hospital, they'd found Darian slumped in a chair, a long-since cold cup of coffee clutched in his hands. Seth remembered how odd it was to find him dressed in a suit and tie on a weekend—had he been at work?—and how his suit and coat were uncharacteristically rumpled and mussed. He'd never seen Darian so disheveled, worn and tired, so visibly damaged. His eyes were heavy and red, his face twisted into an expression of horrific disbelief, like it had frozen that way and he could no longer correct it.

Darian looked up at them with the fear and confusion of an abandoned child as they rushed into the waiting area. Mother always had the answers, always held it together and helped everyone else do the same—that was his way, his trademark—but not on this rainy afternoon. His mouth opened to greet them, perhaps to offer more information, but words never surfaced, only an eventual sigh and a helpless shrug of his shoulders.

"What's happening?" Seth asked, crouching before the chair. "Is Louis—"

"No one's told me anything since they brought him in. I've asked two or three times now but no one seems to know anything. He was alive when he got here but he was badly hurt, Seth, *badly* hurt."

"Did you talk to the cops?"

He nodded. "Briefly. I told them what happened, gave them a statement. When they saw the state of his apartment they didn't seem to care anymore. Just some poor crazy bastard who lost it and pitched himself out a window, right?"

Raymond stayed back a bit, hands stuffed into his jacket pockets, eyes scanning the waiting room and reception desk on the far wall as if he were expecting the sudden arrival of someone or something at any moment. But the ER was unusually quiet for a city hospital, and only a few people were scattered about the large waiting room. An inordinately tall security guard with a shaved head and a utility belt that included a holstered 9mm stood at the entrance, arms folded across his chest and a bored expression on his face. They'd rushed right by him and never seen him.

Seth let a hand rest on Darian's knee. He could feel the tension in him, the trembling. "Take it easy," he said softly.

"You take it easy." Darian sat back in the chair, away from Seth, his hands still clutching the coffee cup. "You didn't see what he'd done to himself, to his arms and—and you didn't see how he'd written on the walls with his blood—his own goddamn blood, Seth. You didn't see him go out that fucking window."

"Look, don't make a scene, all right?" Seth checked the security guard, who had now come awake a bit and was watching them without subtlety. "Keep your voice down."

Darian's eyes shifted, locked on Raymond. He put the coffee cup aside on the chair next to him and slowly rose to his feet. Seth stood as well, making sure he stayed between them.

"And you," Darian said. "He said you knew what was happening to us."

Raymond stood his ground but didn't respond.

"You need to start talking, motherfucker."

"We're all going to talk," Seth said. "But this isn't the time or the place—"

"Oh yes it is." Darian pointed at him. "I want some answers and I want them now."

A sudden rush of activity distracted the three men. The automatic doors slid open with a whooshing sound and a couple came in hurriedly, escorted by two uniformed policemen. Though he had not seen her in quite a while and despite the fact that she looked different than he remembered her, Seth recognized the woman immediately.

"Becky," he said, watching as she and the others disappeared down a hallway and behind a set of double doors. "How did she find out about this?"

"I figured where she's his *ex*-wife they probably wouldn't contact her or even know how, so I called her." Darian's voice and posture settled somewhat, but the power of his tension and emotion remained painfully obvious just below the surface. "I didn't know how to get a hold of his family. I know his sister Claire still lives in Revere but I couldn't remember her married name. Becky was the only one I knew how to reach."

"Did anyone take a look at you?" Seth asked. When Darian shot him a disgusted look he said, "I mean, are you OK?"

"Yeah, just great." Darian's expression changed; fury to sorrow in an instant.

Unsure of what to do with himself, Raymond moved away, closer to the exit and the security guard, who had again slipped into something of a pseudo-coma of boredom.

After a moment Darian snatched his coffee cup from the chair, walked to a nearby receptacle and dropped it in. "I need to get out of here," he muttered. "I need to get out of here but I can't—I can't go home. I don't want to go home."

"You can stay at my place if you need to," Seth offered.

Darian nodded and wandered away among the rows of plastic chairs.

The glass wall at the entrance to the ER was blurred and distorted from rain flowing along the large panes, and the world beyond it had grown dark—too dark for late afternoon. But black clouds continued to linger, and night was coming.

Much like their fear, nothing could stop it.

Raymond stood before the large panel of glass near the entrance, watching the parking lot and street beyond through sheets of rain. They were near. He could feel them.

Slowly and deliberately, he scanned the lot. Rain-blurred cars passed on the nearby street, head and tail-lights distorted like vigilant eyes slithering through darkness.

Nothing else moved out there.

He craned his neck to get a better glimpse of a cement flight of stairs leading down from the street. The parking lot streetlights were already on, and one positioned next to the stairs managed to shine enough through the rain to partially illuminate the steps.

It was then that he made out the umbrella.

It was black and hard to see through the premature darkness and heavy rain, but he was certain it was there. Raymond squinted, realized it was stationary; whoever was carrying it had stopped about halfway down the steps. The umbrella was tilted forward but was also quite low to the ground, signifying someone exceptionally diminutive was in possession of it. Like a child, he thought, or something similar to a child.

He glanced over at the security guard, but he had his back to the glass and appeared to be struggling to keep his eyes open. Raymond turned back, saw the umbrella had not moved and was still tilted forward in a manner that made it impossible to discern anything behind or beneath it.

Slowly, it began to spin, twirling in unseen hands.

Rain spattered against it, ran down onto the pavement into pools already formed there and small streams speeding to nearby gutters. "Come on," Raymond whispered in a tone one might use to call out a shy kitten. "Come on."

Little by little the twirling slowed until the umbrella had come to a stop. Gradually it rose to reveal someone standing beneath it.

A small being stood on the steps dressed in a dull yellow raincoat and matching hat.

Where its eyes and sockets and nose should have been the skin was smooth, flat and blank. Its mouth was impossibly small, but it opened wide then wider still until the sides tore and began to bleed. The twisted, unfinished face froze in a soundless scream of inhuman fury and horror, and as the rain increased, falling in heavy torrents across the cement steps, the being dropped the umbrella.

Raymond watched it tumble off in the wind and blow away across the lot into darkness. The small thing—was it female, a little girl, perhaps?—held its tiny arms out; palms turned to the night sky, and tilted its head back to catch the rain. Behind it, others moved about in shadow, scurrying like rodents, a horde of barely distinguishable beings darting from the light.

Raymond sensed movement behind him. Seth and Darian stood watching the parking lot with him, and from the look on their faces they'd seen it all too.

"Hey," a deep voice said, distracting the three men. They looked in unison at the security guard, who had left his post and was now peering out into the night with a puzzled look on his face. "You fellas OK?"

The beings were gone…if they'd ever really been there at all.

"What the *fuck* was that?" Darian asked, the words spilling from him as if beyond his control and in a tone that was in such direct conflict with his usually casual demeanor, it seemed to surprise even him. He looked suddenly uncomfortable in his own body, his movements economic but anxious. "Who was that, what—"

The guard strode closer. "Something going on out there?"

Darian spun toward him like the guard had snuck up on him. "Stay away from me. Just—just stay away from me."

The guard gave them a quizzical look, the kind security personnel or police often use that wordlessly conveys the question: Am I going to have trouble with you?

"Sorry," Seth said, quickly slinking an arm around Darian and steering him away from the window and back toward the rows of chairs. "We're under a lot of stress. Our friend was badly injured earlier."

After a quick glance at Raymond, who was still at the window watching the rain, the guard acknowledged Seth with a slow nod. "Sorry to hear that."

Seth motioned for Raymond once the guard had returned to his post. Reluctantly, he joined them by the cluster of chairs. "They're getting stronger," Raymond said quietly.

He stared at him, unsure of how to respond to such a statement while still trying to make sense of what he'd just seen. "I want you and Darian to go back to my place," Seth said. "I'll stay and see if I can find out more then meet you back at the apartment later."

"Maybe we better stay together," Darian said.

"Just do what I tell you on this one, Mother. Please."

"I'm not leaving you here alone," Raymond said.

"I'll be fine."

"You're not hearing me, man."

"Go back to my apartment and I'll be there later." Raymond said nothing and made no move to comply. Seth stepped closer and leaned in so only Raymond could hear him. "Darian's ready to come apart and I don't want it happening here, you understand?" He dug his keys from his jacket and pushed them into Raymond's hand. "Get him back to the apartment and explain this to him as best you can. I'll see you back there later."

"Darian drove himself here, remember?" Raymond handed the keys back. "Hang onto your own wheels, man, you'll need them. We'll take his car."

"You be careful, you hear me, Raymond?"

Darian watched the night through the sliding doors, the rain and darkness that had swallowed the visions only moments before still lingering, waiting for them. "Is there another exit?" he asked the guard.

He raised an eyebrow. "There something wrong with this one?"

"We're parked around the other side," Raymond said quickly.

He let a few seconds burn before answering. "Straight down that hall there," he said, pointing. "Take a right at the elevators and there's an exit down the end, put you right into the north-side parking lot."

"Thanks."

The guard let slip a peculiar, rather negligible smile.

"No problem."

"Watch yourself." Raymond turned to Seth sharply. "It's not safe here."

Seth nodded, watched them leave the waiting area and pass cautiously into the hallway. As they rounded the corner and disappeared from sight, Seth glanced back at the guard. He was still staring at him, the same strange grin in place.

* * *

"If you'd rather not, it's OK," Peggy said, ushering him back. "Talk about it, I mean."

"I'm sorry I showed up so late last night, out of the blue and all." Seth looked at the alarm clock on the nightstand. Red digital numbers read: 7:45. He couldn't remember the last time he'd slept beyond seven o'clock in the morning. "I should've called first."

"You're forgiven," she said, smiling casually, "obviously."

"I didn't mean to complicate matters."

"Little late for that, don't you think?"

The wind howled, thrashing branches just outside the bedroom windows. Seth followed the sound, half-expecting to see a face peering in at them, but instead found only shadow and gradually increasing daylight. It rarely seemed to recede now, the uncanny feeling of being watched and on display, gawked at from the far side of some unseen veil.

"I've been under a lot of pressure lately," he said, telling her things he knew she realized all too well. But what was the alternative? To tell her he was losing his mind, or worse, that something had stolen it from him?

"And yesterday, with Louis, I just—I really needed to see you, Peg."

She breached the space separating them long enough to touch his hand with her own. It was a gesture so swiftly and efficiently executed—familiar and reassuring fingers there one moment then gone the next—that by the time he realized what she'd done it was already a memory. But that single move also served to summon up their history together, the longtime familiarity togetherness breeds—which often continues to survive even in the stasis of separation—and the anticipatory instinct one develops for the thoughts and actions of the other, all of which nearly become second nature. And so, an entire conversation passed between them in that now empty space, as if they'd never been apart, none of it spoken until she asked, "Is Louis going to be all right?"

"I hope so," Seth said wearily. "But it didn't look too good last night."

"Awful. Darian must've been really freaked out after seeing something like that."

When he didn't offer an immediate response, the atmosphere in the room again became edgy and still.

"He obviously had issues," she said. "To do something so extreme, he—"

"Peggy, look," he interrupted, the memories of the night before already wrestling his reason away, tearing down his defenses and ravaging the short-lived comfort he'd embraced just seconds before. "I can't—I'm sorry, but I can't stay long."

Her mouth curled into a bit of a smirk. "I don't recall asking you to."

"I just don't want you to think I was—"

"We're adults," she said. "Well, allegedly. Let's behave that way, OK?"

"I'm doing my best, Peg." He looked down at the rumpled sheets between them.

"You didn't promise or imply anything last night." She slowly rose from the bed and moved to a free-standing mirror in the corner, the faint scent of vanilla and baby powder in her wake. "And neither did I."

Seth nodded, though he knew she was no longer looking at him.

Again, the room drifted into silence, but in his mind the maelstrom raged on, growing stronger despite his best efforts to fend it off. He was remembering. Little by little, through the disjointed storm of paranoia and terror, he was remembering more and more about that night at the cabin. Yet it all continued to remain blurry enough to just barely elude him, closer than it had ever been before but still not clear enough to make out, to make sense of.

A familiar thumping sound interrupted the silence.

Petey stood in the doorway, his tail wagging against the floor. The night before, upon seeing Seth, he had celebrated by barking endlessly, nearly tackling him and showering him with a tongue bath. He'd then taken to running around the place in a frenzied expression of glee and celebration until he'd grown exhausted and collapsed on a rug in the kitchen. Petey often seemed to have no clue how big or how old he was, he only seemed certain of one thing: how much he loved Seth and Peggy. Now he watched Seth as he had so many times in the past, his soulful eyes searching, waiting for the signal that it was all right to join Seth on the bed.

Seth couldn't remember the last time he'd felt happy. "Hey, big man," he said. "What are you doing?"

Petey lowered his head a bit, and though he readjusted the position of his front paws he remained in the same spot, waiting.

"Somebody misses his daddy big-time," Peggy said. She reached for a pair of jeans on the nearby bureau but remained in front of the mirror.

Seth grinned at him. "Well…come on."

The lab bounded across the room and launched into the air. He landed on a spot of bed partially occupied by Seth, and as Seth caught him in a big hug, the two fell back on the sheets to the sound of Seth's laughter. Petey lapped at his face until Seth managed to maneuver him off. "I miss you too, buddy, I miss you too!" Seth took the dog's head in both hands and planted a kiss on the bridge of his long nose. "*Who* is my good boy? Petey-man!"

Peggy laughed lightly as she squirmed into a pair of old but tight jeans. "You're like a little boy when you're with him."

"Yeah," he said softly, running his hands over the dog's shoulders. He glanced over in time to see Peggy just pulling the jeans up over her bare ass. "Isn't it great?"

"I have to admit it is."

"Petey's the man. After all, he brought us together."

"This is true."

"I love him."

She faced him now, as she buttoned the jeans closed. "And he loves you."

"What about you?"

"What about me?"

"Do you still love me too?"

Her pale blue eyes gazed back at him. "You're the one who left."

"That wasn't the question."

"Are you fishing for compliments or are we having a real conversation?"

Petey flopped down across Seth's lap, his chin flat against Seth's thigh. "I just wanted you to know how I feel."

"OK." She peeled off the half shirt, tossed it into a hamper in the corner then retrieved a sweater from the bureau. She slipped it on then pulled the sleeves up a bit on each arm. It looked huge on her. "How *do* you feel, Seth?"

He pet the dog a while. "Maybe once I have some things worked out I could come home and we could—"

"Which home?" She folded her arms across her chest. "The home we had, *our* home? Neither of us live there anymore remember? There's only your home and my home now. That's the way you wanted it."

He nodded blankly.

"Love means nothing," she said, "unless we're together in a meaningful way."

He saw his opening, and took it. "Peg, if something were to happen to me and—"

"What's going to happen to you?"

"I said *if* something were to happen to me. I want you to let it go, OK?"

"What are you talking about?"

"Something bad," he said. "If something bad

happens to me and—and maybe it doesn't seem quite right, I want you to just leave it alone and get on with your life."

"I'm already doing my best to get on with my life, Seth."

Petey let out a soft moan as Seth continued petting him gently. "Just promise me."

She came closer, though somewhat hesitantly. "What are you into?"

Seth forced himself to look into her eyes. But when he did he saw another set of eyes. He saw eyes from the night before at the hospital, eyes that belonged not to his wife, but someone else.

"I talked to Becky last night," he told her. "It was…strange."

"Well, Jesus, with the kids and a new fiancé and all, she's in a horribly awkward position." Peggy's posture relaxed somewhat and her expression softened. "But they were married for years, you can't just discount that, and Louis is still the father of her children. Some deep waters running there."

"Yeah," he said, but his thoughts had already returned to the hospital the night before, replaying the moment Becky and her boyfriend emerged from the hallway, moved through the waiting area and headed straight for the exit.

* * *

Arm-in-arm, they walked briskly and with purpose. Becky, who was wiping at her nose with a tissue that had seen better days, and the man, a tall, square-jawed type who looked like he'd just come from modeling sweaters for a catalogue shoot, remained oblivious to Seth's presence until he stood up from the chair he'd been waiting in and crossed in front of them.

The couple slowed but didn't stop. The man offered an annoyed side-glance and said something to Becky only they could hear. She noticed Seth for the first time and a look of instant recognition crossed her face.

Still several feet away, Seth gave an awkward wave and stood his ground.

Becky whispered something back to her boyfriend then patted him on the arm as if to reassure him. After a few seconds of staring, he flashed a blinding smile and nodded to Seth quickly, granting consent, then strolled across the waiting area and out the exit without another word.

Seth slowly closed the gap between them. She'd lightened her hair since the last time he'd seen her, and her makeup wasn't as heavy as she'd once worn it. Still, even under the circumstances, though she looked tired and emotionally drained, all things considered, she looked pretty good. Louis had essentially fallen apart since their divorce, but the opposite seemed true with her. Becky was fit, healthy and seemed together. Her clothes sported the kind of designer labels she hadn't been able to afford while married to Louis, and her fingers, nails professionally manicured and painted a dazzling red, were adorned with several pieces of obviously new jewelry, including a large diamond engagement ring.

"Hi," he finally said.

"Seth," she said; voice weak and drawn. "I'm sorry, I didn't see you."

Though he knew she was lying, he let it go. "It's OK."

They stood looking at each other a moment. In years past, when she and Louis had been married they might've hugged. Instead, Seth offered his hand. She shook it with deliberate indifference. Her skin looked vibrant and well cared for but was cold and clammy to the touch. "Is there any word?"

Becky ran the tissue under each eye, patting away remnants of tears. "The doctor said the next twenty-four hours are crucial. He's got really serious head and neck injuries. He's in a coma."

"Christ." He released her hand and let his own flop to his side lifelessly.

"If he can hang on and make it through the night—and from everything they've told me that's a big if—they said he has a chance." She crumpled the tissue in her hand and shook her head sadly. "Assuming he even gets that far, the question's more about the quality of life at this point. Even the best case scenario didn't sound very promising."

"I'm sorry, Beck." He ran a hand through his hair. "Are you all right?"

She folded her arms and her body swayed a bit, as if with an unseen wind. "I'll be OK. I just have to figure out how to tell the kids. They have to know what's happened but I..." Her head turned suddenly, the sorrow in her eyes replaced with anger. "Why would he *do* this, Seth? Why would he do this to his kids?"

"I don't know. He was having a lot of problems."

"Tell me about it," she snapped. "It's been getting worse for a long time now, and over the last few weeks it's been ridiculous. He was calling four, five times a night, and at all hours. He'd insist I go check on the kids and he kept telling me how sorry he was. He'd cry like a baby, like he'd completely lost his mind."

"Did he say anything specifically about what was wrong?"

"It was mostly rambling stuff. But it was frightening. It was like he was deranged or something. Most of the time he didn't even make sense, and I was worried about him, but I never thought he'd do something like this. How could he be so goddamn selfish?" She drifted closer to the exit, glanced first at the security guard and then out at the rainy night. "Louis was never good at seeing things from anyone else's position. He never sees beyond how things directly affect him."

A strange pulsating sensation tickled Seth's temple. He brushed his fingers across it quickly, the way one might swat away a crawling bug. But it felt like this bug was *beneath* the skin. After a few seconds the sensation became visual, as a small black spot appeared in the corner of his right eye, flickering across his vision. He turned a bit, tried to focus on it, but as he moved, it did too.

The security guard was watching him again from his position on the wall, and though Becky was still talking, for a brief interval all sound escaped him.

When it returned it did so gradually, like a slowly turned dial, and things previously unnoticed became more pronounced: the hum of a nearby cola vending machine, the incessant buzz of overhead fluorescent lights, the raindrops pitter-pattering against the windows, and the sound of Becky's voice.

"...sometimes we have to do what's best for everyone, not just ourselves," she said, her small leather purse clutched in both hands, the delicate chain shoulder strap dangling like a broken limb. "We have to have faith in the bigger picture and not question things so much. We should just go along, you know what I mean?"

Seth realized Becky's voice was out of sync with the movement of her mouth, and he suddenly felt dizzy. "I don't—yeah, I..."

She leaned closer and whispered, "Just let them out."

"What did—what did you say?"

Becky smiled. It was a cold, soulless smile that parted her lips in a manner that should have shown her teeth, but instead revealed toothless gums, bloodied and diseased. Her eyes rolled to black, shiny onyx orbs impossible and inhuman.

Shrieks of terror called to Seth from the past.

In his mind he stepped back in a harried attempt to get away from her, but in reality he stood frozen, the incapacitating horror within him spiking in time with the pulsating black spot. It grew quickly, spreading like spilled ink, the darkness filling his eyes to a point where only peripheral vision remained.

Becky cocked her head. "Seth, are you all right?"

He felt himself nod in agreement. The darkness slowly dissipated, drifting off in different directions, black fingers worming across his eyes until they were gone. In their wake they left the beginnings of a headache that throbbed across his temples and spread slowly to the back of his head.

"Do you need to sit down?" she asked, reaching

carefully for his arm. "You looked like you were going to faint there for a minute."

"I'm good, I'm—I'm OK." He rubbed his eyes, looked around cautiously. "I'm all right."

Becky seemed unconvinced. "Maybe you should sit down."

She, and everything else, seemed to have returned to normal. Or perhaps it was he who had returned to normal and everything else had always been that way. Of course, he thought, of course that's what it was. It was all in his head.

*Do you think you're crazy, Seth?*

"Sorry," he said softly. "I have a splitting headache."

She looked back at the reception desk on the far side of the room. "You want me to see if they have some aspirin or something handy?"

"Thanks, it's OK."

"You sure? I might even have something in my purse come to think of— "

"I'm all right. I..." He watched her, waiting to see if anything else would happen. His chest felt tight and his fingertips tingled, asleep. "Sometimes it just feels like everything's coming apart, like the whole world's falling in on me."

"Yeah, I hear ya." Becky nodded and let out a long sigh. "We were supposed to leave for Montana next week."

"I heard."

"Now, I don't know. I can't just leave him this way, but goddamn it, Seth, we're not married anymore. I have my own life now, you know? And the kids deserve better than this. We have a chance at a life there with my fiancé, a real life. Louis knew how important this was for us, and now he does something like this and what—what the hell am I supposed to do now? Tell me, what do I do now? What do I tell the kids?"

"I wish I knew, Becky." Seth rubbed the back of his neck. The pain was spreading. "I wish to Christ I knew."

She opened her purse, dug another tissue from it then snapped it shut. "You must think I'm some awful coldhearted bitch."

"Look, I never—"

"We were happy once, a long time ago."

"You don't have to get into this."

"But then it died. I didn't kill it, he didn't kill it. It just happened. It just…died."

"It's really none of my—"

"It's like pretending you're dead," she said flatly. "Going through life like that, the way I did before. The way I did when I was with Louis. Hoping every day will be the one when things change, when things get better. But it never gets better, it only gets worse. I was miserable and so were the kids. Now, we're reborn."

Seth found her choice of words unsettling. He could just barely remember a time before all this, when Louis and Becky were still together and happy. Hadn't they been happy once, as she claimed, genuinely happy? Hadn't he witnessed it himself on several occasions over the years? Or had it all been a lie, a big smokescreen?

Becky blew her nose then pitched the tissue into a nearby trash bin. "I should go."

"If you need anything let me know, OK?"

"I loved him once. There was a time when I did love him, Seth."

"I understand."

"But it wasn't meant to be." Her eyes turned brighter, the coldness in her posture and facial expressions slipping away. "*This* was meant to be, my life now."

"Then maybe you should get on it with it, Becky. Go to Montana as planned and start over with the kids. I don't know what else to tell you."

*Maybe he'll do you all a favor and die during the night.*

"Take care of yourself, Seth." A slight grin crossed her face as she casually gave Seth's shoulder a quick pat. "Go home and get some rest."

"You too."

Becky turned and moved toward the exit. Seth noticed again how she and the security guard exchanged glances that seemed oddly familiar, as if they knew each other. Or was it only his mounting paranoia?

As the doors slid open she stopped suddenly, as if she'd forgotten something important, and looked back at Seth. The sudden smile on her face showed off a beautiful set of pearly white teeth. "It's going to be all right," she told him, her voice smooth and unusually whispery. "Everything's going to be all right."

Once again, Seth let the trees beyond the window distract him.

He gave Petey a pat on the head then rose from bed and walked closer so he might have a better view of the backyard. The area possessed a rather indifferent sense of desolation, and reminded him of other memories, other barren landscapes in distant winter dreams, none of which particularly appealed to him at that moment. His eyes moved across a series of stripped trees, black branches dancing in the wind, then along a small patch of dead ground leading to a grassy slope which eventually spilled out into the ocean. Finally, he looked to the sky, dark and ghostly gray. Everything seemed so lifeless out there, so icy and dead.

"We're treading some rather deep water ourselves," Peggy said from behind him.

He'd momentarily forgotten she was there. Several birds gathered on a telephone wire which ran across the back of the house to the street were suddenly disturbed and flew away in unison, forming a synchronized pattern that turned in one direction then the next. The flock disappeared over the treetops. Seth visualized them gliding out over the ocean.

"Or maybe we're just sinking in them," she said.

A chill swept through him, and it was then that he remembered he was nude. "Is it OK if I use the shower?"

"Sure, just leave a quarter on the counter."

Seth responded with a brief, obligatory smile. "I'm sorry, Peg…for everything."

"Last night," she said quietly, arms wrapped around her sides, "you were so sad and helpless. You were so lost. And then later, for a little while it was just you and me and everything was all right again, everything was like it used to be. The storms in you went quiet and there was nothing scary in the dark because there was only the two of us. There was only warmth and love and trust and silence."

"Peace."

"Yes," she said. "Peace."

He stood there naked, numb and uncertain.

"Are you still seeing Connie Farrow?"

It took a moment for the name to register. "Doc?"

"Yes, Doctor Farrow, are you still seeing her?"

When Seth had first considered the idea of seeing a psychiatrist he and Peggy had already split, but when he'd hinted that seeing a doctor might be a good idea, she had found Doctor Farrow through a friend of a friend, a psychiatrist she had personally never met but who was highly recommended and trusted by those who had. Since she was included as one of the doctor's in Seth's health insurance through work, when he learned she was taking some new patients he'd decided to go with her. But he'd never discussed his sessions with Peggy or anyone for that matter. "Yeah, I still see her, but we're on a break. She's on vacation. The Cayman Islands, I think she said."

"How's it been going?"

"All right, I guess."

"From what I hear she's very good."

"Want me to make you an appointment?"

She dismissed his attempt at a joke without even acknowledging it. "My friend Sherry's cousin goes to her. She says Dr. Farrow helped her a lot. Her reputation is impeccable."

"She's OK."

"Just OK?"

"What do you want me to say? I like her all right."

Peggy seemed to weigh the accuracy of his statement. "Maybe she can help you find that peace more consistently."

"No one can do that but you."

"Don't you mean *us*?"

He shrugged. She went blurry.

Peggy saw the tears in his eyes and looked for a moment like she might reach out to him, but instead she cleared her throat awkwardly and said, "You'll find fresh towels in the closet. Be sure to let the shower run a while before you get in. Old pipes, old system, takes a while to heat up."

Seth watched her walk away down the narrow hall with her usual relaxed stride and easygoing pace. She moved like some slightly aging stoned hippy girl, fluid and tranquil, as if all was right with the world and nothing warranted serious concern. And yet beneath that surface he knew how intelligent, soulful and deep Peggy truly was. Was it all a trick to fool the outside world into believing nothing bothered her—the way a child whistles while walking past a graveyard—or was it merely an instinctual act of survival?

As she slipped away into the darkness at the end of the hallway, another face flashed before his eyes.

Christy—eyes wide with horror and her shirt drenched in blood.

And screams, always the goddamn screams tearing through his head.

A low growl turned his attention to the bed. Petey lay watching the window with an unusual intensity, an apprehensive snarl emanating from deep in his throat.

Seth followed his gaze to the window and found only the same tree branches wildly blowing about against a dull sky. But as he stood watching, listening to the dog's barely audible growl, he felt a disturbing sense of kinship to its primal timbre, as if whatever had joined them just beyond that thin pane of glass was more than a trick of the mind. It was something with weight, substance, and a diabolical familiarity that both his and Petey's species recognized intuitively.

Like danger, he thought. And the instinctual fear that accompanies it.

# Chapter 16

The shower in Peggy's bathroom consisted of a portable showerhead strung up over an old-fashioned freestanding porcelain bathtub. A plastic curtain hung in circular formation around it, reminding Seth of those that often separate beds or gurneys in hospitals. The water pressure was less than he was accustomed to but it was hot and felt relaxing against his sore, tense muscles. He soaped up and rinsed, then washed his hair with shampoo he'd found on the counter, a glowing cherry colored concoction that smelled like wild berries. He bowed his head, closed his eyes and let the water pulse against the back of his neck.

For a few moments, it was as if everything had returned to normal. The world was peaceful, safe, warm and calm. He listened to the sound of the water as it dripped from various points on his body to the tub below; heard it swirling down the drain, spattering the plastic curtain.

But even in quiet and relaxing times—perhaps especially so—it was Raymond's face Seth saw in the darkness of his mind. Always one version or another, it was his brother who came to him in those moments, bringing with him the same guilt that had haunted Seth for decades. This time it was memories of Raymond sitting in that locker room in high school, alone with only a small white towel wrapped about his thin waist. His hair, still wet from the shower, dangled in his face like seaweed, barely masking the embarrassment and quiet rage in his otherwise soulful eyes.

As Seth watched him from just inside the locker room doorway, he saw Raymond's clothes laid out on the bench in front of his locker, just as he'd left them. Only now his shirt and pants were covered and smeared with shaving cream and his shoes had been filled with toothpaste. His small nylon gym bag had been emptied onto the floor and his shorts, t-shirt, underwear and socks had received the same treatment. The bag itself was covered with a dark stain. Seth could smell the urine from across the room.

Raymond saw his brother there, looked at him but said nothing. It was a look Seth had never been able to erase from his mind. Raymond had looked so fragile just then, so impossibly young, his body thin and wiry.

The office door opened and Mr. McKenzie, the gym teacher, appeared in his usual polyester coaching shorts and a shirt with the school name and logo emblazoned on the chest. From his brush cut to his wannabe Marine-like demeanor, he was as annoying as he was ridiculous, but on this day he had put aside his usual gruff machismo in favor of a more sullen manner. He looked at Raymond and then at Seth, addressing the latter when he spoke. "Just got off the phone with your mother, Roman. She's running some fresh clothes over to the office, should be here any time now. Soon as they land I'll go down and get them for you. In the meantime you sit tight."

Neither boy acknowledged him.

"We find out who did this, rest assured they'll be punished." He turned and left them alone in the locker room.

Seth walked to the bench and sat down a few feet from Raymond.

"I could've stopped them, but I didn't. I'm so sorry, Ray."

Each time Seth remembered that day he spoke those exact words, but in reality none of them had ever left his mouth.

"You all right?" he finally managed to ask. When Raymond didn't answer, he asked a second time. Again, there was no response. "Do you know who did it?"

"No one's ever going to do anything like this to me again." His voice was cold and detached, a listless monotone. "Not ever."

*It should've been me, Ray. I wish to God it had been.*

Seth opened his eyes.

The drain was slow in emptying and the water had risen in the tub past his ankles. He reached up, turned the nozzle off and stood dripping a moment, the memories fading in favor of darkness more current.

After he'd dried off and dressed he returned to the bedroom, but it was empty, so he moved back through the small house to the kitchen. Beyond it was a modest area where Peggy had been working, a pantry-like room off which was a door that led to the backyard. An easel with a large canvas balanced on it stood in the center of the room but the painting was faced away from him. Shelves along the wall were filled with various art supplies and a few small sculptures.

The room reminded him of their place in Boston. How he missed the smell of her clays and paints and brushes. How he missed watching Peggy work, and those times when she'd finish a project and come to him so he could see and share in it with her.

He remembered how they'd always make love afterward, her clothes and body and hands still stained with the materials she'd used, and how when it was over they'd lay for hours together listening to each other's bodies and the sounds of the city around them. They were so alive then, so utterly, passionately alive. And he'd let it slip through his fingers. All of it gone, stolen by a night he still couldn't completely remember or understand.

This was his salvation. *She* was his salvation.

"I want it back," he whispered. "Goddamn you, I want it all back."

"What?"

Seth spun toward the sound of her voice to find Peggy in the kitchen with Petey at her side. "Nothing, I—I didn't know you were there."

"Sorry, I didn't mean to startle you." She raised an eyebrow. "Did you use my shampoo?"

"It's all there was."

"You smell devastatingly pretty."

"I do what I can."

She smiled, held up Petey's leash. "I'm going to take Petey out for his morning walk. Wanna come?"

The thumping of his tail against the floor let Seth know Petey's feeling on the subject.

"I wish I could," he said. "But I have to go."

Peggy fastened the leash to Petey's collar. "Let me know how Louis is doing, OK?"

"Of course." He watched her a moment, certain he had never seen anyone so lovely. "I'll call you."

As he moved through the room toward the backdoor, he glanced at the painting on the easel. At first all he saw was some subtle splashes of dark red and green on a charcoal-colored background. But something made him stop and consider the piece more intensely, and the longer he gazed at the painting the clearer other aspects became. She had shaded the piece, hidden other things deeper within the coats of paint. Two things in particular, upon closer inspection, became eyes. Black, otherworldly eyes just barely detectable through the dark gray and swirling patterns of red and green stared out at him as if from behind deep shadow. And attached to those eyes was the vague outline of a head and shoulders not quite human, a being purposely concealed and yet, still there, watching, waiting.

He'd seen it before—that thing—in his nightmares, in his memories, and looking into its eyes triggered a relentless fear that came to him in a single violent rush of uncontrollable terror.

"What the fuck is that?" He staggered back, away from the easel. "What the *fuck* is that?"

Peggy froze, the color drained from her face. "A painting I'm working on. Why, what's the matter?"

"What is it, where—where did you see that? How do you know about that?"

"About what? I don't understand."

"Goddamn it, how do you know?"

"I told you I—I dreamed of colors and patterns."

The terror remained, but it was slowly transforming into something closer to blind rage. He felt cold suddenly. His hands clenched into fists. "Answer me."

"I did answer you. Stop it, Seth, you're frightening me."

He grabbed the canvas and turned it toward her. The easel tipped and fell to the floor with a crash. "This fucking *thing,* how do you know about this?"

"I saw color and patterns in a dream against a night sky like that," she said, her voice shaking. "For God's sake, it was just a dream, just—"

"Bullshit! You're fucking lying to me!" Seth dropped the canvas like it was diseased then stepped back. "You dreamed about this? About those eyes and that—"

"What's happening? Please just calm down and tell me what's happening."

At that moment he wanted nothing more than to grab her by the throat with one hand and pummel her with the other. He wanted to hurt her, to beat her face to a pulpy mess, to hear the bones in her face crack and split against his fists.

But some small part of him struggled against it, fought the terror and the rage long enough for him to see that it was only Peggy standing before him, his wife, the only person he could truly trust. It also allowed him to see how truly frightened she was. She was as terrified as he was, but her fear wasn't of the unknown. She was afraid of him.

And it broke his heart.

He ran his hands through his hair, fighting away the anger. It collapsed into him, became raw emotion, tears and sorrow, releasing him. He looked at the painting, which now lay at his feet, but from that angle he could no longer make out the being. Maybe it had never been there in the first place. "Christ, I'm sorry, Peggy, I didn't mean to—I don't know what the hell's wrong with me. I'd never hurt you, I love you."

"It was only a dream," she said again, tears trickling down her cheeks. "You know my dreams inspire me, I—why are you so angry? What have I done?"

"Nothing, I'm sorry," he said again. "I'm so sorry."

"I don't know what to do," she said. Petey sat quietly next to her, head bowed. "I don't...I don't know what to do."

"I can't be here, it's not safe."

With a heartbroken expression of her own she said, "Sweetie, of course you're safe here. It's only me. It's only me and Petey and you."

"It's not safe for you to be around me, Peg." The headache returned, bringing with it spikes of pain that shot up from his jaw to the top of his head. "There's something wrong with me, something's happened to me, something's..."

*In* me.

"Then let me help you, Seth."

"I have to go."

He stumbled through the backdoor and into the yard. He could hear the ocean as he moved around the side of the house to the driveway and the safety of his car, his breath forming clouds around him in the cold air. But it was the vision of Peggy's terrified face that refused to leave him, and from somewhere behind her, the horrific eyes that now watched them both.

# Chapter 17

Edward Brock. Eddie, as his friends called him. He'd been the ringleader, the senior football star who had led the raid in the locker room where Raymond's clothes and gym bag had been defiled. Of average height, he had blond hair he wore in a crew-cut, striking blue eyes and the solid physique of a linebacker. Until that day Seth had considered him a fairly nice kid, the kind of guy who ran with the "in" crowd but who had never given him any problems. He had wondered many times in the years since that day what had made those three young men do what they did to Raymond. Had it been some twisted way of elevating themselves? But they were already the powerful in school, the social elite, why would they bother with him at all—maybe just because they could? Or was there something about Raymond that led them to believe in some twisted sense that he was deserving of such treatment? And regardless, what made them think they had the right to administer it? They didn't even know Raymond, knew nothing about him. How could otherwise everyday young people suddenly become so casually cruel, so thoughtless? How did that happen? Did they just not think about it in any relevant way? Did it occur to them that Raymond was a human being, or to them did he exist as something of less importance, a toy created solely for their personal amusement?

Heartlessness often came so easily, so effortlessly to so many, it seemed.

Seth left Plymouth, pulled onto Route 3 and headed for his apartment, the memories replaying in his mind.

Three days after the incident he'd found Raymond sitting on a stone wall near their home. He often sat there, alone, watching the cars go by. It was an area a few blocks from the main drag in town, but off the beaten path enough so he could hang out there undisturbed. Seth had gone looking for him, concerned over the way his brother had been behaving since that day in the locker room. Raymond hadn't been the same since, something had changed, something inside him. Quiet victim had transformed from prey to smoldering predator.

"Figured I'd find you here," Seth said. "You OK?"

"Fine," Raymond said evenly.

"You wanna go do something?"

Raymond slowly shook his head. "Can't, waiting on somebody."

"Who?"

"Eddie Brock."

Seth felt his heart drop. "Why, what's—"

"His girlfriend Nina lives over on Rutherford." He motioned to a side street a few blocks away. "He walks right by here on his way home."

"So what?"

"So he was one of them. I saw him in the locker room that morning from the showers. He didn't know I saw him, but I did. He did most of it."

"Did you tell—"

"I didn't tell anybody."

"Why?"

Raymond slid down off the wall, landed next to Seth. He was wearing a waist-length jacket and had both hands stuffed in the side pockets. "Because I'm handling it. You told me I needed to start fighting my own battles, right? Well, that's exactly what I'm gonna do."

Seth forced a swallow. His mouth had gone horribly dry. "Ray, listen to me, Eddie's a tough kid. He's not the kind of guy you want to get into a fight with, OK?"

An odd smile creased Raymond's lips. "It's not gonna be a fight."

"This isn't the way to deal with it, you're gonna get hurt. He's older than you, bigger than you and stronger than you, Ray."

"But he's not smarter."

"What's any of this going to prove?"

"I told you," Raymond said. "No one's ever going to do something like that to me again. I've been putting up with this shit for years. You're right; I have to handle it myself. Isn't that what you told me?"

"I didn't mean for you to go getting into fights with—"

"I told you, it's not going to be a fight." Raymond's expression turned cold, mean.

Seth had never seen his brother look that way

before. "Then what's it gonna be?"

"A beating."

The car radio interrupted the memories, dissolved Raymond's troubled face.

He'd forgotten the damn thing was on. Some political pundit just to the right of Genghis Khan was droning on about world affairs and how important it was for everyday citizens to relinquish certain civil rights of their own while also denying rights to other groups of "undesirable" citizens in order for the country to remain free and safe and to be governed with "moral values." "We *must* govern with moral clarity in this country," the man said in an officious tone. "Moral order *must* be maintained for the greater good of all peoples."

Seth glanced down at the digital tuner. Odd, he thought. It was set to an all-talk, ultra-right-wing station he never listened to and couldn't recall tuning in.

He switched to a station near Cape Cod that played classical music, but the phantoms still chased him, jockeying for position in the forefront of his mind: Raymond's face all those years ago, Peggy's face only moments ago, those black eyes in the painting, Christy covered in blood.

The highway rolled past. A bit of sunlight struggled through the gray sky with a dull glint, cascaded along the treetops lining either side of the road. As he drove on, he did his best to keep an eye on the roadside, the trees and the other cars around him. Everything seemed infuriatingly ordinary, yet the strong sense of being watched had returned. If they—whoever *they* were—were truly watching him, then where were they? Where exactly were they watching him from? He wondered. Could they be right next to him, leaned in and only inches from his face, staring at him with those hideous black eyes? That concept sent a shiver-induced tremor through his body.

Maybe they were more a distance away, he hoped, watching from some superior perspective. Were they above him, perhaps, looking down on him the way a child lords over a pile of toys? Was theirs a bird's eye view, a god's view?

Or did they watch him from below?

Seth tightened his grip on the wheel and increased speed. It felt like the universe was slowly closing in on him, becoming smaller and more confining with each passing moment. He drew a hand across his forehead; wiped away the perspiration that had formed there then opened the window and let in some cold, sobering air.

"Madness," he mumbled. "Fucking madness."

*Help me.*

Eddie Brock strolled back across his mind's eye, his letter jacket slung over his shoulder as he walked casually up the street. He acknowledged Seth with a slow raise of his chin then flashed Raymond a smirk.

"Hey, hold on a sec," Raymond said, moving toward him.

Seth tried to reach out and stop him, to grab his arm and hold him there, but he was already gone, already standing in front of Eddie and blocking his way.

"Yeah?" Eddie sized Raymond up.

"That was some funny shit you did."

Eddie smiled. "Oh yeah, what shit was that?"

"What you and your friends did to my stuff in the

locker room the other day."

"I don't know what the fuck you're talking about, dude." He placed a hand on Raymond's shoulder and gave him a quick shove. "Fuck off."

Seth remembered walking toward them, remembered he had planned to say something to distract Raymond. But it all happened so fast.

With one fluid motion, Raymond removed a hand from his jacket pocket and swung it at Eddie's head. It connected near his hairline and Eddie stumbled back a few steps, initially looking more stunned and surprised than hurt.

It was then that Seth saw a large brick in Raymond's hand.

Eddie Brock seemed to realize this about the same time, and he blinked a few times, dazed, as the beginnings of blood began to trickle down across his face. He touched his scalp where the brick had cut him, looked at his bloodied fingers then back at Raymond groggily. "What the fuck?"

Raymond dropped the brick as Eddie's knees gave out. He fell back onto the road, still conscious but clearly hurt.

"Jesus Christ, Ray!" Seth ran forward but Raymond had already straddled Eddie.

With one hand he grabbed his shirt and lifted him up off the ground a bit. With the other he made a fist and pummeled Eddie's face with four or five hard punches. With each strike the blood from the head wound sprayed up into the air, and after the second punch, blood from his broken nose erupted as well.

Seth grabbed his brother and pulled him off before he could hit Eddie again.

Raymond stumbled away a bit, regained his balance and looked down at the fallen boy. "How's that, motherfucker? Feel good?"

Seth knelt next to Eddie, held his head and told him it would be all right and not to move. A passing car screeched to a halt and the driver, an older man, got out.

He remembered screaming at the man to call an ambulance and the confused and frightened look on his face. He also remembered the blood: blood on Eddie, on him, on Raymond, on the pavement—everywhere.

Raymond's childhood ended that day. Seth watched it die right before his eyes as his brother returned to the stone wall, sat down and waited for the police with Eddie Brock's blood sprayed about his face and hands.

Eddie Brock spent that night in the hospital but was not seriously hurt as it turned out, his injuries having looked far worse than they actually were. But no one in town or at school ever forgot the incident, and it earned Raymond an almost mythical reputation as the "crazy kid."

Raymond was arrested for assault and sent off for psychological evaluation as well as a brief stint in a juvenile detention facility. Upon his return, and as time went on, Raymond did as much to perpetuate his newfound reputation as anyone. The person he had been before was gone forever, and the most disturbing aspect of his transformation was that Raymond seemed imminently more comfortable in this new role than he had in his previous one.

From that fateful day forward all that waited for Raymond were stints in juvenile prisons, endless physical confrontations, drugs problems, and when he was older, jail.

A few weeks after his graduation from high school, Eddie Brock was seriously injured when he fell from a ladder while working as a house painter. He lost his balance and plummeted from a high roof to a pavement driveway below, suffering severe neck and spine injuries that left him a paraplegic to this day.

But it was the violence perpetrated against Eddie Brock by his brother that day that changed them all forever. He'd seen fights before, seen violence in many circumstances growing up, but never like that. Never before had he seen someone hit someone else with such a clear intent to seriously injure, if not kill them. That degree of violence forced him to see it for what it was: something beyond controlled teenage bravado and posturing and instead something at home in a realm where all theatrics and glamour was stripped away. In the end it was the sound of that brick striking Eddie Brock's skull, the sound of Raymond's fist breaking bones and the sound of blood spurting all over them both that burned its way into Seth's consciousness. This violence was more determined, more defined. It was real, and it was abhorrent, and it made him feel like he needed to bathe, to cleanse himself of it somehow. And just as the humiliation Raymond had suffered at the hands of Eddie Brock had been worse and more personal than the typical hazing freshmen endured, Raymond's response to it revealed an entirely new terrain of human experience, a place that until that day Seth knew existed but never suspected he'd ever have to explore personally.

Their innocence died a particularly gory death, and

nothing could bring it back.

All these years later, Raymond was still paying for his sins.

*We both are,* Seth thought. *For your sins...and mine.*

Seth focused on the road as he pulled into his apartment building parking lot.

He found a space, parked and shut off the engine.

There'd been so much violence over the years, so much pain. But the violence was Raymond's world, not his. Seth was convinced of this. He was a peaceful man, one who believed violence and anger solved nothing. He hadn't had a physical confrontation with anyone since high school, hadn't even come close. And yet just moments earlier he'd felt a rage so sadistic and encompassing he'd nearly attacked Peggy with a savagery he hadn't even realized he was capable of.

The blood flashed in his mind. Eddie Brock's blood, Christy's bloody shirt, the blood that had leaked from his nose at Nana's—and more blood—*blood in the snow,* in the moonlight, in the woods.

More recollections conveyed piecemeal struck in quick flickering bursts then dissipated, leaving only the memory of Peggy's horrified face.

Seth dropped his head against the steering wheel, let it rest there and whispered, "What the hell's wrong with me?"

After a moment he looked up at the apartment building looming before him. He opened the car door and stepped out into the chilly air.

It was time to find out.

# Chapter 18

"Where the hell you been?"

"I was at the hospital until late." Seth moved past his brother and into the apartment. He saw Darian sitting on the couch, head back as if asleep. "Then I went to see Peggy."

Raymond closed the door and followed him into the living room. "You shouldn't have done that, man, you—"

"I had to see her."

"Yeah well—"

"I *had* to see her, Ray."

Raymond backed down, bowed his head. He looked worse than he had in some time, which was saying something. His eyes were bloodshot and ringed with dark circles, his face drawn and pale. Both he and Darian looked like they'd been up all night.

"Any word from the hospital?" Seth asked.

"We called a few minutes ago," Darian answered for him, head still back, eyes still closed. His suit was even more disheveled and wrinkled than the day before, and at some point he'd kicked off his shoes.

"He's listed as critical, but still alive."

Seth went to the kitchen; he could smell the coffee. He poured himself a mug then headed back into the living room. Darian remained on the couch. Raymond took up position near the far wall, standing there and looking as awkward, nervous and out of place as ever. In scanning the apartment it struck Seth just how sterile it was, this small space he'd run to and been occupying these last several months. Peggy's place had the look and feel of being lived in, but it was different here. His apartment looked more like a demo unit than one where anyone actually resided. Stark and ascetic, it was barely furnished with unimaginative, purely functional necessities, and since he'd become someone that existed rather than lived, it all made perfect sense. Sleepwalking, that's what he'd been doing, working and consuming, a mindless drone unaware of life as it unfolded around him. But the transformation had happened quietly, slowly, like a measured whisper in a silent room.

How had he failed to notice the severity of these things until now?

"Is Peggy OK?" Raymond asked.

Seth sipped his coffee. "Far as I can tell, Ray, nobody's OK."

"We had a long talk last night, Raymond and I." Darian sat up, removed his glasses and rubbed his eyes. "There were things I needed to know, and he shared them with me. Unbelievable as they may seem, I have some equally disturbing information for you. Things *you* need to know, too."

"I'm listening."

He slid his glasses back on. "Ever since that night

at the cabin we've all avoided talking to each other about what happened—what *really* happened—because I don't think any of us truly remember or understand it. But we all know something happened. We all knew that from the start."

"And the sky's blue and fish swim in the sea."

"You're not the only one who's sick and tired of this, Seth." His choice of words seemed to amuse him suddenly. "Sick and tired. How apropos."

"What's your point, Mother?"

Darian found his shoes, a pair of leather tassel loafers, and casually slipped his feet into them. "There are some things I haven't told you. I tried to tell Louis but never got the chance. Last night, I told Raymond."

"Well, I'm glad it's finally my turn."

His smile crept away. "After we got back from the cabin I subscribed to some newspapers in Maine, including a little local rag from Gull's Peak and a handful of others from areas nearby. Every time I got one I'd check it front to back looking for any news about Christy or the man she told us about."

Seth took another swallow of hot coffee. "And?"

"I wanted to tell you, Seth, believe me I did. I did a thousand times in my mind, rehearsed it over and over again driving to work every day. But I couldn't go through with it because it didn't make any sense—not then, not now—and I didn't want you to think I was completely out of my mind." Darian sighed. "Truth is I've spent every waking moment for the better part of a year trying to convince myself I'm *not* crazy."

"Me too," Seth said quietly.

"A few days after we left, at a cabin not far from where we were, they found that man Christy told us about," Darian said. "He was dead, but not from an ax like she said."

Seth drew a deep breath. "OK."

"A brain hemorrhage killed him. One so severe the coroner that worked on the case said he'd never seen anything like it. It was as if a part of his brain literally exploded, Seth, that's what it said in the article. Something of a medical mystery is how they described it."

"Then Christy didn't kill him. Why would she lie and say she'd hit him with an ax?"

"She lied about a lot of things," Raymond mumbled.

Seth looked to his brother then back at Darian. "Go on."

"Apparently this guy was just some retired local yokel, a former mill worker named Clayton Willis. He had a wife in town, couple kids who are grown now and also live in the area. Just a simple backwoods sort, had this cabin where he'd go now and then to hunt and do whatever else it is those types do out there in the woods. The last his wife knew he'd gone to Portland to find some part for one of his trucks or something. He never came home. When his son went out to the cabin looking for him, he found the body. Far as his family knew he hadn't had any plans to go to the cabin the day he left for Portland."

"But Christy claimed he'd picked her up just outside Portland, remember?"

Darian nodded. "It seems at least that much was true."

"Did they find something that tied her to this guy?" Seth asked.

"Well, they didn't find any evidence that Willis was some crazed rapist or serial killer, but they did find something odd: a backpack. Inside it was some clothes and other personal items, including a wallet with an old high school student ID card among other things that made it clear the backpack belonged to a woman named Christiana Miller."

"Christy."

"Subsequent articles in a couple papers ran her picture. It was definitely the same girl." Darian slowly rose from the couch and walked across the room to where he had left his briefcase. "She was a runaway, like she said. Ran away from home and never came back. No one ever saw or heard from her again."

"Then that was all true too."

"Yes." Darian grabbed his briefcase from the corner. "But there's more."

Seth remembered the morning after Christy's disappearance at the cabin, how Louis had awakened him and how they had discussed things quietly in the kitchen area.

*I don't feel the same now, I feel different.*

*Different how, Lou?*

*Like myself again, I guess. Only different.*

Darian retuned to the couch, his burgundy briefcase in tow. "Christy was sixteen when she ran away."

"She told us that too," Seth said.

"She also claimed to be nineteen, which means she would've been on the run and missing from her family for three years." Darian let the briefcase rest across his knees. "And that's where it gets weird."

"So she lied about her age, so what?" Seth shrugged. "Easy enough to believe, she looked younger than nineteen anyway."

The metal clasps on Darian's briefcase flipped up with a loud snap. "Actually, she was older than she claimed." He reached into the briefcase and pulled out a section of newspaper that had been folded down into a manageable size. "I know nothing's made much sense over the last year, but can we all agree on the simple fact that we're currently living in 2004?"

"Of course," Seth sighed, his patience a distant memory. "Will you get to the fucking point already?"

"How's this for a point?" Darian held the paper out so Seth could better see it. "Christy ran away in 1980."

# Chapter 19

The grainy photograph in the newspaper was positioned beneath a headline which read: *Long-time Runaway's Belongings Found Near Local Man's Cabin*, and looked like something out of a high school yearbook. Formally posed, Christy's head was cocked slightly to the right, and a bright smile lit up her otherwise vacant face. As when he'd first seen her in person, it was her eyes Seth focused on as he reached out and took the newspaper in hand. Those same pained eyes were evident even then, signaling so much more brewing just beneath the surface. A small caption under the photograph read: *Christiana Miller, missing since 1979.*

"This isn't possible," Seth muttered. "It can't—she must—I mean—this can't be the same person."

"Look at it, goddamn it."

"I am, but—"

"That's her and you know it." Darian slammed his briefcase shut. "We all know it."

"That would've made her forty-three years old when we saw her," Seth said. "There's no way. She was a kid, for Christ's sake."

Through a hard swallow he said, "Yeah."

"1980 was twenty-four fucking years ago." Seth gripped the paper harder, pulled it closer so he could read more of the article. "The girl we saw wouldn't have even been born in 1980. It's just not possible. This has to be someone else."

"When the police checked out the area, as they always do in an unattended death," Darian said, "and due to the odd nature of Clayton Willis's death, they did a brief search of the forest around the cabin. Apparently it's a procedural thing they do just to see if there's anything in the immediate vicinity that might yield clues as to what happened."

Seth's head was swimming again. "It can't be the same person. It *can't*."

"They found Christy's backpack in the woods," Darian continued. "I think the article said thirty yards or so from the cabin. It was just laying there against a tree. No sign of her, no sign of foul play. But the backpack was twenty-four years old, and it was in better shape than it should've been, so obviously it couldn't have been there long, officials decided, because exposure to the elements over that amount of time would've been evident. It wasn't. It had normal wear but was still relatively new, like it had just been left there recently. They determined it had only been out there a few days. The same amount of time they estimated Clayton Willis had been dead when they found him."

A pain shot through Seth's temple. He dropped the newspaper on a nearby chair and began to pace. "Did they find anything else?"

"Of course his family says there's no connection between Clayton and this runaway girl from twenty years ago, why would there be? Their take is: it's the wilds of Maine out there, that backpack could've come from anywhere or anybody. It's strange, sure, but it's got nothing to do with him. After all it was found *near* his cabin not *in* his cabin. The family wrote it off as an odd coincidence. If there was a connection they had no idea what it could be. The cops wanted to make sure that maybe this guy hadn't come across Christy twenty-four years before, maybe killed her out there in those woods and kept the backpack, hidden it in the cabin all these years, which could explain why it was in such perfect shape. The problem is that you're dealing with a man who's lived up in those parts his whole life, has family and friends all through the area, many of them on the police force investigating all this. According to some articles I found they did conduct an investigation, even had crime scene specialists come in and see if they could find anything in the cabin that might link Clayton to Christy. They came up empty.

"In the end their take was that the two things were in no way connected, because Clayton Willis was a God-fearing Christian family man who wouldn't hurt a fly, a man with a family who kept to himself and never had one bit of trouble with the law or anyone else. His death was strange, but even the coroner said there was absolutely no sign of foul play or any reason to believe there'd been any."

Darian slid his briefcase off his knees and let it drop softly to the floor. "So they ended up with this poor old bastard having some bizarre brain explosion that killed him and an odd coincidence with some old backpack from a girl no one's seen in almost twenty-five years. Weird, but not connected as far as they're concerned. Case closed."

"What about Christy's family?" Seth asked.

"Couple papers looked into just who Christiana Miller was...or is...I don't know which." Darian shrugged helplessly. "She did come from Florida originally like she said, and her father did pass away when she was young. She lived alone with her mother, a real piece of work, drug addict, boozer, mental problems and all sorts of arrests over the years."

"Must've been horrible for her," Raymond said softly. It was the first thing he'd said in some time. "Living like that as a kid, I mean."

Seth barely acknowledged him, his attention still zeroed in on Darian. "And what did her mother have to say about all this?"

"She's lives in upstate New York now, but the years of drug abuse took its toll and she's in some halfway house now," Darian said. "One paper interviewed her by phone. She hadn't seen her daughter in decades, figured she was probably dead. She didn't have much to say about the backpack or how it might've gotten there. I got the impression from the article this woman was pretty much out of it."

"So it winds up being two separate incidents far as the authorities are concerned."

"You've got Clayton Willis who dies from some unknown and almost unbelievable brain hemorrhage, and nearby a backpack's found from some kid who ran away over twenty years ago. But there's no sign of the actual girl or any evidence or indication that would lead them to believe one has anything to do with the other. Both situations were odd to be sure, but as far as they saw it, completely unrelated, particularly after investigating a number of possibilities that yielded no evidence whatsoever."

Seth ran his hands through his hair, tried desperately to think this through. For some reason Doctor Farrow's face blinked in his mind just then and a part of him wished he could be sitting in her office talking this out. Doc could calm him, help him sort his thoughts. This must be what it's like, he thought, to need someone like her to keep someone like me sane and balanced. Is this my life now? Is this what I've become?

"It's going to snow."

Seth and Darian both looked over at Raymond, who was leaning against the wall, watching the sky through the glass sliders. Just beyond them a small balcony overlooked the parking lot and highway junction beyond.

"Soon," he said, finishing the thought.

"And we should give a shit why exactly?" Darian cracked. "What are you a fucking weatherman too?"

"Just telling you," he said, voice laced with emotion. "It's gonna snow soon."

"Great. I'm afraid of snow." Darian let out a burst of awkward, nearly maniacal laughter. "How absurd is that? I've never really liked snow, but the idea of it scares the shit out of me now, can you believe that? Ever since that night up there, I—I can't—why would snow frighten me?"

*Think* kept repeating in Seth's head. *Think.*

"Twenty-four years ago." Seth let the words linger, thought about them from every conceivable angle.

There had to be meaning there. "It couldn't be the same person, Christy couldn't be that old. Twenty-four years ago would make her older than I am."

"Times not always the same," Raymond said softly, eyes still fixed on the sky as if he were talking to himself.

"I'm getting really tired of this cryptic bullshit."

"Time's not always the same...when you're with them."

*Tell me what you see, Seth.*

Darian rose to his feet. "What the fuck does that mean?" He turned to Seth with a frantic expression. "What the *fuck* does that mean?"

"Twenty-four years," Seth said.

*Just beyond the darkness there was something more.*

"You know more than you're saying." Darian aimed a finger at Raymond. "I know it. Louis told me. You know more than you're telling us. You've told us what you want us to know but there's more. You're holding back the rest and you're not fooling anyone, Ray. This is tearing our minds—our lives—apart. You have to tell us what you know. You have to, or I swear to God I'll—"

"I was twelve," Seth said, suddenly realizing the significance of the timeframe.

*Seth? Tell me what you see, please.*

"I was twelve," he said again. "Twenty-four years ago, I was twelve."

*I see Raymond.*

He turned to his brother. "And you were eight."

*And what is Raymond doing, Seth*?

"That's when it began, when all this started. Twenty-four years ago."

*Running. He's…running.*

"And that's how you knew her, wasn't it?" Seth moved toward him.

*Are you running too?*

"That's why you had a look of recognition when you first saw Christy."

*Yes.*

"You hadn't seen her in one of your visions, or whatever the hell they are."

*Is it day or night?*

"She looked familiar because you'd seen her before, really seen her."

*Night.*

"For real."

*What else do you see?*

"You'd seen her twenty-four years ago."

*It's snowing.*

"When you were eight and she was nineteen."

*And he's so lost.*

Raymond, still propped against the wall, began to weep.

*He's so terrified.*

"That's it, isn't it?"

*Why is he so terrified Seth?*

"It's all right, Ray. We'll beat this, we'll get through it."

*How old is he in the dream, Seth?*

"But you have to tell us what you know."

*How old is Raymond?*

"All of it."

*Little, seven or eight. Eight. He's eight.*

"Everything, Ray, do you understand?"

*We're running.*

"You have to tell us everything now."

*We're running in the snow.*

"This nightmare began twenty-four years ago. It's time for it to stop, Ray."

"What are you talking about?" Darian demanded. "This started a year ago. It started that night at the cabin."

"Not for us. Not for Raymond."

Raymond seemed to catch himself, as if he just then realized where he was and what was being said to him. He wiped the tears from his face and staggered away from the wall toward the door. "I have to get out of here."

They all felt insane, but he looked the part now more than ever. A pang of guilt swept through Seth, and he reached out for his brother. "Stop it, Ray. Help me stop it."

"Get out of my way."

"Bullshit." Darian started toward him. "You're not going anywhere until—"

Seth held a hand up like a traffic cop to silence Darian then stepped directly into Raymond's path to the door. "You can't run, Ray. Not anymore."

"Back off me, Seth, I mean it." His hair hung across his face, barely shielding wild eyes. "Back the fuck off me."

He'd seen that exact look in his brother's eyes the day he'd attacked Eddie Brock.

"Don't make me hurt you," Raymond whispered. "Please."

Seth slowly stepped to the side.

Raymond gave him a long look that encompassed such a wide array of emotions it was impossible to discern one in particular. He opened his mouth to say something, then apparently thought better of it and instead hustled out the door, slamming it behind him with a loud thud.

Seth felt nauseated and weak, but forced himself back across the room to the sliders and looked out at the lot below.

Slushy snow began to fall, spitting globs of thick runny ice against the sliders.

The fear was becoming more manageable. Was that a good sign or a bad one?

"We're not going to make it, are we," Darian said from behind him.

Though it clearly hadn't been a question, Seth answered anyway. "I don't know."

"Why the hell did you let him go?"

"Don't worry, I'm going after him."

Darian stood next to Seth. Upon seeing the wet snow he grimaced and turned away, hugging himself as if to ward off a sudden chill. "Don't give him too much of a lead or you'll never find him."

"It doesn't matter." Seth watched the sky. "I know exactly where he's going."

# Chapter 20

*Close your eyes.*

Even then he'd wanted to tell her, to explain his pain and terror, to define it for her. This was no trivial childhood angst, but a remorseless and eternal torment far deadlier than either of them could even hope to comprehend.

But he was as doomed then as he was now, perhaps more so, because as a little boy Raymond had even less capacity to understand and accept the things tormenting him than he did after years of enduring them. Affliction blind no more, the agony remained the same regardless of his years, regardless of time or circumstance. An unending screech in his head, a bloated reptile coiled and trapped within his skull, it nested and waited, its skin leathery, cold and dead, even bathed in the warmth of his blood.

There was no escape. Never had been, never would be. And he knew it even then.

"Momma," he would whisper, snuggled into her arms as she sat on the edge of his bed, "will you sing a song for me?"

"Of course, honey," she'd answer, her beautiful face staring down at him through the darkness, eyes blinking slowly. "Lay back now and close your eyes like a good boy."

"I don't like to close my eyes."

"What an odd thing to say, Raymond." She'd raised an eyebrow and frowned a bit. "Why don't you like to close your eyes?"

"I don't like to sleep."

"But everyone sleeps, sweetheart."

"I'm not like everyone. I don't like nighttime."

"Is that why you don't like to close your eyes?"

*Close your eyes and listen.*

I don't want to close my eyes because that's what they tell me to do too, Momma. That's when they come, when I close my eyes in the night. That's when they see me. That's when I see them. They know it frightens us, the dark; the night.

"I don't know," he murmured.

"Don't look so pained, Raymond. A little boy should never look so pained."

I am pain. Not *in* pain, Momma. I *am* pain.

"Sorry."

"Don't be sorry sweetheart," she'd say, the warmth of her palm pressed tenderly against the side of his face. "Just close your eyes and let me sing you to sleep, all right?"

He knew Seth was in his bed just feet away, listening to everything they said. But his brother never teased him about such things. He was the baby, and sometimes he needed to act like the baby, and that was OK. It was OK with everyone.

Except them.

*Close your eyes and see.*

Silent and watchful, their disapproving grimaces leering from the shadows.

*Close your eyes and be.*

"Does God really see us, Momma?'

"Of course, my love, his angels watch over us always." She smiled. "Remember the story from the Bible I read to you?"

"About the ladder?"

"'And he dreamed, and beheld a ladder set up on the earth, and the top of it reached to heaven, and behold the angels of God ascending and descending upon it.' It's from Genesis, do you remember?"

He nodded. "Jacob's Ladder."

"That's right."

"Are you sure they're angels, Momma?"

Her smile slowly vanished. "What else would they be, sweetheart?"

*Beyond anything you could imagine.*

What he wouldn't give for one more night. To be tucked into bed and to have his mother there with him, singing quietly, her fingers stroking his hair as he drifted off to sleep. What he wouldn't give for that love and warmth just once more.

She only survived in his dreams now, but even then her presence was rare.

Just as well. His dreams were diseased.

*Close your eyes, Raymond.*

White…he remembered the white. How blinding and pure it was, shining there all around him like a flood of fluorescent light. Moving, walking slowly into the light, it bled free to reveal a room—an empty room—everything white. The walls, floor, ceiling, all of it stark white and empty, sterile, soulless and artificial.

"What is this place?"

*Close your eyes and dream.*

Then she was there too. His first memories of her were there, in the bright white room. She was older than he was but still young. And pretty. He remembered he thought she was pretty.

"Where am I?"

*Close your eyes and pray.*

He knew then she was as lost and uncertain as he was.

"What's happening?" she asked, her voice hollow, as if she were much further away than only a few feet. "What's happening to us?"

There was an unmistakable loneliness to this place, and loneliness was something with which Raymond was deeply familiar. Even the silence seemed unnatural here. Forced and staged, it was a space better suited to whispers and mute gesture, like a library, perhaps a church…or a cellblock. He didn't know it then, but in years to come he would learn that in night they often became so very quiet.

Except for those particularly dark nights when screams shattered illusions of safety—

*Close your eyes and see the truth.*

—and all that was evil and vile became close enough to touch. Lucifer's thorny wings, stained with bloody tears of angels and drool of demons alike, flapped through darkness, summoning the winds of Hell against an ancient fresco painted along the interiors of his mind. Monsters, legends, nightmares and myths expertly filed, defined and conjured on command to in some way make sense of the entities pursuing him.

*When you see us – really see us – you want to look away, but can't.*

"Do you know what's happening to us?" she persisted.

Raymond shook his head no.

"It's all right," she said, smiling at him. "Don't be afraid, OK?"

He could tell she was lying, that she was just as scared as he was and only doing her best to comfort him because he was younger than she was. But even all these years later the memory of that smile had never left him. In part because it was so beautiful, in part because for an instant it *had* made him feel better, but more because it was the last thing he saw before he began to fall.

*We are the ground.*

Hurtling, plunging downward, it ended in total darkness, the light reduced to a mere pinpoint from above.

*We are the sky.*

Screams—her screams—echoed down, found him, rained down on him in a horrible shower of lunacy. There was something else up there with her now and it was frightening her, hurting her but—but then a new sound distracted him, and he realized he too was no longer alone, deep in this pit. There was something else down here with him. He could hear it moving. He could feel it near him.

*We are the wind.*

The sensation of being strapped down followed, secured with what appeared to be thick brown leather-like harnesses of some kind, various old and rusted metal contraptions littered along the periphery of his vision.

*We are the earth.*

"Momma?" he gasped, tears spilling free as terror consumed him. "Momma!"

*Devils and gods both.*

Faint wheezing and labored breath swirled in the darkness around him.

Help me, Momma. Please help me.

*We are you, Raymond. We are you.*

"Is this Hell?" he gasped.

Something nearby shuffled closer. "Not yet," it whispered.

And then it was Raymond's turn to scream.

He abandoned his memories, found himself running, staggering across familiar terrain, the cold air burning his eyes and causing them to tear as a wet snow spattered down around him. He knew he was crying and calling out, could hear traces of his voice in the air around him, in the forest before him, but the world was blurry and spinning and he was tumbling to the ground before he could stop himself.

As he rolled onto all-fours, his hair hanging down into his eyes, he glimpsed two dark figures standing at the far end of the field he had just crossed.

One separated from the other and started toward him.

Seth was right. He couldn't run. Not anymore.

# Chapter 21

Darian could tell by the way Seth negotiated the streets that he had driven them before. There had been virtually no conversation on the way there, and he'd decided not to push the issue. Whatever tied these two brothers together bound him to them as well, and any secrets revealed only served to help him too. They were one now, the three of them—four, if Louis lived—and nothing could change that. The idea of unity, of many being one, reminded him of his family. It was the first time in hours he'd thought of Cynthia and Debra in any meaningful context, and he found himself wondering if they'd still be there when he finally gathered the courage to return home. Would things—*could* things—ever be the same?

He considered calling Cynthia on his cell phone but didn't want to have to explain things, not now. Explain things, he thought. Good luck. He didn't even understand what was happening himself. But he felt a strong sense of guilt he hadn't been able to shake since that night at the hospital. What kind of man runs from his family, he asked himself, particularly at a time like this? No, he thought, I'm protecting them. Staying away will keep them safer. What was it Louis had told him?

*I can't ever go home. That's the worst part. I can never go home.*

When he closed his eyes he saw Louis staring back at him, tormented and crazed.

*I can't spread this to her and my babies.*

He saw Lou's face as he fell backwards out the window to the street below. The sound his body made as it hit the pavement ripped through Darian's mind like a cleaver until it came together into those three discernible words.

*Let Them Out.*

Debra's beautifully innocent and loving face flashed before him…covered in blood.

He pushed the horror away, brought his hands to his face and covered his eyes, hopeful they might block the visions from getting to him, from reaching inside him and showing him things no one should ever have to see.

Silently, Darian began to pray.

Within moments of crossing the town line into Adamston, Seth pulled up in front of a modest house at the end of a dead end street. He shut off the engine but left the key engaged, allowing the battery to continue to give life to the car. The wipers continued to squeak across the windshield, accompanied by the patter of wet snow against the roof and the hum of the car heater.

Darian looked up and saw the house before them: small, two-story, yellow with white shutters. What he didn't know was that it had been off-white years before, with light blue shutters, and that the fancy stone walk leading to the front door was new, as was much of the landscaping. A few large bushes were present and several old trees that had sat on either end of the front lawn had, sadly, been cut down, but other than that, the house and grounds looked remarkably similar to the way they had decades before.

"Maybe you should wait here," Seth said blankly, staring at the house.

"Maybe you should go fuck yourself." Darian wasn't sure which had startled him more, the sound of Seth's voice or his response to it. What's gotten into you? Isn't that the expression people always used? If only it were still just an expression, he thought. But something *has* gotten into me. Visions of shelled bugs and writhing maggots slithering beneath his skin, swimming in his bloodstream, colonizing his organs, flashed across his mind's eye. Fighting away nausea, he pushed open his door and stepped from the car. "We're in this together, all of us."

Seth joined him outside the car. "All right, but let me handle it."

Parked at an odd angle near the house was an older car that had obviously been driven to that point quickly then abruptly abandoned. The driver-side door was still partially open, and as they got closer they saw the steering column had been broken.

Both men stood silently in the rainy snow a while, oblivious or perhaps just hesitant, then together walked across the small front lawn to an empty paved driveway. They followed it to the side of the house and through to the backyard.

"This is the house Ray and I grew up in," Seth said.

Without slowing his stride he pointed to a spot now occupied by a large grill covered with a tarp. "There was a picnic table there once, and a birdbath and feeder. Next to them was our swing set." All of that was gone too, replaced by a freestanding screened-in portable patio of sorts. It looked out of place there, odd and worn. "My mother's gardens used to be right over there." Again he pointed, this time to a spot of empty, dead lawn. "She used to work for hours on those gardens. Our father used to lie in a hammock between those two trees there."

It seemed an odd time for a tour or trip down memory lane, but Darian understood Seth was making these announcements more for his own benefit than anyone else's. He was gaining bearing, remembering, focusing, forcing himself to see the house and yard and everything else as it used to be rather than how it was now.

The present was of no use to him here, though that too would soon change.

Darian thought of his own parents, wondered what they were doing, if Cynthia had contacted them. Surely they were all concerned, wondering where he was, maybe even out looking for him? He hadn't been home in more than a day now; he'd never done that before.

Debra. If anything happened to that precious baby he…

"Seth," he said quickly, "do you think Cynthia and Debra are safe?"

"I don't know. Maybe nobody's safe."

Darian pulled his glasses off, quickly wiped them free of snow and rain as best he could, then slid them back on. As they continued on across the backyard toward an open field beyond, he looked back at the house. Curtains adorning a window at the rear of the house moved, swayed quickly closed. He was certain someone had been holding them open then released them when he looked back, but due to the glare and contrast of light mixed with torrents of thick wet snow, he couldn't make out anything beyond the window. "Who lives here now?" he asked.

"I have no idea."

"Then maybe—"

"We never owned the house, my parents rented. I haven't been here in years."

"—it's not the best idea to be traipsing through their property. Obviously Raymond stole that car out front and now we're trespassing. It's only a matter of time before whoever lives here calls the police."

Whether he agreed or not, Seth kept on until they reached the edge of the field. Perhaps seventy yards in length and forty or so in width, it stretched to a distant patch of forest in the distance. "I can't believe it's still here," he said with a sense of wonder. "I figured it would've been sold or built on by now."

Then they heard the crying.

Raymond was on hands and knees at the far end of the field, just feet from the tree line. Overcome, his body bucked as raw emotion poured from him in great roiling, wailing gusts.

Darian had never heard anyone cry quite like that.

The only thing close had been the sounds that night in the woods, the screams and the horrible shrieks. But were those real memories or all in his mind?

He turned to Seth, who was fighting a losing battle to maintain control over his own emotions. "God almighty," Darian said softly. "What the hell happened here?"

Rather than answer, Seth left Darian at the start of the field and moved slowly toward his brother.

# Chapter 22

It shocked Seth to realize how affected he'd felt returning to this place. He had tried desperately to remain aloof and removed, as if he were watching himself from a safe distance, but like a twig swept up by a rising and raging river that carried everything in its path to whatever destination it chose, his control over the situation was only an illusion. He was so certain the person he'd once been, the little boy who had lived here all those years ago had evolved into someone superior, an entirely new person that had mastered this darkness and left it all behind, but now realized he hadn't changed so very much after all. That little boy was alive and well. Here, in this field.

Raymond seemed to notice him as he drew closer, but Seth watched the trees, the sky, the field—all of it as clear and familiar as it was decades before—and let the flood of memories wash over him. He forced a hard swallow. "It's all right, Ray. I'm here."

Stretching his arms toward the sky with open hands, Raymond arched up onto his knees. The wet snow trickled between his fingers, continued to drench his hair and face. A madman, a wild-eyed Rasputin praying to the clouds and whatever lay behind them, hands grasping at the robes of God and all that might save him, deliver him from this evil, he reached for the heavens as if salvation were somehow within his grasp.

And perhaps it was.

He lurched forward, his hands again finding the ground and his head bowed, hair dangling to wet earth. "Get out of my head," he sobbed. "Get—get out of my head. Please…*please*."

Seth dropped to his knees next to him, took his brother in his arms and held him tight to his chest. "Stay with me, Ray. Stay with me, I'm here."

"I've tried," he wept. "I've tried for so long."

All those years, Seth thought. All those years of torment and madness slowly devouring his brother's mind and maybe his own. Their lives had always been about Raymond—about this—about dealing with these demons, literal or otherwise, and now those gremlins in his mind had finally finished the job, rendering Raymond a blubbering and broken husk of what he'd once been in long-ago memories, of what he might have been had they spared him such things.

*I am pain, Momma.*

"It's going to be all right," Seth whispered, clinging to him. "You're not alone."

"No," he said, suddenly fighting his way free. Raymond fell back, away from him, splashing down into a fast growing puddle of mud and ice. A moment of clarity seemed to pass over him the way a rolling cloud passes over the moon. There, then gone. Raymond's tears subsided and he sat there a moment, out of breath, chest heaving. "They took me," he finally said, his voice small and timid like it had been when he was a child. "They *took* me, Seth."

"I know."

"You don't know. You don't understand."

He nodded. "I do know, Ray, I do. I remember you running. You always ran here, to the field, to the edge of the woods."

Raymond turned, gazed at the woods sadly. "They had no—no right to do that to me."

"I remember the first time, Ray. I was twelve and you were eight."

"I was just a little boy," he said so softly it was barely audible. Then, as if to the forest directly, he screamed, "I was just a little boy!" His face contorted and he looked down at the ground, tears overcoming him again and reducing his voice to a quivering murmur. "Just a little boy."

"We were both little boys…with nightmares, horrible nightmares about something in our room, watching us, stalking us." Seth remembered the raw fear that surged through him as a child in that dark room, how it burned through him like he'd swallowed fire. "Only they weren't nightmares were they Ray?"

He shook his head.

"The first time it really happened," Seth said. "It was all real, *they* were real, they really were there, and they took you. We ran but they took you. They took you and left me behind."

"I led them out here," he said, strangely calm now. "I ran because I knew I was smaller than you, faster. I led them out here so they'd take me and wouldn't hurt you."

Seth's heart pounded in his chest and he could no longer be sure where his tears ended and the snow and ice pelting his face began. Even then, his little brother had been the better of them. "You—you saved me?"

"I tried, Seth, I swear I did, but I fucked it up. That's what I do, I fuck things up."

"That's not true. This isn't your fault, it never has been."

"All the times after that night were only dreams, my nightmares and memories of what they'd done to me."

"I thought it was all a nightmare," Seth told him. "I remember something was there with us, in our room." He shook his head, still unable to fathom what he now knew to be truth. "Doc helped me remember that night, that first night. I couldn't remember but she helped me. Before I went to her it was like my memories of that night had been wiped away somehow. What could do that? What could steal our memories like that?"

"They bury them," he said. "But they come back slowly, in pieces. For me the nightmares never stopped, and my mind it—it was different. It was *changed*. They changed me."

"What did they do to you, Ray?"

"You don't come back the same way you were when they took you." His face twisted into a helpless expression, the terror rising in him again. "You come back different."

"Able to do things you couldn't before? Able to see things and know things you couldn't before?"

"Diseased," he whispered.

"Why, for what purpose?"

"Because then we're not like everyone else. Our minds can do things the human mind can't do. They do it so we'll have them with us always. The pain and horror it allows us to see and experience and leave in our wake—that follows us like a storm cloud no matter where we go or what we do—makes us like them, less human. It's a disease—*they're* a disease. Even when it gets quiet sometimes, you know they're still there. You know there's a switch in your head because they put it there, and one day they throw that switch and they move through us to others. Those others become the afflicted, and they change too. Slowly, quietly, it kills everything they were before, destroying them a little bit at a time."

"But why, why now, why did it take years? Why are they doing this?"

"We can't even begin to understand." Raymond's eyes found him through the rain and snow. "They're not human, Seth. Why would their motivations be?"

"But why us? Why you?"

"Chance, luck of the draw, or maybe they know who's more susceptible to them somehow and that's where they start. I don't know how, but they know who we are."

Seth ignored the cold, unable to tell whether it was caused by the snow and rain or the chills of terror running through him. "And Christy was there that night, too?"

"Not just her. There were a lot of us."

"But they let you go, they—"

"They didn't let me go," he said. "They sent me back."

"Why?"

"They kept Christy," he said as if he hadn't heard the question. "For years, I guess. They sent her back later. That's how they do it. Different people, different places, different times and—and like I told you, time isn't the same when you're with them. Nothing's the same."

"But why, Ray? Why did they send you back?"

"Because Christy and me and the others like us are..."

Seth crawled closer and took him by the shoulders. "Tell me."

"We're the carriers."

Seth released him, pushed his hair from his forehead, sweeping away rainwater and snow along with it. "Carriers of *what*, some apocalyptic endgame, murder and disease and famine like in the Bible? Is this how it happens? Not with horsemen galloping through the clouds bringing death and misery, but like this?"

Raymond looked away but didn't answer.

"Or is it something demonic taking us over through our dreams and childhood fears?"

The wind answered with a distant howl.

"Is it some alien species?" Seth asked; searching his mind for any possibility he could grab hold of, however initially absurd it seemed. "Posing as insanity and moving from mind to mind, invading us one at a time?"

"Answer him."

They both looked up; saw Darian standing over them, as drenched and cold as they were.

"It doesn't matter," Raymond said. "If it's one of those things or something else, it doesn't matter." His hair was sodden and clinging to him. He pushed it away from his face so they could better see him. "Because sooner or later they come for everybody."

Whatever was left of Raymond's rational mind seemed to be evaporating right before Seth's eyes. These things revealed had turned back his scalp, exposed his mind to raw and unforgiving possibilities, all of which led to certainties of absolute madness, as if such things could never be faced and survived with a mind healthy and intact.

"You know how they always tell you something's all in your head? It's all in your mind, man, all in your mind." Raymond turned back to the forest, looking for a moment like he might get up and move toward it. "The thing they don't tell you is, just because something's all in your mind doesn't mean it's not real." He shook his head and sighed. "Now you know just how fucking crazy I am."

"How crazy we all are," Darian mumbled.

"None of us are crazy," Seth said.

"Of course we are, don't you see?" Raymond watched them a moment. "It just doesn't make any difference."

"Who are they, Ray? Goddamn it, *what* are they?"

"The end…they're the end." Raymond began to laugh the sad, quiet, hopeless laughter of the damned. "The end of us."

Darian glanced back at the house. Whoever was watching from the back window was at it again, but this time didn't bother ducking from sight. A cross-looking elderly woman in a housecoat glared at them from just behind the pane of glass, one hand holding open the curtains, the other with a cordless phone pressed to her ear. "We have to get out of here. There's a woman in the window on the phone, and I think it's safe to assume she's calling the police."

"They can't help us," Raymond said, still laughing quietly.

"That car's stolen and we're on this woman's property uninvited, Seth. We have to go." Darian stepped closer to him, drawing his full attention. "*Now.*"

Seth nodded, rose to his feet and held a hand out for his brother. "Come on."

"You go," he said, staring at the mud surrounding him. "Leave me here."

"Raymond, they'll arrest you. They'll lock you up, now come on."

He shook his head sadly. "It doesn't matter anymore. It's happening."

"We don't have time for this." Darian turned and started back toward the car.

Seth crouched next to him. "I'm not leaving you here, Ray."

"Remember the man in the sun?" Ray asked. "Remember I told you I saw him when I was a kid? Right here, I—I saw him right here. He was different, Seth, he wasn't one of them, not really. I wanted to go with him but I couldn't, I couldn't. He told me I couldn't because if I did then he wouldn't be there…right there…right then…and neither would I. He told me to hide. He told me to *hide*. The man in the sun told me to—"

"Come on," Seth said, no longer able to cope with his brother's incoherent rambling. He reached down, took Raymond's hand. "I'll take you to Nana's."

Raymond snapped to attention like a child promised chocolate. "Nana's?"

"Would you like that?" he asked, struggling to hold himself together. What had been broken for so long now seemed beyond repair. His brother had been teetering on the edge of a precipice for years, and now he had finally stepped off. Or maybe he'd been pushed. Either way, he was gone, what little was left of him prior finally snapped and destroyed by all this madness, the weight of which he could no longer bear. "We'll go back to Nana's and you can stay with her a while, OK?"

"Nana's." He nodded, a smile slowly surfacing. "OK."

Seth helped him up, put an arm around his shoulder, and together they walked back across the same field they had so many times in the past run across in abject terror. The terror remained, of course, as did the memories the house and field and forest held for them and always would, but as they crossed the backyard and headed for the street, Seth hesitated just long enough to look back one last time.

He knew they would never again return to this cradle of memory, this place that for so long had kept their secrets. Because like so much else it was now lost to them. Forever.

# Chapter 23

On their way out of town they stopped for a red light at a large intersection. Within seconds two police cruisers charged through the intersection but flew right by them, lights blazing and sirens howling. Darian slumped a bit in the passenger seat as Seth watched them in the rear view. They quickly disappeared over a bend on their way to the house. In the backseat Raymond remained quiet, preoccupied, eyes staring and fixed on the mayhem playing across the dark stages of his mind.

"I hope that old lady didn't get your plate," Darian said.

"I doubt it." Seth pulled out as the light changed, turned onto the highway on-ramp and headed back for Boston. "But at this point we can't worry about it."

"Can't worry about it? That stolen car was—"

"I'm heading back home," he interrupted. "We'll figure things out when we get there." He tightened his grip on the steering wheel, increased speed then checked his watch. Still early, traffic through the city would be light. Once through to the other side he'd head south and return to his apartment building. "I'll grab Ray's things," he said, lowering his voice so only he and Darian would hear it clearly. "And we'll bring him to my grandmother's on the cape."

Through slushy snow and set against a dark gray sky, the cityscape of Boston loomed before them as they drove up over the expressway. Seth switched lanes and skirted the city proper, following the tunnel and another stretch of highway to the Route 3 split. No one spoke another word until they reached the apartment building.

Seth parked the car in the first open space he could find. "I'll be right out."

He dashed across the lot, and once inside his apartment, brushed the snow and water from his coat then ducked into the bathroom to grab a towel for Raymond. Once in the living room he grabbed Raymond's duffel bag and Darian's briefcase and was about to head back for the car when he noticed the display on his answering machine flashing 2.

He put the things down and hit the play button.

"Seth, hi," a deep, detached voice he recognized as his boss Bill Jacobs said through the small speaker. "We've of course heard about Louis and I know you two were close so I just wanted to—on behalf of the entire department, of course—pass along my thoughts and prayers regarding that situation. Also, Accounting called looking for Darian Stone and was wondering if perhaps you knew where he was. Under the circumstances and with the whole Louis *thing*, no one's upset, just worried. No one's seen or heard from Darian, and apparently they've tried calling his home phone and cell but haven't heard back from him. If you know how he can be reached give Dave Radcliff over in Accounting a buzz and let him know. Thanks. And I need you to give me a call too, at your absolute earliest convenience, all right? It's imperative that we discuss a few things before the conclusion of your vacation. OK, great. Take care, talk soon."

A loud beep sounded and after a moment the second message began to play.

"Hey, it's me, Ruthie. Give me a call when you get a chance, OK? I'm at work but if you can't call until after five that's cool, you can get me at home. I'll be around." A few seconds of dead air followed, and then: "It's important, Seth, OK? Call me."

Seth thought it odd that Ruthie would call him at home, and her antics were about the last thing he had time for at the moment, but there was something unusual in her tone, something uncharacteristic that sounded almost like fear. He grabbed a pen and small pad from a nearby end table and jotted down her home number as she recited it. Stuffing the paper in his pocket, he next cycled through the calls on his caller ID unit and realized that the call from Bill Jacobs had come in the day before. Ruthie's call had been two days prior and he'd just not seen it with all that had been going on.

He picked up the phone and first called the hospital.

Louis was still alive and still listed as critical.

Seth then called work.

"Severance Corporation, how may I direct your call?"

"Bill Jacobs, please."

After a series of clicks his secretary answered.

"Good afternoon, Bill Jacobs's office."

"Judy, Seth Roman returning Bill's call. Is he available?"

"Yes, he just got out of a meeting. One moment, Mr. Roman, I'll transfer you."

After what seemed like an inordinately long time, Bill Jacobs finally came on the line. "Seth, it's Bill, hi. Listen, I was so sorry to hear about Louis over in Shipping. My God, what a terrible thing, how is he?"

"Still listed as critical," Seth answered. "I just got your message, sorry it took me so long to get back to you but—"

"No, no, that's fine. First, any word on Darian? They still haven't heard from him."

He hesitated only long enough to make a quick decision as to what his answer would be. "I haven't heard from him since yesterday myself. Last I knew he was going home to be with Cynthia and his daughter. If he's not there maybe they all went to his parents' house."

"Right, OK, well if you hear from him have—"

"Yeah, I'll have him call in. Was there anything else, Bill? I'm kind of right in the middle of some personal business at the moment."

A long pause followed, and for a time all Seth heard was shallow breathing.

"Look," Jacobs eventually said, "I know you're on vacation and it's been a tough couple days with the Louis situation and all, but I need to discuss a few things with you. It's important Seth or obviously I wouldn't bother you at a time like this."

"OK, what is it?"

"Why don't you come in and we'll talk about it?

"You mean today?"

"That'd be super."

"I'm kind of busy, Bill, I—"

"It won't take long but it's important."

"Is everything all right?"

"Everything here's fine. But we need to talk and I really don't want to get into it over the telephone."

Seth checked his watch. "Give me a few hours and I'll be there."

"Andrea's throwing a dinner party tonight so I'm leaving at five on the button and—"

"I'll be there before five, Bill."

"Super. Talk to you then."

Seth hung up, went to the bedroom and found a fresh shirt. About the last thing he needed at this point was Bill Jacobs's bullshit, but he figured if he didn't stay long at Nana's after dropping off Raymond, he could be back in Boston before five and find out what was so damned important. As he tossed his soaked shirt aside and pulled on the fresh one, he contemplated calling Ruthie back but decided to save time and just talk to her when he got to the office.

As he left the building and headed across the parking lot, he saw Darian step out of the car, close his door and walk around the front of the car, nervously glancing back through the windshield at Raymond, who was still in the backseat.

"They're looking for you at work." Seth handed him his briefcase. "I lied, said I hadn't seen you since yesterday, figured you could call in if and when you felt like it."

"Thanks," he said awkwardly, taking the case.

"Bill Jacobs is insisting I come in and talk to him

about something."

"What the hell does *he* want?"

"Who knows?" Seth shrugged, walked around to the trunk, opened it and tossed Raymond's duffel inside. "I told him I'd be there in a few hours. By the time we drop Raymond off and get back there'll still be time to—"

"I'm not going."

"Then you can stay on cape with Raymond but I told him I'd be in."

"No," Darian said. "I mean, I'm not going with you."

Seth slammed the trunk closed. "What are you talking about?"

Darian hugged himself and looked to the sky. The snow was changing, becoming thicker and fluffier as the last remnants of rain retreated. Large flakes suddenly filled the air, flitting about all around them. "Seth, I need to be with my wife and daughter. I need to be with Cynthia and Debra."

"I'm not sure that's the best idea right now."

"It very well may not be, but I have to go home."

Seth watched him through the sea of snowflakes. He'd never seen him look quite so defeated and drawn. He reminded him of a pummeled boxer unable to answer the bell and opting to remain on his stool. He pictured him for a moment as he'd looked so many years before as the best man at his and Peggy's wedding, and how he'd so graciously stepped in when Raymond didn't make it. But the memory was short-lived, because remembering such things also forced him to remember Peggy on that day as well, and at the moment it was simply too much for him to endure. All the happiness, the purity of that day and the promise it held seemed little more than a fading dream, a storybook tale not quite as real as it seemed when told over time, remembered and reflected upon. "There's no way to tell for sure what'll be waiting there for you," he said.

"I know," Darian said. "But whatever this is, I have to face it with them, not running away or leaving them on their own. I've got to make sure they're all right. If something happened to them and I could've prevented it by being there I'd never forgive myself. I need to be with them. It's where I belong." His entire body trembled. "I'm Debra's father, her daddy. I'm supposed to protect her and keep her from harm no matter what. That's what daddies do. No matter what, I have to be there to make it right, or what the hell good am I?"

Seth offered his hand. "Good luck, man."

"You too." Darian took his hand, shook it slowly.

An empty hush filled the air. Even nearby traffic sounds softened, and they stood quietly in the parking lot, hands still joined, the snow falling heavily now, accumulating and turning the world white.

"We had some good times over the years, didn't we?"

Though the smile on Seth's face didn't last long, it was accompanied by the first genuine feeling of happiness he'd felt in recent memory. But it too withered quickly. "Some real good times, Mother, some real good times."

Though neither man spoke again, they searched each other's eyes in the way good friends often do, and the rest of what both men felt and needed to say was realized and understood amidst the silence of a cold, quiet, sad winter day.

# Part Four:
# Talk of Wolves

"We are dealing with a yet unrecognized level of consciousness, independent of man but closely linked to the earth...Human beings are under the control of a strange force that bends them in absurd ways, forcing them to play a role in a bizarre game of deception."

—Dr. Jacques Vallee, *Confrontations,*
*Messengers of Deception*

# Chapter 24

Of all the memories Seth had of growing up and spending time with his parents, most involved his mother. Despite his somewhat avant-garde personality, after Raymond's problems as a child began, more often than not their father seemed to exist on the periphery of their daily lives. But then, Raymond's tribulations had caused changes in all of them, and to some extent altered their entire family structure. Because it involved recognizing and coming to terms with certain facts he was still not comfortable with—for Seth specifically—their family dynamic had never been something he'd spent a great deal of time thinking about. And yet now, driving through the mounting snow toward their grandmother's house, he could think of nothing but.

Raymond was not quite nine years old the first time he went away. Seth was just thirteen. His parents told Seth they had taken his little brother to see sleep specialists, doctors who could help him solve the night terrors problem. When they left early one morning Seth was told all three would be back later that same day, but when they returned it was without Raymond.

His mother, already in tears when they got home, hurried by Seth and disappeared into her bedroom without a word, leaving him and his father alone in the kitchen.

He remembered how deathly quiet the kitchen was that late and dreary afternoon.

His father, with an uncharacteristic scowl, eventually went to the refrigerator and found a bottle of beer. He drank most of it before he made it to the table and sat down. "Your mother's upset," he said flatly. "She'll be OK."

"Where's Ray?"

"He had to stay with the doctors a while." He took another swig of beer. "It's not safe for Raymond to be having these *attacks*, or whatever they are, Seth. Thing is, he could hurt himself running around in that state."

"When's he coming home?"

"Soon, son, real soon—couple weeks."

Seth had never been apart from his brother more than a day or two. Visions of this vague place he'd been taken to and what went on there filled his head and set his imagination running wild. "Why does he have to be there so long?"

"Well, because they have to watch him sleep—monitor it, they call it—and they have these machines that let them watch his brain patterns and whatnot. I don't fully understand it all myself, son, but they need to keep an eye on him for a bit so they can figure out what's wrong. Once they know, they can help him, see?"

Neither spoke for a long while.

"Is Ray going to be OK?"

His father gave a strong nod, as if the force of his conviction could make it so. He finished his beer then held the bottle before him like it warranted study. "He's going to be just fine, don't you worry."

"How come you didn't tell Ray he was going to be gone so long?"

"We didn't know." The last word snagged in his throat. "We have to pack some of his things and bring them to him tonight." He put the bottle aside, folded his hands together and leaned into the table, closer to Seth. "Son, I know you've seen this stuff with Ray up-close. You've followed him out back, been there with him. We've all seen it and know how scary it is. Ray needs help before this gets too out of hand. Believe me, I hate turning him over to those guys too, you know I've always preached to you boys to be your own people and never trust The Man, but hell, son, there's not much else I know to do at this point." He attempted a relaxed posture but his awkward hesitation and the deep look of concern on his face betrayed him. "Son, I'm going to ask you something, and I need you to tell me the truth, OK? It's very important that you be totally honest with me on this."

"OK."

"Have you had nightmares like this too?"

Seth thought on it a moment. "I get scared sometimes when he has them."

"That's not what I mean. You're always with him, I just want to—it's important that—Seth they told us—the doctors, I mean—they told us it's important to find out if you're having problems like this too, OK? The two of you always end up outside when this happens, now is that because he wakes you and you follow him, or is it because the same things are happening to you?"

"I told you and Mom before that Raymond has the nightmares, Dad, not me."

"Thing is, these problems can be hereditary, meaning they can—"

"I know what hereditary means."

"Sorry, I—yeah, of course you do."

"I don't get them too, OK?"

"OK." His father's normally playful eyes were dull and red and lost. His long and unruly hair and bushy mustache had both been neatly groomed and combed into place, and even his clothing was different on this day. Always clad in either jeans or work clothes, on this day he'd worn a pair of penny loafers and khaki pants with an oxford shirt. He'd even taken the earring out of his right ear. But he was fooling no one, least of all Seth. "I forget how fast you're growing sometimes," he said thoughtfully. "It's hard for a father to see his kids objectively. You'll know what I mean one day when you have your own children. Hell, when I look at you I still see a little boy. But it's time I started treating you like a young man. And I want you to act like a young man, too, and to know it's OK to tell me the truth, son. In fact it's real important that you do."

"I am telling you the truth, Dad."

"Have you been having headaches?"

"No."

"Do you ever smell freaky odors, hear things inside your head or see things, like funny colors or—"

"No."

"Have you ever had one of these night terrors like

your brother?"

*There was something in our room.*

"Why do you keep asking me that? I just try to help Ray when he has them."

*I saw it too. I saw it in our room.*

"It's important if you're not feeling well to tell your Mom and me, OK?"

"OK."

"You don't have to be afraid, but if things get to bothering you and you feel you need to talk to somebody and—well, maybe your mom and me are too close or whatever—you just tell me and we'll get you someone to talk to, OK? If need be, I mean."

"I don't need anybody to talk to, Dad."

"I'm not trying to hassle you, I—look I'm doing my best. I promise you I am."

Seth wasn't sure what to say. "I know."

"Sometimes these things just happen, OK? It's nobody's fault. Ray has problems and he needs help working through them. He's not strong like you. Some people need help more than others is all, and that's why he needs you the way he does. You're a good brother to him, son, and I'm proud of you."

Seth felt like he should smile but couldn't quite manage it. The words seemed particularly poignant coming from his father. "Is Mom OK?"

"She's upset but she'll be all right. You know your mom. She's not used to being apart from you boys. But Raymond's going to be home before we know it, and this'll all work out fine. Those doctors are gonna get this all straightened out, you wait and see."

His father's voice—trying so desperately to sound convincing—echoed in memory then faded beneath the squeak of windshield wipers and the hum of the car heater.

The snow was a bit lighter as they crossed the bridge and headed onto the cape and it seemed to lessen in strength the further along they went.

Seth checked the rearview mirror. Raymond was leaned toward the backseat passenger side door, head rested against the window and eyes fixed in a glassy, faraway stare that Seth now knew held more secrets and housed more shadowy caverns than either of them would ever fully be able to comprehend.

Seth had only begun to understand in any genuine sense how truly alone his brother was and had been for most of his life, and that realization not only brought forth in him tremendous sorrow, it chilled him to the very core of his being.

Images flashed: The cabin, night, snow, blood, screams, visions of running through dark forest, bitter cold…and the same omnipresent terror.

*I'm beginning to remember, Ray,* he thought. *Why am I finally beginning to remember? Am I getting closer to the truth…or is it getting closer to me?*

Eyes back on the road, Seth watched the snow blow across both lanes in furious gusts, carried and shaken by nearby ocean winds.

He remembered his father a second time, not long after Raymond's assault of Eddie Brock. Only this memory revealed him standing on the back steps of their house, staring out at the field Raymond so often ran to in the night. As Seth came upon him he realized his father was crying.

Despite the fact that he was often quite emotional, Seth had only seen his father cry once before, when as young children he and Raymond presented their father with a handmade birthday present, a peace sign made from elbow macaroni painted with sparkly paint and glued to a sheet of heavy construction paper.

But on this day and in this memory, his father's tears had not been born of joy. They fell across his cheeks in a steady stream as he smoked a cigarette and glared at the field and forest like they were to blame, and maybe in some way they had been. A red bandana he often wore as a headband was tied and in place, and he still had on his work pants and shirt with his name embroidered on the pocket.

For a long while he and Seth stood silent on the steps, together in thought.

"I always tried to teach you boys right from wrong," his father finally said, voice gravely and raw. "From the time you were old enough to understand I talked to you about the value of peace and understanding. I always tried to teach you violence is never the answer."

"They mess with Ray at school, Dad, they do it all the time and he finally snapped."

"He hit that boy in the head with a brick."

"He was—"

"In the *head*, Seth. With a *brick*."

"I was there, I know."

His father looked at him, smoke leaking from his nostrils. "He could've killed him."

"But he didn't." Seth knew had he not been there to stop him Raymond just might have, but he defended him anyway, in the only way he knew how. "Eddie isn't even hurt that bad. His nose is broken and he has a concussion and some stitches. He'll live."

"That's not the point and you know it. Violence isn't the way, not ever. All it does is make things worse. It's a lie The Man teaches innocent and impressionable children so they'll kill and die for some ideal the government and a handful of corporations sell them and say is right and just and *necessary.* But it's all a lie designed to convince people that murdering each other is the answer. It's bullshit."

"Ray went too far," Seth said, "but people have the right to defend themselves, Dad, and sometimes violence is the only way."

"Violence is never the only way, just the easier way." He took a hard pull on his cigarette and exhaled angrily. "You know the cops and the juvenile courts are talking about charging your brother with attempted murder? Did you know that?"

Seth shook his head no, watched the empty field.

"Fascist bastards," he growled. "Like assault with a deadly weapon isn't bad enough. They talk about my boy like he's some crazed killer or something. Nazi motherfuckers, he's fourteen years old, for Christ's sake. Goddamn freshman in high school."

A gentle breeze blew through the distant trees, and Seth could smell alcohol on his father wafting toward him now and then. Visions of Raymond running across the field in terror came to him quickly then retreated back into darkness.

Where was all this anger and cries for justice when Eddie Brock and his friends were terrorizing Raymond every day at school? Seth wondered.

"Ray needs help, Dad. He's—"

"You think I don't know that?" He swallowed back emotion, quickly wiped the tears from his cheeks as if he'd only just then realized they were there. "But all these big-shots with their fancy degrees and dime store crap don't know Raymond, they don't understand him and they don't care to. We've been down this road before; they don't want to help him, not really. They want to turn him into some zombie that'll do everything they say, make him into some fucking houseplant. All they want to do is punish him. Nobody ever wants to help, but start talking punishment, and oh, they line up, don't they? People love that shit. We got no help, no prevention, but break a rule or step out of line and we got more punishment than you can shake stick at. We love it, can't punish people enough, it makes all the self-righteous pricks out there feel better about themselves."

*Out where*? Seth wondered. "Is Ray going to go to jail, Dad?"

"They offered us a deal Eddie Brock's parents had already agreed to." He took another drag off his cigarette then flicked it out onto the grass. "Ray's going to have to go away again for a while, get his head straight. If we play along and pay Eddie Brock's medical bills no criminal charges will be brought against your brother."

Seth reached out awkwardly, touched his father's shoulder then let his hand drop.

"So, The Man pulls the strings and we dance for him," his father mumbled. "Because it's a fixed game and nobody gives a streaming pile of dog-shit about justice. Long as there's some punishment, a little coin to cover expenses and peace and quiet, they're happy. They don't care if a bunch of witchdoctors are gonna fuck with my boy's head, long as they make him a robot like everybody else they're happy."

"Where's Raymond going, Dad?"

He looked at him, eyes bloodshot and glazed. "Where the hell you think, son?"

His father left Seth standing alone on the steps and walked across the field to the edge of the forest, hands in his pockets and face turned to the sky.

"He's had too much to drink," his mother said from behind him.

Seth turned and saw her standing in the back doorway. He could tell she had already shed her tears, and now resolve was setting in.

"He's feeling like he's failed Raymond," she said. "Failed as a father."

"It's not his fault."

"No, it's not." Her large eyes blinked at him slowly. "But sometimes feeling something's enough. It hasn't been easy with Raymond for any of us, but we have to be as strong as we can, for him and each other. You have that strength, Seth, you always have and you always will. Unless you give it away no one can take it from you. It's God-given, your strength and faith. It's what makes you, you. It's just like in the Bible with Adam and Eve, only in reverse. My hope—our hope, came first, in you. It's why we named you Seth." She joined him on the steps. In a rather frumpy, casual cotton dress, she looked thin to the point of frailty, like she was in need of a good solid meal. "In the story, Seth was Adam and Eve's third son. Eve gave him the name Seth as she put it: 'For God hath appointed me another seed instead of Abel, whom Cain slew.' Amidst the bad that had come before him, Seth was her hope."

"I'm no better than Raymond, Mom."

"No, you're not, just different. You're his pillar."

She smiled, as if this should have pleased him. "Raymond's afflicted with things he can't control, burdens or crosses—whatever you want to label them—that none of us asked for, least of all him. But remember, Seth, *blessed are the afflicted.*"

"What about the unforgiven?" he asked. "Are they blessed, too?"

She raised an eyebrow, startled by the question. "God forgives everyone, Seth."

"But only if they seek His forgiveness."

"Yes, only if they seek it."

"Otherwise God just looks down with anger?"

"No, Seth, with sorrow."

The memory left him, swallowed by swirling snow just beyond the windshield and the flash of memories more recent. Memories unlike those from so long ago, that played out across cold and distant landscapes, these were growing stronger and more vivid with each passing moment. Memories of that night at the cabin—the sounds and smells and feel of that dark night were calling him again, beckoning him—drawing him back to the secrets and horrors they held and the spells of black magic they cast.

*Christy running through the snow…blood…the cabin…screams.*

"You're remembering," Raymond said suddenly. "Aren't you?"

*Sounds of things tearing, ripping…*

Seth found him in the mirror, nodded slowly.

*Cold winds and labored breathing…and then a shift…that night and the dark forest gone, replaced by the hospital Louis had been taken to…the child beyond the glass twirling the umbrella in the rain…its face…what—what had happened to its face?*

"The child at the hospital," Seth said, "we all saw it, Ray, we—"

"Wasn't a child."

*A small being on the steps dressed in a dull yellow raincoat and matching hat.*

"Why was it there?"

*Where its eyes and sockets and nose should have been the skin was smooth, flat and blank. Its mouth was impossibly small, but it opened wide then wider still until the sides tore and began to bleed.*

"What did it want, Ray?"

*The twisted, unfinished face froze in a soundless scream of inhuman fury and horror.*

"The thing we have that they don't."

*Had he seen it before—or something like it before?*

"Tell me, Ray."

*In the woods, running, screaming, had he seen it there—or others like it?*

"What do we have that they don't?"

With an intuitively devilish smile, Raymond looked back out the window and watched the snow. "Souls."

# Chapter 25

The dark drop hit the pool and immediately began to dissipate, turning the previous clear water an inky maroon. A second drop splashed into the toilet, followed by a third, and within seconds the blood had overtaken the water, running in finger-like strands and veins across the bowl, alive and swimming for the edges where water met porcelain.

Standing above the toilet and bent slightly forward to allow the blood dripping from her nose to fall directly into it rather than onto the floor and nearby carpet, Nana reached for the roll of toilet paper on the wall dispenser and carefully removed several sheets. Folding them into a single small pillow, she brought them to her bloody nostril and held it there, then applied pressure to the bridge of her nose with her free hand.

Her heart raced, and, despite the chill in the old house, her skin had become clammy, leaving her feeling sticky and unclean. Two doors down the hallway her grandsons were waiting. Prior to all that was happening, she hadn't seen either of them in months , but now they had come to her for the second time in just twenty-four hours, as she knew they eventually would, seeking her out like moths to flame in an otherwise dark void.

Though she could do them little good, still they had come.

At least for Raymond, it made perfect sense.

The end—his end—would come here with her, where they could face the final chapter as they had all those chapters before it since he'd been a child: together. Even when they were apart, separated by miles or oceans or prison bars or locked hospital doors, they had been together.

But the same had not and would not be true for Seth.

Alessandra pulled the paper from her nose and inspected it. A circular stain filled the center of the wad but the bleeding itself had stopped. She dabbed her nose a few times with the paper and it came back clear, but she knew what was happening in her now. She was no exception to the rule, no safe harbor, just another of the infected, one more victim in an endless circle of many. For so many years the disease in Raymond had remained dormant, coming alive to attack only when those responsible for it chose to do so. But now the sleeping period was over, what lived in her grandson had awakened beyond the borders of his own tortured mind, able to reach out and slip into the dreams and thoughts of others. The end result could not be stopped, and as she understood it, only Raymond and those like him would remain free of transformation, though even he would pay further penance. While he carried their sickness and spread it for them, they would never gain his body and soul. But they already had dominion over his mind, or what was left of it, so there could be no end for him but to live the remainder of his life in some padded cell, deemed insane, dangerous and beyond repair, a useless machine tossed aside and forgotten, just another carcass on humanity's junk heap. The only choices that remained for the rest of them were submission, persecution until insanity or death ensued, or suicide. Odd, she thought, how subtle this all was, how similar it was to normal, everyday reality, nothing at all like prophecies and nightmares depicted such things.

People were running now, as they had for centuries, but in these days of horror, conquest, infiltration and occupation, they were running into the flames rather than away from them; embracing the twisted and sick values that these things fed upon while hiding behind rigid social and manipulated religious fears camouflaged as morality. The things that made them strong and the human race weaker, like a narcotic that initially induces bliss but eventually brings only death, helped to bring even the common man to the trough to feed without even fully realizing all they were ingesting and forfeiting.

Sad, she thought, how cheap, expendable and ultimately irrelevant the human soul and all the potential it possessed had become to so many. A commodity, for sale or even given away for mere illusions of happiness, like all else, it held little or no enduring value.

And what of Rolf, she wondered, poor, dear, oblivious Rolf, tinkering with his models or watching his news programs and sipping his tea? What a magnificent, loving and selfless companion he'd been these past years. For him it would be quiet and peaceful. She would see to it.

Alessandra wiped the remnants of the nosebleed from her face, and, mostly from habit inspected herself in the mirror over the sink. Her instincts were to fight, but it all seemed so futile now. "You've still got backbone, haven't you?" she asked the mirror and those that watched her in it—those ghostly apparitions writhing in her head like maggots and worms swimming behind her eyes, squirming deeper and deeper, gnawing, nibbling like termites, slowly eating their way into her brain.

She squeezed shut her eyes. The visions and nausea weakened, and she steadied herself against the sink until the feelings passed. She had excused herself moments earlier, when she felt the wave of dizziness and the beginnings of the nosebleed, and had escaped into the nearby bathroom down the hall. But she knew she would have to return to them soon. Time was short for them all now.

Alessandra opened her eyes, stared at her reflection with sadness, and then defiance.

* * *

In those rare instances over the past year when he'd allowed himself to daydream, some separation from the nightmares that plagued him in both light and darkness, Darian always dreamt of a grand ballroom similar to the one where he and Cynthia had celebrated their wedding reception. Only in the dream it was far more glamorous than it had been in reality.

*Arched high above the glossy dance floor, a ceiling covered in sprawling paintings with a medieval motif of heroic angels and great bountiful clouds looks down upon him with equal parts majesty and menace. Surrounded by tables draped in white linen and set with expensive silverware and beautiful crystal centerpieces, each holding a white lighted candle, the dance floor is occupied by only two people: Darian, in a sleek black tuxedo, and Cynthia in a strapless white gown.*

*Sitting in a chair near the edge of the dance floor is Debra, in a beautiful little gown of her own, watching with an excited and favorable grin.*

*Though there are no musicians Darian can see, somewhere nearby a band plays the most mesmerizing music he has ever heard.*

*Cynthia smiles at him, and they begin to dance with such grace, it feels for a moment as if they're gliding, their feet not quite touching the floor but hovering above it somehow.*

*He remembers the feel of her lower back, the bend just above her buttocks, and how his hand has always seemed to fit the spot perfectly. He remembers years before when they were dating and how he would touch her there and say, "See? A perfect fit. God made that spot on your back so my hand would fit it perfectly. We were meant to be."*

*Her arm wraps around him and her other hand slides into his as they move across the floor, effortlessly twirling like seasoned partners that have danced this same routine for years and know it by heart.*

In those moments he could remember happiness, conjure it, make it so, make it real and of value. Those fantasy moments of dancing with this woman he so adored and who so adored him while the result of that loving union—their daughter—watched on, made their problems and terrors fade to nothing, leaving only their love and the power of their family, kept him moving and provided the strength and conviction he needed to stay alive. But those moments were fleeting and always left him too soon; escaping his senses like drifting tendrils of smoke, gone so completely they left little or nothing behind, phantoms vanished with a sigh or the blink of an eye…

*This time as they dance it begins to rain. Somehow the painted clouds turn black and rain falls across the dance floor in a slow but steady trickle, splashing about on the tables and snuffing out most of the candles.*

*Yet they remain oblivious to it all…until that spot on Cynthia's lower back, the spot where his hand has always fit so perfectly, begins to change, to move beneath his fingers.*

*Like another hand beneath her skin pushing to get out, stretching the skin and muscle in an effort to break free of her body, it squirms about beneath his touch with jerking, spasm-like movements, and from the periphery of his vision Darian sees more movement, the shifting, scurrying, ascending movement of small dark beings scaling the walls around them like fleeing insects.*

*They stop suddenly, turn and look at him in unison with their dead black eyes.*

*He has seen them…and they have seen him. They are not fleeing. They are preparing, organizing. It's a formation, a positioning for attack.*

*Debra's smile turns to sorrow, then to terror and agony.*

*The ballroom grows darker, and whispers swirl around them from unfamiliar voices speaking in alien and ancient tongues, but Darian and Cynthia continue to dance, the pressure in her back mounting, pushing against his palm. He tries to remove his hand but something within her grabs it, the hand beneath her skin holding him now as Cynthia's face contorts and her eyes look to him with confusion and horror.*

*Blood slowly drips from the corners of her eyes. She opens her mouth to speak but instead vomits blood. Hot, sticky and foul, it spatters Darian's face as the pressure in her back mounts, bubbles out as first flesh and then fabric rips in a gush of blood and fluid, leaving a raw cavity and the play of spidery fingers reaching at air.*

*Whatever thrashes about from within her skin finds his wrist with those blood-soaked fingers and yanks his hand back inside of her along with it. Darian struggles to break free but cannot, screaming now for it to stop, but the blood and rain have become one, falling down on him in great torrents, splashing against him, momentarily blinding him and filling his mouth until he gags and is certain his lungs will fill and drown in all the gore.*

*Cynthia's body goes limp but continues to jerk about, a lifeless being operated now by a demonic hand living inside her.*

*But their macabre dance continues, spinning them both without consent, two marionettes performing on a stage and unable to stop, twirling uncontrollably, their bodies moving so quickly they become a blur and Darian can no longer distinguish the room from the blood and rain. Debra and Cynthia's faces are swept into a single distorted and hideous image, as the whispers become growls and shrieks.*

*Debra – he is certain it is Debra – begins to scream.*

*Darian has heard these screams before – perhaps even from himself – though never from his daughter. But he hears them now. He hears them so clearly he knows he will never again be able to completely eradicate them from memory.*

*They are a part of him now. There, in the dark, amidst a*

*bloody rain.*

Darian remained in the car a while, parked across the street from their townhouse, watching and waiting, a cold sweat peppering his forehead. He blinked rapidly and shook his head until the hellish visions cleared. They could find him even in his private dreams and fantasies now. Find him and fuck him and destroy him.

*They show you things,* Louis had told him, bloody and perched in the window to his apartment, the sickness in him already in control, his friend already dead, already gone.

*Horrible fucking things.*

Cynthia's car was there, but if she and Debra were home, why hadn't they answered the phone when work had called looking for him? What were they doing in there?

*Have they shown you yet, Mother*?

Darian forced himself from the car.

*Game over, man.*

The snow was falling heavily now, accumulating quickly. Soon the entire city would be cloaked in white, buried in snow and ice and cold. If they were going to get out of there, away from the city, he'd have to convince them quickly.

*We're done.*

"Fuck you," he told the voices in his head. "Not me."

Gritting his teeth, Darian crossed the street and headed for the townhouse.

* * *

In the darkness of their room, as children they had laid next to each other, just feet apart, listening to the night and the rhythmic sound of each other's breathing. On the first night back from the sleep specialists, Raymond had said little. Their parents had thrown a small party of sorts, with Raymond's favorite foods for dinner and even a cake for dessert. They had all made an effort to make his homecoming a happy event, but Raymond was anything but festive. He returned home more removed and sullen than when he'd left, and on that first night, lying in their beds as they had hundreds of times before, Seth finally stopped listening to the questions filling his head and said, "It's OK if you don't want to talk about what happened there. You don't have to tell me." He propped himself up on an elbow so he could see his brother in the bed next to his own. "But if you want to you can, OK?"

"Thanks," Raymond whispered. "All I know is I just don't ever wanna go back, Seth. Not ever."

Seth leaned far enough out of bed so he could reach across the space separating them and muss Raymond's hair with his hand, a brotherly ritual he had often executed over the years that signaled he loved him and was there for him and had missed him.

Raymond responded with a restrained smile. Though just barely visible in the sparse moonlight, it was a smile as effortless as it was genuinely affectionate, and revealed in him an expression as close to peaceful contentment as Seth had ever seen in his little brother. For a few seconds, everything was right with the world, with their world and his world and all the noise in his head. Seth had never forgotten that smile, and though he knew it was something relegated only to memory, even all these years later he would've given anything to see it just once more.

Now Raymond sat just feet away from him again, this time in an upstairs bedroom Nana had taken them to and then excused herself from. Three tall windows overlooked the dunes and ocean, but with the snowfall there was not much to see but curtains of white flakes and a distant monochrome sky. Still, Raymond immediately took up position in a wide window seat and watched the snow with unusual intensity, seeing something more beyond the whiteout.

Seth stood in the center of the room feeling lost as ever. He wanted to leave as soon as possible, to get away from here and confront those things that needed confronting. But he also understood this could conceivably be the last time he saw his Nana and little brother, at least in this way, and in this world, and that possibility kept his feet firmly planted.

"Were you thinking about Mom and Dad?" Raymond asked without turning around.

"Yes."

"I always try to remember the last time I saw them alive. What we did and said; how we felt and what we all looked like then...but I can't. I can't ever remember any of that. Some days I have to think really hard just to remember their faces."

Seth nodded even though Raymond couldn't see it. "Me too."

"It's always made me sad," Raymond said softly. "I want to remember but some days I just can't. I remember the things I want to forget and forget the things I want to remember. What a bitch, huh?"

"Ray, I—I have to go soon."

"You can't win, man."

"Doesn't matter, I can't just lie down."

"Is that what you think I'm doing?"

"I didn't say that, I—"

"If you're going, go to Peggy. Be with her now."

"I will." He pushed visions of her away for the moment. "But is it Peggy I'll find, or something else?"

"Maybe she's wondering the same thing."

"Nothing's as it seems now, is it?"

"Never is." Raymond slowly turned, looked over his shoulder at him. "Never was."

"No, I guess not."

"They'll try to break you," he said suddenly, as if he had just remembered to tell him. "And if they can't, they'll try to make you think you're crazy. Maybe by then you will be, but don't listen to a fucking word they say. It's all illusion, a mind-fuck."

Seth nodded awkwardly, unsure of how to respond.

"I'm so fucking tired, Seth. Nobody should be this tired at thirty-one."

"You don't owe anybody anything, Ray. You don't deserve this. You never did."

A quick smile came and went, as if without his knowledge. He needed a shave and bags even darker than usual hung beneath his bloodshot eyes. "It's all fluid, all constant motion, that's what life is. Our bodies and brains are just energy surrounded by doors and windows, realities side by side and stacked one on top of the other. We know nothing, Seth. *Nothing*. People talk about other realities and the afterlife and all the things we don't understand like they're things out of children's books. They're not. The mysteries surrounding us are just that—mysteries—and they stay that way because we can't even begin to understand any of it. We're not wired to. We don't have the ability to. But it *is* human nature to try, isn't it? To try and to fail, because it's a shell game on a street corner, man. People want everything explained and tied up with perfect pretty ribbons, but it's not like that. It's so far beyond our ability to comprehend it's like an ant trying to grasp calculus."

Seth felt numb. His brother laughed lightly, and at that moment, appeared to be completely out of his mind and as lucid as he'd ever been all at once.

"That's why we have faith," Raymond said. "It fills in the gaps, counters nihilism, but the enlightenment people look for never amounts to much of anything because they expect human explanations given from human perspectives and carried out with human comprehension. They're just running blind. They forget... the Devil ain't human."

"Neither is God."

Raymond returned his gaze to the endless white swirling beyond the windows. "You're the one who says you lost your faith, Seth, not me."

"How could you still have faith?" Seth felt anger rising from deep within him, the same kind of anger he'd felt when their parents were killed in a seemingly meaningless accident, and when his once innocent little brother had been taken from him by whatever dark demons now haunted them both. "Faith in *what*? God turned His back on you and left you to rot here with the rest of us. He does nothing to help us, so what good is He? Tell me, what good is He, Ray? What good has He been for you?"

"Human explanations, that's what you want."

"Yes, that's exactly what I want. He made us human, didn't He? And as far as I know I'm still a human being."

"For now, though that's never been anything to brag about far as I'm concerned."

Quiet fell over the room, leaving only the sound of snow ticking against the windows.

"When we were little," Raymond said a moment later, "and in our room in the dark, sometimes even when nothing happened I'd be afraid. It was like knowing there really *was* a monster in our closet, and that it was only a matter time before it came to get us, so even in the quiet, I was afraid a lot of the time. Most nights I never said anything to you, and you never said anything to me, remember? You didn't do anything, you were just there. I knew you were there, and that was enough."

"Well I'm sorry, but I expect a bit more from God than His simply being there."

"And who the hell are you to expect anything from *God*? Can you even hear yourself? You expect more from God. Shouldn't it be the other way around?"

"I don't know, you tell me."

"There's sickness everywhere, spilling over. It's a plague now."

"How do I stop this, Raymond?"

"You don't."

"But I— "

"You *don't*." He stood up, touched the glass pane in the window with his fingertips. "They'll take you places, Seth. You'll see things they want you to see, awful things. And you won't be able to look away.

Time and space—reality—it's all different with them. They know how to control it, to bend it. We're just game pieces."

Seth wanted to reach out and touch his brother, to hug him and tell him he loved him and that everything would be all right. But such things seemed pointless now.

"I need to sleep. I'm so tired." Raymond shrugged, laughing a bit, perhaps at what he'd said, perhaps at the snowflakes dancing beyond the windows. "Sometimes I think maybe that's all any of this really is. Maybe we're still just two scared little kids in the dark late at night, watching shadows and moonbeams and imagining what our lives might be like when we grow up...*if* we grow up."

"Wouldn't we imagine something better?"

"Nobody ever imagines anything better in the dark, Seth. There's only hope in daydreams, never in nightmares."

"I'll see you again, Ray." Seth moved closer. "Won't I?"

Raymond looked at him sadly. "Go do what you got to do."

Seth took the final step separating him from Raymond, put his arms around him and told his brother he loved him.

Even before he'd let him go, perhaps for the last time, Seth knew he'd been wrong.

Such things were never pointless.

* * *

The front door was unlocked, which was unusual. Though this was a good neighborhood with little crime to speak of, one rarely left one's door unlocked in the suburbs these days, much less the city.

He pushed the door open enough for him to see inside before crossing the threshold.

The house was quiet, the front hall and living room empty. "Cynthia?" he called. Silence answered. Darian stepped inside, reached behind him for the door then slowly pushed it closed as he moved cautiously into the den. "Cyn?" he called again. "Are you here?"

He walked down the short front hall to the foot of the stairs and looked up at the landing above. Darkness concealed most of the area beyond the last few steps, and though he hesitated a moment to listen, none of the normal sounds associated with their home answered. The television in the den was off, the stereo was off; the entire place was draped in a silence indicative of no one being home. Yet Cynthia's car was out there. Could she have gone for a walk? She enjoyed walking around the city, but rarely during winter months.

As he began to slowly climb the staircase, eyes trained on the darkness beyond the landing, he wondered if perhaps she'd gone off with one of her friends or business associates and they had taken their car instead of Cynthia's. Yes, he thought, that must be it. She just isn't home. She's gone off to…to do what? He'd been gone overnight and she decided to go out for lunch with a friend? It made no sense.

Then he thought of his parents. She might've gone with them somewhere. It would be just like his father to insist upon driving so—

An odd sound interrupted him. Darian froze on the stairs, about halfway up, and strained to listen.

A wet sound, water or fluid of some kind splashing about, like a large sponge being wrung out into a bucket of soapy water. Yes, that was it. That was the sound exactly. He listened a moment longer. The sound was coming from the end of the hall upstairs. From their bedroom, or perhaps Debra's, but the sound was definitely emanating from one of the two bedrooms, no question about it.

There's someone in the house, he thought. Someone in the bedroom but...

He drew a slow breath, wrestled his nerves into some semblance of control then grabbed the rail and leaned forward a bit, hoping to hear more. He was still only about halfway up the stairs. Darian looked back in the direction from which he'd come. The front door was still relatively close. If need be, he could turn and run back down the stairs and straight out of the house if...if what? Goddamn it, stop being so frightened of everything, he told himself. Stop being such a pussy. Get a grip.

"This is *my* fucking house," he muttered, unaware that he'd said it aloud until he heard the sound of his voice. "Cynthia?" he called out, much louder than he had twice before. "Are you up here?"

"Dar?"

His heart slowed and he let out a long sigh of relief. "Yeah, it's—it's me."

"Come on up, I'm in the bedroom cleaning."

He climbed the remainder of stairs and was already nearing their bedroom when it occurred to him that her response had been anything but usual. She should've been furious over his being out all night. She'd have come running the moment she heard him, if only to make certain he was all right and to then demand an explanation.

And what could she possibly be cleaning in their bedroom by slopping around in a bucket of soapy water?

Darian stopped again. Framed pictures of he and Cynthia and Debra stared at him from both walls of the hallway, their history together frozen in time and sitting in judgment over him, detached spectators watching to see what he might do next.

He moved slowly down the dim hallway, stopping long enough to glance into Debra's bedroom. Nothing out of the ordinary there, everything in place just as it always was, just as it should be.

A wave of cold swept through him. It was decidedly colder here, upstairs. He shivered but kept on, doing his best to ignore it. Darian had been perpetually cold since that night in the forest a year before. Even in the dead of summer he'd been chilly most of the time.

Three more steps and he'd be at their bedroom doorway.

Again, but for the sounds of water splashing in a bucket, silence overtook the house.

* * *

Nana emerged from the bathroom just as Seth was nearing the end of the hallway. He stopped, looked back at her. "Are you all right?"

With a quick, nearly dismissive nod, she joined him at the top of the stairs. "Is Raymond—"

"In the window seat watching the snow," he told her. "And whatever else he sees out there."

She gazed into his eyes knowingly. "You could stay with us."

"I can't, I—you know I can't Nana."

She took his hand and together they descended the stairs to the landing below. The old house was quiet, but Seth could barely make out the sounds of a television newscast coming from somewhere nearby, probably Rolf's study. A reporter's voice was describing something about a violent incident in a town near Boston.

Nana realized he'd heard it and said, "It's been all over the news today. A man in Dedham murdered his entire family with an ax then put a gun to his head and pulled the trigger. That was this morning. This afternoon a woman walked into a restaurant in Revere and slit her throat from ear to ear in the middle of the dining area. They say she was crazy, heard voices in her head, saw things. She'd told some friends apparently, and they'd begged her to get help. She didn't and this was the result…or so they tell us."

Seth ran his hands through his hair. "How can this really be happening?"

"They talk of wolves, these people on television," she said softly, as if she hadn't heard him. "The politicians and the clergy and these so-called journalists, all those we've been raised to believe we should trust. They use it as metaphor, of course, with their usual flair for mistakenly thinking themselves clever. They talk of wolves that will tear us apart and destroy us, and yet, those posting the warnings are themselves wolves. Who will protect us from *them*? They speak of individuality and freedom, the power of the individual, and yet, should a true individual ever emerge, he or she is systematically discredited, made the fool, dismissed and disenfranchised from the alleged mainstream. So true individualism isn't really celebrated or even desired in our world, is it? It's a disingenuous fairy tale ideal, told to people who themselves will never be individuals; a distant dream they can imagine happening somewhere else to someone else. A Shangri-La that never was and never will be anything but a broken promise and a concept that once put into the real world can never truly be allowed to exist, much less flourish, because God help us all it might just work. No, fall in line. That's the order of our day. Follow, obey, be the same—the same ideals, the same beliefs, the same approach, the same religion—the same, always the same, nothing varied or out of step, rather a uniform world where one is either a cooperative slave to the state or its sworn enemy, with no middle ground existing between the two. Conform, play the game, do it the way everyone else does, don't vary, stick to the program, be a member of the team. Free thought, diverse thought becomes traitorous thought. Thoughtful dissent becomes a campaign of terror, violence and servitude to some faceless, vague antichrist. They talk of wolves, these antichrists who claim to protect us from evil. And we follow, Seth. We follow. Heads nodding, guns blazing and flags waving. Bigotry, ignorance and hatred disguised as mindless patriotism, nationalism and a supposed spiritualism as corrupt as the horror it spawns and the truths it will stop at nothing to conceal and destroy. Death, destruction, greed, hatred and fear—always the fear—because none of it can exist or grow without fear, the fuel that keeps the wheels turning and the machine alive."

Seth nodded gravely. "These are dark days, Nana."

"They're all dark days, my love. It's why we cling to those moments of joy and bliss so desperately, because joy is many things, but rarely abundant. Those exceptional glimpses and fleeting sensations of wonder, love, clarity, joy and freedom—*real* freedom—are so powerful precisely because they're so scarce. And it's been this way for a long time. This is nothing new, this darkness. It's only more out into the light now than before, more legitimate in appearance somehow, which in itself makes it even more repugnant and evil. We've hurtled toward this place and time for hundreds of years, and we're finally reaching our destination, our end not in a final scream of fury but in a bored, apathetic, inconvenienced sigh."

Seth paced about, wringing his hands as they had begun to tingle and fall asleep. He felt lightheaded and even more exhausted than before suddenly. "Is it some kind of invasion? Little green men in spaceships? Demons, angels, what?"

"No one above the age of four or five with a fully functional brain and even the sparsest ability to understand the laws of physics truly believe in little green men and spaceships from other planets flying about in our skies, do they?" Nana reached out and gently took his wrist to stop his pacing the way one might grab hold of a jittery child. "This is no invasion, Seth. They're already here, and have been for thousands of years. I believe they were here long before we were and will continue to be long after our kind is gone. We serve a purpose and that purpose is ending, changing, becoming a purpose of theirs rather than ours, because ours makes no sense and has no bearing, no eventual resolution, just an unending caravan of greed and arrogance."

"And their purpose is better somehow?"

"Not to us. But as their purpose becomes ours, our metamorphosis begins. Think of it as emerging from a dark chrysalis, we become something else, a new and darker version of ourselves better equipped to survive in a new and darker version of the world. The susceptibility of human beings to the very real presence and power of evil is nothing new, but there's always been a saving grace, a return to our senses even at the very brink of self-destruction that has always rescued us. Now the darkness has found another of our weaknesses, and in exploiting it succeeds, as the growing oppression and tyranny it so desperately seeks to control us with, rises. And it is in succumbing to that weakness that our true nature emerges, both good and bad. More worker ants are born but so are more rebels, prophets and saviors, because in the end there are no monsters, Seth, only varied versions of ourselves. In the end butterflies are still caterpillars, but were the process reversed, if the beautiful butterfly became the caterpillar rather than the other way around, the difference would be more than simple aesthetics, wouldn't it? In the end it would be more profound than that."

Seth took her face in his hands, leaned in and kissed her on the cheek. "You've always known this was coming, haven't you? It's why you've lived your life the way you have."

"I suppose it was selfish, but I'd always secretly

hoped I might pass away before this all began. Yes, I knew. I knew because Raymond told me."

"And you believed him."

"Even though you wish you didn't, and every fiber in your logical being tells you not to, don't *you*?"

Seth dropped his eyes to the floor.

"Raymond's a prophet, Seth. I've known it since he was a young child." She took his hands in hers, held them down between them. "We've all known it, even you."

"And if you're wrong?"

"I'm not wrong."

"But if you are, Nana. What then?"

"Then we're all just frightened children hiding under our covers at night." Her hands gripped his a bit tighter. "And sooner or later, despite how hard we may fight it, we'll all eventually drift off to sleep and let night take us. All of us, Seth...*all* of us."

# Chapter 26

By the time Seth had returned to the streets of Boston most of the day was gone. Though it was still light out the early darkness of winter was on its way, and the sky had turned a deep and vast gray. The snow covering the city was fluffy and full, the flakes plump and tumbling from the sky with exquisite beauty. He'd once loved the snow and all its grandeur, but that was before the night at the cabin. Now it just made him uncomfortable. It didn't frighten him, as Darian had admitted, not exactly, but produced in him an uneasy feeling more akin to sorrow and doom.

He rolled to a stop at a red light not far from the office. A smattering of lights had already come on inside many of the buildings a bit prematurely, and people were bustling about on foot and by car in an attempt to either get home or out of the city before the storm got too out of hand.

Seth barely paid attention to the tail end of a weather forecast on the radio as his mind changed gears in anticipation of his meeting with Bill Jacobs and whatever the hell he wanted. He switched the radio off and looked out the window a moment at a newsstand he'd patronized countless times over the years. The same grizzled old man who always worked there was huddled near the corner of the stand clad in a badly worn knit hat and a coat easily as ancient as he was. He held a steaming Styrofoam cup of coffee in both hands and was gnawing away on the customary already chewed, unlit cigar stub jammed into the corner of his mouth. He looked miserable in the snow and cold. But then, the old man at the newsstand always looked miserable, and at that moment, even such seemingly blasé familiarity and normalcy was comforting.

With no idea who he could trust or what exactly he needed to do next, Seth took a few seconds to ponder the Bill Jacobs situation. Should he even go? Maybe the smarter move was to go get Peggy and just get the hell away from there for a while. What could Jacobs possibly have to tell him that he'd be interested in hearing now anyway?

Then again, he needed to see what was happening at work. Maybe he'd find things different there too, changed and oddly menacing, or maybe he'd find a safe haven instead. Maybe he'd find some answers there.

And what about Ruthie, he wondered, what about her phone call?

His mind was overloading, exhausted and beginning to shut down.

The blare of a horn behind him snapped Seth back into the moment. He waved an apology into the rearview mirror at the cab behind him and drove through the now green light, heading toward the Park

Plaza Hotel. Severance was only a few blocks away.

He slowed for a cluster of jaywalkers half a block later, coming to a slow creep so they could cross the street before he reached them. He looked at everyone differently now, with suspicion and uncertainty and—

Something on the edge of his peripheral vision caught his attention. He glanced to the sidewalk on his left. A figure moved through the falling snow, a figure that stood out from those around it, and as Seth focused it quickly became more defined.

A woman in a long and expensive black wool coat and black leather boots walked along the crowded sidewalk with a particularly confident and purposeful stride. On her head was a black beret, her thick blonde hair sticking out from either side of it hanging just a few inches from her shoulders and bouncing in time with each step she took.

Horns blared behind him again, but Seth sat frozen, watching her.

"Doc?" he muttered, astonished.

One car roared around him while two others behind him continued to lay on their horns. Seth pulled as far over to the left as possible but kept the car at a slow roll so he could keep the woman in sight. He drove a bit ahead of her to the first available space on the next block and took it. She was still a bit behind him, though she seemed intent on getting to wherever she was going relatively quickly. He stared at her as she drew nearer.

She stopped on the corner to let a car pass, and her face came into full view. Even from this distance and through the thick snow he was certain it was her. There was something missing, though, something not quite right. Her eyeglasses—the turtle shell eyeglasses—she wasn't wearing them. But it had to be her. Strange, he thought, he'd never seen her outside her office, and there was something odd about it, the way seeing a teacher outside of a school setting when he was a child always seemed strange. Still, it *was* her, he was sure of it.

But she was supposed to be in the Cayman Islands for another week, why would she be back already? Had something brought her back? Could she know what was happening? If she did, could he trust her?

He quickly dialed her service on his cell. On the second ring a woman with a bored tone answered: "Farrow and Associates."

"Yes, hello," Seth said, "is Doctor Farrow in by any chance?"

"I'm sorry, she's not. This is the answering service."

"I'm a patient of Doctor Farrow's." Seth stepped from the car and dug in his pocket for change to feed the meter, craning to keep an eye on the woman as she continued on along the street. "I was hoping maybe I could speak with her."

There was a slight hesitation, and then: "I'm sorry, but Doctor Farrow is out of town. She's out of the country, actually."

"Yes," he said, doing his best to feign sincerity, "I knew she had gone to the Caymans on vacation, I just couldn't remember if she'd gone for one week or two."

"Doctor Farrow will be back the week after next, sir, but if you have an emergency or need to speak with someone I can page Doctor Kowalski for you, he's covering Doctor Farrow's patients while she's away,

Mister…"

"No that's fine, no emergency, thank you." He snapped the phone shut, dropped some change in the meter and moved quickly down the street in an effort to close the gap between them before she got too far ahead of him.

Why was she lying? If she wanted to duck her patients and not be disturbed she didn't have to lie about leaving the country. Or did they really believe she *was* in the Cayman Islands? Did she want everyone to think she was, and if so, why?

Seth checked his watch. There was still plenty of time to see where she was going and to make it to Severance before five. He wasn't certain why he felt so compelled to follow her, but something was drawing him to her. Though her office wasn't far from there, she was out of place on the street, going somewhere or up to something, and deep in his gut, an instinctual urgency told him he needed to follow her and see for himself.

* * *

When Darian was a step or two from the bedroom he noticed what looked decidedly like smoke wafting about the hallway directly in front of him. But it was too fleeting to be smoke, too thin and wispy. It wasn't until he was standing fully in the doorway that he realized the smoke was his own breath hitting the cold air.

The bedroom windows were open all the way, the curtains billowing, and on the floor next to the bed, on hands and knees, was Cynthia scrubbing the hardwood floor with a large sponge. Next to her sat a plastic bucket of soapy water.

The walls were streaked and wet where she'd run the sponge along the paint, smudging whatever had been there into dark splotches. But he had gotten there before she could finish with the floor, or adequately disguise what she was cleaning there: blood smeared into large letters that formed three words finger-painted just beyond the foot of their bed.

*Let Them Out.*

Cynthia was dressed only in panties and a snug t-shirt, both of which were spattered with small bloodstains faded a bland pinkish color, most likely diluted by the splashing water. She looked back over her shoulder at him casually. "I'm almost done."

Darian felt his bowels clench and nausea rip through him from the pit of his stomach clear to the bottom of his throat. "Where's Debra?" he asked, voice trembling.

"It's OK." Cynthia resumed her scrubbing. "Everything's going to be all right."

His hands tightened into fists. "*Where* is my daughter?"

"You don't understand," she said smoothly. The sponge dropped into the bucket with a loud plopping sound, splashing water over the edges and onto the floor. "Something's happening…something extraordinary…something amazing."

It was so cold in there, so cold and dead. Darian felt things watching them.

"You don't have to fight it anymore," Cynthia said. She slowly rose to her feet and faced him. The wounds on her arms and thighs now evident, and the large kitchen knife she had used to inflict them tossed onto the nearby bed. "You're remembering. It's all right to remember now, Darian. It's all right."

He brought his hands to either side of his head. "This is *not* happening!"

"That's right." Cynthia smiled, but it was as counterfeit as the rest of her. "It's all in your mind."

"Where is she?" Darian took a step toward her, a rage building in him he was not certain he could control much longer, while memories of the night at the cabin returned to him in a rush, more vivid and exact than he'd ever known or remembered before. Razors of pain fired through his temples and across his eyes in one direction and down along his jaw and into his shoulders in the other. It felt like his head was being slashed to pieces from the inside out. "Where's Debra!"

Cynthia's eyes shifted, looked beyond him. Her smile faded.

From behind him a small voice said, "Hi, Daddy."

* * *

After following Doctor Farrow for a few blocks, Seth found himself in the theater district and heading in the general direction of Chinatown. He stuffed his hands deep into his coat pockets, tucked chin to chest and quickened his pace. For a woman of average height Farrow walked with an unusually long stride and moved so briskly she was nearly at a slow run, but wherever she was going, it seemed she had no doubt of her eventual destination. She looked as if she'd walked this exact route many times before, and though the neighborhood was getting worse with each step, from what Seth could see she seemed completely at ease.

Before reaching Chinatown she crossed the street and headed down into a small area near the outskirts of the theater district. Seth stepped off the curb, careful to avoid a car that darted in front of him, splashing up some slush from the gutter across his shins. He ignored the wet and cold seeping through his pants and socks and into his shoes and remained focused on Doctor Farrow, who slipped into a narrow side street, the focal point of which was an old rundown tenement that had apparently been turned into a church or revival house of some kind. An enormous red neon cross on the face of the building served to light up the otherwise dim street.

As Seth started after her, he slowed his pace, careful not to get too close now. The street was deserted and garbage-strewn and quite short, and at the far end was a vacant lot covered with piles of bricks and debris where a building or buildings had recently been demolished. Across from the building with the cross was an equally old tenement, but this one vacant and boarded shut. But for a few street people sitting on the steps and huddled in the dull neon glow emanating from across the street, the area was void of people.

Doctor Farrow disappeared into the open front door of the building without once looking back or slowing her stride. The men across the street noticed her but seemed to take little interest, which struck Seth as odd, since she was even more out of place in this area than he was, and since it was clear they had not only noticed him, but were paying particular attention to his presence.

The muffled sounds of a live choir singing with the

accompaniment of a slightly out of tune piano bled into the open air from somewhere deep inside the building, and an array of smells ranging from soup to body odor to urine wafted about, some from within the building, some from the street. Seth gazed up at the huge cross. A small scarred sign at its base and just above the front door read: *Savior House*.

Seth could feel eyes following him as he walked closer to the steps. He looked back over his shoulder at the men across the street. They stared back.

He turned away, and against his better judgment, slowly entered the building.

# Chapter 27

Seth moved through the open doorway Doctor Farrow had crossed just seconds before and was met by a short hallway. It was a bit warmer than the street, though not by much.

There was nowhere to go but straight, so he followed the hall until he'd reached a room to the left. Several tables were scattered about in a cafeteria style setting, with a series of long tables set along one wall like a makeshift buffet. Through a cutout at the rear of the room, Seth could see a small kitchen area, where an older Hispanic man in a white apron stood stirring a huge pot of soup. The man didn't notice him, so Seth continued on.

What would Doctor Farrow be doing here? Had she come to see a patient, or did she volunteer here perhaps, counseling the homeless and downtrodden on her free time? But why the lies about the Cayman Islands, and why was she walking by herself in an area like this? Why not drive or take a cab?

The deeper into the building he ventured the louder

the choir became.

At the next open door he stopped and saw a large function room with a stage and several chairs set up into a makeshift church setting. A robed, multiracial choir consisting of both men and women was onstage, and an older woman who also seemed to be directing them played a nearby piano. They all seemed consumed with happiness.

Seth quickly looked from one end of the room to the other, but Doctor Farrow was nowhere in sight.

He kept moving through the building until he came across two closed doors. He stopped and listened at both, but the rooms beyond were still and quiet. A staircase to his right lead to a second floor but was cordoned off with yellow police tape. Seth hesitated to inspect the tape a bit more closely. It looked quite old, as if whatever crime scene it had once served to secure had taken place many years before but the tape had never been removed. Odd, he thought. Why would…

Seth craned his neck to try and see up the stairs but it was dark and seemed unoccupied, at least at the moment. Besides, the tape was arranged in a way that would make it highly unlikely Doctor Farrow would or even could climb over it without disturbing it. So she hadn't gone that way.

Through to the end of the hallway was another door. Seth turned the knob and opened it into an extremely narrow outside alleyway. Beyond it was a small section of ground and the back of another large building, the alleyway separated from it by a tall, severely tattered chain link fence.

Somewhere nearby but out of sight an angry dog barked and snarled.

Seth looked down the alleyway. It led to another small building next to the church. Behind him the hallway remained empty. He closed the door and stepped down into the constricted alleyway, careful not to catch his coat on the rusted fence.

What the hell am I doing? What am I doing here? Seth shook his head and pushed on, ignoring his fears. He'd come this far, he had to see it through.

At the end of the alleyway he walked into an open area and approached the doorway to the other building. Whatever door had once been there was long gone, leaving only an open and rotting doorway. It was quiet inside, no choirs or pianos, and though there were some pungent smells few could be attributed to a soup kitchen. Though two stories, the building was significantly smaller than the one which housed the church, and even more rundown and unkempt, clearly abandoned.

What in God's name was Doctor Farrow doing in such a place?

Seth stepped cautiously into a foyer of sorts, the ceiling low and the floor covered in aged, stained and cracked linoleum. It was darker here, as most of the windows in the room beyond had been blacked out or boarded over, and only those that had been broken clean through allowed for any outside light. He squinted through the near-dark, trying to gain his bearings, and he noticed a slight trace of light at the far end of the otherwise dark room just beyond the foyer. But this light was different than the small bit leaking from broken windows. It was less pronounced and...was it *moving*?

Candlelight, it—was it candlelight?

From the darkness to his right came a disturbing noise that sounded like labored breath. He spun quickly in that direction and saw a dark figure sitting on an old bench against the wall. "Jesus Christ!" He staggered back a few steps and nearly lost his balance. As his eyes focused and adjusted to the sparse light he realized there was a woman sitting there. She had to be well into her nineties and was dressed as if in mourning—entirely in black—including a kerchief that covered her head and tied beneath her chin. At her feet was a small chipped basin and a scrub brush, but she looked so old and frail surely her days of scrubbing floors were well behind her. "I'm sorry, I didn't see you there," he said, deliberately keeping the volume of his voice low. "You startled me; I wasn't expecting anyone to be sitting there."

He attempted a quiet bit of nervous laughter but the woman simply looked at him as if she were not quite sure what she was looking at. Even in meager light Seth could see the network of deep spidery lines traversing her face and neck. There was a palpable sorrow to her, but despite the cold temperature her body remained eerily rigid and still. She wheezed with each breath she drew or expelled, and she held something in her arthritically gnarled hands he couldn't quite make out.

"Ma'am?" he asked, heart still racing. "Are you all right?"

She continued to stare at him, her eyes dull and covered in milky cataracts.

"I'm looking for someone," he told her.

No response, no reaction.

"A woman just came in here a minute ago, a

woman with blonde hair and a black beret. Where did she go? Ma'am, can you tell me which way she went?"

Very subtly, the old woman's eyes shifted to the dark room then back to him.

Seth looked to the room and the odd light flickering deep within. He forced a swallow and felt a current of terror surge through him. His hands were so cold they were growing numb. "Is there anyone else here?" he asked. When the woman didn't answer he turned back to her. "In the building, ma'am, is there anyone else here?"

This time her eyes looked up to indicate the floor above them.

"Who are you?" he asked, moving closer to her. "Why are you here?"

The woman stared at him.

"You need to get to where there's some heat. You'll freeze to death if you stay here after dark. You'll die, do you understand?"

Her mouth slowly curled into a toothless grin.

"What the hell is this place?" Seth backed away. "What are you doing here?"

The woman's smile faded, and her dead stare returned. Her hands moved about slowly in her lap, tinkering with whatever they were holding, but he still couldn't quite see what it was.

In the distance the faint sounds of the choir could just barely be heard, but they seemed so far away now, so very far away.

The woman watched Seth without comment as he searched the foyer quickly for anything of use he could find.

Just inside the door, amidst a pile of debris, junk

and scraps of metal and wood, he noticed a small length of old pipe. He bent down and carefully pulled it free of the pile, feeling the weight of it in his hand. If necessary it would make a passable weapon.

With the sound of his own frightened breathing ringing in his ears, he glanced at the old woman a final time then walked into the dark room, heading directly for the flickering light at its far end.

* * *

In an instant, Darian's entire life with his daughter flashed before his eyes. Every vision of her, every moment he'd ever spent with her from the moment he saw her born to the present exploded across his mind in one whirlwind of panic and terror.

He spun around and saw Debra standing behind him, so small and innocent, so pure. "Baby," he said, collapsing to his knees before her, hands reaching for her tiny body, "are you all right?"

Debra nodded calmly, her focus solely on her father, as if all that was going on behind him with Cynthia no longer existed, as if they were the only two in the room, in the entire universe. "Don't be mad, Daddy," she said quietly.

"I'm not mad, sweetheart." He touched her shoulders, expecting her to react as she always had, by nearly throwing herself into his arms in a loving hug. But instead she stood curiously taut, arms at her sides. "Are you all right?" She nodded with a look of confusion. Darian's eyes inspected her frantically, but she seemed physically unharmed. He looked back over his shoulder at Cynthia. She hadn't moved but was watching him intently. He turned back to his daughter. "Don't be frightened. Mommy's not feeling well. I want you to go to your room for me and wait for me there, all right? I'll be right there, I promise."

Debra looked past him to her mother.

He tightened his grip on her shoulders until her eyes returned to his. "Debra, I need you to do exactly as I say now, do you understand? Go to your room and I'll be right there."

"But I need to tell you something, Daddy."

"You can tell me in a minute, right now I want you to—"

"I need to tell you something now, Daddy, *right* now." She leaned in close to his ear so only he might hear. *"Let Them Out."*

Darian fell back, scrambling to get away from her while also attempting to regain his feet in one frenzied motion.

Cynthia grinned at him, standing there in her underwear.

"What did you do to her?" Darian moved toward her. "What have you done to her? If you've harmed one hair on her head I swear to God I'll kill you. You hear me? I'll fucking kill you."

The sound of furious movement behind him stole his attention. He turned in time to see his daughter—or something like his daughter perhaps, something that had once been his daughter—shaking about like she was being throttled by some invisible force. With movements inhumanly fast and spasmodic, she jerked about as if electrocuted, her small body jolting about with such speed she became blurred.

Cynthia began to laugh. It was a hollow, lifeless

sound.

Debra grew still. Blood leaked from the corners of her eyes and something moved beneath her skin, crawling along her throat and across the side of her face as she broke into a wide smile, laughing with her mother now.

Small dark things joined them. On the walls…in the doorway…from the closet and beneath the bed…scurrying across the ceiling and gawking at them through the open windows.

Horrible pains fired through his temples, and the night at the cabin came to Darian at once, no longer in flashes and pieces but in one tremendous flowing wave where sight and sound and sensation blended into a single ghostly memory. And all he had been unable to remember for so long, he suddenly remembered.

The others watched as Cynthia and Debra moved closer, grinning and circling him the way lions size up wounded prey.

Darian dropped to his knees, hands desperately clutching either side of his head as the pain became too much to bear.

Something blurred his vision. Blood or tears—perhaps both—he couldn't be sure which. The only thing Darian Stone could still be completely certain of was that his mind was ripping apart and that something was trying desperately to crawl inside of what was left of it, something ancient and deadly and alien, something that brought with it the winds of time and space, something that wanted to coil there and nest in his warm blood, in his memories and dreams and fears.

He closed his eyes; saw Louis falling out the window of his apartment.

And then he felt their hands all over him—their repulsive inhuman hands—and a thousand whispering voices screeching in his head.

*Let Them Out*, the voices told him. *Let Them Out.*

And finally, screaming in furious agony, he did.

* * *

Seth crossed the dark room carefully but quickly. Debris scattered about everywhere made it tough going, and though he lost his balance more than once as he made his way toward the flickering light, he managed to reach it without falling.

Sounds of the city had all but vanished, relegated to distant hums overpowered by faint whistles of wind passing through various openings in the building.

The light was not a candle, rather a small hurricane lamp sitting atop an old crate. Seth approached it cautiously, searching the small area the light provided.

A middle-aged man sat on the floor, his legs out straight in front of him and his back against the wall. His hands sat in his lap lifelessly. He looked as if he'd been dropped there from some great height and seemed too weak and disoriented to pose a threat. Obviously homeless, he was filthy, dressed in tattered clothes and had several days growth of salt and pepper beard. He saw Seth but didn't seem terribly interested in him. Beyond the crate and lamp was a staircase leading up into the darkness of the second floor. Checking first to make certain the stairs were clear, Seth crouched before the man. Up close he looked even more unhealthy and lethargic.

"Are you all right?" Seth asked quietly.

"Sick," the man said in a gravely voice. "We're all sick."

"What is this place?"

"Don't nobody use the building but us. Sometimes the church and shelter next door gets full—no more beds—so we stay here. Sucks, but it's better than outside." He looked at Seth listlessly. "Nice coat you got on."

Seth again glanced at the stairs. He could hear occasional muffled voices seeping down through the darkness from the second floor. "The woman that just came through here," he said, "did she go up there?"

The man nodded.

"How many others are up there with her?"

"I don't know, maybe four, five. Looks warm, that coat."

"Do you know who they are?"

"Just guys like me. Always some new guys passing through, staying here to beat the cold. Tough times, chief. Lots of homeless in the city, but that's changing. It's *all* changing now."

"What's the woman doing up there?"

The man shrugged. "Same as always."

His answer stopped Seth in mid-thought. "She's been here before, the woman?"

"Couple times I know of."

"For what—why?"

"The sickness." He coughed and spat a ball of phlegm to the floor. "We're all sick."

Seth's head was spinning. "She counsels you, helps you with your sickness? *Here*?"

"Got to get sick before you can get better." He gave a tired sigh. "She spreads it like the rest of them, makes us sick. Then we get better."

Seth stood up, his entire body trembling. He tightened his grip on the pipe.

"But you already knew that." The man's bloodshot eyes glistened in the dancing lamplight. "'Cause you got it in you too, chief."

Seth backed away from him as a pain shot through his temple, bringing with it flashes of memory.

*He is on his knees in a clearing ringed by a thick forest of enormous trees.*

The pain disappeared faster than it struck, leaving more memories in its blurry wake.

*Snow blows about like dust, but just above the treetops, through the darkness and swirl of flakes, he makes out a section of cobalt sky.*

"You're still sick, though," the man said softly. "I can tell. It's bleeding out of you."

*Breath surges in thick clouds from his nostrils and open mouth.*

"I died here once," the man told him. "In this place."

*His chest rises and falls, lungs sore from the cold and straining for more oxygen.*

"Where'd you die, chief?"

Seth defiantly turned away and started up the stairs. Hugging the wall, he moved as quietly as possible until he eventually neared the second floor landing.

*Screams hemorrhage the silence; explode through the trees surrounding him in squealing waves of agony and terror.*

Trying to clear his head, Seth hunched low and squinted through the darkness to a large open area where two more lamps had been lighted and left on the floor. But for a small circle of eerie light provided by the lamps, the room was draped in pitch-black.

*Sounds of skin splitting and clothes tearing trail the screams still echoing through his mind, screams from familiar voices...and...and Christy...visions of Christy running through the snow ahead of him...and the blood – so much blood – blood in the snow and those horrible sounds of suffering...*

The memories of that night dissolved but lingered in his mind, hanging on now and drawing him back, deeper each time.

As his head cleared he saw Doctor Farrow standing in the pool of light.

From his position on the stairs Seth was closer to her than he'd been the entire time, even closer than when he'd first spotted her on the street, and whatever vague uncertainties he may have harbored to that point vanished instantly.

There was no question. The woman was Connie Farrow.

If she knew Seth had followed her she gave no indication. In fact, she seemed preoccupied, her expression one of deliberate contemplation coupled with her usual smug air of superiority.

She removed her beret, slipped it into her coat pocket, then despite the cold, opened her coat, pulled it off over her shoulders and let it fall to the floor.

But for the knee-high black boots, she was dressed as she might have been at her office, in an attractive sheer silk blouse and a black skirt. Without her coat she should've been freezing, but instead seemed unaffected and completely in control.

## Deep Night

As shadows crept from the darkness surrounding her, skulking closer toward the pool of light, she turned to them, smiled, and slowly began to unbutton her blouse.

# Chapter 28

The shadows closing on her from the darkness became men, filthy and scarred and dressed in threadbare clothing. They reached for her with grimy hands, their faces eager, eyes wild and ravenous and looking as if they could hardly believe this beautiful woman was there for the taking.

One man circled behind her, pulled her blouse back off her shoulders and down to her wrists, pinning her arms back behind her in the process. But Doctor Farrow gave no indication of fear or resistance. Instead she laughed seductively, threw her head back and leaned into the man while the others in front of her ran their hands over her body greedily, jockeying for position with one another.

Her bra was torn free and thrown aside, and another man began fumbling with her skirt, at first attempting to pull it off but then opting to simply hoist it up over her buttocks until it was a tangled mess around her waist.

"Get her on the floor," one man said as he opened his pants.

While one ripped a gold necklace from her throat and stuffed it in his pocket, a third man violently yanked her panties down and off over her boots. The man behind her pushed a knee into the backs of her legs, collapsing her.

She sunk to the floor with him, lying on top of him as he held her, arms still pinned behind her back. Two men each took one of Doctor Farrow's legs, holding them up and open as the lead man, now fully erect, fell across her.

Seth sat in the darkness on the stairs, unable to fully process what he was seeing. He contemplated helping her, stopping this, but not only was she not resisting, she was clearly enjoying it.

The man on top of her slammed into her repeatedly, his guttural laughter quickly turned to moans of ecstasy. The men released her legs as it no longer seemed necessary to hold her, and one dropped his pants and straddled her face while the others laughed and encouraged him. As the man on top of her finished with a loud groan and rolled off, another quickly took his place.

Seth shook his head, trying to clear it. He had to stop this. But that man had told him she was spreading the sickness, she was…

The second man finished, stood up and staggered off into the darkness, still laughing. The other man finished as well, then pulled free of her mouth and crawled away, gasping.

The man beneath her rolled Doctor Farrow off and got to his feet. He reached down, grabbed her by the hair and pulled her to her knees. She looked up at him, grinning maniacally. She whispered something through heavy breath Seth couldn't make out, her breasts rising and falling, nipples full and erect in the cold air. She took her breasts in her hands and crushed them together enticingly.

Seth watched as the man turned her around so that she was facing away from him and on all-fours. He mounted her from behind in the dull yellow pool of light, her body nude but for her boots and the skirt still tangled up around her waist, her flesh covered in gooseflesh and grime from the dirty floor.

Sounds began to emanate from the darkness, where the others before him had disappeared to.

And then someone began to scream.

Seth had heard those screams before…in the woods, in the dark, in the snow.

Something brushed against his leg.

He glanced back down the stairs. The lamp at the base on the crate had either gone out or had been taken away. A syrupy darkness washed up the stairs from the first floor at him, but even through the solid black, he was able to make them out.

There were at least eight or nine of them—including those who had watched him from across the street when he'd entered the church—slowly crawling up the stairs toward him, silently emerging from the darkness, their eyes dead, their hands reaching for him, tugging at his legs now, fingers fastening on his flesh.

He kicked at them, catching one man full in the face. As he fell away Seth kicked again and again until he had enough space to stand. He got to his feet but nearly lost his balance as one man yanked at his coat.

He swung the pipe down and hit him on the side of the head. It made an odd clanging sound as it smashed against his skull, and the man howled and fell back, tumbling down the stairs and into the dark. The others hesitated, still lying on the stairs, many of them frozen in mid-crawl, watching him but still now.

Seth looked back at the pool of light, the sick stage where Connie Farrow was still performing. Her head snapped up, her hair flying up and back, away from her face.

She looked directly into Seth's eyes and smiled.

More screams pierced the darkness.

Memories flashed in Seth's mind.

He darted down the stairs, swinging the pipe wildly as he went, bringing it down and across in front of him in wide arcs, knocking men out of the way with each step and moving quickly enough to pull free of those grasping at him.

At the base of the stairs he fell, and threw his hands out in front of him to help break the fall. The pipe flew off into darkness and he landed hard, the air leaving his body as his chest crashed to the floor. He slid a few feet forward on his stomach and rolled over, through the fall as best he could, scrambling back up to his knees and struggling to draw breath.

Seth got to his feet and ran through the dark room toward the only source of light he could find, light from the door he'd entered the building through. It provided a beacon of sorts, and he followed it until he had nearly reached the exit.

Just inside the door, the old woman was still sitting on the bench, the basin and scrub brush at her feet. She looked at him, expressionless, and released whatever she'd been holding in her lap. It dropped to the floor and moved toward him quickly, making strange squeaking and scratching sounds as it scurried closer.

Seth moved laterally, slowly inching toward the door. The thing stopped, as if anticipating his next move.

Shuffling noises came from behind him. The others were giving chase.

The thing in the dark crept closer.

Two red eyes materialized first, followed by a hairy body and long tail.

A rat, one of the largest he had ever seen.

Seth was within a foot or two of the door when he saw the rest of them.

The light from outside revealed dozens of them in the darkness just beyond the woman, waiting and watching him, along the floor, perched on beams and along the piles of debris, an army of rats poised to strike in a single wave.

*We're just game pieces.*

Beyond the rats, deeper in the corner of the building, almost entirely concealed in darkness, other entities watched in silence. Small beings the size of children huddled like dark statues, waiting. Right there with him and yet…not quite.

The woman parted her lips as if to speak, something fleshy dangling from the corner of her mouth. Like rare beef, it hung in thin pink strips, dripping blood.

When it began to move he realized it was her tongue…or what was left of it.

The old woman's body convulsed and she vomited it forth, spitting it out onto the floor as she began to pick at the loose skin on her face, tugging, peeling it away like clay to reveal the raw network beneath.

Seth looked back at the room from which he'd come. The others were coming, running now through the darkness toward him.

Darting for the doorway, Seth launched himself through and into the alleyway with such speed he nearly fell forward and tripped from the sheer force of his momentum. But he managed to catch himself on the fence, crashing a shoulder into it. It bowed but held him, then sprung back, pushing him further along the alleyway as he continued running for the back door to the church building. Though he heard things behind him, chasing him, within reach and snapping at him, he ran on without looking back, crashed into the door and fell into the hallway. He slammed the door shut behind him and leaned his full weight against it, bracing himself for the impact he was certain would follow.

But no one or no thing tried to open the door.

Seth held his position nonetheless, struggling to catch his breath.

The choir down the hall had again begun to sing.

He stepped away from the door carefully, and once certain he was no longer being pursued, moved quickly down the hallway toward the exit.

When he hit the street he broke into a full run until he'd reached the outskirts of the theater district. He slowed his pace to a quick walk and headed back to his car, looking behind him every few seconds just to be sure no one was following him.

His head still spinning, he grabbed his cell phone and dialed Peggy's number, watching the people in front of him now, those that passed him on either side, moving in the opposite direction. Most walked by without noticing him, but every third or fourth person seemed to look directly into his eyes, as if to let him know they had seen him, were aware of him, were watching him. He pressed on, blinking away the snow as it hit his face.

Peggy answered the phone. "Hello?"

"Peggy," he said excitedly, "listen to me, I need to talk to you."

"Seth? Are you all right? What is it, why are you out of breath?"

"Just listen to me," he snapped, moving along the increasingly congested sidewalk. "I want you to stay there, do you hear me? Stay right there, in the house. Don't go out and don't talk to anyone. Just stay put until I get there, all right?"

"For God's sake, what are you—"

"Goddamn it, Peggy, just do what I tell you for once, will you?"

"Who the hell do you think you're talking to?"

"Sweetheart, please, I—"

"Oh, now it's sweetheart suddenly."

"This isn't a fucking game!"

"No, I don't imagine it is," she said. "Though I almost wish it were."

The people passing him took closer notice. One man winked at him, mouthed something he couldn't quite make out.

"Please, for the love of God, just *listen* to me." He brushed past a small group of people waiting for a light, hurrying even faster once he had his car in sight. "Promise me you'll stay put until I get there. I'll explain everything then."

"I don't need this drama. I can't take much more of this."

"I'm sorry about earlier, I didn't—you don't understand—I didn't mean to—"

"Calm down, Seth, please just take it easy."

A woman emerged from the crowd, moving toward him. She too mouthed something, and this time he knew exactly what she was saying.

*Let Them Out.*

He watched her, sliding further away from her toward the curb until she had passed by him and vanished, absorbed by the snow and a blur of moving cars and hustling people.

"I'm sorry about before, losing my temper like that. It won't happen again, I promise."

"You're really frightening me. You're acting like you're out of your mind."

*I am out of my mind.*

"Please wait for me, just—just please wait for me. I'll be there soon."

There was a pause so lengthy he thought for a moment she had either hung up on him or the signal had been interrupted.

"Peg? Peggy, are you there?"

"Yes," she finally said. "Yes, I'm—OK, I'll be here, fine. When are you coming?"

"An hour or so," he told her. "I'm in Boston, not far from the office, but I'll be leaving the city soon and coming directly there. Just wait for me, and don't let anyone else in the house. I mean it, *no one* but me."

"I'm not expecting anyone, why would—"

"I'll be there soon as I can."

"OK, drive carefully, I'm not going anywhere. The weather guy on TV said this storm's going to get a lot worse before it gets better. They're saying we'll get well over a foot by the time it's done."

Seth reached his car, leaned against it and took a series of deep breaths. He hadn't even noticed until then how heavy the snow had become. It was accumulating rapidly now, swallowing the city. He was within a few blocks of the office, and in these conditions walking would be easier than driving, so he started in that direction on foot. "One more thing—just in case—I know it sounds strange but please listen. If for some reason I'm not there within an hour or so, I want you to take Petey and get the hell out of there, all right? Don't go to family or friends. Go somewhere anonymous, like a motel or something, and don't tell *anyone* where you are. Then tomorrow, I want you to go to where I proposed to you, the exact spot, OK?"

"What? What the hell are you talking about?"

"Go there and wait for me in the morning. If I'm not there by noon just leave. Get as far from the city as you can, just go. Promise me."

"I don't—I don't even know what to say to you at this point, honestly."

"Promise me you'll do it. I know it sounds crazy but you have to believe me and trust in me. I'll explain everything when I see you. OK?"

A heavy sigh and then, "OK, Seth."

"I'll be with you soon."

After another lengthy pause, Peggy softly said, "All right."

He snapped the phone shut and walked on through the snow. Visions of soiled hands reaching for him through the darkness, leering rats and Doctor Farrow nude and laughing still filled his mind, but memories of the night at the cabin pushed them aside. Before he could fully comprehend them, they too had slipped away, though they were no longer simply nightmares or disjointed phantoms drifting through his mind.

These were real memories of real things.

He knew that now, could no longer deny it. He could no longer hide behind vague explanations and systematic disbelief. It no longer mattered what he believed or disbelieved. Perhaps it never had.

It was all there, all in his mind, and at last almost fully within reach.

And all of it was real.

# Chapter 29

Seth entered the Severance Building and made his way to the first floor bathrooms, which were right around the corner from the elevators. Like all bathrooms in the building it was immaculately clean, with large mirrors positioned over a series of shiny sinks, floors polished to a literal glow and urinals and stalls along the opposite wall that sparkled. The innately unflattering fluorescent lighting always left him looking washed out and deathly pale, but this time his reflection was as accurate as the mirrors suggested.

Dark bags hung beneath his eyes, his hair was mussed and his face, hands and clothes were soiled from when he'd fallen. He'd torn his lapel and a portion of one coat pocket when he'd collided with the chain link fence. Seth looked at his hands. Both palms were scraped from his slide on the cement but neither was still bleeding. Despite his best efforts to stop them, they continued to tremble. He turned the water on and ran them under the faucet.

The door opened and George Walker, one of the

young lions from the sales department, hurried in toting his briefcase, a cell phone to his ear. "That's not the point, Jimmy," he said, catching Seth's eye in the mirror and shrugging, like doing so would somehow allow Seth to understand what he was referring to. "I had fifty pieces ready to ship and your department blew the deal because somebody down there can't process a standard credit agreement within a reasonable amount of time." He went to a urinal, put his briefcase down and began fumbling with his slacks.

Seth did his best to ignore the conversation. He'd dealt with Walker several times and found him relentlessly arrogant, not terribly bright and difficult to stomach. He finished washing his hands then bent down to the sink and splashed a bit of warm water on his face.

The urinal flushed and Walker joined him at the sinks. "Fine, Jimbo, you tell him that when he's tearing you a new asshole, OK?" He flipped his phone shut, returned it to his belt and nonchalantly inspected himself in the mirror. "Douche Bags in the credit department," he said, rolling his eyes at Seth. "Fucking Mongoloid Central down there. Like this goddamn snow shutting everything down isn't a big enough pain in my ass, I have to deal with those pencil-pushing dipshits taking money out of my pocket, too." He smirked then seemed to notice Seth, really notice him, for the first time, and his demeanor changed. "Jesus, Roman, what the hell happened to you? You look like shit."

Seth slid down to a half-wall where the paper towel dispenser was located and pulled a sheet free. "It's been a tough couple days."

Walker's expression changed again, a dawning

slowly spreading across his face. "Oh shit that's right, the Lou from shipping thing, you two were friends, weren't you?"

"*Are* friends," Seth said, drying first his hands and then his face. "Not were, George. Louis is still alive."

"Just barely from what I heard," he said crudely, lightly combing his already perfect hair with his fingertips. "They said he fell out a window, what was he shit-faced?"

Seth tossed the paper towel into the trash. "Never thought I'd say this, but it's good to see you're still you, George."

Walker gave him a puzzled look. "What's that supposed to mean?"

With hands now clean but still shaking, Seth turned and left the bathroom.

He crossed the lobby to the first set of elevators, rode one to his floor and stepped out into the hallway leading to the sea of cubicles beyond. It was even more quiet than usual, and the hallway was empty.

Seth looked out over the mass of cubicles. All were unattended and the area was dim, the main lights having already been shut down. The large windows on the far wall revealed that darkness was closing over the city quickly. Bill Jacobs's office was located in the rear right corner of the floor, and he could see it perfectly, as the lights inside were still on, making the fishbowl glass front more obvious from this distance than usual.

"What are you doing here on your vacation?"

Joe Levin, one of the more jovial customer service reps from his department appeared to his right, having just emerged from his cubicle.

"Hi," Seth managed. "Just came to see Bill for a

minute."

"I'm sorry, did I startle you?"

"Yeah, I thought everyone was gone."

"Everyone is, except for Jacobs." Levin buttoned his coat then pulled on a scarf and flung it around his neck. "Management sent everybody home about an hour early because of the storm. I got tied up with an account but it's taken care of so I'm heading out, too. Getting pretty bad out there from the looks."

Levin seemed all right, like his normal self, the same as Walker had.

"Yeah, coming down pretty good," Seth said. "Drive carefully."

"No worries, I took the train in." His expression grew unusually serious. "Hey, I was really sorry to hear about Louis in shipping. How's he doing?"

"The same, last time I checked." He glanced over at Ruthie's cubicle. Empty. "Joe, was Ruth Chandler in today?"

"Yeah, but she blew out of here a while ago. When they first said it was OK to leave for the day she left smoke trails." He chuckled. "You know Ruthie, last one in first one out."

"Thanks." Seth started toward the office. "I'll talk to you later."

Levin headed for the elevators. "OK, Seth, take care."

Even before Seth had reached his office, Bill Jacobs noticed Seth coming, stepped out from behind his desk and offered a warm smile while he was still several feet away. A tall, trim man in his early fifties, Jacobs had neatly styled silver hair, rather angular features, and wore expensive hand-tailored suits with suspenders that always matched his ties. "Seth, hi, thanks for coming in," he said in his deep voice, the usual odd cadence evident in his delivery, where each word was spoken slowly and drawn out longer than seemed necessary. As Seth stepped into the light of his office Jacobs blanched, shocked by his ragged appearance. "My God, are you all right? What's happened?"

"I'm fine," Seth lied. "I slipped on the ice outside and fell."

"Are you hurt? You look—"

"Bill, I'm fine. What was it you wanted?"

Slight annoyance joined the concern on his face. "Have a seat."

Seth collapsed into one of the two chairs positioned in front of the desk.

"Andrea's beyond upset," he said, feigning sincerity. "She's been planning this dinner party for weeks and now the storm hits and the odds of anyone showing are virtually nonexistent. Suffice to say she is not a happy camper at the moment, so I need to get home, and with this snow getting out of the city is already going to make me late, but—"

"Why did you want to see me, Bill?"

"I was trying to get to that, if you'd let me finish, I..." He seemed to catch himself, and his anger drifted off, replaced by more concern. "The point I was trying to make is that this is important. *You* are important, Seth." Jacobs nodded happily, apparently pleased with himself.

Seth watched him, trying to gauge his behavior to determine whether or not he could be trusted, but it was difficult. Jacobs oozed insincerity on his best days.

After a lengthy and rather dramatic sigh, Jacobs sat

on the edge of his desk and folded his arms across his chest. "First off, I want you to know how sorry I was to hear about Louis in shipping."

"Dodge."

Jacobs raised an eyebrow. "Pardon me?"

"Dodge," Seth said. "Louis Dodge. His last name is Dodge. Not *From Shipping*."

"All right," he said with condescending patience.

"Louis can be annoying sometimes. He can be a misogynistic, crude, argumentative know-it-all. Other times he can have a heart of gold and be the best friend anyone could ever hope to have." The words caught in Seth's throat. He cleared it awkwardly, battling back the emotion. "He's a human being, Bill, flaws and all. He's a father to two kids and he has a last name. It's Dodge."

"I certainly didn't mean any disrespect to your friend." Jacobs forced a phony smile. "Look, Seth, I know you've been having a difficult time, and that you're under a tremendous amount of stress and not yourself right now. I know what close friends you and Louis were. I'm sure his accident has made things even worse for you, and clearly you're quite vulnerable emotionally. I also know you and your wife have been having some problems, and that you've split. I'm sure that, coupled with—"

"Leave my wife out of this. She has nothing to do with any of this."

"I just want you to know I understand."

"Well, thank you, but my marital problems are none of the company's concern, Bill."

"Yes, of course." He paused, struggling to sustain his patience. "I'm simply trying to let you know that I understand you're having some personal problems right now and that I'm here for you. The company is here for you. You've been with us a long time, and you've always been an outstanding member of the team. But now and then things happen and we all need a bit of help. There's no shame in that, Seth. If a person falls and breaks his or her leg, for instance, are they embarrassed about going to a doctor to have their leg fixed? Of course not, so why then should we feel embarrassed if we need to see another kind of doctor to help us fix some other part of us?"

Seth pushed his hands deeper into his lap for fear Jacobs might notice the tremors wreaking havoc with them. "Any doctor I see is my business."

"We provide you with the health insurance that pays for your visits," Jacobs said flatly. "And we're glad to do it, don't misunderstand. But you're right. Normally, as you say, frankly your personal life is your own. The difference in this instance is that I've been *asked* to get involved and help out if I can, and that's all I'm trying to do."

"Asked? Asked by whom?" Seth stood up. "Help with what?"

"Don't get upset." Jacobs held his hands up in front of him. "This isn't about making you upset, all right?"

"Then what the hell *is* it about?"

"Getting you the help you need, Seth. Please understand that. I'm not the enemy. None of us are. We're all your friends, Seth. We're all very concerned about your well-being."

"Who the hell are *we*?"

"Because ultimately, that's all that matters: your health and well being."

"My well-being, I see."

"Now I know you've been acting strangely lately and that there's a lot happening right now, but Doctor Farrow can help you work these things out." Jacobs smiled, though Seth could tell how nervous he'd become. "We all just want to help you."

Seth looked back at the dark cubicles. A beeping sound in the distance indicated the elevator doors at the end of the hallway had just opened.

"Please, let us help you, Seth."

"Who told you to do this?" Seth shuffled back and forth like a cornered animal, his mind racing. "*Who*, you sonofabitch!"

"It's important that you remain calm."

"Was it Farrow? I saw her, I saw her in the building with those men, I—"

"No one wants to hurt you, Seth, we only want to help."

"I know who you are," he growled. "And I know *what* you are."

"Of course you do, you've known me for years," Jacobs said, smiling like an imbecile.

Seth saw two uniformed policemen walking quickly toward the office. "I know what's happening."

"Seth, look at me. It's me. Bill. Bill Jacobs. I'm your boss, your friend."

He grabbed Jacobs by the front of his shirt and shook him. "You hear me? I *know* what's happening!"

"Seth, stop!" Jacobs cried. "I'm only trying to help you!"

Seth released him with a push that was hard enough to send him crashing to the floor.

"Hold it right there," one of the cops called out.

"Stay right where you are!"

Seth darted out of the office and stumbled down one of the paths between the cubicles, eluding the grasp of the first policeman by mere inches.

He ran as hard as he could, his coat flapping behind him, and as he turned down another pathway and charged toward the elevators, he stole a quick glance back over his shoulder. One officer was still giving chase but was several feet behind him. The other had apparently gone into the office to aid Jacobs or was so far back he could no longer see him.

Seth heard the policeman behind him relaying information and instruction into a radio clipped to his shoulder as he ran, but kept on. Just before he reached the elevators he veered off to the right and disappeared down another pathway. He crouched low and followed it to the next opening, which put him at the exit leading to the stairs.

He slammed into the door and found himself half-running and half-falling down the first flight. He just managed to grab hold of the railing in time to prevent himself from falling head over heels, but slid down several steps until he again had his feet under him. Seth bolted down the remainder to the first floor then hit the exit door with his shoulder with such force it swung all the way open, hit the outside wall then slowly closed back.

A burst of cold air and snow hit him as he surged from the building into an alley, twirling awkwardly as he caught his balance then ran for the street.

At the corner of the building he stopped and looked around. There were fewer people on the street than before, but the area was still fairly congested, and traffic remained heavy. Two police cruisers were parked at the front of the building. Both were empty but the occupants from one were standing at the entrance to the building waiting for him.

He was just about to make a break for it in the opposite direction, when a woman in a dark coat and hat emerged from the other people bustling about. She moved toward him deliberately, and with a barely controlled look of panic on her face. A Walkman was draped around her neck, the headphones dangling loosely at her side, but it was her lipstick that stood out. A retro bright shade of red few women wore these days, it contrasted sharply with her short jet-black hair.

*Ruthie.*

She turned into the alley, but as Seth opened his mouth to say something, her eyes widened and she walked right by him. He turned to follow her, but saw the door open and the officer that had been chasing him stumble through into the alley.

Before he'd even seen her, Ruthie had closed on the policeman, and in one fluid motion spun around and fired an elbow into his face. It connected just below his nose, the point of it hitting him full in the mouth. He fell away from her with a muffled grunt, the back of his head slapping the wall as he smashed into the building.

Astonished, Seth watched as the man slid to the ground in a heap, unconscious.

Ruthie looked back at Seth and smiled self-consciously.

Seth stared at her, dazed.

"I watch a lot of Steven Seagal movies," she said, slipping her arm into his. "Walk, don't run, and do *not* look back. Come on."

She nonchalantly led him out to the street, and arm-in-arm they headed away from the Severance building, rapidly blending in with everyone else.

As they walked on Seth could only hope the cops watching the front doors hadn't seen them. The snow was heavier now and the temperature had dropped considerably in the brief amount of time he'd been inside. "My car isn't far from here," he told her. "If we can get back to it we can—"

"Too dangerous, there's a cab waiting for us a block over."

As a thought occurred to him Seth slowed his pace and turned her toward him. "Ruthie, how did you know I'd be here?"

"Relax, keep moving."

"Answer me."

"Keep *moving*." She shot him a look, daggers in her eyes. "I overheard Jacobs on the phone telling the big-shots upstairs you were coming in to see him. He's been bugging everyone for the last couple days about getting in touch with you. I was trying to get to you before he did, that's why I called you at home and left the message. By the way, thanks so much for getting back to me at some point this century."

Relieved, Seth lowered his head and continued on, attempting to be as inconspicuous as possible. "I just got the message earlier today," he explained. "I'm sorry. I didn't know who to trust. I ran into Joe Levin and he told me you'd left a while ago, so—"

"Yeah, well when I heard Jacobs say you'd be in I decided to wait on you. I figured if you showed maybe I could help. I left the building but hung around the neighborhood waiting and watching. I was out there a while and it was so cold I was freezing my tits off, so I went to that place just down the street to get a cup of coffee, you know that bagel place I like that has that killer Columbian coffee? Anyway, I figured it'd keep me warm while I was waiting, you know? I got back just in time to see you going into the building. I tried to catch you but when I got to the lobby you were already gone, guess you were already on the elevator."

Seth had never been so happy to hear her endless chatter. "I was in the restroom."

"No matter," she said, walking a bit faster. "We're almost out of here."

They reached the next block without incident. Just as she'd promised, a taxi was waiting for them. They slid into the backseat. Ruthie thanked the driver for waiting then gave him an address.

"Where are we going?" Seth asked.

"My apartment, it's only a few blocks from here. No one knows we're together so I figure it's about the last place they'll look for you."

The cab lurched off into traffic. "That cop hit his head awfully hard on that wall, do you think he's—"

"Shhh," she whispered, a gloved finger pressed to her lips. She indicated the driver with a slight nod of her head.

"You knew all along what was happening, didn't you," he said softly, stating it rather than asking. "That's why you kept trying to get me to go to your rallies and meet your friends. That's why you kept saying there was hope for me. You were trying to help me. You knew what was happening even before I did. That whole bit about—what were they—*Piggyback Fish,* it was all a test."

"Complete crap, I made them up." Ruthie smiled demurely. "Sounded good, though, no?"

"You were trying to find out what I knew."

She gave him a cynical look. "Gee, you think?"

He rubbed his eyes, a headache was settling behind them. "Then there are others like us who know and—"

"Now's not a good time to talk about it," Ruthie said, eyeing the driver.

"Right, sorry, I just—"

"Seth," she said, taking his hands and holding them tightly in her own, "I know it's hard but you need to try to calm down. Take a deep breath and chill, ratchet it down a few thousand pegs. Neither one of us will be any good to each other if we go bat-shit and lose it. We need to stay cool and think this through or we'll make a mistake. And if we make a mistake, we're fucked. OK?"

"OK." Seth nodded, doing his best. "Thanks for helping me back there."

"No sweat, but right now I just want to get off the street, it's too dangerous out in the open like this." Ruthie let him go then straightened the frumpy winter hat she was wearing and leaned forward. She watched the route the driver had taken to make certain he was going the right way. "Dude, bang a left right here, much shorter that way." She looked back at Seth, lowered her voice. "If Magellan ever finds it, we'll clear our heads and figure out what to do next when we get to my place."

Seth nodded in agreement. "And you're sure it's safe there?"

"It's safer than the street, I'm sure of that much."

"I need to get to my wife," he told her. "I told her I'd be there soon to—"

"Where is she?"

"Outside the city, but she's alone."

"If you call her don't use your cell, it's not secure. If it's totally necessary you can call her when we get to my apartment, just be careful, don't tell her where you are and keep it brief. Even landlines aren't totally safe."

He thought about it. "I just spoke to her a while ago, but I called her on my cell."

"Nothing you can do about it now."

"We have to get to her and—"

"After we get to my place we'll figure out our next move, then you can get in touch with her and we'll go from there, OK?"

"I just hope she's still all right," he said grimly. "Petey's with her, he'd die protecting her if he had to."

"Who the hell is Petey?"

"Our dog."

"Cool." Ruthie smiled, but it left her quickly. "Listen, don't get your panties in a knot, but I have to ask this. Your wife, we can trust her, right?"

"Yes."

"You're sure?"

"She's my wife, I know her, all right? Sometimes you just know, the way you knew when it came to me. How did you know *I* could be trusted?"

"I didn't."

"Well obviously you trust me now."

"I like you Seth—I always have—so I'm taking a chance." As the cab took a sharp corner, Ruthie frowned. It didn't suit her. "But I don't fucking trust anybody."

# Chapter 30

Ruthie's apartment was a modest three-story walkup on Washington Street, not far from Saint Elizabeth's hospital. The apartment itself was small, and consisted only of a kitchen, bedroom, bath and living room. Seth expected it to be decorated as flamboyantly as Ruthie's personality, and was surprised to find it furnished instead with very drab and purely practical furniture and accoutrements. Everything was dark and dreary, and the shades had all been pulled, giving it the charm of a cave.

"It's not much, but it's clean and warm," she said, switching on a small lamp. "Severance doesn't exactly pay me what they pay you."

"It's very nice," Seth said, looking around.

Ruthie tossed her purse on the couch and made her way to the tiny kitchen. "I've got some kick-ass winter comfort tea, want some?"

"Thanks." Seth joined her in the kitchen. An inexpensive table and chairs filled most of the room. He pulled out a chair and sat down as Ruthie retrieved two cups and saucers from a cupboard, placed them on the counter then ran water into a basic silver kettle.

"Give me a sec, OK?" She switched on the stove and slid the kettle onto a burner. "I need to get out of these work clothes."

Seth sat at the table trying to collect his thoughts as Ruthie disappeared down a short hallway off the kitchen and slipped into her bedroom. He looked around a bit from his position in the chair, noticing how impersonal her living space was. Though it was nothing like he'd expected, it also made him realize how lonely in many ways her life probably was. For all her talk of friends she seemed more a confirmed loner, and her apartment only further illustrated that. There were no photographs of family, friends—of anyone or anything—and no sense that she was in any way connected in a personal sense to other human beings. It was an apartment that revealed no past or present, no future. It told one nothing about who lived there, and Seth wondered if she'd done this purposely. Perhaps her life before this place was not something she was comfortable with. Perhaps it had been horrible and was something she wanted to forget and leave behind.

He couldn't be sure. In fact, Seth knew very little about Ruthie other than what she'd told him, and virtually none of that had included personal information. She was a woman that worked for him in the department, the eccentric and politically-charged girl on the other side of his cubicle who seemed to only exist between nine and five. Still, as ambiguous as the apartment was, it somehow made her more complete to him, this life she possessed outside the office, this place where she came to sleep and eat, to read and watch television and to listen to music.

A twang of pain trickled across his temple, followed by flashes of memory.

He brought his hands to his head, holding his temples and slamming shut his eyes in an attempt to deflect the pain. It left him, leaving more ghostly memories in its wake.

*Christy running through the snow.*

"You OK? Seth, what is it?"

He looked up. Ruthie was standing barefoot next to the table in a small black top and a pair of matching panties. "What are you doing?" he asked.

"What am *I* doing?"

"That's quite an outfit, Ruthie."

She looked herself over, as if she hadn't realized what she was wearing. "I wasn't done. You were screaming. Are you all right?"

Seth sat back a bit in the chair. "I was screaming?"

"You let out a scream," she told him. "I didn't know what was happening."

The kettle began to whistle.

"I'm sorry, I…I'm remembering." He suddenly felt lightheaded.

"They say that's how it happens, that it comes back to you slowly, in pieces." Ruthie turned her back to him, pulled the kettle from the stove and made the tea. A small tattoo of a tribal art design adorned the small of her back just above her buttocks, pieces of it still hidden behind her panties. The shirt was a t-back that allowed another tattoo on the back of her left shoulder—a yin and yang symbol—to be seen. She turned back to him and placed the tea in front of him. "Here, drink this. It'll make you feel better."

Seth brought the cup to his mouth with both hands then swallowed some tea. It had a vague mint taste and was very smooth. As he took another sip, the warmth spread through him, traveling slowly through his body. "Thanks."

"Dude, I need to know some things," she said, "and I need you to be totally honest with me, OK? No bullshit."

"OK." Seth tried not to notice how tight the little top was, or how it revealed quite a bit of cleavage and only reached to just above her navel. He tried not to notice how smooth her legs were, how delicate and cute her feet were, how the panties were tight yet rode up enough to reveal the underside of her ass. He tried not to notice how amazingly sexy she smelled. "But maybe you should finish changing first, Ruthie."

He thought she'd respond with one of her typical wiseass comments. She didn't. Instead she stopped halfway to the refrigerator, leaned back against the counter and folded her arms across her chest, crushing her breasts into an intentionally erotic swell. "Tell me what you know," she said, clearly enjoying his embarrassment.

Leaning forward so that his arms could rest on the kitchen table, he sipped more tea then relayed to her everything he knew and everything that had happened to the best of his ability. He told her all of it—from Raymond and his experiences as children, to the night up in Maine, to everything that had happened since—and the more he told her the better he felt, like a huge weight had been dislodged from the back of his neck. But even as he explained things to her, despite all that had happened, it still sounded absurd, still sounded like the ramblings of a madman, and in expressing this all at once for the first time, the thing he realized most profoundly was the full extent of what he still *didn't* know.

Throughout, Ruthie stood perfectly still, leaned against the counter and listening intently to each word. She never had any reaction or give any indication that what he was saying was bizarre or frightening or troubling her in any way. In fact, she seemed almost bored, like she'd heard this many times before. He might as well have been talking about some mundane television show he'd seen or a typical project at work.

When he'd finished she sighed long and hard, blowing a renegade piece of hair away from her face. "You don't remember anything else about the night at the cabin?"

"It seems to be coming back to me slowly, but only in flashes." He sipped his tea. "But the memories are getting longer and more vivid. Stronger."

"And it hurts?" she asked. "It hurts to remember?"

"Doesn't it always?"

She arched an eyebrow. "Good point."

"Now you."

Ruthie squirmed a bit but remained leaned against the counter, arms folded. "I'm not from here originally," she said a moment later. "I was born in Delaware, grew up with my mom. My father died of cancer when I was little, so it was just my mom and me. We were really close. When I was a senior in high school we moved to Massachusetts. We lived in Dorchester for a while, then Jamaica Plain. She was a waitress mostly, made shit but we got by. It was tough because my mom had problems. Like your brother."

"They took her?" Seth asked.

Ruthie nodded. "When I was about thirteen, she had this…experience…and she was never the same. Gradually, she went crazy. About a month after I graduated high school it all got too much for her and she had a breakdown. They locked her up in a psychiatric ward, medicated the shit out her and threw away the fucking key. She's still there, rotting." She cocked her head to the side to indicate the psych ward at nearby Saint Elizabeth's hospital. "That's why this apartment's perfect. I can stay close to her. She usually doesn't recognize me anymore, though. All the drugs over the years have fried her brain like you wouldn't believe. Maybe in the end that's a good thing. Maybe it's more merciful to *not* know what's happening. I don't know."

"I'm sorry, Ruthie."

"Like Raymond, she's a carrier. For years she just thought she was going nuts, and maybe she was. Either way, eventually it crippled her. Even though those *things* hadn't set all this motion yet, she knew what she was carrying. She understood what her role would be in all this when they finally did. Like the rest of us, she just couldn't get it all to fit in her mind. Square peg in a round hole, you know?"

Seth wanted to tell her how deeply he understood everything she was feeling, everything she had felt over the years, and that she no longer needed to feel so alone because now neither did he. Instead, he asked, "How did you come to know all this?"

"Same way you did. My mother finally told me just like Raymond finally told you. The rest I got on my own by finding other people who were going through the same thing or who had loved ones who were."

"But your mother, she didn't spread it to you?"

"Did Raymond spread it to *you*?"

He shook his head. "If it even has been spread to me then it came from Christy."

"And if it has you've been able to fight it off, just like me. Some of us can…for a while anyway."

"How do we do it?"

She smiled slightly. "You still don't know?"

"Do I look like I'm playing games to you?"

"Love," she said softly. "And faith."

"Ruthie, when my parents were killed I lost my faith."

"You only thought you did."

"No."

"You only *thought* you did," she said again. "What you did without even realizing it was the same thing I did when my mother had to be institutionalized. We got so angry with God we stopped talking to Him. It took me a while to realize that only made my faith stronger. Your anger, my anger, it made Him even more real to us. No one's angry with someone or something that isn't there, that doesn't exist, right? That makes no sense. In being so angry at Him for allowing the things that happened to our parents and to Raymond, we only made our belief in Him stronger. And the stronger you believe, the more you love. We're angry because we loved God and felt like He'd let us down, abandoned us."

"And this stops the spread, or slows it?"

"Our minds are the battleground, Seth. That's how they move and breed and control us, through thoughts and dreams and nightmares. There are only three avenues they haven't been able to break in human beings: our free will and our proven ability for boundless love and indestructible faith. My mother didn't spread it to me and Raymond didn't spread it to you because they love us and would never do anything to hurt us. They weren't capable of it. Others, yes, they can't control what's inside them in those instances, but with those they love, these things are powerless to turn us. That's why they send others to do it when the time comes, other carriers at other times and in other places."

"Christy," he mumbled.

She nibbled her lower lip a moment. "It's not like the movies. Monsters and lizard people jumping around, bug-eyed gray aliens flying in spaceships and all that shit, that's all human invention, people putting a face on the boogeyman so they can make some sense of it in a way that even a child could understand. The reality is these things are far more complicated than that. They abducted people, like Raymond and my mother and that Christy girl who came to you in the forest. They've done it for years, taking hundreds—maybe even thousands—from everywhere, every walk of life. Then they sent them back, at different times and to different places, so when they finally flipped the switch and set this all in motion, none of us would have a chance."

*Time isn't the same when you're with them.*

"It's not about flying metal ships or wars or big explosions. Just madness, a sickness in the human spirit no one can see or put their finger on. They're phantasms traveling through our minds, never provable, never seen and always hidden in the dark."

Seth finished his tea. His hands had again begun to tremble uncontrollably. Even when he concentrated and stared at them, the shaking refused to stop. "What are they, Ruthie, do you know? These things, what the hell are they, aliens from some alternate existence?"

"I've read everything on these subjects I can get my hands on," she told him. "Most of the serious, highly-educated, scientific researchers that investigate the whole alien angle no longer believe these things are from distant planets. Most believe this phenomenon is much closer to Earth and the origins of Man. Ever heard of the French National Council for Scientific Research?"

Seth tiredly shook his head in the negative.

"It's pretty prestigious stuff. Trust me, we're not talking a bunch of UFO geeks and alien enthusiasts sitting around jerking each other off, these are serious scientific people." Ruthie left the kitchen long enough to rummage through a small bookcase in the living room then returned with a dog-eared paperback. "They quote a guy from there in this book, some big-shot." She rifled through the pages, many of which had been flagged with sticky notes, until she found what she was looking for. "Here it is: Dr. Pierre Guerin, from the French National Council for Scientific Research. He said the alien phenomenon and its behavior—and I quote—'*is more akin to magic than physics as we know it.*' And there's another one where he says the demons of yesterday and the aliens of today are probably one in the same." She tossed the book onto the kitchen table. "Basically, a lot of these guys believe that what people used to worship as gods and angels or fear as devils or demons, and what people are encountering today are the same beings."

"But they've changed over the centuries."

"No," Ruthie said. "We have. And so they have different faces, different looks to fit different, constantly changing cultures and times. Our minds do the rest, filling in the blanks and trying to make sense of something that makes no sense. Our minds define things as best we can so we can understand or at a minimum identify them, right? They used to burn crazies as witches. People used to see fairies and gnomes and shit running through the woods. Now we lock people like that in institutions, the way they've locked my mother away and the way they've locked Raymond up before too. But it's been a slow burn, the world's gone nuts, and the whole mess is entirely fucking *human*. Turn the TV on, dude, read a newspaper. The whole planet's going to snot. Chaos and violence rules, nothing makes any sense anymore, good countries, good people gone mad and nobody even seems to give a shit when they're lied to or manipulated by the government. Long as the cable TV works and the cell phone bill gets paid, who gives a shit what's happening in the rest of the world or even your own backyard, who cares what the price is as long as we don't have to pay it right here and right now? If they ain't taking a big steamy dump on my head or someone's head I love, who cares? And if you fight it or stand in the way or have even the slightest dissenting voice, *you're* the bad guy, right?" She reached for her tea, took a quick sip. "It's over, life the way we knew it once. It's changing, the planet and everything on it is changing, being altered. Maybe like when the dinosaurs were wiped out, or evolved and became something else. Maybe the same way we have again and again from the time we crawled out of the water. Maybe this is just the next evolutionary step, the next big shakeup on Planet Earth. Maybe it's as natural as life or death and everything that happens in the middle. Either way, it's all controlled by these fuckers and we can't stop any of it anymore than we can stop a hurricane, a blizzard or an earthquake."

"And who do *they* answer to?"

"Maybe they *are* angels, or demons. Maybe they're something in between, something we can't even begin to comprehend. Maybe they're us, or some form of us. Maybe they *are* gods in a way, lesser gods that answer to the Devil. Maybe in the end we don't answer to anyone but ourselves. Or maybe we all answer to the same God."

"What about Him?" Seth asked. "Where is God in all this?"

"Personally, I think He's always with us," she said. "But it's the way parents are still with us once we grow up and move out, you know? Maybe when it's all said and done, when it's all over, maybe He's there to make it all better, to make sense out of it for us. I don't know. But out in the real world, we're on our own."

"Then Raymond was right." Seth brought a hand to his head and rubbed his temple. "We can't stop this."

"How do you stop something that uses your own weaknesses against you?" Ruthie pushed away from the counter. "That's the vehicle they use for movement, for infection from one person to the next. Sin. They use our sins against us."

Seth looked at her, speechless.

"Because what is sin? Think about it, Seth, what is

it really? I mean once you strip away all the bullshit and religious definitions and all that, what is it?" Ruthie moved closer to the table and put her hands on the back of one of the chairs. "It's human nature. Sin's just a label we use to hide the facts that those things we do—both good and bad—are simply human nature. *Our* nature, Seth, it's how we're made. It's our own nature used against us, to control us, to destroy us. Human beings are amazingly flawed, each and every fucking one of us, and they use that against us."

Lust. Christy had used lust. Whenever Seth remembered her, he remembered lust.

"They use the dark half of human nature—greed, arrogance, fear, violence, gluttony, sloth, hated, jealousy, *depravity*—it's all as much a part of us as love and affection and compassion are. And they know it."

Doctor Farrow, in that building, had used lust as well. It was lust and greed and anger that had incited those homeless men not only to rape her but to steal from her as well. Like offering an alcoholic a drink, it was something they should have been able to resist, but simply couldn't. Sin. Ruthie was right, everyone was susceptible to it.

"Like some sort of perfect weapon," he said.

"They know all our secrets, Seth. All of them."

And what about Raymond, what had he used?

"Violence," he said aloud.

"What about it?" Ruthie asked.

As a boy Raymond had used his position as a victim to bring out the worst in people, to bring out the violence and cruelty in people. It was so typically Raymond, to martyr himself even in the destruction of others. And then later, through committing crimes and giving opportunity to others to join him, his comrades and victims both were caught in the web. Infected.

"My brother Raymond didn't have much of a choice, did he?"

"I don't think any of the carriers do. I'm not even sure the infected have any choice once it's inside them, once they've begun to change or revert or whatever you want to call it. We might all be fucked, Seth."

Seth felt suddenly dizzy. Flashes of the forest came to him again, visions of Christy running through the snow. Screams, the horrible screams…

"What happened out there," he muttered, "wha—what did we do?"

Ruthie moved to the refrigerator. "When's the last time you had something to eat?"

"I don't—hell, I don't even remember."

"You need to eat, keep up your strength. You'll need it." She bent over to rummage through the refrigerator. "I've got some sandwiches in here."

"I need to get to Peggy and…and…"

Ruthie returned to the table with a plate holding two roast beef sandwiches. "Eat," she said firmly, sliding the plate in front of him. "I'm going to finish getting changed then we'll get Peggy and Petey and get the hell away from here. I have some friends who can help."

Nausea throttled him and the lightheadedness grew worse. "I can't eat, Ruthie, I…"

"Take it easy, breathe," she said. "Try to eat, you'll feel better." She grabbed one of the sandwiches and took a big bite. "They're good, see?"

Seth managed to get to his feet, but his legs felt weak. "What are you doing? That's roast beef."

"Don't you eat roast beef?"

"*You* don't eat roast beef, Ruthie. You're a vegetarian."

She grinned, mayonnaise and strings of chewed red beef on her teeth. "Not anymore."

The room spun, and Seth felt his legs give out. He hit the floor, and through the blur, Ruthie came into focus above him, looking down at him with that same grin. She winked, took another bite of sandwich. Something trickled slowly from her nose. Blood. She seemed not to notice. "Don't be afraid, I put something in your tea to calm you."

"But you—before, you—you helped me," he said groggily.

"It's always better for these things to happen privately, without a lot of attention."

"What did you do to me?" he asked, his voice sounding abnormal and disconnected.

"You've told me what you know." She straddled him, her eyes turning dark. "Now let me tell you what *I* know. You can make it all stop, Seth. All the fear, all the pain, you can make it go away. I saw how you looked at me. All that lust, give it to me."

He tried to struggle but his body was limp, paralyzed. He fought to keep his eyes open but they slowly slid shut.

Darkness engulfed him, and as he slipped into unconsciousness, he felt Ruthie's hot breath in his ear. "Make it all go away, Seth, it's so beautiful once you do, you'll see," she whispered. "Make it all go away. They're already asleep inside you. Wake them up and *let them out.*"

# Chapter 31

He remembered moving briskly along the street. Hurrying, but not quite running. The streets of Boston were impossibly empty, abandoned and deathly quiet as heavy snow continued to fall over the city. Seth approached the corner, hands in his pockets, the cold tearing through him despite his heavy winter coat.

Where was everyone? How could he be alone here, in the heart of the city?

As he turned the corner his question was answered. He wasn't alone at all.

An enormous wave of people were walking in his direction, a sea of humanity going about its business, moving together and coming his way. None of the people seemed to notice him, even when he began walking directly into the heart of the mob in the opposite direction. A space opened that was just barely able to accommodate him, so he pushed his way through, fighting his way upstream while the others brushed past.

"Let them out," one man said as he passed.

A woman talking on a cell phone stopped her conversation as she neared him. "Let them out," she said dully, then was gone.

Each face, young and old, male and female, all began to recite the same mantra in monotone, one voice blending into the next.

The crowd slowed and began to close in around him, and the harder Seth fought and pushed against it, the harder it became to break through. The mob had grown stronger and larger and was swallowing him, burying him. It surged in one direction and then the next, knocking him off-balance, and Seth crashed to the cold ground, legs and feet stomping down around him, the hems of endless coats closing off the sparse bit of sky above him he could still make out through the snow.

And then the darkness returned.

His eyes opened but his vision remained blurry and dull. Something was passing overhead slowly, as if in timed intervals. Lights, flashes of light were passing overhead every few seconds. That was it but…no, he thought, no the lights aren't moving…*I am.*

He tried to speak but couldn't seem to open his mouth. His hands and legs were paralyzed, and when he tried to raise his head someone behind him put a hand flat on his forehead, holding it down, the touch of their skin cold and slightly moist. Seth tried again to move but could not. In his mind he cried for help at the top of his lungs, but still couldn't get his mouth open, much less scream. The best he could manage was an odd croaking sound strangled deep in his throat, and the harder he tried to scream and make noise or move, the less he seemed able to. He rolled his eyes to one side and then the other but could only make out bare white walls. They had no markings or identifiable features of any kind and seemed to go on for far as the eye could see.

An odd sound distracted him, rhythmic and squeaky—a wheel in need of oil—and it was then that he realized he was on a gurney of some kind. That was it, he was being wheeled on a gurney down a long white hallway, and the lights passing overhead were fixtures on the ceiling glaring down on him as he swept by.

Seth felt the gurney turn to the right. A doorway passed over him and he found himself in a small room. Again he tried to move but could not. Only his eyes still had life, but as he darted them back and forth all he could see was the endless white. Though he knew he was not outdoors, in the distance he could hear the wind, a blowing, howling, winter wind. He could also hear subtle shuffling movement behind him.

The hand on his forehead tightened its grip, and Seth felt breath against his face.

He lifted his eyes in an attempt to see as far back over his forehead as he could to whoever was standing at the head of the gurney, but he strained so hard he became dizzy and the blurriness of his vision grew even worse.

Whispering. Whoever was back there was whispering something in a chant-like cadence, but in a tone so soft Seth couldn't make any of it out. But he knew from the direction of the whispers that it was above him now.

He forced his eyes open and up.

Its horrible skinless face, unfinished and otherworldly, gazed down at him.

*Who is in the room, Seth?*

Its body was perched on the gurney and crouched over him in an awkward, inhuman stoop more reminiscent of a bird or a gargoyle balanced on the ledge of a bell tower. It held his head in both hands and whispered to him, its breath humid and foul.

*There's something in the room, it—*

Thick drool dangled then dripped from its repulsive mouth onto Seth's face. He felt it run down his neck in hideous wet strands.

Seth tried to scream but was still unable to make a sound.

*Who is this person, Seth?*

His heart pounded like it might rupture at any moment, and his throat constricted to the point where he could barely draw a breath.

*It's all right, you can tell me.*

And as his terror became unbearable, the white walls turned to black, and all that was light became dark.

*Who is this person?*

The quiet returned…but for the steady breathing and the soft whispering murmurs behind him.

*It's not a person.*

A violent chill shook him awake.

"Raymond!"

A ring of trees in the forest. A slow, steady snow. Night.

He and Raymond were alone in the clearing, standing in snow past their ankles. Seth had a flashlight and pointed it upward, moving the beam slowly toward the treetops and sky above. The light illuminated the barren trees, made them look like a vast network of old bones. Death.

The light swept back to the ground, to the clearing, to Raymond, who stood staring at him. "Am I dreaming, Ray?" Seth asked, his breath a cloud in the night.

"You're remembering," he answered sadly. Raymond motioned to the woods beyond the clearing. In the deep darkness the outline of a cabin was just barely visible in the distance. Swaddled in shadow and the intermittent touch of muted moonlight, a woman ran through the snow.

Christy.

"Why did she bring us out here, Ray?"

"She brought you here to die."

Seth's arm fell to his side, the flashlight beam aimed at the ground. Blood seeped up from under the snow, leaking at first in small specks but growing gradually into wide blossoms, staining the snow, littering it like blooming flowers sprinkled about his feet. "Am I dead?"

Raymond crouched in the snow, grabbed a handful and crushed it, letting it fall in chunks back to the ground. Slowly, he looked up at the moon. A slow trickle of blood leaked from his nose. "Not yet."

The blood in the snow grew worse, spreading and encircling Seth. "How can this be happening? How can God let this happen, Ray? Why has He abandoned us?"

"This is all His," Raymond said softly, his voice blending with the wind. "He can come and take it back whenever He wants. He can save us whenever He feels like it."

"Then why doesn't He?"

"Maybe we're not worth the time or effort anymore. Maybe we blew it."

"Are you a prophet, Raymond, like Nana says?"

"You're the prophet." Raymond smiled one of his heartbreaking smiles as the falling snow collected in his long hair. "I'm just your little brother."

"I know the secret." Seth felt himself sink a bit in the moist, blood-red snow. He felt wetness soak through his pants and onto his skin. "Ruthie made a mistake. She talks too much, and she told me the secret, Ray. Faith and love."

"Don't forget free will." Raymond's dark eyes looked out at him from behind the hair hanging across his face. "Submit, suicide, insanity or eventual overload and death like that poor bastard back at the cabin—Clayton Willis—head popped like a fucking grapefruit on the business end of a Louisville Slugger. Use your free will and choose. Go ahead, pick one. Free will. Shit. Gets us every fucking time. The game's rigged."

Deafening screams rained down as if from above, exploding through the forest.

*Darkness, the night unfolding before him, the snow draping everything and coming down with unusual ferocity now. Sounds of his boots crunching beneath him, and his own gasping, labored breathing. The flashlight in his hand bouncing and shaking, its beam cutting enough of a fissure in the night to reveal blurry views of Christy running several yards in front of him, maneuvering through the trees and along the uneven terrain, her nude body impossibly pale amidst the darkness. Another cabin coming into view, the door open…*

Seth suddenly found himself back on the street.

Falling, his balance lost, he staggered to the side, the world tilting and spinning. He struggled to gain his bearings and right himself, but it was too late, he was already crashing to the ground. He hit the sidewalk, bounced his shoulder on the curb and rolled into the gutter. Snow and mud splashed up around him.

Seth lay there a moment until the world slowly came back into focus.

Standing over him were two of the same homeless men from the building he'd followed Doctor Farrow to. One knelt down next to him, smiled, and slammed a fist into his face.

Pain and an explosion of purple-blue light erupted behind Seth's eyes, and as his vision eventually cleared he flopped back into the mud and slush.

Seth tried to move but his arms and legs had gone limp, lifeless.

The man rummaged through Seth's coat, yanking his wallet free, grubby hands searching his pockets and moving over his body while the other stood watch.

The man finished his search and left him, but his partner stood over Seth a moment, looking down at him with a curious expression. Assuming a wide stance, the man reared back and kicked Seth in the side again and again until he had rolled completely over, and collapsed face-down in the gutter.

After a moment, Seth managed to get up onto all-fours, his hair and face dripping dirty water and slush as he crawled back toward the safety of the sidewalk. He tasted blood, and pain rifled across his ribs. His jaw and face ached where he'd been punched.

His arms gave out and he collapsed again to the

pavement. He rolled over onto his back with a moan and lay still. A horrible smell wafted up from the gutter, a combination of dirt and motor oil and shit and cigarettes and God knows what else.

Someone walked by, Seth could sense them. He tried to reach out for their ankle. "Help me," he gasped. "Please—help me."

The person muttered something unintelligible and was gone. Others came and went, passing by or simply stepping over him, but no one stopped to help.

"Get a job, you fucking lowlife," a man snapped.

Seth's head lolled to the side. His cheek pressed into the icy snow as his eyes focused on the street, and eventually the sidewalk on the far side of it.

Across the street Ruthie stood watching, smirking with satisfaction, arms folded and hips cocked. Christy stood behind her, arms slipped around Ruthie's waist and her chin resting on Ruthie's shoulder. She said something and Ruthie laughed, leaning her head back until their cheeks met.

They watched him like sated vampires, faces smug, sexy and evil.

Almost human. But not quite.

Seth's vision blurred again, turning the world into little more than indistinct shapes and vague colors amidst the drifting, ever-present shadows.

And the winter wind began to sing to him like the seductress it was.

*She brought you here to die.*

# Chapter 32

Light, dull with a yellow hue…the steady hum of nearby city streets…the slow and steady rhythm of breath…and the soft scratch of an expensive, metal-tip pen on paper. A musty smell…followed by the faint aroma of perfume…familiar perfume.

All of it was familiar, in fact.

His brother's face flashed in his mind, sitting in the window seat and watching the snow. Nana stood behind him with sorrowful eyes, blood dribbling from her nose.

*Raymond*!

Seth's eyes opened, and he sat up quickly as the small, windowless room around him whirled into focus. He realized he was lying on a bed, and someone was there, just beyond the foot of it.

"Easy, Seth, it's all right. You're in no danger, easy now."

That forever-accommodating voice, he'd have recognized it anywhere.

Doctor Farrow sat in a chair, smiling at him,

piercing blue eyes watching him through turtle shell glasses. The bedroom door behind her was slightly ajar, allowing a sparse bit of light to seep in from the rest of the apartment. The only other light in the dim room came from a small lamp on a nightstand next to the bed.

Seth reared back, pushing against the headboard as if hoping to dissolve through it while frantically searching the room to see if they were alone.

They weren't.

Just beyond the door, shadows moved and muffled voices carried, though he could not discern anything they were saying.

"Don't be frightened," Doctor Farrow said in her smooth voice. "You're perfectly safe, I promise you, perfectly safe. Take a few deep breaths and do your best to remain calm, everything's all right."

He saw her in the abandoned building, nude and dirty, taking homeless men one after another with that wild look in her eyes.

"Do you recognize me?" she asked through a placid smile.

Seth nodded grimly. "Why wouldn't I?"

"I'm sure you're a bit disoriented," she said. "That's to be expected, but you're all right, you're in Ruth Chandler's apartment, in her bedroom, in fact, and you're safe and sound now, Seth, all right? Safe and sound."

"What are you doing here?"

Rather than answer she motioned calmly to a small cup of water on the nightstand. "Would you like some water?"

"What are you doing here?" he asked again. His

entire body ached.

Doctor Farrow wrote something on her little pad. "Do you remember coming here earlier?" When he stared at her without response she said, "Can you tell me the last thing you *do* remember?"

He planted his feet on the floor and stood up slowly. The dizziness did not return.

"Sit down so we can talk, Seth."

"I'm not talking to you." Despite the fear and confusion, and soreness in his jaw and ribs, he felt stronger and more rested than he had in recent memory. "Who's out there?"

"I received a call that you were in trouble and came as fast as I could." She smiled. "I thought we could talk here, rather than in a more *formal* setting."

"Fuck you, lady," he said, pointing at her. "I'm not staying here."

Doctor Farrow sighed. She even did that calmly. "Seth, there's no reason to be childish. Now we can discuss this, but—"

"I know what's happening," he snapped. "I saw you."

"Seth, please sit down."

"You can't keep me here."

Doctor Farrow uncrossed her legs and sat forward a bit in her chair, pad and pen still held in her hands. "If you don't sit down and remain calm so we can talk sensibly about what's happened I won't be able to help you."

"I don't want your help, asshole. You let me the hell out of here or I'll give you a psychotic episode like you've never fucking seen."

Doctor Farrow looked at him as if to say: *Are you*

*finished*?

"I know what's happening," he told her again.

"Seth," she said patiently, "I understand you're frightened, confused, angry and experiencing all sorts of varied emotions—and that's OK—but you need to understand that you've been through a terrible trauma and if I'm to help you I need you to be more cooperative than you're being right now. I thought you and I had developed a certain trust, and I'd hoped we could do this here in Ms. Chandler's apartment, in surroundings you'd be more comfortable with. You've never expressed any aggression before, never given any indication of being a violent individual whatsoever, and I was reasonably certain you posed neither yourself nor the community at large any threat. Now I'd like very much to address what's happened, and to help you in any way I can, but these things *must* be addressed, Seth, do you understand? The choice is yours. We can either try to handle things here, or I can have you hospitalized and we can proceed with your care from there. Which would you prefer?"

Seth stopped cold, glanced first at her icy eyes and then at the door. The word *hospitalized* rang in his ears. He moved away and sank back onto the edge of the bed.

"Good." She quickly consulted her pad then said, "Can you tell me the last thing you remember?"

"Why are you doing this?"

"What am I doing, Seth?"

"I know what's happening and I know what you're doing. I saw you."

"Saw me?"

"I followed you."

"Followed me where?"

"The abandoned building behind the old church shelter."

Farrow creased her brow in confusion. "Do you remember that I was on vacation until recently? I was out of the country, Seth. Could it have been someone who resembled me?"

"What's the point of this? We both know what's happening here."

"I'm not sure we do," she said evenly.

* * *

*Alessandra sits with him a long while. She neither speaks nor cries. Instead, she gently strokes his cheek and does her best to remember the happy years they spent together.*

*His study, with all his leather-bound classics neatly displayed on tall bookshelves, its mahogany furniture, ostentatious world globe and enormous grandfather clock, its numerous model airplanes he'd spent hours building himself hanging from thin plastic wires attached to the ceiling, seems so quiet and still now, and lacks the warmth that once existed here in abundance. Rolf took such pride in this room and in the things he kept here, things others might find silly and inconsequential, but then, it was his simplicity that made him so attractive to Alessandra in the first place. Rolf was not a stupid man – on the contrary – he was quite bright, albeit in a bookish sense. But there was a minimalism to his manner Alessandra had always envied.*

*Sitting in his high-back leather chair and slumped forward over his desk, he looks so peaceful, head turned to the side, one cheek pressed flat against the desk blotter where his head has come to rest. Beyond one outstretched hand sits the model he'd been working on when Alessandra brought his lunch: a steaming bowl of minestrone soup, his favorite. He'd not quite finished it when the poison sent him drifting off to eternal sleep…quietly, painlessly, lovingly. She looks beyond his peaceful face to the snow blowing about outside. The storm has grown worse over the last few hours.*

*Alessandra stands up, straightens her dress and draws a deep breath. She leans over, kisses Rolf gently on the side of his forehead and runs her fingers once more through his neatly cropped hair. She will see him again soon, in a place where forgiveness is inherent and explanation unnecessary.*

*She walks slowly into the dining room and eventually the kitchen. But for the sound of her heels along the floor and the baying wind just beyond its borders, the house is silent. The putrid smell is everywhere.*

*Raymond is waiting for her in the kitchen. At her request, he has showered, shaved and changed into a clean sweatshirt and pair of jeans, his freshly shampooed hair pulled back into a tidy ponytail. On the table next to his cigarettes and lighter are two small glasses and a bottle of Crown Royal sitting in a purple cloth bag. As they have for years, he and Alessandra have an entire conversation without ever uttering a word. The look on her face and in her eyes tells him everything he needs to know, and vice versa.*

*Nana moves to the table, carefully pours a bit of liquor into both glasses then replaces the crown-shaped cap. She takes both glasses in hand and holds one out to Raymond. He takes it, watching as she slides into the chair next to his.*

* * *

"Would you like to answer my original question?" Doctor Farrow asked, her pen gliding across paper. "What is the last thing you remember?"

"I remember being here, at Ruthie's apartment," he said in an annoyed tone. "She lured me here to find out what I knew and to try to turn me. She drugged me."

"Ruthie *drugged* you?"

"Yes. I woke up here, with you staring at me. This is ridiculous, I—"

"You said she tried to 'turn' you. What do you mean by that?"

"I'm not playing these games with you."

She studied him a moment. "So you remember being here prior to what happened?"

"You asked me the last thing I remembered. I told you."

Doctor Farrow let the pad rest in her lap. "Seth, on the day that took place, you had a significant amount to drink at a string of bars in the downtown area. You went to your office, and upon leaving, apparently walked here, to Ms. Chandler's apartment. An argument ensued and you left, still quite inebriated. Ms. Chandler, concerned about your behavior and well-being, followed you. You had a few block lead on her, however, and wandered a ways from here where you were mugged and beaten. Luckily, Ms. Chandler found you lying semi-conscious in the gutter. She managed to get you back here to her apartment and phoned for help. I came right away, as I said."

"Explains why I'm so sore. But how did she know to call you?"

"She's your friend, Seth. She knew you were under my care."

"Ruthie had no idea I was under your care."

"I gave you a mild sedative for your own safety," she said, ignoring his response. "You had awaked suffering from nightmarish episodes and hallucinations. These things happen sometimes when a person suffers intense moments of fear, anxiety or even physical duress, which obviously you had. Thankfully, the physical injuries you sustained weren't life-threatening. Some cuts, bumps and bruises, and I imagine you'll be sore for a few days, but you'll be all right. It's your psychological and emotional well-being I'm concerned with at this point, Seth. When you awakened just now, understandably, you were disoriented and frightened." She offered her best impression of a concerned smile. "And obviously you're still rather upset, but can you tell me how you're feeling otherwise?"

"Let's just cut to the chase. I'll ask you again. What's the point of all this?"

Doctor Farrow brought a hand to her chin as if wildly fascinated by his question. "What do *you* think the point is?"

He swallowed. His throat was raw and sore. "I'm not insane and you know it."

"No one's suggesting you're insane."

"How long has it been?"

"How long has what been?"

"How long has it been since the day I was attacked on the street?"

"The assault and mugging took place late yesterday afternoon. It's now the early morning of the following day."

"I've been here overnight?"

She nodded. "I could've had you moved but you

were comfortable here, had no serious injuries, and Ms. Chandler didn't mind, so it was best for you to stay put."

Seth immediately thought of Peggy and the timetable he'd established for their meeting when he'd spoken to her on his cell. He looked to his wrist but his watch was gone, apparently taken in the mugging. He searched the room for a clock, came up empty. "What time is it?"

She glanced at her watch. "Nearly ten o'clock. Why?"

"I'm the curious type." Thank God, he thought. There's still time.

A long, thoughtful pause, and then: "Seth, do you have any recollection of yesterday at all, or to the events that lead up to what happened? Do you remember why you started drinking heavily that morning?"

"I wasn't drinking," he said. "And we both know that."

"According to Ms. Chandler you were extremely intoxicated. She tried to sober you up with some tea. Or are you saying she was mistaken? Are you saying you *weren't* drinking yesterday?"

Seth rubbed his eyes. "Doesn't much matter what I say."

"It matters a great deal to me. Why do you say that?"

"This is the part where you make it out like I'm crazy and lock me away because you can't get to me any other way." He looked to the cup of water on the nightstand. It was appealing, but after Ruthie's tea he didn't want to risk drinking anything else he hadn't prepared himself. "Even now, I'm sounding like a paranoid nut, aren't I? Isn't that the point? Every time I open my mouth I walk a little deeper into your trap."

"Is that what you think this is, Seth, a trap?"

Seth stared at her dully.

"Is that how you're feeling, trapped?"

*They'll try to break you,* Raymond had warned.

Seth's heart was racing again. The fear was returning. Perhaps it had never truly left. "It's just the two of us," he said. "There's no reason to pretend."

Doctor Farrow's expression remained neutral as ever. "What is it you think I'm pretending about, Seth?"

*And if they can't they'll try to make you think you're crazy.*

"I know what happens next," he said. "You lock me away, pump me full of drugs and throw away the key. What are you waiting for?"

"Why would I want to do that?" she asked innocently. "Do *you* feel you need to be locked away?"

*Maybe by then you will be, but don't listen to a fucking word they say.*

"I feel I need to get the hell out of here and away from you, that's what I feel."

"Why do you feel that way, Seth?"

*It's all an illusion, a mind-fuck.*

"What do you want from me?"

She sat back, assuming a more casual posture, and again crossed her legs. "I'd like to talk about your sudden hostility toward me. Do you think maybe you're directing it at me because I'm your doctor and you trust me, and because it's easier that way? It's not uncommon for patients to direct anger toward their doctors in certain situations."

"We both know why I'm directing my anger toward you."

She let the tip of her pen rest on the edge of her bottom lip. "What I'd like you to do is to think about yesterday and the events leading up to it, all right? How much do you remember?"

"I remember everything," he told her.

"Would you like to tell me about it?"

"Maybe you should tell me. Your version's already a lot different than mine."

She flipped a few pages on her pad and briefly consulted it. "Do you remember meeting with your boss William Jacobs?"

"Yes."

"Do you remember physically assaulting him, Seth?"

"Yes, I do."

"All right, would you like to talk about why or how that happened?"

Seth would've laughed had he not felt so utterly hopeless. "Just do whatever it is you're going to do to me and get it the hell over with."

"Luckily, Mr. Jacobs has been wonderfully understanding about this and has chosen to try to help you rather than press charges." Doctor Farrow was quiet for a time then said, "Let's go back a bit. What can you tell me about your friend Louis?"

He felt anger rise alongside his fear. "He threw himself out a window to get the hell away from all this. It's one of the options, suicide. He took it."

She flipped through her pad, read over the various notes jotted there then looked up from it. "Louis is still alive."

"But in a coma?"

She nodded. "How did Louis's actions make you feel?"

"Why are you doing this to me? You've won, OK? You win."

"Seth, I want you to revisit some of these things with me because they all play a part in what's happened since, do you understand?"

"Oh, I understand, believe me."

"You've suffered a tremendous trauma, and many things have happened. It's important for you to retrace some of these events so you can better understand them, and also to better understand the subsequent impact they've had on you. It's all tied together, and these things have helped to contribute to what's happening now." She tried on another smile. "Make sense?"

Seth clenched his trembling hands into fists but kept them in his lap.

"All right," she said in her velvety voice. "Do you remember the conversations we had about your vacation trip to the cabin in Maine with your brother and your friends, and how you felt upset about the things that happened during that vacation?"

"Yes."

"And do you remember our discussions about how mental illness is often hereditary?"

He nodded.

"Would you agree you haven't been acting like yourself for some time now?"

Seth glared at her. "Why don't you go ahead and explain it to me? Lay it all out."

Doctor Farrow put the pad aside and folded her hands delicately across her knees. "Seth, your grandmother and brother both suffered from mental illness."

"Nana's always been eccentric, not mentally ill."

"That illness is something you've been dealing with for some time now," she said, dismissing him. "That doesn't mean you're insane, and no one is suggesting that you are. But you are struggling with some problems right now. Problems I fully believe we can resolve with your cooperation, but problems nonetheless. You began to not feel yourself some time ago, and things have been steadily unraveling since that time. Things at home became difficult, and then at work as well. You vacationed in Maine, had the episode at the cabin where your brother disappeared for a time, at night during the snowstorm, and that triggered many terrible childhood memories for you. I believe it also served as a trigger to some of the things you've been dealing with since.

"When you returned from that vacation," she continued, "your problems escalated. Within weeks you and your wife had separated. From there, problems at work began to mount. You decided to come and see me, and we began having these sessions together. Not long afterward, your friend Louis, struggling with his own inner demons regarding his divorce and his ex-wife's attempt to relocate with another man and take their children with her, attempted suicide. The shock, stress and depression associated with this made matters worse for you, and your problems escalated again."

"I knew you'd have it all figured out, Doc." Seth felt a smirk dance across his upper lip. "Somehow, I just knew it."

Her eyes again dropped to her pad. "A few moments ago, just before you woke up, you called out your brother's name. Do you remember doing that?"

"Raymond."

At the mention of his name, Doctor Farrow's expression changed ever so slightly, and Seth's heart plummeted as an overwhelming rush of realization and sorrow engulfed him. "Oh, Christ," he said softly. "*Raymond.*"

* * *

*Raymond takes another sip of whiskey; feels it warm his throat. Though he is nearly finished with his drink, Nana has yet to even taste hers. Neither has spoken in some time, choosing instead to listen to the wind and their thoughts and memories.*

*At one point Raymond can almost hear his mother singing to him again, nearly feel her arms around him, her love absorbing him and making everything all right. And in these memories he can see her face clear as day, like she is sitting right there at the table with him. His father is there too, standing a bit to the side with that wry look he so often had. Only Seth is missing from the picture. It is his time to be alone now, to fight the battles he feels he needs to.*

*"I know you're feeling tremendous sorrow," Nana says, her voice shattering the silence. "So am I. But there are far worse things than sorrow, my love."*

*Raymond nods. He knows this all too well. He wipes at his nose. The smell grows worse here with each passing minute. He remembers reading somewhere once that they put something in it so it would smell like this. A safeguard, they called it.*

*"I've always believed what's important is how one confronts and deals with those things, how one maintains one's poise and self-respect in the face of chaos. But it can't be an exercise purely for show. It needs to go deeper into one's soul than that because its very essence is more profound. It has no choice but to be what it is." She holds up her glass until the light from nearby windows catches the golden tint of the liquor. "In the early 1980s I visited Israel. One of the more fascinating sites I had the privilege to experience was The Masada. Are you familiar with it, Raymond?"*

*"Not really, no."*

*"It's an ancient mountain fortress that overlooks much of the Dead Sea." She takes a dainty sip from the glass. "It has an intriguing history, would you like to hear it?"*

*Raymond nods sullenly. The memories of his parents melt away to darkness.*

*"In 1st Century B.C., due to the threat posed by Cleopatra and Egypt, The Judean King Herod the Great had Masada built. At Herod's death years later, it was captured by the Romans and turned into a stronghold for the empire. It remained under their control for years until it was captured by the Zealots, a group of approximately one thousand people, including women and children, known for their strong positions and outlook on life. When Jerusalem fell under Roman occupation, the Zealots took refuge in Masada. The Romans responded by attacking the fortress. After years and numerous attempts to take the fortress, and eventually, due in large part to an enormous assault ramp the Romans built, it became apparent to the Zealots that Rome's victory was imminent.*

*"And so the Zealots had a choice to make," she continues, "a literal life or death decision."*

*Raymond reaches for his cigarettes, pulls one from the pack and holds it in his free hand, rolling it nervously between his fingers.*

*"Their decision was death. They chose suicide rather than slavery at the hands of the Romans, death over enslavement, dignity and principal over degradation and submission. Quite heroic, I'd say."*

*"Yes," he said softly.*

*Visions of Seth come to Raymond suddenly. He sees him in the bed next to his own, the two of them young and vibrant, laying in the dark, talking quietly then joking and laughing with each other before sleep takes them. There had been happy times, playful and carefree times when they'd been allowed to behave as young boys should, times before the darkness had become something hideous and frightening, a predator constantly on the hunt. It is that image of his big brother – the image of him laughing – that Raymond will take with him.*

*"To the Zealots," Nana says, raising high her glass.*

*He gently clicks his glass against hers. "To the Zealots."*

*Together, in single quick swallows, they empty their glasses then return them to the table.*

*Something in the next room creaks…a floorboard, perhaps a window casing.*

*Or something else.*

*Raymond's smile fades, gone like the innocent laughter and young faces in his mind. "They're here."*

*"I know," she whispers.*

*From the nearby corridor come the shuffling sounds of small, deadly things.*

*Raymond slides the cigarette into the corner of his mouth then carefully pushes his lighter across the table to her.*

*She takes the lighter in hand, flips it open with her thumb and holds it up for him as her eyes slowly fill with tears. "Come for one more walk in the rain with your Nana, my love."*

*Holding her gaze throughout, Raymond takes her free hand and cradles it gently in his own, remembering the gentle rain against his face, the smell of the ocean, the breeze and fresh sea air filling his lungs and making him feel so alive. And the love, most of all he remembers the love. Despite it all, there was so much – then and now – and try as it might, no madness, no amount of darkness has been able to kill it.*

*Raymond wants to believe that there is something fundamentally human about that, even as he leans across the table until the tip of his cigarette is within inches of the lighter.*

*He feels himself smile. It seems an odd thing to do just then, yet strangely fitting.*

*Alessandra's eyes slowly roll shut…and she ignites the lighter.*

* * *

"Would you like to talk about Raymond?" Doctor Farrow asked.

Seth shook his head no.

"I think it's important that we talk about him, Seth, don't you?"

"Raymond's dead," he said.

She watched him, offering nothing.

"I know that now."

"Why do you say that?"

"Do you have any brothers or sisters?"

"I'm an only child."

He pawed at his eyes, certain he'd find tears there, but they remained dry. The time for crying was over. The time had come for something else. "Then you wouldn't understand."

"Can you explain it to me?"

"Raymond's a part of me, and that part of me is gone. I can feel it."

She nodded, presumably satisfied with his answer. "Seth, the day before yesterday your brother, grandmother and her husband were involved in a terrible accident in your grandmother's home. Apparently there was a gas leak authorities believe came from the stove. There was an explosion. I'm very sorry to have to tell you this, but it's important that you know. They were all killed in the blast."

This time it was more difficult to restrain his emotions, but he managed it.

Once the slightest traces of tears had left his eyes and the lump in his throat had subsided, he did his best to stare Farrow down and reveal nothing in his expression. "Let me guess," he said a moment later, "I already knew that, right? It was just another *trigger* for my breakdown, one more thing, one more excuse to prove my insanity."

"I understand you and your brother were close," she said softly, "but do you think maybe the reason you were so sure he had died was because you *did* already know?"

"Whatever you say, Doc, whatever you say."

"I'm more interested in hearing what *you* have to say right now."

"I've heard that line from you before. You need new material."

She drew a slow breath, held it a beat. "After hearing the news about their deaths, you went on a drinking binge. You went to your office and assaulted Mr. Jacobs. The police were called, but you fled the area before you could be apprehended. You continued your drinking binge then wandered around the city until you found your way here, to Ms. Chandler's apartment. You left after an argument with her, came upon the wrong neighborhood at the wrong hour and were mugged and assaulted."

Seth grabbed the cup of water. The hell with it, he thought. Not much else to lose. He downed it then returned the cup to the nightstand. It felt nice on his dry, scratchy throat. "I guess I'm just trying to figure out whose benefit this is for."

"Why, yours, of course."

"Congratulations, you've got it all tied up with a pretty bow, nice and neat and making perfect sense right from the moment I supposedly heard this news," he said. "But there's one problem."

"And what would that be?"

"There may be a tiny bit of truth in what you just said, but the rest is bullshit." He leaned forward. "And you and I both know it."

"Why do you feel that way, Seth?"

"I *saw* you, you're not fooling anyone. I *know* what's happening."

"Seth, obviously the person you saw—or think you saw—wasn't me. It couldn't have been because I was in the Cayman Islands on vacation. And even if I had returned in time for it to be me, why would I be in some abandoned building, Seth?" She gave him one of her classic condescending looks. "Just the same, I do think we should discuss this, because obviously it's important to you. You keep saying you saw me and that you know what's happening. Talk about that a bit."

"I'm not doing this anymore. I'm done."

"You act as if this is some sort of conspiracy."

"That's exactly what it is."

"Seth," she said in a breathy voice, "do you know what an *intervention* is?"

He nodded.

"It's often a very effective tool in helping someone see and understand things they might not otherwise," she explained. "I don't think a traditional intervention is needed or appropriate here, but I do think briefly involving someone other than myself, someone in your life you know and trust who shares my concerns and who can express them to you from another perspective could be very helpful. It's all part of the process, Seth, a very important process where you'll be able to come to terms with some of the things that have happened to you over the last year or so. In the end, you'll be better equipped to confront your own actions since then, so that together, you and I can effectively deal with them. You've been experiencing a downward spiral for some time now, do you understand? Everyone around you and in your life has been a witness to it, and everyone wants to see you get well as quickly and as painlessly as possible. You haven't been yourself for a long time, and the point of this is to help you find yourself again so we can get to the heart of these problems and resolve them for you in a healthy manner." Doctor Farrow absently brushed a thick strand of blonde hair from the side of her face with a finger. "Now since we began today, I've gotten the impression you think I have some personal stake against you, or that I'm lying to you or manipulating the truth."

Seth gave a smirk Raymond would've been proud of. "Where'd you get that idea?"

Her expression revealed the full extent to which she had not found his comment amusing. "Sometimes when you hear the truth from multiple people rather than one, from people you love and respect and trust, and who love and respect and trust you, it can make quite a difference in one's overall perception of a situation. Do you understand?"

Seth swallowed nervously but said nothing.

Doctor Farrow stood up, straightened the hem of her skirt and with pad in hand strolled to the bedroom door. She opened it enough to squeeze her head through into the other room, and the murmur of nearby voices ceased. "All right," she said. "We're ready."

She returned to her chair with a quick smile.

The door opened slowly, and a larger shard of light bled into the otherwise murky room. An indistinct figure stepped through, closed the door behind it and stood awkwardly in the shadows beyond the doorway.

"Hello, Seth."

# Chapter 33

Seth watched him emerge from the shadows and move deeper into the room, coming to a halt just to the left of Doctor Farrow's chair.

"Hello, Mother."

Darian stood there calmly, his old smooth manner returned to him, his face markedly different than when Seth had last seen him. He looked rested and fresh, free of the worry and terror that had been consuming him previously. "You know, I really wish you wouldn't call me that," he said without a trace of anger or even annoyance. "I've never really cared for it."

"It's a term of endearment, you know that."

"I prefer Darian. That's my name."

"You've never had a problem with it before." Seth held his expression, doing his best to match Darian's composure. "What do you want?"

"Doctor Farrow asked if I'd speak to you. She thought it might help." He adjusted his eyeglasses and moved a bit closer. When Seth offered nothing, he said, "Just like everybody else, I'm worried about you. How are you feeling?"

"How are *you* feeling, Mother?"

He blinked slowly. "I know you've had some hard times recently, and I wanted to let you know how sorry I was to hear about Raymond and your grandmother."

"Tell me, D., what'd you find when you went home looking for Cynthia and Debra?" Seth asked. "Find what you were looking for?"

"I never knew Ray that well," he said, dismissing Seth's question, "but those few days we stayed at the cabin in Maine I really enjoyed his company—other than that one night where he had too much to drink and wandered out in the middle of the night into a snowstorm, that is." He attempted some light laughter. "I know at the time it was really frightening and you were worried—we all were—but we can look back on it now and laugh, right?"

Memories of the night at the cabin came at Seth again, this time in quick, stabbing, violently stunning flashes, and the closer he looked into Darian's eyes, the more vivid the memories became.

Screams echoed in his mind as Christy peered at him from some distant darkness, the corners of her eyes leaking blood.

"What about Christy?" Seth said defiantly. "Want to laugh about her for a while too?"

Darian turned his head a bit, as if to better hear him. "Who?"

"Yeah," Seth sighed. "That's what I figured."

"You haven't mentioned anyone named Christy to me before," Doctor Farrow interjected. "Would you like to share that with me now?"

"No thanks." Seth remained focused on Darian.

"What about Louis?"

"His condition hasn't changed," Darian said.

"Oh, Louis you remember."

"Of course I remember Louis, Seth."

"Do you remember him going out that window, or did I make all that up too?"

"That's nothing to joke about." Darian's expression grew grave. "Louis is still in a coma, and I was *there* when he tried to kill himself."

"Where are you now, Mother?"

"Look, we've been friends a long time," he said softly, moving a bit closer still, "and that means a lot to me, I want you to know that. I'm here for you if you need me, and I'm here to help in any way I can, OK?"

Seth tried to find the man he knew, the man he'd known for so long. He tried to find the man that had stepped in for Raymond at the last minute and been an excellent best man at his wedding to Peggy. He tried to find anything that might link this person standing before him to the person he'd known and trusted for years, a person he'd laughed with and experienced so much with over the years. But all he was certain of was that whoever or whatever this was, it certainly wasn't Darian Stone.

"What the hell have they done to you?" Seth whispered.

Darian exchanged an awkward glance with Doctor Farrow then moved away and took up position near a bureau on the right-hand wall of the bedroom, arms folded and a look of deep concern on his face.

The door opened again, and two people filed in.

Ruthie came first, followed by Bill Jacobs. They stood on either side of Doctor Farrow's chair, Jacobs smiling incessantly and Ruthie shooting him self-conscious sideways glances. Initially neither said a word, looking to Farrow for some indication that it was all right to speak.

Rather than acknowledge them, Seth tried to listen subtly to determine if there was anyone else beyond the bedroom door. The moving shadows and muffled voices had stopped.

"Go ahead, William," Doctor Farrow said.

"Seth," Jacobs said cheerfully, "I want you to know I don't have any hard feelings about what happened at the office. We're going to just pretend all that never happened, all right? Let's move forward, that's what's important. Moving forward and making sure you're well. OK, buddy?"

Ignoring an intense desire to assault him again, Seth gave instead a slow nod.

"Are you feeling any better?" Ruthie asked, looking at her feet like a guilty schoolgirl. "You scared the hell out of me when you ran out of here before. Those guys could've killed you. I'm just glad you're OK."

Silence filled the room.

"Finished?" Seth asked a moment later.

"Perhaps you'd like to thank them?" Doctor Farrow suggested. "After all, Mr. Jacobs has been good enough to forget about your earlier violent outburst, and Ms. Chandler has let you stay here and recuperate."

Seth stared at her.

"Talk about how you're feeling right now," she pressed.

"Is there anyone else here?"

"Why do you ask?"

He shrugged, feigning nonchalance. "Wondering

what other surprises you might have for me on the other side of that door."

"Is there someone else you were hoping to see?"

He knew at this point he could only hope Peggy was still safe, but realized the odds of that were probably low at best. "Is my wife going to walk in next?"

"We haven't been able to get in touch with her just yet," Doctor Farrow said, "but I do think it's important we do. Though you're separated at the moment, I assume you'd still like her involved in your recovery?"

Seth felt an enormous weight lifted from his chest. There was still hope, but he had to get to where he'd proposed—the banks of the Charles River—by noon. "Leave her out of it," he said evenly.

"If you want me to talk with her, I'd be happy to," Darian offered.

"You stay the fuck away from her or I'll—"

"Now, Seth," Doctor Farrow said suddenly, "it's that type of behavior we cannot tolerate. No more violence, no more outbursts, do you understand?"

He rose slowly from the edge of the bed. If he made a break for the door and was able to force his way out, he was relatively certain he could outrun all of them.

"Sit down, Seth." Doctor Farrow watched him a moment, and when he didn't do as she'd instructed, called, "Mr. Gordon, would you come in here a moment, please?"

Seth looked to the door. A rugged middle-aged man in a white shirt and pants stepped into the room. "Everything all right, ma'am?" he asked, eyeing Seth.

"This is Mr. Gordon. He works for Saint Elizabeth's hospital, just up the street. He's here to help transport you safely to the psych ward there, should it be necessary." She offered a triumphant smile. "*Is* it necessary, Seth?"

Seth considered Gordon's muscular physique, and with a sigh, shook his head no.

"I'm sorry, I didn't quite hear you."

"No," he said softly, lowering himself back onto the bed.

The doctor gave Gordon a dismissive glance and he left the room.

"Very impressive," Seth said wearily. "Does he roll over and fetch too? Hump your leg when you get lonely?"

Farrow's smile slipped away, and her face turned dark. "Destruction isn't always necessary, sometimes control is enough."

*It's all a mind-fuck*, Raymond whispered to him.

"Do you understand now, Seth?" she asked. "Do you see how easy this all is?"

Ruthie stepped forward and crouched down in front of him. "Why rot in some mental hospital when you can be reborn?"

"Love, faith and free will," he said. "Remember, Ruthie? You can't take them from me. I have to give them to you, and I won't. You hear me? I won't. Not ever."

"You're already infected, just let it go. Set it free." Ruthie smiled. "It's so easy."

Doctor Farrow rose from her chair, put the pad and pen aside. "It's all about bridging the gap from here," she said, pointing to her temple, "to here." She made a slow sweeping gesture with her hand, indicating everything around her, the world.

"You can have anything you want," Jacobs said. "More money, a better position with the company, better place to live—it's all right there for us to reach out and take, Seth, don't you see? It's our time now. We can have and do anything we want."

"What about everyone else?"

"Long as we get ours," Jacobs said, his ridiculous grin finally leaving him, "fuck 'em."

Seth could only hope the sickness he felt in the pit of his stomach translated to the look on his face as he glared at his former boss. "It's not such a big leap for all of us, is it, Bill?"

"Forget him then," Ruthie said, moving her hands seductively across her body, down onto his knees and then Seth's thighs. "I've seen the way you look at me. You always tried so hard to look like you didn't notice me or think of me that way, but I could tell. I could tell how much you wanted me, and it's OK."

Seth glanced at Darian. He smiled encouragingly. "Do it."

Ruthie stood before him, offering her hands. "Come on, it's easy."

He hesitantly reached out, took her hands and allowed her to gradually pull him to his feet. He stood there awkwardly, as Ruthie pulled him closer, wrapping her arms around him as Doctor Farrow and Darian watched.

"Think about how you feel," Ruthie whispered in his ear. "Think about all the things you want to do with me...*to* me. Just close your eyes and think about it. The violence and anger you feel is good, OK? Let it go, set it free, use it, give it over to them."

Doctor Farrow moved closer, reached out and ran a

hand along Seth's back. "Let them out," she whispered. "Let them out, Seth."

Seth looked at her and nodded slowly, submissively.

Then in one quick move, pivoted around, scooped the pen from the chair where Doctor Farrow had left it, and stabbed it down into Ruthie's face.

He didn't realize he'd buried it halfway into her eye until she began to scream and staggered back, the pen protruding from her socket.

Seth grabbed the chair and swung it at Darian, slamming it into his head before he had time to react. It connected with an odd clanging sound as it bounced off his skull, and Darian collapsed into the bureau then tumbled to the floor.

Whirling like a dervish, chair still in hand, Seth swung it around and smashed it into Doctor Farrow. It hit her with such force he felt the impact reverberate up his arms and into his hands as the chair flew free of his grasp and crashed into the far wall.

Doctor Farrow left her feet and vaulted back, eyeglasses and one high-heeled pump sailing into the air before she landed, flopping onto her back a few feet away. Lying motionless, her eyes rolled back to white and a trickle of blood leaked across her face from a wound beyond her hairline, the crimson hue contrasting with her blonde hair.

Though the entire thing had taken only a matter of seconds, it unfolded in nearly silent slow-motion.

Until Ruthie's screaming snapped him back.

She had dropped to her knees and was screaming unintelligibly, hands clutching the pen embedded in her eye as blood and other matter ran from it like water from a faucet.

Realizing what he'd done, Seth's stomach twisted and he nearly vomited.

Ignoring the nausea, he ran for the door in an attempt to gain as much momentum as possible. Just as Mr. Gordon stepped quickly into the room, Seth squared his shoulder and launched himself toward the doorway.

They collided with a sickening thud, and Seth felt himself drive through the man, ignoring the pain and impact, his feet still under him somehow and moving, running, carrying him forward as Gordon, off-balance and caught off-guard, received the brunt, taking Seth's shoulder in the chest. In a continuous frenzied run, Seth knocked him out of the way and ran right over him, sending him sprawling to the floor.

On pure adrenaline, he ran through the apartment, out the door and continued at a full run until he'd reached the street.

It was no longer snowing but the storm from the day before had left an enormous amount of accumulation on the city streets. Much of it had yet to be sufficiently plowed, but that which had was pushed into mountainous drifts on either side of the street that helped to provide him some cover. The temperature had plummeted since the last time he'd been outside, and the cold hit him like a sledgehammer, particularly since he was without a coat. Regardless, he pressed on, still running but a bit slower now and checking back over his shoulder every few seconds until he'd put several blocks between himself and Ruthie's building.

But even when he shifted to a brisk walking pace, he realized he had no money, no car keys and no means of doing much of anything but walking.

The city streets were nearly empty, and quieter than usual, locked down and barren after what had turned out to be a fairly major snowstorm. His destination was a long walk from where he was, particularly in those conditions and in that temperature. It would take him a while, but he felt he could reach the banks of the Charles River well within the timeframe he'd given Peggy if he kept a steady pace and didn't encounter any other roadblocks.

And, of course, *if* Peggy had done as he'd asked.

There was still hope while she was alive and not afflicted.

*You're already infected,* Ruthie had told him.

But that was no longer Ruthie. Something like Ruthie, or maybe just one part of her, of what she'd once been, the rest destroyed and devoured, gone.

The endless white everywhere reminded him of the forest, of that night. Things flashed in his mind, but he could not be distracted now, could not remember now. He stuffed his hands into his pockets and hurried on, fighting them off with one goal and one goal only.

He had to find Peggy. It was his only chance…*their* only chance.

And probably the last one they'd ever get.

# Chapter 34

The Longfellow Bridge spans the Charles River and connects Cambridge to the city of Boston. On this cold day, the river was calm, its normal glistening beauty and vibrancy replaced with a look and feel of deserted inertia. The normal steady traffic associated with the bridge was absent, and even in the distance it—along with the rest of Boston's skyline—was dressed in white. Seth could've been the last person on Earth, there on the banks of the Charles, amongst the barren trees and long stretches of snow-covered ground, as the area had taken on an uncharacteristically apocalyptic look, frozen and bleak.

Bound by the surreal sights, sounds and feelings the icy landscape produced in him, he could do nothing to stop the frenzied cries from that night in the forest a year before from returning. Frantic cries, not quite human, had surged through the trees surrounding him as he fell to his knees in a clearing ringed by enormous trees. Snow had blown about as the sky shook and burst apart, showering the darkness down around him like water from a bucket, drowning him, pulling him under, down into its depths of its mass until he and it were one.

Seth closed his eyes. A violent shiver throttled him.

The visions retreated, and as he opened his eyes and returned to the world, through the swirling clouds of breath encircling him with each exhale, he saw Peggy's car pull into one of the nearby parking spaces adjacent to the park. He was so cold he could barely feel his hands and feet, and his shivering had become so violent his muscles had begun to tire from it. But he remained concealed behind a tree, watching the bright yellow Volkswagen Bug idling in the space, its startling color standing out on the otherwise drab landscape like a neon sign. He could see Peggy behind the wheel and Petey in the passenger seat.

She looked around for a moment then rather hesitantly stepped out of the car.

Dressed in a heavy coat, boots and a big knit hat, she was the most beautiful sight he'd ever seen. She scanned the area subtly, and as she turned in his direction, Seth stepped out from behind the tree.

She saw him immediately and began moving toward him with a look of deep concern, her boots crunching the frozen top layer of snow. "Are you all right? You scared the shit out of me with that phone call, I—where's your coat? You'll freeze to death out here dressed like..." She came to a slow stop once she was within a few feet of him. "Is that blood?"

He looked down, saw a small bit of blood spattered there he hadn't noticed before. Ruthie's blood. "It's OK—it..." Her screams echoed in his mind, along with the horrible crunching and squishing sounds of the pen bursting into her eye. "It's all right."

"What happened to your face?"

"My face..."

"Did you get into a *fight*? You've got to be kidding, that's beyond juvenile."

He hadn't seen himself in a mirror in some time, but apparently the beating he'd suffered had left visible marks as well as the aches and pains he'd been feeling since returning to consciousness. "I had some trouble, a couple guys mugged me and—"

"*Mugged* you? Jesus, are you all right?"

"Yeah, I—it doesn't matter, I—are you alone?" he asked, still watching over her shoulder.

"Petey's with me." She motioned in the direction of the car.

Seth managed a weak smile. "Does anyone know you're here?"

"I thought I wasn't supposed to tell anyone."

"Where are you staying?"

"A motel, like you said. Despite my better judgment, I did as you asked."

"Thanks for coming through, Peg."

"You're welcome." She crossed her arms. "Now maybe if it's not too much of an inconvenience you could see your way clear to letting me in on just what in the *fuck* is going on!"

He nodded, watching her, gauging her. "Did you talk to Doctor Farrow?"

"Your psychiatrist? Why would I talk to her?"

"You didn't hear from her then?"

"Was I supposed to?"

She looked like herself, but then so had Ruthie. "I thought she might've tried to contact you."

"If she did it was after I left the house. Why would she be contacting me?"

He stepped a bit closer. "Should I let them out, Peggy?"

A look of confusion joined the frustration already present in her expression. "Let who out where? What the hell are you talking about?"

"Thank God," he said through a heavy sigh. "Thank God, thank God."

"Why would Doctor Farrow contact me? Did something happen?"

"She's a part of it now."

Peggy shrugged. "She's a part of *what* now?"

He looked out at the water, and to one particular patch of snowy ground. Though the cold made his eyes tear, he could still recall blurry images of standing with Peggy in that precise spot—so much younger then, so full of hope and love—her face so bright and happy, eyes wide and slowly filling with tears as Seth, grinning from ear-to-ear, took the ring from his pocket and slowly dropped to one knee.

Peggy followed his stare then looked back at him, the cold causing her eyes to tear as well. Or perhaps it wasn't the cold at all.

"It was a whole different world then, wasn't it," he said softly.

"The world's the same as it's always been," she told him. "It's people who change."

He went to her and they embraced much as they had so many years before, the steady pulse of her breath against his cheek and her arms wrapped tightly around his neck. "What's this all about, Seth?" she whispered. "Please, I can't take anymore of this."

She smelled good—familiar and safe—and her body felt strong and warm and perfect against his own. The rollercoaster ride that were his emotions took another quick turn, and he quickly kissed Peggy, first on the lips and then on the forehead, holding her face in his hands and looking deep into her eyes. "We have to get out of here," he said. "How far is the motel?"

"Little over half an hour, it's just a small roadside place in Kingston."

"Take me there," he said wearily, "and I'll remember."

"Remember?"

Seth let his eyes wander about the small park. Memories of the night at the cabin came at him again, attacking him, and he could no longer stop them. But then, he no longer wanted to. He reached out, gently wiped a tear from her cheek. "Take me there and I'll tell you everything."

With a heavy sigh, Peggy took his hand and slowly led him back toward the car.

# Chapter 35

Seth emerged from the bathroom, one towel fastened around his waist and another draped over his neck. Though his body still ached, the hot shower had helped, and had served to clear his head somewhat.

The motel was a small, one-story, unremarkable series of connected rooms on a rural road a few moments from the highway. Though Kingston was only one town over from where she resided in Plymouth, Peggy had made a solid choice by renting a room here, Seth thought. The room was close enough to the highway if escape became necessary, but also secluded enough to provide a sufficiently clandestine hideout.

Peggy was at the window, gazing out at the parking lot, which was empty but for her car. When Seth stepped out of the bathroom she let the curtain close, and the level of darkness in the room swelled, as with the curtains drawn the only light came from the television, which was tuned to an old black-and-white movie, the sound turned down. "I think we might be the only people staying here," she said.

"Good." Seth went to her, kissed her lightly on the cheek then moved to the bed and sat down at its foot. He glanced at the TV. John Garfield and Lana Turner were locked in a primal embrace, the picture casting beams of contrasting light that played across the walls and floor in odd, ghostly patterns. He watched the movie a moment. It was one of his favorites, *The Postman Always Rings Twice.* Garfield and Turner kissed with abandon, unaware that they were doomed, the walking dead.

Seth glanced at his wife, curious if they ought to feel the same.

*You can't win,* Raymond had told him.

Maybe not, he thought, but I *can* remember.

"Peggy," he said softly, "I need to tell you about Raymond."

She looked at him, nodded.

"He's dead."

She brought a hand to her throat. "Raymond's *dead*?"

He fought back the tears, cleared his throat loudly. "He, Nana and Rolf are all dead."

"My God, what—what happened?"

"The papers will say it was all an accident, a gas leak in Nana's home that led to an explosion." He took the towel from his neck, slung it over his head and began to rub his hair dry. "But suicide is probably closer to the truth."

Peggy's face reached a new depth of paleness but she stood awkwardly still. "I don't—what—Seth, what are you talking about? They killed themselves? Why would they do that?"

They watched him now from the shadows in his

mind as well, vague and indistinct, like the faces of his parents, faded from this reality and already absorbed into another. Quiet sentinels seeing everything…and nothing at all.

"How do I tell you the world's gone crazy and that there's a good chance you and I could be one of only a handful of sane people left?"

"I don't understand."

"Neither do I," he sighed. "But it's happening, Peg. Not like in novels or the movies, but it *is* happening."

"What's happening, Seth? *What*?"

"When you and I were still together," he said, "and I went on the trip to the cabin with Darian and Louis…something happened out there, Peg, in the woods, something I couldn't remember, and that I'm still remembering even now."

"You weren't the same when you came back," she said. "I tried to reach you, God knows I did, but you wouldn't talk to me."

"I had trouble sleeping and I was having these terrible nightmares, I—I was on edge and—"

"Rage, Seth, that's what it's called," she said flatly. "You'd fly into these rages and it scared the hell out of me because that wasn't you, it wasn't the man I knew and loved."

"I was…changed."

"Yes," she said, not yet understanding what she was agreeing to. "And those changes led to our separation, and you know it. We had some problems before that trip, but your behavior after you got back became too much for me to deal with. I loved you then and I love you still, you know that, but you were impossible."

"I'm sorry. I'm so goddamn sorry, but—"

"I know my not being able to have children was always an issue, but I—"

"*No,*" he said firmly. "No, this had nothing to do with us, Peg."

"Then tell me what it does have to do with. And I suggest you do a good job of it because right now you're behaving like someone desperately in need of psychiatric care."

He nodded, fought the impulse to reach out and take her hands and instead pulled the towel from his head and tossed it aside. It landed in the corner near Petey, who had curled up there to take a nap. The dog raised his head a bit, sniffed the towel, glanced at Seth then resumed his slumber with a soft sighing moan. "The things that happened were a part of something much bigger that had been going on for years. But none of us knew that then, except for Raymond. Remember how he just showed up unannounced right before we left? I was so glad to see him, remember?" Seth felt an involuntary smile on his lips. "I was so happy he was coming with us. Hell, we were all excited about going. Louis was a little upset that Raymond showed up like that—they never got along that well, they both had too much alpha male in them, I guess—but he got over it and even they were getting along great once we got going. We were all so thrilled to get a break from the company, some down time up in the woods just hanging around, playing some cards, drinking too much and relaxing, it was like nothing could ruin it. Christ, it was supposed to be *fun* but..." The smile slipped away as Seth drew a deep breath, closed his eyes and let the memories flow over him like slowly breaking waves. "Then Christy showed up."

"Christy. Who the hell is Christy?"

"This girl," he said, eyes still closed. "She just appeared out of nowhere, running toward our camp and covered in blood like some madwoman. She was terrified and in shock and told us this local guy had kidnapped and abused her and that she'd killed him in self-defense. But from the moment she came over that ridge, nothing made any sense, nothing was ever right again."

"You never mentioned any of this to me before, why—"

"We took her in, tried to help her, but—but we didn't know, we didn't understand."

Flashes of his dream came to him—

*Lightning...lightning between the trees...blood in the snow.*

—then receded, left him covered in the dark and terrible memories of that night.

"There was a snowstorm coming, a bad one, and we were trapped there with no clue as to what was happening," he continued, eyes clenched. "Raymond knew more than the rest of us, of course, but I don't think even he completely realized what was happening, at least not at that point. Even he didn't know what was out there yet, what was coming for all of us, infecting us...and what's still asleep in me now, trying like hell to come awake."

# Chapter 36

Christy walked slowly and with a degree of effort, her legs neither as strong nor steady as they needed to be, but still capable of carrying her. As if to be certain they were still there, she gave a final glance over her shoulder at the men then slipped into the bathroom, closing the door behind her…

"You've been awfully quiet through all this, Ray," Seth said. "What do you think?"

"I think I'll go have a smoke." Raymond moved toward the door, cigarettes in hand.

"Great," Louis cracked. "Thanks for your input, man."

Ray shook a cigarette free from the pack, rolled one into the corner of his mouth and lit it with a Zippo. "Storm's already here, snow's already falling, what's there to talk about? Like Seth said, nobody's going anywhere anyway." He extinguished the flame with a quick snap shut of the lighter then pulled open the door and stepped outside. "Least not any time soon."

"I guess he's right," Seth said. "Not much else we

can do at this point."

Louis swatted at the air between them. "Fine, but I don't have to fucking like it."

"No, you don't," Darian agreed. "None of us do, but it's the way it is, so we better deal with it. Like it or not that storm's not going to accommodate us, Lou."

"True enough." Louis slapped Darian on the shoulder and headed for the door. "Come on, man, let's get whatever else we need inside, straighten up camp and hunker down before it gets real bad out there. Seth, you keep an eye on her."

Once they had left him alone, Seth stifled a yawn, realizing he had begun to crash rather suddenly from the earlier adrenaline rush. He walked to the bathroom at the rear of the cabin. He'd expected to find the door fully closed, but it was ajar enough for him to see inside. Though he glimpsed only shadows he looked away quickly so she wouldn't think him intrusive. "Christy, are you OK in there?" When she didn't answer he stepped closer and looked up, this time focusing on the room beyond the door. "Christy?"

She stood in the center of the small room, staring at him. The bloody shirt she'd been wearing was tossed on the edge of the basin sink, and the sweatshirt Seth had given her to change into was clutched in both hands and pressed against her chest in an attempt to cover her breasts. She had not yet pulled it on.

Their eyes met.

"I'm sorry," he said. "I just wanted to make sure you were all right."

Christy slowly dropped her hands, bringing the sweatshirt with them. Though she was nude from the waist up, at that moment there was little erotic appeal to her presence, and it struck Seth that the frail and terrified girl she'd been earlier was now cold and somewhat detached in an almost predatory way. Yet she seemed altogether ill at ease in the role, as if she had little choice in the matter.

"Get dressed," he said in what he hoped was a fatherly tone. "You don't have to do that sort of thing here, all right?"

Making no attempt to cover herself, Christy moved toward him, her legs still shaky.

Seth reached out and slowly closed the door, but before he moved away he heard her on the other side, her breath heavy and loud, as if her face were pressed up against the casing. "It's OK," she whispered to him. *"It's OK to scream."*

He backed away, and though he was not certain he'd heard her correctly, there was no mistaking the chill than rippled across the back of his neck and down across his shoulder blades. Obviously the poor girl had been through hell and might even still be in some form of shock—he couldn't be sure—but there was an undeniable uneasiness he felt toward her he hadn't previously. Something had changed. Or perhaps he'd only just then noticed it.

*It's OK to scream.*

Why would she say that? She wouldn't. Surely he'd misheard her.

He walked back to the main room and stood near the stove to warm himself. Through the windows, he saw the snow—like tiny kernels of salt blowing about the sky—the kind of snow that always signaled an incoming storm of enormous proportions. The worst blizzards always began that way, with barely perceptible flakes that slowly mounted then suddenly grew to impenetrable walls of snow and ice within minutes. That's how nature often behaved, it seemed, slowly at first, lulling the world to sleep and then striking rapidly, mercilessly. Perfect, really. Perfectly deadly…but perfect nonetheless.

Seth watched as Louis closed up the SUV and grabbed the last of the essentials from it. Darian gathered the wood he'd been carrying previously, but had dropped upon Christy's arrival into camp, and headed for the front door.

As his chill dissipated, Seth moved closer to the window and scanned the area for his brother.

Raymond was leaned back against the woodpile in one of his typical casual cool poses, a large ax in his hand held down against the side of his leg and a burning cigarette dangling from his mouth. Through the bursts of snowflakes, Seth found his brother's eyes, and realized they were looking directly into his own.

"Come on," Louis said, waving at Raymond. "Get inside before we start really getting shit-hammered."

Raymond smoked his cigarette, said nothing.

"There's already plenty of wood inside, Ray," Darian called from the front porch. "And I'm adding this to the pile so we should be fine." He raised the pieces cradled in his arms to emphasize his point.

"And long as Lizzie Borden's visiting," Louis quipped, "leave the ax outside."

"Jesus, Lou, she might hear you," Darian snapped. "Be quiet."

"I don't have to watch what I say in my own place, Mother."

"It's not your place. And a little common decency

wouldn't kill you, would it?"

Seth's eyes remained locked with Raymond's as Darian and Louis crossed into the cabin, still bickering.

Darian carried the wood to a large bin near the stove and dropped it in. "Besides, that's nothing to joke about," he said quietly, "a man's been killed and she's the one that did it. She's been through an ordeal we can't even begin to imagine, show some sensitivity, for God's sake. What the hell's the matter with you?"

Louis, carrying a cooler and other assorted supplies, flashed Darian an annoyed look then turned to Seth. "Your brother having a seizure out there or is he just being his typical rude motherfucking self?"

Seth ignored him as well, and continued watching his brother. Raymond had an odd quality that often surfaced in times of extreme stress or trouble, something he'd developed once he'd left childhood behind, and something Seth had seen many times over the years and developed a talent for spotting. Unlike the frenzied horror of his night terrors years before, as an adult, Raymond tended to react quite differently. Rather than outwardly lose control, he'd become spooked—the way wild animals often do in certain dangerous circumstances—and while in this state remain calm and composed, the terror contained, hidden.

"Must run in their family," Louis said, placing the cooler on the floor next to the table.

"Sorry." Seth finally broke eye contract and acknowledged him. "Just let him be, Louis, he'll come in when he's ready."

"Hey, whatever, he can freeze his hog off out there if he wants, I don't give a shit. But it'd be nice if we could close the fucking door at some point before spring sets in." Louis took up position next to the stove, slapped his still gloved hands together, shuffled his feet furiously and cocked his head toward the bathroom. "What's she doing in there?"

"Changing," Seth said absently.

"How long does it take to change into a sweat-shirt?"

"Maybe we should check on her," Darian suggested.

Seth was about to tell them he already had when the bathroom door opened and Christy stepped out. She approached them slowly, self-consciously. "I wanted to…I just wanted to thank you guys for helping me."

"It's the least we could do."

Everyone turned in unison to the front doorway. Raymond stood watching her.

An awkward silence fell over the cabin.

"Yes—well—once the storm passes we'll sort all this out," Darian said suddenly. "For now, none of us are going anywhere so let's just try to make the best of it." He went to the wood stove and removed the cover from a large pot on one of the burners. "The stew's almost done. Another half hour or so and we can eat."

Louis pulled a chair out from the table and collapsed down into it. He found a beer in the cooler next to him and opened the tab with a loud pop. "Until then, I suggest we all start drinking heavily and get knee-deep in some good poker. Who's in?"

"I'll play," Seth said, doing his best to relax. He went to his suitcase, grabbed a small jar of change and joined Louis at the table. "Toss me one of those beers, too."

"Is it OK if I lay down for a while?" Christy asked. "I still don't feel very good."

"Of course," Darian led her back to the bed where she'd been previously. "Get some rest and I'll wake you when dinner's ready. Some hot food will do you good."

She settled into bed, allowed Darian to cover her with the blankets and smiled at him appreciatively. "Thank you."

"You don't have to thank me," he said, smiling back. "Just rest, OK?"

She nodded.

Darian gave her a quick wink then took a seat at the table. "Deal me in."

"How about it, Ray?" Louis asked, shuffling the cards. "Feeling lucky?"

"Not a minute in my life."

"Maybe today's your day, man. Never know."

Raymond looked at him as if to say: *I know. Believe me, I know.*

After a moment he closed the door, secured it and walked casually across the room to his duffel bag. He rummaged through it until he found a bottle of Jack Daniels then went to the fireplace, turned the chair there so it was facing the beds, and after taking a long pull from the bottle, sat down. "Think I'll sit this one out, fellas."

Louis stifled a laugh. "Thought we weren't supposed to be too obvious about keeping an eye on her," he said under his breath.

"That was the plan," Darian muttered.

"Well, at the moment he's about as subtle as a bean

fart in church."

"You are a piece of work, Louis," Darian laughed, "a real piece of work."

With a wide, shark-like grin, Louis dealt the cards.

Seth glanced over at Raymond. He was watching Christy, a dead look in his eyes.

"Ante up, ass-munch."

He turned to Louis. "Huh?"

"You're light." He indicated the pot. "No pay no play, sailor."

"Sorry." Seth tossed a quarter in and picked up his cards. Full house: aces over tens.

He should've been happy but a horrible restlessness churned through him, playing across his mind like distant storm clouds roiling over an otherwise clear horizon, promising only imminent darkness and the arrival of those that existed within it.

And come they would.

* * *

They played sloppy poker, ate enormous helpings of stew, drank more than was necessary and did their best to laugh and pass the hours. Outside, the storm raged on.

Christy ate when the stew was served but did little else. Napping in bed beneath a pile of blankets, she came awake only a few times in short intervals while the others played cards. Throughout the evening, Raymond remained in the chair next to the fireplace, smoking a cigarette now and then or taking an occasional quick pull of JD, watching her all the while with the same lifeless look in his eyes.

# Deep Night

After putting the inevitable off long as possible, they eventually decided to turn in.

Everyone, that was, except Raymond.

* * *

At some point after they had all drifted off to sleep, Seth came awake to find Raymond still in the chair near the fireplace. Instead of watching Christy, he had now taken to staring at the fire.

They had agreed to take shifts keeping an eye on her, but it seemed pointless now, as she had been asleep for most of the evening.

"Ray," he whispered, "you OK?"

He offered a slight nod.

"I'll take the next shift. You take the bed, OK? When I'm done I can use the sleeping bag, it's not a big deal."

"It's OK. Wanted to watch the fire a while anyway. Not real sleepy."

He looked over at the bed where Christy lay sound asleep. "You sure you're OK?"

"Too much to drink, that's all." Raymond held up the bottle of Jack Daniels and gave a feeble smile. He'd had a lot to drink that evening, the bottle was nearly empty. "Go ahead and get some more sleep, I'm cool."

"Something's got you spooked, Ray, I can tell. What is it, what's wrong?"

He was quiet for a very long while. "Don't have a good feeling about this," he finally said through a sigh. "It's probably nothing but…" He took another swig of whiskey. "Like Darian said, we can sort it all out come morning. Until then I just feel better staying up and keeping an eye on things, OK?"

"All right," he agreed, albeit reluctantly. "Wake me when you've had enough and I'll take over for you."

Raymond nodded, his attention again focused on the fire.

Seth lay back, closed his eyes and some time later slipped back to sleep.

* * *

Night. Late Night. Deep Night.

The wood stove had burned out and the Coleman lanterns were extinguished, but the fireplace still burned strong, filling the small cabin with a thick, stifling heat and a centralized but fair amount of flickering light. The cabin was silent but for sporadic pops or crackles from the fire, and even the wind had softened.

There in the woods, isolated and alone, they might as well have been on some distant planet, the cabin a solitary man-made intrusion on an otherwise pristine and natural vista. The unique hush of a forest in winter—a quiet stillness unlike any other—fell over the camp as snow spiraled delicately but steadily through the trees, veiling the star-filled night sky, nothing moving in the darkness and soft moonlight but the never-ending cascade of white flakes, curiously beautiful as petite pieces of intricately etched glass.

*Wake up.*

A voice, oddly monotone and hollow—soulless—spoke to him in not quite a whisper.

*Wake up, Seth.*

Echoing softly through his mind, it roused him

from sleep.

Consciousness, if that's what it was, came to him slowly. His vision cleared gradually but remained somewhat blurred, as if something thick and gummy had been rubbed across his eyes. Patterns on the wall flickered, and he realized he was seeing shadows cast from the fire. He blinked and gently rubbed his eyes, but still saw the world like a camera lens smeared with Vaseline. His arm felt heavy and weak, and it flopped back to his side lifelessly. His head lolled to the side. The chair in front of the fireplace was empty. The bottle of Jack Daniels, also empty, lay on its side next to it on the floor.

He closed his eyes.

*Wake up, Seth.*

Movement—a quick, scurrying sound—came from somewhere above him.

There was something on the roof, something moving. Quickly, like a pebble rolling across it from one side to the other, it scraped and clicked across the darkness above him as whatever it was negotiated up one side of the sloping roof and down across the other. But the snow that had surely accumulated on the roof would pad such noises and make them impossible…wouldn't it?

Seth opened his eyes. The blurriness had lessened but he still couldn't see clearly.

The sound on the roof ceased.

All sound had, it seemed, and now there was only silence. Impossible silence.

*Can you feel it?*

The wind's whisper returned, but softly, gently.

*Can you feel us?*

"Raymond," he said in a gurgling, barely audible voice.

Shuffling sounds distracted him. He listened.

The porch, something was moving on the porch just outside the cabin door.

Shuffling movement—closer and louder, more intrusive, bolder than before—and then a pitter-patter sound like…like children running closer.

"Raymond?" he said again, louder this time, with more force, his voice clearing.

*Can you hear the night, Seth*?

The gauze-like film over his eyes weakened, and the cabin slowly blended into focus.

*Can you hear it coming alive*?

A shifting of shadows and a break in the moonlight drew his attention to the floor. Someone was whispering nearby, but Seth could not make out any specific words or phrases. He peered through the semi-darkness, following the sound.

*Our minds are the battleground, Seth.*

Silhouettes moved together on the floor, near the sleeping bag. Seth's vision was still cloudy, but better, improving with each passing second, and he was able to discern three distinct shapes. The closest to his bed was Christy. He could see the side of her face in the moonlight. She knelt next to the sleeping bag and Louis was lying on the floor, looking up at her with a mesmerized expression. But there was something wrong with his eyes, something slightly off, as if he were sleepwalking with them open. Yet he could see and was clearly cognizant of what was happening. Also on the floor but a few feet away, Darian sat watching them; a strangely docile smile on his face that looked almost drug-induced. *Raymond,* Seth thought. *Where's Raymond?*

Christy slowly pulled the shirt Seth had given her off and tossed it aside. Completely nude beneath it, she knelt before them, her face pale as the rest of her body.

*They're phantasms traveling through our minds, never provable, never seen and always hidden in the dark.*

She went to Louis, and he welcomed her in his arms as they both disappeared into the darkness, falling back beyond the scope of moonlight. Darian watched them silently until two small hands reached up out of the darkness. He took them, allowed them to gently pull him down, out of the moonlight as well.

Time seemed eerily malleable just then, moving like dark liquid behind his eyes, slowly flowing and shifting from one point to the next. Silently. Deliberately.

*That's the vehicle they use for movement, for infection from one person to the next.*

Seth felt a sudden pressure on the bed. Christy's sorrowful face appeared above him, slinking closer, her hands gliding up across his body. He wanted to move, wanted to call out, but found it impossible to do either. Christy's face hovered above his, her hair dangling down, the ends tickling his cheeks. She looked so devastatingly sad, yet the heat from her body was undeniable, pulsing from her in waves. Her small breasts pushed against his chest, and her hands slid down his chest, across his stomach and into his underwear, gripping him. He felt himself harden against her cold touch.

*Sin. They use our sins against us.*

Christy's lips brushed his ear. "I'm sorry," she

whispered.

*Because what is sin? Think about it, Seth, what is it really?*

He watched her slide back down his body until her face—like a pale ghost hovering near the foot of the bed—was within inches of his erection. She removed him from his clothing, her fingers moving deftly as she stroked him then pushed him into her mouth.

*It's human nature. Our nature, Seth, it's how we're made.*

The wetness engulfed him, but it was cold inside her, cold and disturbing.

*They use the dark half of human nature against us.*

Seth's tongue felt dry and heavy, the words like lead blocks in his mouth. "Stop," he managed, slurring the word badly. "Don't—what—what are you doing..."

*Greed, arrogance, fear, violence, gluttony, sloth, hatred, jealousy, depravity—it's all as much a part of us as love and affection and compassion are.*

She released him with a loud popping sound and he felt a tingling sensation vibrate up through his body. "It's all right," she whispered. "It's all right to scream."

*And they know it.*

As she took him back in her mouth, suckling loudly, darkness rolled over him like an incoming fog, dense and alive.

*They know all our secrets, Seth.*

He reached up through the inky blackness, took either side of her head in his hands and tightened his grip, locking his fingers in her hair.

*All of them.*

The black void parted, Christy's slowly gliding

head came into focus, her eyes looking at him, her mouth tight around him and drawing him deeper and deeper.

*Like sin itself it lies dormant, sleeps within us only to come alive later.*

Seth began to thrust into her, ignoring the overwhelming feelings gushing through him, feelings that told him what was happening, what he was doing, and why.

*But we have to allow it.*

He thought of Peggy, and of how young Christy was, how wrong this all seemed, but the thoughts tumbled free of his mind even before he could focus on them.

Gone, like rolling mist.

All he could see was the pretty, innocent, sad face of a young and willing girl, and the sensation and vision of her mouth on him, sucking him so greedily, so savagely now.

*No one will know. No one will ever know.*

His body bucked, slamming into her harder, and he felt himself come, exploding into her as she received him.

*Free will, Seth.*

"It's all right to scream."

Christy's head snapped back, as if yanked away by invisible hands, her back arching to an impossible angle and her body rigid in seizure. Things moved beneath the skin on her face, stretching it like rubber as they darted back and forth across her features and throat until they had formed a large tumor-like bulge in her temple.

With a single unexpected surge of mental clarity

and physical prowess, Seth shot up into a sitting position. For several seconds he couldn't breathe, couldn't seem to draw any oxygen into his lungs at all, and sat gasping, his mouth opening and closing with frenzied repetition like a fish out of water struggling for life.

Finally, as if suddenly remembering how, he began to breathe, pulling in deep breaths one after the next until he felt the panic passing, giving way to another kind of fear.

He looked around frantically as he scrambled to his feet. Both beds were empty, and so was the other sleeping bag. He was alone in the cabin.

More footfalls on the porch, small and fast, scurried about.

Seth rubbed the remnants of sleep and blurriness from his eyes and dropped into a crouch. The blood in his ears pulsed violently, and his heart pounded with such force he could hear it thudding in his chest. Despite the terror consuming him, he forced himself to trace the faint moonlight to the windows at the front of the cabin. Through the small segregated panels of glass in each, snow continued to fall across the black background of night.

In an attempt to make as little noise as possible, he did his best to take slow and shallow breaths, but his entire body was trembling. Everyone was gone, and there was something…some *things* out on that porch…on the roof.

Wait, he wondered. Am I…Am I awake?

*Wake up, Seth.*

A shadow darted across the lower part of the window, interrupting the moonlight long enough to catch his attention.

"Open the door."

Seth spun toward the voice. Christy stood in the corner behind him, half concealed in shadow, eyes closed as if in prayer. "Christy?" he whispered loudly. "What—what's happening?"

"Open the door."

"Be quiet, there's something out there."

"Yes," she said, "there is."

As she stepped deeper into the room and into the moonlight, Seth noticed she was no longer wearing the sweatshirt he'd given her, but rather the blood-stained shirt she'd had on when she first ran over the ridge. She looked cold and pale and horrifically sad, a bloodied waif lost in the night, a night that owned her.

"Where the hell is everyone?"

Christy sorrowfully raised a hand and pointed to the door. As if in response, something scratched at the outside wall, something short and low to the ground.

Seth backed away, stumbling over the sleeping bag while still trying to keep Christy in his line of sight. "What the fuck's happening!"

The noises on the roof returned...scurrying, scraping noises.

"Raymond!" he called. "Raymond, where are you!"

*He can't hear you, Seth.*

A gust of wind kicked up, smashing into the cabin and blowing open the door in a furious rush. Snow blew about the doorway and over the threshold.

Night slipped in.

Christy moved to the door, her stride otherworldly and erratic—stiff and jerky—like a doll walking without jointed limbs. As she crossed to the porch and stepped out onto the ground, her bare feet sunk into the snow until it had reached her mid-calf. She turned and looked back at Seth a moment and the bloody shirt rode up a bit, billowing slightly in the wind. She was nude beneath it.

A plethora of distorted, tormented voices swirled through the night, between the trees beyond camp, mixing with the gusting wind. As Christy ran for the forest, shuffling through the heavy snow with an awkward and ponderous gait, they turned to screams.

Hideous screams beyond anything Seth had ever conceived possible.

With a scream of his own—a scream of unbridled horror—he followed, running out into the snow. But his was a panicked run, one with no rhyme nor reason, just terrified flight, and he found himself staggering through the heavy snow in only socks and long underwear, his arms flailing about and the forest and the night and the falling snow and his cloudy breath all blending together in a montage of uncontrollable terror. Rational thought and logic were left behind, fallen away from him like some lost article of clothing, caught up and carried away on the night winds, swallowed by the forest.

"Help me!" someone screamed in the distance.

He fell forward into the snow but scrambled back up to his feet quickly. The world tilted and swirled around him then came into focus. His chest wet and heaving, Seth looked to the thick forest ahead of him. It stood silently draped in white, the flakes falling through the massive trees in an oddly serene contrast to his fear.

Christy was nowhere in sight.

He looked behind him. The cabin sat in the distance, the front door open, smoke rising from the chimney. The SUV parked alongside it now little more than a large lump of snow. He'd covered a larger distance than he'd realized.

More faraway screams tore through the night.

Seth turned toward them, watched the darkness.

A rapid blur in the night ahead of him—someone—someone or something was running behind the trees, running parallel to him at inhuman speeds.

Horrible sounds of things ripping and shredding echoed through the forest.

Seth pushed forward, up a steep slope of drifted snow, and realized he had reached the ridge overlooking their camp. As he turned, he lost his balance and nearly fell backwards into the snow, but as he caught himself, he saw Christy several yards ahead of him in the forest, running. Ignoring the cold and snow, the icy wetness that had soaked through his socks and into his feet, through his underwear and into every pore in his body, Seth ran on, following her.

Night became day in a brilliant flash then returned to darkness.

Lightning? During a snowstorm? It was possible but…

Though his eyes were tearing from the cold and his breath-clouds obscured his range of sight, Seth ran even harder, the pain in his feet increasing with each step.

The sky blinked bright and faded back to black again.

It *was* lightning, or something comparable to lightning, but it lacked the neutrality of nature. This possessed a consciousness, specific purpose and intention.

And it had found him.

"Raymond!" he screamed. "Ray!"

The fear fired through him like electrical current, and he thought he might pass out, but instead he staggered forward, tripped and catapulted through the air. He crash-landed in the snow a few feet away, his fall causing a puff of it to rise up from the ground like an explosion of powder.

Seth rolled over onto his knees and looked around frantically. He was in a clearing ringed by a seemingly endless expanse of enormous trees. Snow blew about, but just above the treetops, through the darkness and swirl of flakes, he could make out a section of cobalt sky. Breath surged in thick clouds from his nostrils and open mouth, his chest heaving rapidly, lungs sore from the cold and straining for more oxygen.

He attempted to push himself back up onto his feet, but the freezing temperatures had left his hands numb and nearly useless. More tears from the cold, fear, frustration or all three, filled his eyes, and he whimpered helplessly.

Screams hemorrhaged the short-lived silence.

Exploding through the trees surrounding him in squealing waves of agony and terror, the shrieks circled and cornered him there in the clearing like a pack of ravenous coyotes closing on wounded quarry.

The sky trembled and cracked as an unearthly storm coursed across the heavens, stealing his eyes and sending him plummeting into horrible darkness.

"Raymond," he gasped, "what have they done to you?"

Sounds of skin splitting and clothes tearing trailed

the screams still echoing through his mind, screams from familiar voices.

The darkness, thick and endless, encircled him in a slow sweep, a series of black waves crashing over him, swallowing him and pulling him deeper into nothingness, it filled him like a cancer invading his body against his control. He breathed the darkness into his lungs, felt it bleed through the corners of his eyes, rush deep into his ears and absorb into his pores until there was no longer physical separation. He and the darkness had become one, the same.

Seth realized his attempts to struggle against the night he'd found himself lost in were futile. He felt the rigidity in his body slowly uncoil and release, submissive now, he became a lamb led to whatever slaughter the darkness had planned for him.

*This is home*, something whispered to him from not so far away.

Seth forced his eyes open. The huge trees loomed over him like sentries.

The strange light returned, blinking through the forest in rapid intervals like a strobe. Flickering across the sky, it illuminated the barren trees with a color similar to lightning, causing their enormous branches to appear as giant tentacles reaching down through the darkness. Those that intertwined and formed a canopy high among the treetops, bathed in the blue hue, looked like a vast network of old bones.

Death.

It wasn't until Seth had regained his feet and looked more closely that he realized the branches didn't simply look like bones, they *were* bones. Bones that had once belonged to human beings somehow fused with the trees and strung among the branches as if to mark a passage or gateway between this world and some other.

The strobe shifted and swept back to the ground, to the clearing, to Seth, who stood staring at it, terrified but mesmerized.

It moved away, revealing trees beyond the clearing, and through the dense woods, the outline of another cabin became visible in the distance.

And then quickly as the strange light had appeared, it vanished.

Swaddled in shadow and the intermittent touch of muted moonlight, a form moved, a woman running through the snow toward the cabin.

Christy.

Something moved neared Seth's feet.

He looked down at the snow. Like demonic acorns scattered from above, countless eyes buried in the snow stared back at him: human eyes opening, lids brushing aside the powder, lashes blinking away the flakes so they might see him.

Blood seeped up from beneath the snow, swallowed the blanket of eyes and grew gradually into a wide blossoming stain, covering it like a carpet of blooming flowers sprinkled about his feet.

Seth's mind began to rip like the faraway screams fracturing the silence, and he felt a sudden release and rush of warmth across the front of his thighs. It trickled down his calves and into the snow, gold mixing with crimson.

Was he laughing hysterically, crying uncontrollably, or wedged at some point between the two? He could be sure of nothing...except that they were shredding his mind and determined to frighten him to the point of absolute, irreversible madness.

And they were succeeding.

The blood grew worse, spreading along the snow, encircling him.

The screams became deafening, raining down and exploding through the forest. Seth felt himself moving forward again, and though he was running it was at a much slower pace than before, his body numb and wet as he staggered into the forest, following the pale specter of Christy loping ahead of him, leading him to the cabin in the distance.

With low branches whipping past his face, Seth slogged toward the cabin.

Christy vanished inside the open doorway.

His lungs burned and his muscles ached, but he seemed to be moving now as if without his consent, continuing his course on automatic pilot.

He tripped over a drift, rolled through the fall and struggled back to his feet. The cabin was within a few feet of him now, the door open and snow blowing about on a slowly strengthening wind.

An old pickup truck was parked nearby, almost entirely concealed in snow.

Unlike their cabin, this one had no porch, only a small single step up to the front door, and was markedly older and not as well cared for. The windows were dark, and though he was sure he'd seen Christy go inside, he could no longer see her.

Whispers, or the wind, swept past his ears.

Seth stumbled forward until he'd reached the front step then pushed himself across it to the open doorway. The interior of the cabin was pitch-black but quite a bit of snow had accumulated in the threshold. The door had been open for some time.

"Christy?" he called. His voice sounded unfamiliar. Weak, slurred, tattered.

Seth stepped through, shuffling through the snow in the doorway and into the main room of the cabin. His feet became tangled in something, and he felt his knees buckle. As his hands reached the floor he felt around in the darkness for what he had tripped over.

Loose shelves and an array of items lay scattered about the floor. A storage unit, a freestanding closet-type piece of furniture from which they had apparently come, lay smashed to pieces in a heap just inside the doorway.

Seth searched the items, feeling through the darkness and using the moonlight for guidance until he located a large flashlight alongside one pile of debris. He scooped it up frantically and switched it on.

Light splashed into a pool at his feet.

He swung the flashlight around the cabin in a slow arc.

The furniture was sparse, but most of it was overturned and scattered about, indicating a violent struggle of some kind. The bed in the corner was standing straight up on end and leaned against the corner, like someone had picked it up and tossed it there, and a chest lay open and on its side, various items of clothing and a few basic supplies spilled across the floor next to it.

But for the mounting wind, the night had again turned silent, the screams gone, swallowed into darkness.

Seth struggled to keep his legs under him while

continuing to play the flashlight beam across the walls. As the light crept along, it revealed an enormous spray of blood along the back wall of the cabin. It looked as if someone had thrown a full can of dark red paint against the wall then allowed it to freeze there. He dropped the beam a bit, following the arc of gore until the light found a dark form slumped to the side and sitting on the floor. Seth took a shaky step closer, the beam widening against the wall.

The man on the floor was dressed in old jeans, boots and a heavy flannel shirt. His hands lay in his lap, clutching a large ax. He looked to be in his late fifties or perhaps earlier sixties. Gray stubble covered his face and neck, mixed with snow and bits of ice. His eyes were open and appeared to have been locked on something directly in front of him when he'd died. His mouth was agape and coated with blood, frozen in a silent shriek, his expression one of horror and agony. The front of his shirt was covered with a thick red coating of blood, like he had vomited it onto himself at the moment of death, and congealed paths of blood that had leaked from the corners of his eyes still stained his cheeks like smeared war paint. Both ears were caked with globs of crimson that were connected directly to the enormous spatters on the wall next to and above him. Though his skull seemed to be intact, it appeared as if the man's brain had exploded within its confines, the blood detonating from every orifice in his head in a single volatile blast.

*Submit, suicide, insanity or eventual overload and death like that poor bastard back at the cabin – Clayton Willis – head popped like a fucking grapefruit on the business end of a Louisville Slugger.*

Seth tried to pry his eyes from the man's body but could not. He stood spellbound, an icy chill coursing through his veins.

He was not certain how long he stood there staring at the dead man and listening to the angry wind whip through the forest, but it seemed like hours. The cold had rendered his body nearly useless. His feet were so cold and wet he could barely feel them, and his entire body ached. How could he still be alive in these temperatures dressed only in wet and soggy long underwear? Nothing made any sense.

But his terror welcomed bedlam, and as the screams returned, calling him back from the precipice of absolute madness, Seth granted his fear exactly what it wanted.

This time the scream sounded like it might be Louis.

Seth returned to the cabin doorway, bringing the light with him. He staggered forward until he'd again reached the snow. The forest remained dark but for the moonlight and falling snow, and the wind had quieted somewhat. But the screams continued, emanating from just beyond the tree line and ringing through the night, sirens calling, enticing him to come closer and investigate.

Seth moved the light across the forest, following it through the spaces between the huge trees, but there was nothing but falling snow and darkness. He stumbled through the snow, closer to the woods from which he'd come. "Louis!" he called; voice gruff and weak. "Louis!"

And then he saw them.

Standing shoulder to shoulder to form a boundary

that surrounded the entire stretch of forest, countless dark beings waited in silent vigil. Thin and short, with long spindly arms that proportionately didn't quite match the rest of their bodies, their black silhouettes stood out even against the backdrop of night, just barely detectable in the sparse moonlight.

The screams were coming from somewhere behind them, deep in the woods.

*It's all in your mind,* a voice whispered, *all in your mind, Seth.*

"This isn't happening," he muttered. "This isn't happening."

*It is happening, Seth. It's happening in your mind, but it* is *happening.*

The screams that sounded like Louis stopped.

Seth felt his legs give out, and he sank down onto his knees, the flashlight at his side and casting its beam over the snow. His eyes wide and mouth open, he stared at the beings, trying to understand what he was seeing. Something unholy and terrifying, something his mind had become infected with and now fought to make some sense of. Were they really there? Did they really look like that? Or was his mind filling in the blanks to give them faces and bodies—substance—so he might comprehend even on some fundamental plane what was taking place?

Kneeling in the snow before them, body convulsing and shivering, mind melting as all sanity abandoned him, he realized it no longer mattered.

"I'm dreaming," he heard himself say through tears of horror. "I'm—I'm dreaming."

A horrendous pain fired through his skull like an electrical charge. He dropped the flashlight and brought both hands to his head, clutching it violently. And as the flesh across his temples began to bubble and extend, the sounds of skin and bone tearing and cracking beneath it, he realized the beings were no longer stationary. They were moving slowly forward through the swirling flakes of snow.

Closer…and closer still.

Darkness fell over him—a cold and inexorable darkness—and within it, things began to touch him. Inhuman things. Foul, vile things walking across his bare skin with long, spidery fingers.

As Seth's mind finally ripped open and split in two, they slithered in, submerging themselves in the warmth of his bloodstream and the endless hiding places in the vastness of his human brain. He felt them passing through him like a contaminated wind, sneaking across his dreams and nightmares, his thoughts and fears, all the places his soul might rest. Coiling and sleeping within him forever.

*Forever, Seth. Forever.*

This time when the screams returned, they were unmistakably his own.

* * *

Seth could see them, but from a distance. Raymond and Christy were in the forest together, unaware of him and encased, as if he was watching them through some large crystal without their knowledge.

*Where am I?*

Dusk settled and the horizon loomed above the trees, an endless canvas painted with great brushstrokes of celestial blue and black. Amidst the slowly dying light, the moon sat high in the sky like a hastily hung ornament pasted above the darkened edges, and but for the beginnings of delicate snowfall, all was quiet.

Raymond watched her awhile, careful not to reveal himself too soon.

Christy lay on her side at the edge of the forest, her weight supported on one elbow, her face turned to the sky. The snow increased a bit, becoming a light flurry, but she seemed unaware of it, absently blinking away flake after flake while sorrowfully gazing straight ahead, seeing everything, and nothing at all.

"Where are they?" he asked softly, still concealed in the shadows behind her. When she didn't answer he asked again, this time more forcefully. "Christy, where are they?" He stepped forward, allowing the moonlight to touch him. "Where are they?"

"Where do you think they are?"

"Where's my brother, Christy? Where are the others?"

"It took them," she said, this time looking back over her shoulder at him.

"The snow?"

"The night."

Raymond looked out at the vast expanse of forest. Blood dribbled from his nose. He touched a finger to it, held it away from his face so he could see. It ran along the space beneath his nose to his upper lip, seeping in and trickling along the line of his mouth.

"I'm sorry," she said sullenly.

"No, you're not." He stepped closer, an ax clutched in one hand and held down against his leg.

"Weren't you all the times you did it?" she asked.

"I'm always fucking sorry."

Seth reached out and tried to touch the scene playing out before him, but he could not reach them. When he touched the strange material separating them it rippled like water disturbed then slowly returned to normal.

"Raymond!" Seth called. "Raymond!"

*Whatever it is I'm able to do, to see and sense, it helped me to see something that night at the cabin, Seth. Something I shouldn't have seen. Something I wasn't supposed to see. So I ran.*

Seth continued to call him even though he knew he couldn't hear him.

*I ran, don't you get it? I ran.*

"We don't have any choice," Christy said softly.

*I ran. Like a coward. Because I knew what was coming.*

Though it was still down against his leg, Raymond gripped the ax with both hands and assumed a wider stance. "But they might."

Christy glanced at the ax, just then noticing it. After a moment she turned away and looked again to the sky.

"Raymond!" Seth called. "Stop!"

Distant echoes of screams leaked through, accompanied by visions of Louis and Darian on their knees in dark and distant snow-covered landscapes, their heads splitting open, cracking apart like shattered eggshells and crumbling to pieces. Christy was there too, standing over them and reaching inside their opened bodies, pulling things loose and holding them up in the moonlight the way a chef rips things free of an animal's carcass and dangles them over a boiling pot.

Then Seth was there in the vision with them, collapsed in the bloody snow, the world around them exploding into a whirlwind of rapid images and memories, their lives from birth to death—cradle to the grave—and all that lay between playing out beneath the flickering pulse of the eerie strobe-like lightning.

The visions ceased, returned him to the forest where Raymond held the ax.

As Christy watched the sky, a small smile on her lips, Raymond raised the ax and brought the blade down into the top of her skull with a single savage swing.

Seth closed his eyes as the ax made impact.

Blood droplets sprayed his face and eyelids, somehow transcending the material.

Without bothering to wipe it from his face, Seth opened his eyes and watched Raymond plant a booted foot against the side of Christy's face and yank the ax free of her head. He let the ax rest against his shoulder, and with his free hand took Christy by the ankle and dragged her deeper into the woods, her limp body leaving a deep and bloody corridor through the snow in its wake.

Raymond buried her in the snow, along with the ax he'd used to end her misery, leaving her body for the thaw and the wildlife, out there in the deep forest...the same forest where they'd all died on that strange, cold and snowy night.

# Chapter 37

Peggy stood staring at him, the dark curtains drawn behind her.

"The next thing I remember," Seth said softly, "I was waking up and the door to the cabin was open. Raymond was missing. We went looking for him but couldn't find him. We were getting ready to go back out searching for him when he turned up at the door with no real explanation that made any sense. None of us remembered what had happened before all that. It was like we'd all been drugged, or like our memories had been erased or altered somehow. We knew *something* had happened but we couldn't remember exactly what. It was only flashes, hints…until now."

"I don't know what to say, Seth."

Still sitting at the foot of the bed, he looked down at his hands. The tremors wreaking havoc with them were in full swing, and the things he had just remembered and stated continued to swirl about in his mind, leaving him shaky and lightheaded. His face was wet from tears that had fallen just seconds before. "I know it sounds crazy," he finally offered. "And it *is* crazy. But it's the truth, Peg. Whether you want to believe me or not, whether you even have the ability to believe me, it's the truth. It happened. It's what's happening now."

Peggy nodded; her expression one of sympathy peppered with consternation.

"It's why Louis threw himself out that window, why Ray and Nana killed themselves."

"What about Darian?" she asked.

Seth stood up, ignoring the lightheadedness and the sudden vision of the pen smashing into Ruthie's eye. He removed the towel from his waist, tossed it aside and began to dress. "It's too late for him."

"Is he dead too, Seth?"

"No," he said, thinking, *but Ruthie might be.* "He's..."

"He's what?"

Seth pulled on a shirt, buttoned it. "He's one of them now."

"One of *them*...I see."

"Do you?" He looked at her. "Do you see?"

"All I know is that we have to fix this, we have to find a solution."

"We need to get away from here," he said. "You and me and Petey."

Upon hearing his name, Petey's tail thumped the floor a few times but he remained curled up in the corner, eyes closed.

"Where would we go?" she asked.

He returned to the foot of the bed, put his shoes on. "I don't know," he sighed.

"Seth, I...I need to know you're OK. I need you to *be* OK. I can't do this alone. I either need to know you'll be here and together, or I need to know you won't be."

"You think I'm out of my mind, don't you." When she didn't answer he felt himself deflate. "I don't blame you, but as God is my witness, sweetheart, I'm not."

Peggy slinked across the room with her usual effortlessly seductive gait and crouched before him. With tears in her eyes she took his hands in her own. "You're trembling," she whispered.

"I can't seem to stop."

"There's something you need to know," she told him, gently rubbing his hands. "You have some…some *problems* right now…and we need you to get help regardless. But something's happened, something important, and you have the right to know. But I also have the right and the responsibility to do what's best for both of us. I wanted to tell you a few minutes ago, but you started explaining about that night so I couldn't."

The trembling grew worse. "What is it?"

"Seth, I'm pregnant."

He stared at her, unsure if he'd heard her correctly.

Her grip on him tightened. "I need to know you'll be in our lives, and that you'll be well and able to function. I'm going to have a child, Seth. *Our* child."

"But you—you're not able to have children, Peg. It's not physically possible."

She smiled somewhat condescendingly. "That was before."

"Oh, Christ," he said, voice cracking, "*no*."

"It's all right, Seth. It's all going to be all right."

"That's why they didn't chase me when I ran from

Ruthie's apartment." He looked at her, watched her distort and blur through his tears. "They knew where I was going."

Peggy reached out, stroked his cheek, clearing the tears away with her thumb. "I'm still me and you're still you. It's the memories we have to deal with for now, but like all memories they'll only stay with us for so long. Doctor Farrow, Ruthie, Darian—the others—it's all happened to them, to me, relatively recently. They all still remember it now, like I do and like you will, but none of us will remember it forever. Eventually it'll slip away, become absorbed into our consciousness. Then, for a while, this will all just be another random memory. It'll be something more, something less, confusion, a memory, a dream—just a nightmare—a fantasy, something thought of but not realized. And eventually, it'll vanish altogether, gone like memories from when we're young. Do you remember anything from when you were two or three? You were here. You had experiences and memories of them for a time. But you lose them, they fade, we change. We're not the same people at twenty-three that we are at three. We're not the same people at thirty-three that we are at twenty-three. We change, and yet, do you remember all those changes? It's all so vague, isn't it? Do you remember being born? Do you remember taking your first step or speaking your first word? Do you remember any of it? Photographs we look at in albums, with relatives bouncing us on their knees, relatives we have no memory of because they died when we were so young—were they real? Was any of it? Is it real to you? Was it ever? Does it even matter now that all this time has passed? They're all just other people's memories told to you. But to you, they're nothing. There is no memory. Just like that, these memories will go, too. They'll change, grow, go to the next step and they'll just be. *We'll* just be. Whoever and whatever we are, we'll just be. With no memory of any of these things, because we don't need to remember, we don't need the memories."

"So during the spreading of this fucking disease we all know and remember what we're doing and what's happening, but in time, we forget, it all goes away, it's all absorbed into who we become. The thoughts and memories of who we were and what we are now are gone, they cease to exist. Forgetting is the final stage, and that's supposed to make it all acceptable? That's supposed to make it all right? We sell our souls for pocket change but we won't remember so what difference does it make?"

"We only need the transformation," she said, "the evolution and the chance to be reborn. Come with me on this, Seth, just come with me. Trust me."

Seth wanted to pull his hands free of her, but couldn't. In his mind he pulled away and ran from her, but all he could truly feel was a sense of loss and dim hope that perhaps this woman he loved so desperately might somehow be telling the truth, a truth that could somehow include him, deliver him from this horrible and relentless evil. "Whatever's growing inside of you isn't ours. It's not human."

"Don't be absurd. Of course it's human, what else would it be?" She released his hands and stood up out of her crouch. "This isn't some science fiction movie, it's real life. There's no such thing as monsters. There's only us, Seth, and we're still who we always were. It's all an illusion—life, being alive, what we know and feel and see and hear and think—all of it. For God's sake, do any of us really know who the hell we are or where we came from? Do any of us really know what we've evolved from or what we're truly evolving to? All we know is what we've been told to believe. Do you really know what swims in your blood, what sleeps in the deepest recesses of your mind? Do you have *any* idea?"

"Do you, Peg?"

She sat next to him and put an arm around him. "Are you prepared to say the rest of the world is crazy and you're the only sane one left?" she asked. "Are you really prepared to believe that?"

"Yes," he said, angrily wiping away the remaining tears. "Because there *are* such things as monsters. I've seen them. We give them power with our apathy. We hand it to them through our sin and our very natures. Maybe I am the last one left, maybe not. Maybe there are others, I don't know."

"They're us, Seth," she told him. "They make us possible, not the other way around."

"They're a lie."

"We're a lie." She stood up, paced a few steps away then turned back to him. "Don't you care about the baby at all?"

"It's not a baby."

"Yes, it is, and it's growing and forming even as we speak. It's possible now. Anything is. It's a miracle, an intrinsically beautiful creation, don't you see? There's exquisiteness in every living thing if only we're willing to see it."

Seth's shoulders slumped, and the breath seeped out of him with all the grace of a punctured and deflating dirigible. When he looked at her now, he saw the same woman he'd always seen. His wife, his soul mate, the woman he'd watched paint and create and laugh and cry, who had fascinated and intrigued him even when engaged in the most mundane of daily activities. He knew every inch of her body, how it tasted and felt and responded. He remembered how they'd make love then snuggle against each other in the night, hands together, fingers locked, her breath on his neck. He remembered her in the kitchen, making them tea, smiling, and the way the sunlight through the windows there would lighten her hair and brighten her eyes. He remembered having some of the best conversations in his life with her, and how just lying together on the couch watching an old movie, reading, or doing nothing at all, had been a wondrously loving affair for them both. He remembered her as his best friend. Maybe those memories too were fleeting, destined to be lost in some dusty corner of his mind. Maybe they were all an illusion, as she said, maybe they always had been. Other people's memories from other times; told to him and blindly accepted as truth.

*Time isn't always the same when you're with them.*

"Are they coming?" he asked.

She wrapped her arms around herself, looked away and responded with an understated nod. "It doesn't have to be like this."

Something scratched the windows under the cover of drawn curtains.

"Yes," he said, standing. "It does."

He walked over to her, opened his arms. She gave a semblance of a smile and embraced him. Her arms felt so good around him, her hair so nice against his cheek, and just for a moment he closed his eyes and remembered them one more time. Not him, not her, but *them,* happy and together, as he was certain they'd once been.

Peggy said something but he didn't quite make it out. He brought his hands to either side of her head, kissed her cheek then moved his mouth to her ear.

For the first time in years, in a soft whisper, Seth spoke to God. "Forgive me."

# Chapter 38

His concept of physical self was all but lost. It was like swimming up through black water without ever reaching the surface, hands sweeping, feet kicking, head back and eyes straining to find even the slightest indication of light. His limbs no longer felt like natural extensions of his body, though. In fact, they didn't feel like anything. They, like so much else, had been reduced to phantoms. He couldn't be certain they were even still there, still a part of him, but he sometimes tried to remember what it felt like to touch something…anything. He could hear and he could sense things—movement nearby, the touch of nurses or doctors, the smells of the hospital, and most of the things they said even in soft whispers—but he couldn't see, at least not in the traditional sense. In this strange and boundless space he floated free of his body, only reminded of it when someone in some way altered his physical existence. Drifting through endless canals of darkness and armed only with memories of what it once felt like to be alive in a physical sense, he had begun to wonder of late if he was still simply suffering from injuries or if they had done something to him to make certain he remained in this state. Did he feel so free of his body because they had taken it from him somehow? Had they cut his arms and legs off, gouged his eyes from his head and mutilated his mouth beyond repair, leaving him a hideous bandage-clad aberration tucked into some hospital bed in the bowels of an institution where he'd never be found?

He had done nothing to them. Yet they were tucking him away, leaving him to wither and die, because he was of no use to them unless or until he was able to walk with them as others did. But Louis walked alone. In some ways he always had. Now, he always would, alone in the dark, forever searching for light where no light could ever subsist.

Flashes of earlier days came and went, blinking across his mind in brief intervals before vanishing into the night. His children, his former wife, the family they had once been, it all seemed so long ago now, so alien. Like the life they had all led, and the world in which they had led it, everything had changed. The metamorphosis had happened blatantly, and yet, no one seemed to care. The war had been won without much of a fight. They had offered virtually no resistance until it was too late, and by then it didn't much matter. No one cared about him here. No one was coming for him, to rescue him. He understood that now.

Louis remembered his friends differently. When he remembered them here, in the void, he remembered himself with Darian, Seth and Raymond in the forest. But it was so dream-like, something he could not be certain of. Were they genuine memories or only fantasies and tales his mind needed to tell him, placating fairy tales whispered to sleepy children to chase the boogeyman away?

He knew there were many other experiences they'd had together over the years—good and bad—but the only thing he could seem to see in his mind when his friends came to him was the forest. And Christy was always there too, not running in blood-soaked clothing but already dead, her head open and grisly, body pale and frozen and stained in the early morning light…

*On hands and knees, they dig her out of the deep snow. Her hair is the first thing they see, tangled seaweed and dead tendrils fanned out around her head like a halo of snakes. No one speaks. They continue digging, pulling the snow away until more and more of her body is revealed. Raymond is the only one who doesn't help them. Instead, he stands to the side, quietly smoking a cigarette and watching the sky the way he so often does.*

*Once her body is rested free of her snowy grave Darian gently scoops the ice from her eyes then closes them with his fingers. He brushes the rest from her face lovingly, like the father he is, caring for this girl that is technically young enough to be his daughter.*

*Seth gathers her hair in both hands, rings it out like a cloth and binds it together, laying it against her neck neatly while Louis straightens the sweatshirt, pulling it down below her crotch to better cover her. Darian looks to Raymond. He nods quickly, flicks his cigarette away and finally joins them.*

*Together, they lift her from the ground and carry her on their shoulders, Seth and Louis on one side, Darian and Raymond on the other. They carry her above them the way one might transport a casket, trudging methodically through the heavy drifts back toward their cabin.*

*When they finally reach their destination, they lay Christy on the floor in front of the fireplace. Darian gets a fire going as the others look on, standing vigil around her until the fire burns strong and bright.*

*Seth disappears into the bathroom then returns with towels and a small basin of soapy water. He kneels next to the body and the others follow suit. Darian, ignoring the gore there, cups the back of her head, gently sits her up and holds her steady as Louis and Raymond remove her sweatshirt. Pieces of her brain fall free from it, from the bloodstains pasted across it, but the men seem not to notice. The sweatshirt is discarded and Darian delicately lays her back down, resting her head on a folded towel.*

*Nude in front of the fire, Christy looks so young, so innocent lying there; the reflected flames dancing across her hopelessly pale skin. She could be a porcelain doll or a statue carved from ivory. She is beautiful, but not in a carnal or sexual way, rather the way a rose or a sunset is beautiful, the way a child is beautiful. Seth takes a towel and dips it in the soapy water. He begins to wash her hair, cleaning carefully around the gaping wound left by the ax. Darian soaps her torso, washing it painstakingly as Louis washes her legs and feet. Raymond uses a cloth to clean her face, wiping away the blood and brain matter spattered across it.*

*When they have finished, the men dry her from head to toe. Darian pulls a large and heavy blanket free from one of the beds, and they wrap her in it, carefully folding it closed over her so that only her face remains uncovered. She looks like she's alive again, but sleeping.*

*"She's just a kid," Raymond says, gazing down at her. "We both were."*

*It is the first thing anyone says during the entire process.*

*It is also the last.*

*Clean and dry and wrapped in the blanket, the four men again lift her to their shoulders. They return her to the forest, laying her at the base of a small crest deep in the woods. It is a beautiful spot, a place where nature unfolds without the intrusion and manipulation of Man. It is still a place where Christy will be left to the ravages of the wild, but it seems different to them now, better somehow than burying her in the snow like trash, hiding her from the very things she brought to them. They have transcended her victimization, the victimization of them all. Only they will not remember any of it. They will return to the cabin and sleep like they have never slept before. They will be devoured by it, swallowed by their dreams, and left alone in the dark with their demonic trophies, each with their own separate piece of deep night.*

The scene played again and again whenever he thought of them, and though he couldn't be sure of its authenticity, in those rare instances when he allowed himself any hope at all, Louis hoped they had done with Christy's body what his memories assured him they had.

Someone came into the room, disturbing his thoughts. Though soft and delicate, he could hear their footfalls. As whomever it was hovered about, making quiet noises as they tended to things, his other senses kicked in. A faint smell of very light cologne came to him. It was a familiar scent, probably the same nurse or orderly of some sort that had been caring for him since he'd gotten there.

He focused with all his might. Open your eyes, Louis told himself, open your eyes. The darkness rippled, moved like liquid, but refused to part. My God, he thought, this must be what its like to be a quadriplegic, screaming for your body to respond and watching helplessly as it ignores you. He might as well have been trapped beneath a pile of dirt, buried alive in darkness and unable to move or see regardless of how hard he fought.

Wrestling with the frustration and panic, Louis swam on through the darkness, doing his best to listen. But the sounds had stopped and the smell was gone. Or perhaps he'd just grown used to it, he couldn't be sure. He listened a while, floating aimlessly. Yes, he thought; whoever it was is gone now.

His mind shifted gears, and he allowed himself to think about the day he had tried to kill himself and all that lived within him. He couldn't remember the actual act, only the few seconds he had free-fallen through open space toward the pavement. It had unfolded so slowly, and when he hit, there hadn't really been any pain he could recall. Everything simply exploded in a bright light and then collapsed into total darkness.

A darkness he had still not found his way out of.

"And you never will," the someone he thought was gone whispered to him. A female voice belonging to some sadistic nurse waiting for him to die, someone he would never see but only feel and hear as she lurked nearby. "Because you're not alone in the dark, Louis, it only seems that way. Look closely, we're there too."

*Home*, Louis thought. *I just want to go home.*

From the depths of the hospital the faint sounds of a bloodcurdling scream trickled down a lonely and deserted hallway.

Unnoticed.

# Omega

"My form of religious and political fanaticism is linked directly to these other manias and to paranoia and schizophrenia. We are meant to be crazy. It is an important part of the human condition...This planet is haunted by us; the other occupants just evade boredom by filling our skies and seas with monsters."

—John A. Keel, *The Mothman Prophecies*

# Chapter 39

Detective Datalia drew a deep breath then let it out slowly. He'd heard more than enough. "I want to thank you for agreeing to speak with me, Mr. Roman, and for your honesty regarding the situation with your wife."

"Funny how you'd believe that but nothing else I've told you." Seth smiled, he couldn't help it. "That's what we do though, isn't it. We pick and choose what we believe, what we'll allow ourselves to believe, and we throw the rest away. You may not be able to believe me now, but you want to—I can see that—and one day you'll understand how much I loved my wife. You'll understand how much love it took to do that to her."

Datalia stared at him blankly.

"All through the ages people have talked about what's happened, about what's happening even now," Seth said. "Every culture, every civilization has had them— demons and monsters and ghosts and gods, aliens and serpents—every one without exception. And I know what you're thinking. It's because every culture and every civilization we're discussing involves Man, and wherever there's Man there's imagination and dreams and nightmares, there are those with mental illness, those who are delusional and those who con and outright lie. But what if it's because they're a part of us, these things we see and hear and dream about? What if they're a part of who we are, right down to our very souls, and one can't exist without the other? What if it's a constant struggle in dominance between the two? What are the odds that the people who see and talk about these things are *all* liars, frauds and crazies? Isn't that just as illogical as believing they're all telling the truth? What if even some of them were telling the truth, Detective Datalia? What if I am? What then? Do you still just pick and choose what to believe then?"

Again, Datalia offered no response.

"This is an interesting room," Seth said, eyes slowly following the ceiling and walls. "The way there's nothing in here but these chairs and this table, nothing on the walls or the floor, nothing to distract us or to focus on except each other and the things we say. It's a place where the truth almost has to come out, isn't it? It has nowhere to hide."

"I think we're through for now." Datalia pushed his chair back from the table and stood up. "Your attorney should be here any minute."

"It's also a good place to think," Seth said, undeterred. "And when I started to think about things, I thought about what my brother had told me."

The detective hesitated, looked down at him.

"And it made me realize something very important. If they're really asleep inside me, waiting for me to awaken them and set them free, then they really are with me. They're with me, and I'm with them." Seth's eyes slowly traced the far wall and the tabletop before finally settling on the detective's face. "And if I'm with them, then just like Raymond said, time isn't the same."

"OK, Mr. Roman." Datalia gathered the file from the table. "You can discuss this with—"

"It occurred to me that what made them so effective was their ability to use our own weaknesses and natures against us," he continued. "So why couldn't we do the same thing? With faith and love—selflessness—we can find a way, because it's all in our minds, Detective Datalia. Our *minds*. And anything is possible there. Anything is possible, because time isn't the same when we're with them."

Datalia sighed through his obvious discomfort. "This is fascinating, but I—"

"Detective, could you do one thing for me?"

"Depends what it is."

"Petey, my dog, he'll be safe?"

"We had someone take him to your in-laws. That's what you wanted, wasn't it?"

"Yes, thank you." Seth remembered Petey's boundless and unconditional love, and all the things he'd learned from him. How he'd miss that dog. "He's too old to be in some place with people he doesn't know. He needs to be with family, where he feels safe and loved. Peggy's parents adore Petey and he loves them. He'll be happy there."

The detective acknowledged him with a quick nod then turned to leave.

"You were wondering why I'd only talk to you."

Datalia hesitated.

"It's because you're a good and decent man," Seth said. "You don't always think you are, but you are. I can tell. Trust me."

"Thank you," Datalia said awkwardly, and again headed for the door.

"It's important for us to know who we are, and you should know that about yourself," Seth told him quickly. "I never did. I never knew. But now I know. I know who I am."

Datalia came to a halt near the door and slowly looked back. "And who are you, Mr. Roman?"

Seth's eyes filled with tears—tears of joy—and he managed a trembling smile.

When he gave no answer, the detective looked to the floor, embarrassed for him. "We'll send your attorney in the moment he or she arrives."

"I won't be here," Seth said, choking on the emotion but still smiling. "I'll be gone by then. Just…gone. Like you imagined me."

Datalia turned toward the door.

"Detective?"

Again, he looked back over his shoulder.

"Keep the faith, huh?"

Datalia stepped into the hallway and closed the door behind him.

Clarke was waiting. "Guy snaps his wife's neck in cold blood—his pregnant wife no less—but he wants to make sure his fucking dog's OK. Christ almighty, the hits just keep on coming. Guess it's a good sign he loves something, but—"

"He'll never do a day in prison," Datalia interrupted. He took up position in front of the two-way mirror with his partner, watching as Seth sat still as a statue, staring straight ahead.

"He confessed to killing her, Frank," Clarke said. "He admitted to stabbing that poor girl in the eye with a pen at the intervention the shrink set up for him, and he admitted to assaulting all those other people, every bit of it. He's fucked right in the poop-bin. Couldn't happen to a nicer guy."

"He's out of his mind, Dex. He's certifiable, belongs in a hospital."

"He belongs on the lethal injection table, you ask me, but I'd settle for seeing him rot in a cell for the rest of his miserable fucking life. Him and the aliens taking over his brain. Lunatic fuck." Clarke chuckled, apparently amused with himself. "Unless it's all an act so he can cop insanity."

"No," Datalia said, "this guy's deeply disturbed. It's pathetic."

"That'll be the day my heart bleeds for a hunk a shit like that." Clarke looked back through the mirror. "He'd burn if I had my way."

Datalia continued to stare at Seth through the mirror. "You just might."

He had long since figured out what it was in Seth Roman's eyes that hadn't seemed right to him earlier, but try as he might he couldn't shake the unmistakable look all his years of experience and expertise had taught him to recognize.

The look of someone who was telling the truth.

"You all right, Frank?" Clarke asked.

Datalia forced himself to look away. "I don't know," he said softly.

"Come on, you need to clear your head." Clarke slung an arm around his partner. "His lawyer's probably here by now, we'll let him in and go get some coffee."

The two detectives left the hallway and headed back into the station.

But Frank Datalia couldn't help but wonder—only if even for a brief moment—if Seth Roman would still be there when they returned.

Or if he'd ever really been there at all.

# Chapter 40

It was quiet there. Quiet the way a small town is quiet on lazy summer days.

A delicate breeze blew through the open field, causing the grass to sway and bend. The sun shone down like a spotlight from Heaven, flooding the field with a warm and golden hue and peeking out from between treetops in the thick forest beyond. The sky was a startling blue, decorated with lavish clouds that rolled slowly across the top of the world, and the air was warm but clean, the humidity low.

A modest home sat alongside the field, the back door open but the screen door closed and intact. Through the shadows inside and those created by the slanted beams of sunlight, it was difficult to see into the house, but the silhouette of the woman standing a few feet beyond the screen door was unmistakable. Though one could not see her clearly or discern exactly what she was doing, she was thin and seemed to be standing in front of a sink, presumably doing dishes.

As she began to sing, her voice carried from the

kitchen out into the open field, soft but exquisite, and strong enough to be heard quite a distance away. It filtered through the screen door in perfect harmony with the beautiful day, having just as much business in nature as did the trees and grass and dirt and sky.

Beneath the immensity of the sky and clouds, a little boy played in the field, crouched in the grass with a handful of plastic toy soldiers. Only seven or eight, he wore shorts and sneakers and a striped pullover shirt. His face was smudged in places with dirt and grass from when he'd been rolling around in the field moments before. His knees were scraped and sported scabs from various falls and tumbles he'd sustained while playing, and his hair was mussed and looked as if someone had just stooped down and ruffled it with their hand. Though perhaps thirty yards or so from the house, he looked up in notice of his mother's lovely voice, smiled then returned to his toy soldiers and their battle. But the little boy was not oblivious to the singing, rather he seemed to take particular comfort in it, the way a child takes comfort in a nightlight or a bedroom door left ajar.

It wasn't until something partially blocked the sun and darkened the battlefield where his toy soldiers stood fighting, that the little boy realized the man was there in the field with him. He looked up, into the sun and sky, and though he couldn't make out the man's face, he could see that it was, in fact, a man, standing there gazing down upon him. He had neither heard him approach, nor had any idea who he was or where he'd come from. It was as if he'd materialized out of thin air. But the little boy was not afraid. He could see the man's eyes and knew he was a good man and not someone who would hurt him. In fact, the little boy had the sudden urge to go with this man, to leave this place with him.

The man smiled, reached down and touched the side of the little boy's face. "You can't go with me," he said as if he'd read his mind. "Because if you do then I wouldn't be here. Right here. Right now. And neither would you."

*I led them out here. I ran because I knew I was smaller than you, faster.*

"Don't be afraid," the man said. "I'll protect you."

*I led them out here so they'd take me and wouldn't hurt you.*

"Don't come to the field at night."

*You – you saved me?*

"One day you'll understand."

*I tried, Seth, I swear I did but I fucked it up. That's what I do, I fuck things up.*

"Don't go to the field at night. Hide," the man told him. "Make sure you hide."

*That's not true. This isn't your fault, it never has been.*

"Hide and everything will be all right."

*Even then you were the better of us. I'm so sorry, Raymond.*

The little boy rubbed his eyes.

*It should've been me. I wish to God it had been.*

And the man was gone, just—just gone.

*Now, it will be.*

Like maybe the little boy had only imagined him.

*I never knew.*

Another soft breeze blew through the field.

*But now I know.*

The little boy dropped his toy soldiers and looked

after it, as if hoping to see the man again, perhaps carried away on it somehow.

*I know who I am.*

But he was gone.

*And who are you, Mr. Roman?*

The forest watched him silently, the light between the trees revealing nothing.

*I'm the man. The man Raymond saw that day in the field. I'm the man in the sun.*

The little boy stood there awhile…

*I tell you what's coming before it comes, and this time you do hide, Raymond…and they take me instead of you.*

…then looked to the sky…

*I'm gone, vanished in the night like so many others. Like Christy.*

…and studied the clouds…

*A tragedy, a mystery – but you're safe now. You're all safe now.*

…all the while listening to his mother's beautiful voice…

*And one day they send me back. I see you in this field and tell you the secrets.*

…singing to him from the kitchen until...

*Because time is not the same when you're with them.*

…the song came to an end…

*And this is how we beat them, Ray, with love, faith and selflessness. They're all timeless.*

…and her voice drifted slowly to silence.

*So are they. So are we.*

"Raymond!"

The little boy turned and looked back at the house. His mother had opened the screen door and was leaning partially through it.

"Come in and wash your hands for lunch, please."

"OK, mama," the little boy said with a wave.

His mother stepped back into the house, the screen door slamming behind her.

He wondered if he should tell his mother or maybe his older brother Seth about the man. Maybe he could tell Nana.

No, he thought. It's my secret.

The little boy gathered his toy soldiers and started back across the field to the house. As he reached the steps he stopped, and looked once more to the sky.

He thought he'd seen something from the corner of his eye.

But there were only clouds and sunshine.

In time the light would turn to darkness, and with it would come the sleep and dreams of a rambunctious and innocent little boy. And as surely as the sun would rise, darkness was bound to follow.

But the night, it seemed, had lifted.

# About the Author

Greg F. Gifune's critically acclaimed work has received a nomination for the British Fantasy Award as well as multiple recommendations for the Bram Stoker Award. For several years now his fiction has been published in numerous magazines and anthologies all over the world. In addition he has authored several books that have been highly praised by critics and readers alike, including the short story collections *Down To Sleep* and *Heretics,* and the novels *Night Work, Drago Descending, Saying Uncle,* and *The Bleeding Season.* Additional sales include numerous nonfiction articles, and over 100 published short stories in a wide array of commercial and small press magazines and anthologies. Also an editor, Gifune served as Editor-in-Chief of the celebrated fiction magazine, *The Edge* for over seven years, and now works as a professional freelance editor, primarily editing manuscripts for other writers when not hard at work on his own projects. Greg and his wife reside in Massachusetts with a bevy of very cool cats.